KT SALVO

Idol Moves

JETSPACE STUDIO

First published by Jetspace Studio 2023

First edition

ISBN: 979-8-9884454-3-2

Contents

Content Warnings

This book contains descriptions of acts of physical violence and emotional abuse, including scenes of physical and emotional abuse from parents or authority figures and scenes where characters are bound against their will. This book also contains descriptions of acts of homophobia and mentions of abusive parents and authority figures and teen suicide.

01

"Once more from the top!"

Tae Hyun nodded, his ragged breath heaving. Sweat dripped from his brow as he rested, bent over while he slowly massaged his knuckles. His pounding heart echoed the song's thumping bassline as a stark reminder that, despite his best efforts to maintain his fitness routine during and after his military service, he'd still fallen seriously out of shape. "Please, hold on. I'm still catching my breath."

"Oh, come on, Tay!" Alex playfully scoffed. "Do you really think a stadium full of screaming fans is gonna wait for you to catch your fucking breath?"

Tae Hyun groaned as he straightened his posture. "I have to survive your dance practices first. Then I'll worry about my screaming fans."

Alex casually shrugged. "Hey, I'm just doing what you hired me to do."

Tae Hyun tried very hard not to regret that choice because he knew how much he needed her. When he first started working on his new album's stages, he quickly realized he was in over his head. It wasn't a matter of skill or experience. Tae Hyun had been dancing for much longer than he'd been an idol. And he'd been *XTC*'s leader and lead dancer, so he'd done plenty of choreography work during his years with the group. But that was all carried out under the watchful eyes of KBR's stable of dance instructors and choreographers–support he no longer had. And, while he enjoyed the freedom of finally being on his own, Tae Hyun missed the comforting structure that came with being part of the KBR family. When he complained about it, Jason suggested he hire someone.

It was strange that Tae Hyun hadn't thought of that himself. The freedom to work however and with whoever he wanted was one of the biggest theoretical perks of going solo. But he soon discovered that the reality was much different. None of the choreographers he'd worked with at KBR were options. And many of the independent choreographers he'd spoken with said they would've loved the work, but KBR's vengeful gaze and long reach prevented them from taking it. It was like that with everything. Resources Tae Hyun had easily accessed before were suddenly beyond his grasp. It was a frustrating situation that he'd often used as an excuse to put up with the terrible downsides of being a closeted idol. And it had led to several moments dealing with the aftermath of coming out when he almost regretted it.

But Jason came to his rescue again, introducing him to a choreographer he knew as a friend of a friend in Hollywood. Alexandra Payne had spent years working as a backup dancer before becoming a choreographer herself and had since worked with many artists, including several well-known American pop stars. Best of all, she had no problem working with Tae Hyun. "I could give two shits about KBR," she gleefully explained. "Plus, I'm a total dyke, and I love working with family. Especially when I don't have to pretend they're not."

Of course, working with Alex meant working in English. While Tae Hyun had gotten much better at that after speaking it every day, Alex's colorful language often made it hard to understand her.

"I know, I know." Tae Hyun stretched his shoulders and neck before returning to the first pose. Then he checked to ensure the dancers surrounding him were ready. "Okay. Let's go."

Alex nodded and started the song track. Tae Hyun pointed his nose at the floor and took a pair of slow, even breaths to calm himself, composing his face while the digital metronome clicked through an eight count. He looked up just as the first boom thundered through his body, slinking from side to side in time to the song's deep, bass-heavy intro. A dozen hands reached for him as he gradually rose from his crouch, surrounded by a circle of six prone dancers arcing up from their prayer poses. It was a highly sensual display, and Tae Hyun's expression smoldered to match. He was emerging from the proverbial shadows, no longer held down by the soulless corporate demons controlling him or the many lies he'd told to earn their favor.

Tae Hyun thrust his hands skyward as the vocals began. He ignored his voice, not even lip-syncing as he focused on his face and body. Arching his back, he pushed forward, trusting that the twins, Daniel and Jenny, would twist from his path. Then he reached out, finding their heads where he knew they'd be, and guided them both to his sides. Javi and Malik, still kneeling behind him, rose and mirrored his movements with Skylar and Ember, the remaining dancers. Tae Hyun momentarily froze, captured by Daniel and Jenny's sizzling gazes. Then, the four kneeling dancers rose in time to the beat.

The twins pressed themselves against Tae Hyun's body, their hands caressing his chest as they bent toward him, craning their heads as if to take a bite from his neck. When the beat shifted for the pre-chorus, Jenny slinked around behind Tae Hyun while her brother dropped to his knees before him. Tae Hyun's lip curled into a sneer as their bodies painted a sultry, suggestive scene that he never would've been allowed to create in his *XTC* days.

Jason's jaw dropped the first time Tae Hyun showed him what he'd been working on. And Tae Hyun had needlessly worried that Jason might be jealous. But Jason only smiled.

"We already talked about this," Jason reminded him. "I'm insanely jealous. But you don't belong to me. And I wouldn't dream of trying to hide you away anyway. I say let the world see how amazing and sexy you are." Then he flashed a mischievous grin. "Now, show me that one move again."

The seductive choreo was far beyond anything Tae Hyun had ever previously done. Not that *XTC* never had any sexy concepts. But those had never gone beyond opaque, mesh shirts or the occasional bare arms or midriffs. Between the notoriously prudish Korean media censors and a small but irritatingly vocal segment of fans who'd undoubtedly lose their minds at seeing such a thing, sexy was never *XTC*'s brand. So Tae Hyun had pushed the envelope, and himself, as he'd developed the stages for his upcoming album–especially for the title track. And that put him well outside his comfort zone.

"No, no, no!" Alex huffed with frustration as she stopped the track. "I'm not seeing sexy here. Only tortured."

Tae Hyun groaned as he wiped the sweat from his forehead with the back of his hand. Alex had said essentially the same thing the first time they'd run through the song that day. Hearing it again a dozen more times was eroding his confidence. "I don't understand what the problem is."

Alex heavily exhaled through her nose as she bit down on her lip. Then she nodded. "Alright, everyone. Let's take five. I need a few minutes with our idol."

Daniel patted Tae Hyun's shoulder and flashed him a sympathetic grin. "Don't worry," he said in Korean. Like Tae Hyun, he and his sister had grown up in Korea. But they'd both fled to Los Angeles as teen dancers looking for better opportunities than the local entertainment industry allowed. Also, like Tae Hyun, Daniel was gay. "You'll get it."

Tae Hyun nodded, forcing himself to smile as Daniel joined his sister and the other dancers at the water cooler. He held that smile as Alex approached him, reminding himself again that she was just doing her job. He was the problem, not her. He was the one holding everyone back.

Alex's pouty frown suggested that she didn't buy his smile. Unlike most dancers, her broad shoulders and imposing frame betrayed her second career as a boxer and MMA fighter. It would've been intimidating if her posture and stance weren't so casual and relaxed. Despite dressing for a workout in simple lycra shorts and a sports bra with her thick, wavy, black hair tied back in a ponytail, the bright overhead lights reflected off the sheen of sweat on her walnut brown skin. The studio's A/C could barely keep up with the heat from seven performers and an instructor. And that was another in a long list of things Tae Hyun missed from KBR's state-of-the-art practice facilities.

Alex stopped before him and silently brooded long enough that Tae Hyun began to feel anxious. But he pushed the anxiety back down. He didn't need to please her. He wanted her honest opinion. Then she finally spoke. "So. What's up?"

Tae Hyun snorted. "I thought you would tell me that."

Alex shook her head. "Nah. I ain't no mind reader, Tay." She'd never asked Tae Hyun if it was okay to call him that. But it was the least of his irritations, so he allowed it. "Something's blocking you, that's for sure. But you're the only one who knows what it is."

"But I don't know." Tae Hyun gently sighed. "Maybe I need more practice."

Alex shook her head. "Nah. You already got the moves down. It's gotta be something else." Her well-shaped brows fell as she regarded Tae Hyun with narrow-eyed judgment. "Hell, it's your choreo and your song. The feelings should come naturally. But they're not. Maybe it's too much." She shrugged her broad shoulders. "Maybe you're not ready."

Tae Hyun frowned. "I'm–" He stopped, swallowing a sudden burst of surprised anguish as he shook his head. "I have to be ready. But I don't know what I'm missing."

"Well, something's holding you back." Alex's eyes narrowed further. "Why do you do that?"

Tae Hyun's eyebrows fell. "Do what?" Alex nodded toward his hands. He'd started massaging his knuckles again without realizing it. "Oh." He stopped, shaking his hands out to loosen them. "It's an old dance practice thing." He paused, hoping Alex would accept the easy answer, but she gestured for him to continue. He quietly sighed. "When I was a new trainee, my dance instructor used a thin bamboo rod to rap the parts of our body where we'd gotten a move wrong." He began massaging his knuckles again, not quite purposefully, but at least aware that he was doing it. "I had a lot of trouble with gestures at first. My fingers always seemed to have a mind of their own."

Alex's shocked expression suggested that wasn't typical behavior in her experience. "Are you for real?"

Tae Hyun nodded.

"Okay. Wow." Alex slowly shook her head. "You know that's fucked up, right?"

Tae Hyun shrugged. That was probably true, but it didn't change that it had already happened. "Are you telling me you were never hit as a child?"

Alex snorted. "Are you shitting me? My mother would–" She stopped. "Nah, let's not go there." Then she slowly nodded. "But I got an idea. Do you trust me?"

"Is this some kind of exercise? Because I can assure you I've tried them all."

Alex rolled her eyes. "Listen, Mr. Big Time Idol. If you don't like how I do things, you can always find someone else to–"

"No," Tae Hyun interrupted. "No. I'm sorry. Please, tell me your idea."

Alex nodded. "Okay." She turned toward the other dancers, motioning for them to return. "Everybody, Tae Hyun needs our help."

Although Tae Hyun didn't necessarily mind his nickname, he appreciated that Alex didn't use it when she addressed the others. Shortening names like that was a very Western thing and one of the many daily reminders that he was abroad. Being in Los Angeles felt disturbingly but unsurprisingly comfortable most of the time, owing to how deeply ingrained some parts of American culture were back home. But so many little things still surprised him, reminding him he wasn't in

Korea. And sometimes, it felt like he wasn't even on the same planet.

"Okay, kids," Alex continued, "here's how we're gonna do this." She pointed at Tae Hyun. "You're gonna sing. No music. Just your voice." Then she looked at the others. "And I want you all to freestyle based on what you hear him singing. Don't fall back on the choreo. Just move how the song tells you."

Tae Hyun frowned. "What about me? Do I just stand here?"

Alex shrugged. "Up to you. See, here's what I think. That bamboo rod thing? It's about control." She paused, letting her point hang between them as it sank in. "You're too used to being in control. Or, maybe, more importantly, being controlled. You might be the first K-pop idol I've worked with, but you're hardly the first pop star." She quietly chuckled. "So, I know how the global entertainment machine works. And I can't tell you how many times I've had to pull a giant stick outta somebody's ass to get them to loosen up after spending years under the thumb of some overbearing record label creative team."

"Excuse me?" Tae Hyun understood about half of what Alex had just said.

"She means you're too uptight," Daniel translated, "after working with KBR for so long."

"Ah, okay." Tae Hyun nodded, frowning at the mental image of his movements being so stiff it looked like he had a stick in his ass. "I think I understand what you're asking. But I don't understand why."

Alex chuckled. "That'll have to do." She stepped back to give Tae Hyun and the dancers some room. "Whenever you're ready."

Tae Hyun nodded and closed his eyes, trying to find

the song. All he'd thought about that morning was the choreography, so he shook that away. The melody was there, but he reached further, digging beneath it for something else, something primal. Jason once tried to teach him that when he first learned how to act. He needed a memory that held the feelings he was trying to express through his song. So he thought back to that morning as he stood in the shower. Jason had joined him under the warm spray, seductively soaping and caressing his naked body until he couldn't stand it anymore and begged Jason to fuck him right there. The memory unleashed a surprising spark of warmth in his body. Yes. There it was. He took a breath, opened his mouth, and sang.

In a neon world of lights and haze,

I danced to their rhythm, got lost in their maze.

Tae Hyun's powerful voice filled the tiny studio, echoes bouncing off the mirrored wall and polished wooden floor.

But deep within me, a fire burned bright,

I burst from the darkness and reached for the light

Javi was the first dancer to move, approaching Tae Hyun from behind and surrounding him in a not-quite embrace. Javi slowly let his hands fall, mere inches from contact, as his warm breath sprayed across the back of Tae Hyun's neck.

Now I emerge from shadows' hold,

Unveiling secrets yet untold.

Skylar and Ember stepped up next. Skylar began to circle them in slow, broad strides like a ferocious predator sizing up her prey. Ember circled the opposite way, mirroring Skylar's movements with a dark, wicked grin.

I shed their chains, break free of their game,

As I become the boy with no shame.

Malik soon joined Javi, tracing the outlines of Tae Hyun's body in the air from behind, while Daniel and Jenny joined the circle, playfully reaching toward Tae Hyun before quickly pulling their hands out of reach. And a strange sensation settled on Tae Hyun–as if his weight and mass had disappeared. Only the slow orbits of the dancers and Malik and Javi's near embrace kept him rooted in place. Tae Hyun closed his eyes as he started singing the chorus. The room's energy was electrifying, and he fell into the song's choreography without even thinking.

I'm the boy with no shame, a phoenix aflame,

Rising from the ashes, my body reclaimed.

Alex whooped. "Hell yeah! That's it!"

The dancers unhurriedly moved into their positions, following Tae Hyun's lead.

I dance to my own beat, no longer restrained,

Revealing my true self in passions unchained.

As he sang, Tae Hyun finally understood what Alex had done. He'd been so wrapped up in perfecting the choreo that he'd completely lost the song's essence. It was an old habit drilled into him from his years as a trainee that she was helping him unlearn. Because those old songs weren't his. Even when he'd contributed to the arrangements or lyrics during his later *XTC* years, the songs had come from KBR's in-house writers or were purchased as part of their catalog. But Tae Hyun wrote *Boy With No Shame*. And it was more than just his song. It was him.

Tae Hyun's movements felt natural and relaxed as he sang, inspired by his lyrics and buoyed by his choreography's energy. He held his final pose at the end of the song, the dancers arranged around him in a rising spiral as he reached for the sky. His breath rang heavy, and sweat poured from his brow. But he knew he'd finally gotten it right. Alex found what he'd been missing, making all the difference.

"Well?"

Tae Hyun lifted his head, looked at Alex's expectant expression, and nodded. "Yes."

"Fuck yeah." Alex smiled. "Okay, let's run it again with the music."

They ran through the *Boy With No Shame* choreo a dozen more times before the end of the day. It wasn't perfect yet, but it was far closer than they'd been before Alex's little exercise. And they were close enough to perfect that Tae Hyun knew it was only a matter of time before they got there.

Seong Min had come in sometime during the final run-through and leaned against the wall near the door. He usually waited outside the studio during practice but knew they'd be done soon. He explained that he preferred waiting outside because it got too hot inside the studio. But Tae Hyun suspected it was really because he was so popular with the dancers, most of whom had already confessed to having a crush on him. Tae Hyun understood the appeal. Both the Song brothers were attractive. But Seong Min had the generous build and striking looks typical of Korean action movie stars. And he and his brother had also long ago done away with their simple black suit and tie uniforms, varying their looks to blend in better when required. For Seong Min, that meant more jeans, sweatshirts, and baseball caps. But even a bulky sweatshirt did little to hide his muscular frame.

While the dancers toweled off or changed, Tae Hyun retrieved his phone from his bag. He woke the screen to discover messages from Jason and Yun Seo. He read Jason's first.

Nobody told me being a producer meant going to so many fucking meetings

Tae Hyun quietly chuckled. While he'd been practicing, Jason met with Naomi and Seong Woo to discuss arrangements for Tae Hyun's upcoming tour, among other things. He felt guilty even as he was glad Jason had taken that on. And for all Jason's complaints, he'd never shied away from taking care of anything Tae Hyun needed.

I promise to make it up to you later, Tae Hyun replied before checking his sister's message.

Yoo Mi wants to know if you've done your fitting yet

Tae Hyun chuckled again, grateful he'd talked Yun Seo into becoming his Korea-based assistant. Not that it took much convincing. He'd offered her more than she would've made in whatever entry-level position she would've gotten after she graduated, thanks to KBR exercising his contract buyout. He'd almost refused it, given that it would mean forgoing any future royalties from his work with *XTC*. But Seong Woo suggested he take it after having his financial analysts run the numbers. It hadn't made Tae Hyun wealthy by any means. But it did make him temporarily comfortable. And he appreciated having Yun Seo be a buffer between him and an increasingly neurotic Yoo Mi as her wedding fast approached.

Yes, last week, Tae Hyun replied. *I must've forgotten to send you the confirmation. Sorry*

"Here, have a drink."

Tae Hyun looked up from his phone to see Alex holding a water bottle. He smiled and took it. "Thanks."

Alex nodded. "For sure. So, tell me more about that song. I feel like I'm seeing it in a new light after your little performance."

Tae Hyun quietly chuckled. "I think the lyrics speak for themselves."

"Maybe, yeah. But the music is so much different than your old stuff."

Tae Hyun knew Alex was a casual K-pop fan and was familiar with *XTC*'s old sound. "I never wrote any of those songs."

Alex frowned. "Really?"

"Yes." Tae Hyun snorted before unscrewing the water bottle's cap and taking a drink. "Someone else did. Just like someone else made all our other decisions. What to wear. What our choreography would be. What we'd post on social media about it."

"So you really were, like, an employee?"

Tae Hyun shook his head. "No. KBR treated their employees much better than us." He took a long drink from his bottle, downing half of it. "Not that being an idol didn't come with many perks. But we were definitely the product."

"Ah, yeah. I suppose that's true. But you're not someone else's product now." Alex snorted. "Hell, imagine if you showed the Tae Hyun from those days what you're doing today."

Tae Hyun chuckled. "I'd probably die of shock."

"Good. That's what you want, right? What's the line from your song? *Rising from the ashes, my body reclaimed.* It's powerful stuff. I honestly can't wait to see it on stage." Alex's smile was a little wicked. "It'll have a lotta folks talking."

Tae Hyun's ears warmed as he grinned. *Boy With No Shame* was the first song he'd written after his public coming out. It was an anthem to all the years he'd spent living a lie, both as an artist and a person, hiding his true self for safety or convenience's sake. "I think so, too. That's the whole point."

Alex chuckled. "Well, I guess we all got our battles to fight. Right? Speaking of which, do you know how to box?"

Tae Hyun shook his head. "Only what I learned in the army. Why? Are you offering to teach me?"

Alex's smile fell away, replaced by an expression that could've been caring. Or concern. "Maybe. I know what you're trying to do here. And I know what you're about to go up against."

Tae Hyun snorted. "You think I'll be able to box my way to the top of the charts?"

Alex rolled her eyes and shook her head. "No, of course not. You probably already know how to defend yourself, anyhow. But I bet there'll come a day when you really want to hit something." She grinned. "And when that day comes? Call me."

02

Jason stifled his bored yawn as Camilla, BigCloud Arena's sales manager and their tour guide, led them into the open dressing room. It was a sterile space, with softer lighting than the corridor and a collection of bland office-style furniture that looked stiff rather than comfortable. It was smaller than his last dressing room, the trailer in a Sherman Oaks warehouse parking lot with an A/C unit that barely kept up with the sweltering valley heat. But it was still far and away better than the cold, dusty prefab shed hastily erected on the grounds of an ancient, crumbling castle outside of Budapest. Not to mention the one before that, where–No. Jason shook his head to derail the aimless and unhelpful train of thought before he got caught up in his feelings and refocused on the tour. Even as a Best Actor award winner, he still struggled to act interested.

"And, as you can see," Camilla gushed, her smile just on the cheerful side of unhinged, "our facilities are sure to satisfy even the most demanding and temperamental artists."

Jason quietly snorted, figuring that remark might've been directed at him, considering his prior dealings with BigCloud. Then again, they didn't own the arena. They'd only bought the naming rights. He caught a bit of side-eye from Lily, his former personal assistant who'd graduated to become Big Hammer's office manager. She knew him well enough to divine exactly what he was thinking. He rolled his eyes at her, only to catch a subtle glare from Naomi, who'd already lectured him on the importance of behaving before they had a signed contract.

Naomi returned her attention to Camilla. "It's very nice." She was Camilla's focus since she'd led the negotiations between Big Hammer Entertainment and the arena. As much as being a media mogul stressed Jason out, it had the opposite effect on Naomi. His former business manager turned business partner had absolutely come alive when presented with the challenge of coordinating Tae Hyun's international concert tour. She'd even traded up from her previous, sixties-inspired boho chic wardrobe, choosing a royal blue power suit with a more modern cut for their tour. But she still made it her own, pairing it with a multi-color silk polka dot blouse and pushing her poofy afro back with a lime green silk scarf. The bright colors looked great against her mahogany complexion and black hair. "Could we see the production offices next?"

Camilla's smile widened as she nodded. "Of course." She gestured toward the door. "This way, please."

Naomi shot Jason a second warning glance before following the sales manager to the corridor. Jason ignored it, trailing behind Naomi, Lily, and Seong Woo as they continued their tour. He was behaving fine, especially considering how much of an asshole he used to be when dealing with corporate lackeys like Camilla. He'd been excited to return to the venue where he'd first met Tae Hyun all those years ago. It felt like a full-circle moment. But that had worn off fast, and his limited interest in wandering the concrete bowels of the gargantuan DTLA arena was rapidly waning. And the harsh overhead lighting and dry, slightly too-cold air had conspired to give him a growing headache. It was his third meeting of the day, and they'd been at it for over an hour. Jason was definitely nearing his limit.

Seong Woo stopped when his jacket suddenly chirped. Unlike Jason, who'd gone strictly casual with a thin, eggplant sweater and khaki pants, Seong Woo looked magazine-cover sharp in a navy blue, Italian-cut pinstripe suit and maroon tie. He pulled out his phone and looked at the screen. "It's my office," he explained. "I have to take it."

Seong Woo answered in Korean, which meant it was his Seoul office, not the newly christened Los Angeles branch of the Vital Agency, his marketing, management, and PR firm. His mouth slowly drooped into a frown as he listened. Not good news, then.

"Are you sure?" Seong Woo sighed. "Alright. Forward the details to my email. I'll follow up when I'm done here." He hung up without saying goodbye and stuffed his phone in his jacket pocket. "Camilla?" He switched back to English for their host's benefit. "Could you give us a few minutes?"

"Of course!" Camilla smiled and gestured toward the dressing room door. "Feel free to talk in there. I'll wait for you out here."

Jason was sure Seong Woo had just received bad news about the tour but waited until they were behind the closed dressing room door before asking about it.

"So, what did they say?"

"What do you think?" Seong Woo huffed. "Officially? They said they don't have any open slots during the dates we requested, but they'd put us on the waitlist."

"The fucking waitlist? Shit." Jason shook his head as he plopped down on a small, peach-colored sofa that would've been at home in any plastic surgeon's waiting room. He doubted it would satisfy even the most demanding and temperamental artists, but it wasn't bad. "And unofficially?"

"They said KBR would pull all their concerts if they booked us."

"Fuck." Jason groaned as he pressed himself into the couch. "So, that's it? That's all of them?"

Jason's heart sank as Seong Woo nodded. They'd unsuccessfully tried booking every medium to large-sized venue in the Seoul Capital Area–a not inconsiderable number. Of course, many of them were genuinely booked. But enough of them had given Seong Woo the same answer that the situation was clear. KBR wouldn't allow Tae Hyun to perform in Seoul. Just thinking about it stoked the fires of Jason's fury, which would've led the old Jason into an angry rant or, worse, a fight. But he wasn't that person anymore. Or, at least, he was trying not to be. It was inappropriate in most cases. Or, at least, unproductive. But, mostly, he didn't want to disappoint Tae Hyun.

"There's still the other thing," Lily suggested.

Naomi shook her head. "Not happening. We'd never get a permit for a public performance with his name on it. And if we snuck him into someone else's lineup, the lawyers say we'd have the city down our throats before he'd even finished his set." She spun the dressing table chair around and sat on the edge. "Look, the news isn't all bad. We've got three dozen dates already or almost secured, including this place. So, it's a bona fide tour. And, once people realize there's no Seoul dates, it won't take very long to figure out why."

Seong Woo frowned as he slowly paced the length of the room. "KBR will never publicly admit to stonewalling Tae Hyun."

"Maybe not." Jason grinned. "But we sure as hell can."

Seong Woo shook his head. "We don't want to make any claims we're not ready to back up in court." He quietly snorted. "Not even my father would take on Pak Jun Ho without an army of lawyers backing him up." The KBR CEO was well known for ruthlessly protecting his company's interests by whatever means necessary. The fact that KBR had essentially locked up every auditorium, concert hall, and stadium in Seoul was good evidence of that.

"I'm not talking about running to the *K-Star Daily* with this directly," Jason assured him. "But something back channel, maybe. Hell, we've always got the *U4*s." After several flame wars broke out on the official *XTC Dream* fansites, the mods started handing down permabans to anyone who even mentioned Tae Hyun, leading to a mass revolt and the creation of *U41A*, or *Euphoria,* Tae Hyun's official fan club. The members referred to themselves as *U4*s. "You know they'd love a chance to shit-talk KBR."

"Let's not weaponize Tae Hyun's fan club just yet," Naomi suggested. "One of the reasons we're not KBR is because we don't play dirty."

Lily scoffed. "There's a long list of reasons we're not KBR."

"But Naomi's right," Seong Woo said. "Besides, they're already doing a good job supporting Tae Hyun. Especially the fans in Korea. We don't want to make it more difficult for them." His phone chirped again. He chuckled after taking it out to check it. "Yoo Mi wants to know if you've done your fitting yet."

Jason chuckled, too, nodding. "You'd better believe we did. I'd sooner piss off Naomi than mess with Yoo Mi and her wedding plans."

Naomi frowned but didn't take the bait. Seong Woo nodded as he tapped out a reply.

"Let's just finish up this tour and get the paperwork signed," Naomi suggested as she stood. "We can worry about the rest later."

Seong Woo nodded again. "I'll have my people start working up some language for the inevitable questions around the lack of Seoul tour dates. Maybe we could even put together a tour package for Korean fans to see the shows in Japan?"

Naomi nodded. "That's a great idea. Lily and I are meeting with Min Ji after this, so I'll discuss that with her." Kwon Min Ji was the manager of the Vital Agency's LA office. Part of Big Hammer's business deal with Seong Woo was that Vital would handle all their marketing and PR. Jason was fine with that, considering how well they'd handled everything during the early days after Tae Hyun and, by extension, Jason, had come out.

Lily looked at Jason and frowned. "Hey, boss. You're looking a little rough. Are you gonna make it?"

Jason nodded. The way he'd slowly sunk into the waiting room sofa probably indicated otherwise. But he'd endured far worse. "I did a week of twelve-hour shoots in a Hungarian castle's damp, freezing basement. I'll be fine."

Camilla was waiting for them in the corridor as promised. And Seong Hyeon had somehow found her there. He politely listened while she half-explained, half-bragged, about a concert they'd just had with J-pop superstar Azuma the week before. She probably thought Seong Hyeon was Japanese. Hell, she probably thought they all were. But he looked sharp in a smart, oxford blue suit with a pale green shirt and bright orange tie. It was a nice change of pace from the plain black suit and tie he used to wear. Nearing thirty, he wasn't quite as jacked as his younger brother but still had the Song family's rugged good looks. And he'd probably look thirty for the next twenty years.

Jason's pocket buzzed, so he grabbed his phone and checked it, smiling at the thought of a message from Tae Hyun. But his smile dipped into a frown when he saw the message from Tony Ruiz. He didn't even need to read it to know what it said, considering he hadn't yet responded to Tony's last message, wondering if Jason had read his script yet.

Antonio Ruiz had written and directed *The Moon Shines Madly* and given Jason the part that made him the youngest-ever Best Actor award winner. He and Jason had fallen out of contact after the incident in *The Long Evening Sunset* that got him fired. But Jason's star had recently been on the rise again, prompting Tony to reach out with an offer to produce and star in his newest project about a powerful congressperson's Chief of Staff who becomes unwittingly embroiled in a dark and dangerous political cover-up, called *The Devil's Detail.*

"Everything okay, boss?"

Jason looked up at the sound of Lily's voice and found himself the center of everyone's attention. He forced an insincere smile. "I'm fine. Just an unexpected message." Still, it was as good an excuse as any to break away from the tour. Being back in the corridor's intense lighting only made his headache worse. And he didn't have to sign any of the paperwork anyhow. "But I should probably deal with it." He turned to Naomi. "You can handle the rest of this, right?"

Naomi quietly huffed. She hadn't given Jason any lectures about following through lately, so he knew he'd just earned another one. But she also knew him well enough to know when he'd reached his limit. "Yes, I can handle this. I'll leave you with Seong Hyeon. You can listen to his security report when you're done with–" She waved toward his phone. "–whatever that is."

"Great!" Jason didn't care that Naomi was saddling him with a security report as long as it got him out of the remainder of the tour. "Then I'll catch you all after."

Seong Hyeon patiently waited while Jason tried his best not to actively shoo Camilla and the others away. His faintly amused expression suggested he didn't believe for a moment that Jason was interested in the facility's security.

"I assume, sir," Seong Hyeon said, switching to Korean since they were alone, "that you don't actually want to hear my report."

Jason sheepishly grinned. "No. But I know I should. Just tell me the fastest way outta this maze first."

Seong Hyeon pointed back toward the way Jason had come from. "The outside exit is some distance in that direction." Then he pointed the other way. "But there's a stairwell this way that leads up to the arena."

"That'll work. I've had about enough standing under fucking overhead fluorescents for one day." Jason huffed. "You can give me your report on the way."

Seong Hyeon explained what he'd learned while meeting with the arena's production and security teams, but Jason only half-listened. It wasn't entirely because of his disinterest. He also trusted the man and had no doubts about his capabilities. After learning that Seong Hyeon had served in the Korean special forces with Yu Min Kyu, Seong Woo's head of security, Jason offered him the role of Big Hammer's security chief. He'd never had much in the way of security before he'd met Tae Hyun and everything that went down in Seoul. And certainly not a whole security team. But Jason's needs had changed a lot since then. Hell, almost everything about his life had changed since then.

Given his tendency to get fired, Jason had originally proposed Big Hammer Entertainment as a way to produce projects for himself. And Tony's script was the first real role he'd been offered in years. But taking on the role of producing Tae Hyun's album meant his acting aspirations had competition. His turn would have to come once they released Tae Hyun's album and started his tour. And that was probably fine. He was doing it for Tae Hyun, and there wasn't anything in the world he wouldn't do for the man he loved.

As much as Jason's new profession impacted his life, being in a relationship changed things even more. And the biggest change was always taking someone else into consideration when, for the longest time, he only thought about himself. Naomi had been the first to point out when Jason had started doing that, much to his irritation, when he'd first confessed that he might have feelings for the idol. *I never thought I'd hear you talk about someone other than yourself that way*. But Jason hardly ever thought about himself anymore–or only himself, at least–except maybe when he was stuck in an endless series of boring meetings. He was otherwise almost always thinking about his idol boyfriend. Even when meeting with blandly racist arena sales managers, Jason powered through by reminding himself that it was all worth it for the man he loved. And, hopefully, it helped make him worthy of the man who loved him.

It took climbing three flights of concrete stairs to reach the door that opened to the arena proper. Jason had completely stopped listening to Seong Hyeon by then. He was just excited to be in a space larger than a cinder block corridor. The covered arena was more of the venue's blandness but on a much larger scale, with acres of blue plastic seats stacked in rows that stretched higher than Jason remembered. Even the floor was just a giant segmented slab of smooth, gray concrete. At least it felt more airy and open. Even having seen it, Jason could hardly imagine the space filled with tens of thousands of screaming fans. Even harder to foresee was what the space would look like once it was dressed for Tae Hyun's concert. They hadn't even settled on a look yet.

"Mr. Park, sir?"

Jason sighed as he realized he'd tuned Seong Hyeon completely out. So much for not being an asshole anymore. "Sorry. I guess you lost me about halfway up the stairs."

"I know, sir. I asked if you were alright."

Jason frowned. "Don't I look alright?"

Seong Hyeon's carefully composed face betrayed little about his thoughts. "You look lost in thought," he finally admitted.

"Ah." Jason chuckled. "Yeah, that's definitely not one of my strengths. I was thinking about Tae Hyun and the tour." He walked over to a nearby row and sat a few spots in. "I won't ask you to repeat your whole report. Just tell me that you can keep him safe here."

Seong Hyeon nodded. "Yes, sir. I have every confidence.

And the security staff here seems to know what they're about."

"Good enough." Jason glanced at the empty seats beside him and gestured for Seong Hyeon to join him. "You may as well sit. They'll let me know when they're done."

Seong Hyeon remained where he was for a few moments before taking the seat beside Jason. "If I may, sir–"

Jason chuckled again. "I wish you'd speak informally, but I know that makes you uncomfortable."

"You're my employer. It would be inappropriate."

Jason snorted. "Well, we wouldn't want that. What were you about to say?"

Seong Hyeon's sigh caught Jason a little off guard. He'd grown so used to the man's absolute stoicism that any show of emotion at all seemed like a big deal. "I can see how much Mr. Woo means to you, sir. And I know things like security reports aren't something you're used to dealing with. But I can't stress how important they are. Especially given your and Mr. Woo's status as–" He paused. Had he already used up the rest of the day's word allotment? "As controversial public figures."

Jason frowned. "Controversial?"

"Because you're both gay, sir." At least Seong Hyeon had the good sense to look embarrassed when he said that.

"Oh, sure." Jason shook his head. "Except I've always been gay. The only controversy is that everyone knows now."

"I'm aware, sir."

Jason examined Seong Hyeon's expression a little more closely. But there was no hint of malice or bias. His matter-of-fact delivery always seemed to signal his acceptance of whatever situation he was generally in. "Okay, fine. So, what's the latest from the Big Hammer security team?"

"Fortunately, this has been a quiet week." Seong Hyeon pulled his phone from his jacket and navigated to his notes app. "We only identified a dozen credible threats among the many more you and Mr. Woo receive daily. Most of the responsible parties reside in Seoul, so we sent the information to Yu Min Kyu's team for possible action by the Seoul Metropolitan Police. One of the responsible parties lives here in Los Angeles, but my investigation determined the individual was not a threat."

Jason nodded, stalling for time because he had no idea what to say. So he guessed. "Good work." Seong Hyeon nodded without replying and put his phone away. An awkward silence settled between them. Jason was fine with companionable silences. But awkward ones drove him nuts. "Can I ask you something?"

"Of course, sir."

"I–" Jason paused, unsure how to say what he wanted to say. "Okay, I guess it's not really a question. I'm honestly a little surprised you and your brother have never had a problem with Tae Hyun and me being gay. I don't mean to stereotype you boys, but you definitely fit the anti-gay mold."

Seong Hyeon didn't immediately comment or reply. Had Jason finally managed to offend his Security Chief? "I understand, sir. It's because my brother's also gay."

Jason's jaw fell open. "Wait. Seong Min is gay?"

"No, sir." Seong Hyeon half-smiled and almost chuckled. "My older brother. I never considered myself to be homophobic, but when Seong Hun came out to us, it became important to me to ensure that I wasn't."

"Wow. I had no idea." The concept of siblings was somewhat foreign to Jason, having grown up as an only child.

The closest he'd probably come was with the core cast of the *Monday Night Club* movies since he'd worked so closely with them during his formative teen years. And most of them had turned out to be even messier than he had. "But that makes sense, seeing you and Seong Min together. You're a good hyung to him, too."

Seong Hyeon actually smiled then. It was a rare occurrence that Jason appreciated. "Thank you, sir. If I might ask something–"

Jason groaned. "Let's just assume you always have blanket permission to ask or say things to me."

Seong Hyeon nodded. "This is well beyond my place to inquire, sir. But, are you really alright?"

Jason frowned. Seong Hyeon had just asked him that. Why would he ask him again? Unless, of course, he meant something different the second time. "I feel like we already covered that. "

"Providing personal security requires me to always be mentally present and highly observant. Sometimes, that puts me in situations where I have to witness things that are none of my business without comment. But, mostly, it means I get to know my clients very well. I doubt most people would notice, but you seem more distracted than usual lately."

Jason considered the implications of Seong Hyeon, a man who'd rather say two words than twenty, wondering if he was alright. Of course, he was alright. How could he not be? Tae Hyun's album and tour were practically guaranteed to be successes. And his own career was on the verge of taking off again. He'd never been happier in his life.

Then again, Jason still hadn't responded to Tony asking if he'd read the script yet, even though he'd read it the same day it had been delivered. And then again a few days later. While ostensibly a political thriller, *The Devil's Detail* was also a meaningful conversation about the outsized influence corporate interests had in politics. It featured a lot of clever, sharp dialogue that Jason knew he'd really sink his teeth into. And the main character's arc included coming to terms with the moral gray areas he'd had to live with to be accepted into an elite political circle. It was the perfect role for him and could realistically put him in the running for a second Best Actor award. But committing to it would mean diverting some of his attention from Tae Hyun, which he wasn't willing to do at the moment. He knew he should just explain that to Tony. Surely, he'd understand. But he still hadn't. Hell, he hadn't even told Tae Hyun yet. That was probably his biggest sin. But he wasn't officially thinking about it. It was just a conversation he'd had with his former director. There was no need to distract Tae Hyun from what he was doing.

"Yeah," Jason finally replied. "Of course, I'm alright. I've never been better."

Seong Hyeon nodded. "If you say so, sir. I'm sorry to bring it up."

"No problem." Jason quietly chuckled. "As long as you realize that makes us friends, now."

Seong Hyeon actually snorted. "Alright. If you say so, sir."

03

Tae Hyun's triumphant dance practice left him feeling weightless. He practically floated on air when he finally arrived home. It was an intoxicating sensation he hadn't truly realized was missing until he'd finally caught it again. He couldn't wait to share every moment with Jason when he returned in just an hour. That left him enough time for a quick shower and a change of clothes before he lovingly prepared a meal for their evening together.

Tae Hyun delighted in so many things about Jason's Hollywood Hills home, including its generous size, breathtaking view, and downstairs gym. But nothing could touch the enormous, slate-tiled main bathroom. Like the rest of the house, its grand size was almost decadent. The shower alone was larger than the entire bathroom in his last Seoul apartment. And he wasn't sure, but the bathroom may have been bigger than his entire dorm bedroom back when he was a KBR trainee.

Stepping out of his clothes and into the shower, Tae Hyun luxuriated under the chrome rainfall showerhead as a cascade of steaming-hot water wiped away the sweat and aches from his long day of movement. As he bent under the water, one arm braced against the slate-tiled shower wall for balance, the delicious memories of what he and Jason had gotten up to in there earlier resurfaced again, still fresh on his mind from dance practice. His breath quickened at the thought of Jason's tanned skin glowing from an early morning run. His heart pounded as he smoothly caressed his soap-slicked body just as Jason had done, starting at his sensitive nipples and meandering south across his flat stomach toward his cock. But he quickly pulled his hand away. It would be so much better to wait until he was with Jason again and entice him into an encore session. And, recalling with a wicked grin how Jason reacted to seeing him dance, Tae Hyun knew just how to make it happen.

Sex with Jason was so easy and carefree. He was such a thoughtful, attentive, and experienced partner who was nearly always ready to do it but never tried guilting or shaming Tae Hyun in those rare moments when he wasn't in the mood. In his last relationship, he was lucky if they managed once per week. Even then, it was rarely more than a handjob or blowjob. The demands on their time and being under near-constant watch made it challenging to do much more. And they'd often had to get creative just to do that–sharing a bathroom or shower stall or some other similarly cramped space where they found a few moments away from prying eyes.

After drying off and dressing in simple shorts and a t-shirt, Tae Hyun headed for his other favorite place in the house: the kitchen. While the shower may have dwarfed his old bathroom, the kitchen would've encompassed the entire main room of his old apartment. It was more space than any couple—let alone a single person—would ever need. And the giant marble-topped kitchen island was angled so that whoever used it would be treated to a panoramic view of the Los Angeles skyline via the expansive window wall on the back of the house. Tae Hyun doubted he'd ever grow tired of it.

Jason's kitchen had everything. Once Tae Hyun had settled in, he'd spent many hours exploring the contents of the kitchen's glossy, smokey gray cabinets. Most of the small appliances they contained were restaurant-grade, like their larger counterparts. And nearly all of them were totally unused. Jason obviously didn't cook much. So Tae Hyun promptly claimed the kitchen as his domain, much to Jason's delight.

Tae Hyun took a quick inventory of the refrigerator and decided on tteokbokki and dakgalbi for dinner. Then he grabbed the ingredients he needed and set the rice cakes to soak while he chopped the chicken thighs. He'd learned to make both dishes during his trainee days since they were simple, cheap, and delicious. He hoped Jason would enjoy them. Tae Hyun always had to do some guesswork with Jason when it came to his Korean heritage. Although his parents were Korean immigrants to the US, it seemed like they'd given him a very American upbringing. Not that they'd insulated him from Korean culture. The fact that Jason spoke Korean with near-native fluency was evidence enough of that. But he drank bourbon instead of soju. His favorite food was Mexican. And his favorite sport was American football.

One of the reasons being an idol initially appealed to Tae Hyun was the opportunity to see more of the world. Debuting meant he could travel and experience other cultures firsthand. Seeing the Americas and Europe opened his eyes to how different other parts of the world were–and how much those cultures influenced his own. It wasn't like he didn't know fried chicken had come to Korea from the US. But seeing the same familiar fast-food fried chicken outlets in Los Angeles that he knew from home was a stark reminder of how pervasive Western cultural influences were. And Tae Hyun was excited to see how the reverse was also becoming true. K-pop was a verified global phenomenon. And even just scrolling through BigCloud's streaming app on Jason's giant TV, he'd come across dozens of movies and series he knew from back home.

The rich, spicy dakgalbi sauce had just started to simmer when Jason messaged to say he was nearly home. Tae Hyun smiled, gave the sauce one more stir, and headed to the bar cart to pour Jason a neat Kingston and mix himself a gin and tonic. Jason hardly drank as much as he did when they'd first met, which Tae Hyun appreciated since he rarely drank. But a celebration was in order. And drinking with Jason could be fun–especially when things turned raunchy. He chuckled as he set Jason's drink on the kitchen island and brought his with him while he finished preparing the food.

Tae Hyun did a final taste test of the dakgalbi–perfect–just as Jason and Seong Hyeon came inside. Hopefully, Seong Hyeon had other dinner plans. Tae Hyun didn't make enough for three.

"What is that gorgeous smell?" Jason poked his smiling face around the corner from the main room. "You made dinner?"

Tae Hyun grinned as he nodded. "I did. And welcome home." He pointed toward the hall leading to the main bedroom. "Now, go wash up so we can eat."

Jason nodded. "Yes, sir. I just need to grab something for Seong Hyeon first."

Jason's head disappeared as Seong Hyeon wandered around the corner from the main room. He briefly sniffed at the air and nodded. "That smells like my mother's dakgalbi."

Tae Hyun smiled. "I hope that's a good thing."

Seong Hyeon nodded. "Definitely. My mother's from Chuncheon. Based on the smell alone, I think she'd approve."

Tae Hyun smiled. "That's good, then. I'm sorry I didn't make enough to share."

Seong Hyeon politely waved off Tae Hyun's apology. "No need, sir. I have to check in with Seong Min now so he can take a dinner break."

Jason reappeared a moment later after changing into shorts and a t-shirt and handed Seong Hyeon a thumb drive. "Here you go. And thanks again for everything today."

Seong Hyeon pocketed the thumb drive before offering Jason a quick bow. "Just doing my job, Mr. Park, sir. Good night, Mr. Woo."

Seong Hyeon saw himself out as Jason helped himself to his waiting bourbon. Despite sounding happy, Tae Hyun also saw Jason's fatigue. The first fingers of guilt crept into his thoughts, but he quickly pushed them away. If Jason didn't think what he did was important, he wouldn't do it. It's not like Tae Hyun wasn't working his ass off, too. And Jason still looked good, his muscular form nicely filling out the thin fabric of his tight t-shirt.

"Enjoying the view?"

Tae Hyun's ears warmed as he turned his attention back to his sauce. "Just making sure you saw your drink on the counter."

Jason picked up his glass, had a generous swallow, and contentedly sighed. "This is perfect. It's like you read my mind."

Tae Hyun playfully snorted. "Because I poured you the same thing you always drink?"

"I never said my mind was complex." Jason walked over to stand beside him, gently kissing his neck before leaning in to smell the food. "That smells amazing. What did Seong Hyeon call it?"

"Dakgalbi. It's chicken thighs with rice cakes, perilla leaves, cabbage, and onion in a chili sauce. It's supposed to have sweet potatoes, too. But we don't have any."

"I'm sure it'll still be great." Jason moved directly behind Tae Hyun, wrapped his arms around his waist, and nuzzled his neck. "But I'm surprised you cooked after practicing all day. I'd planned on ordering delivery."

Tae Hyun shivered from Jason's touch and nearly moaned. "Stop being naughty, hyung. I need to serve this."

Jason quietly chuckled as he ran his hands down Tae Hyun's torso and slipped them under the waistband of his shorts. "Here, let me help."

Tae Hyun playfully smacked Jason's hand before picking up a pot. "How about you help me with this instead?" He handed the pot to Jason, who took it without complaint. "And I had a breakthrough working with Alex and the dancers today," he explained as they carried the two pots to the table. "So I felt like celebrating. I hope that's okay."

"What? Of course, it's okay." Jason set his pot down and walked around to sit at the opposite side of the dining table, allowing Tae Hyun to enjoy the view. It was a sweet, thoughtful gesture that always reminded Tae Hyun of when he'd done the same thing for Jason back in Seoul. "I always prefer to eat something of yours," he added with a wink.

Tae Hyun snorted at Jason's incessant flirting as he spooned some of each dish on a plate and handed it to him. Jason immediately tried one of the tteokbokki rice cakes as Tae Hyun served himself.

"So, how'd the arena visit go?"

"It went well enough." Jason stuffed a forkful of the dakgalbi into his mouth. It was so weird to see him use anything but chopsticks–another thing that made it clear he was American. But Jason's face lit up as he chewed. "Oh, this is so good! This one goes on the menu, too."

Tae Hyun grinned. What had once been the source of their worst fight had turned into an inside joke. Every time Tae Hyun cooked something Jason liked–which was nearly everything Tae Hyun made–he insisted that they add it to the menu of the restaurant they'd open together one day.

"I mean, you've already performed there before," Jason continued. "But it's been heavily remodeled since you were last there, so at least it feels new." He gave a brief but surprisingly detailed rundown of everything he'd seen, down to how comfortable the furniture was in the dressing rooms. "Even Seong Hyeon gave it his seal of approval. Then he asked me if I was alright."

"Why? Were you being difficult?"

Jason snorted. "I assure you I was on my best behavior." He shook his head. "But that wasn't what he meant. He basically said I didn't seem happy."

Tae Hyun frowned, revisiting his earlier worries. "Are you happy, hyung?"

"Well, yeah." Jason nodded for emphasis. "I mean, I think so. I feel happy. I was just cranky from the tour. And the lighting gave me a headache."

Tae Hyun's eyebrows fell. "A headache? Are you okay now?"

Jason smiled and nodded again. "Of course! Once I was outside again, everything was fine."

"Good." Tae Hyun couldn't deny that Jason looked and sounded fine. But he also couldn't deny that Jason was doing a lot of things lately besides acting. "You'd tell me if you weren't happy, wouldn't you?"

"For sure." Jason smiled. "I may be a Best Actor winner, but that doesn't mean I can hide my feelings from you. Speaking of which, how was your day? You mentioned something about a breakthrough?"

Tae Hyun didn't want to let the topic go so quickly but was also anxious to share his success. He smiled and excitedly nodded. "You know the choreo for the title track?"

"I do." Jason grinned. "It's super hot."

Tae Hyun chuckled as his ears warmed. "Well, Alex kept telling me the opposite. I think she said it looked tortured."

Jason frowned. "Wow, okay."

"She said something was holding me back, and it turned out she was right. She had me do this free movement exercise with the dancers, where we had to just do what the song made us feel. It reminded me of when you were teaching me how to act. You know? How you had me think back to times I felt a certain emotion?"

"Oh, yeah." Jason's smile returned. "Is that what you did? Think of a memory to bring out an emotion?" Tae Hyun nodded. "What did you think of?"

Tae Hyun's ears warmed to the point where he was sure they were bright red. "I thought about this morning when you joined me in the shower."

"Oh." Jason chuckled low and deep. "Really?"

Tae Hyun nodded. "Yeah. I mean, the song's title is *Boy With No Shame*. So I can't exactly be ashamed of my own choreo while I'm doing it, right?"

"Was that the issue? Were you ashamed?"

Tae Hyun shook his head. "No, not that, exactly." He wasn't entirely sure he understood the problem himself. "I think it's more discomfort than shame. The song is so much different from what I'm used to. So, I think I fell back on my old practice habits to make it more familiar and comfortable. But I got stuck trying to perfect the motions to the point that I forgot about the vibe."

"Ah. So you thought about me fucking you?"

Tae Hyun nodded as the warmth in his ears spread down through his body. "Yes. And it totally opened me up."

Jason chuckled. "Just like I did."

Tae Hyun playfully grinned. "Maybe." He'd planned to wait until after dinner to seduce Jason, but the growing stiffness in his shorts refused to be held back. He wickedly licked his lips as he pushed back from the table. "Want to see how it looks now?"

"You mean your dancing?" Jason enthusiastically nodded. "Shit. Yes, please."

Tae Hyun got up and walked to the open space between the dining area and the upstairs lounge. The sun hadn't yet fallen beyond the roofline, but its light gave the room a warm, golden glow. He crouched to assume the first pose and mentally gave himself an eight-count before looking up at Jason. He rose to the timing of his mental beat, reacting as if his dancers surrounded him, reaching for him, before lifting his hands toward the ceiling. His movements were fluid and sensual, even without the music and the other dancers. As they should be. Then he arched his back and stepped toward Jason. He made eye contact, his smoldering expression giving pure lust. That wasn't exactly how he did it during the song. But this performance wasn't for a stadium of screaming fans. It was for his lover, who watched him with rapt attention.

Tae Hyun slowly swayed his hips as he gently bit down on his lower lip. Then he beckoned for Jason to come over. Jason wasted no time, practically leaping from his chair to approach him. Tae Hyun held a hand to his chest and stopped him before he got too close. Then he shifted right, slowly dancing a lazy circle around Jason as he sensually dragged his hand across Jason's chest and back. Once he completed his circle, he flashed Jason the lurid sneer from his dance. Then he took hold of Jason's shoulders and gently pushed him to his knees.

Jason didn't need any further commands. He reached out, slipped his fingers under the waistband of Tae Hyun's shorts, and slid them down. The erection pressing against them sprung forth, and Jason took it into his mouth. A low moan escaped Tae Hyun's lips as Jason inhaled him. He ran his fingers through Jason's thick hair as Jason reached around and grabbed him from behind, firmly cupping his ass and pressing Tae Hyun into his mouth. But they'd just been eating dakgalbi, and Tae Hyun soon realized his mistake. He quickly pulled himself out, gripped Jason's arms, and pulled him to his feet.

"Spicy," Tae Hyun said with a grin. Then he pulled them together and planted his mouth on Jason's lips. He tasted the dakgalbi sauce on Jason's tongue, but it was much more pleasant in his mouth than on his cock.

Jason took hold of Tae Hyun's arms as they kissed and

slowly pushed him back toward the giant couch behind him. When Tae Hyun bumped against it, he let Jason help lower him onto the soft, dove-gray leather before Jason climbed atop him, balancing his weight on his hands. But Tae Hyun wanted all of him. He pulled Jason onto him, lifting his shirt so he could trace the muscles on Jason's back before sliding his hands under the waistband of his shorts to caress his firm, round ass. He pressed down until he could feel Jason's hard, throbbing erection rub against his. Jason quietly moaned as he pushed himself against Tae Hyun's crotch. Then Tae Hyun pulled his mouth away, forcing a pair of words through his heavy, panting breath.

"Fuck me."

Jason's eyebrows rose in surprise. "Again?"

Tae Hyun nodded. "Please, hyung. I want you inside me."

Jason bit down on his lip for a moment, but that was all the time he needed to decide. He pushed himself off Tae Hyun, helped him off the couch, and led him into the bedroom. The bed still sat unmade since neither of them had time that morning to do it. But Tae Hyun didn't care. He walked up to it, bent down to put his hands on top, and presented Jason with his ass.

"I'd offer to eat you out first," Jason said as he stepped out of his shorts, "but I think we'll run into the same issue as before."

Tae Hyun snorted. "I'll be fine, hyung. We already did it once today. Now stop stalling and fuck me."

Jason's jaw dropped. "Stalling? I–"

Tae Hyun insistently raised his eyebrows and nodded over his shoulder toward his waiting behind. Jason thankfully took the hint and shut up. He grabbed the lube bottle from the top drawer of his nightstand and applied a generous amount to himself. Then he stepped behind Tae Hyun and used a lubed finger to gently tease around his asshole. Tae Hyun immediately squirmed as jolts of pleasure ran up his spine. Then he bucked, nearly losing his balance when Jason stuck one of those fingers inside and found his prostate.

"Fuck, hyung," Tae Hyun gasped.

Jason chuckled. "That's the plan, sexy." He pressed his finger inside again, and Tae Hyun lost his words, only managing an animal growl. Then Jason replaced his finger with his cock. As expected, it didn't take much effort to slip in. Tae Hyun nearly cried out as he felt Jason throbbing inside him. It was perfect.

Tae Hyun moaned as the fuck really started. He grabbed handfuls of bedsheet to brace himself against Jason's increasingly powerful thrusts, pressing his eyes closed to let his other senses take over. The warmth from Jason's breath and body heat on his back. Jason's subtle grunting timed with every thrust. The mingling smells of lube, musk, and dakgalbi spices. It all transported him as he felt his impending climax. Before he'd been with Jason, Tae Hyun had never cum just from being fucked. But he hadn't touched himself at all and could feel his orgasm building every time Jason's cock speared him.

Then Jason stopped. Had he already cum?

"Hey, could you turn over? I want to see your face."

"Oh. Okay." Tae Hyun pulled himself off Jason's cock and rolled over. "How come?"

Jason shrugged as he grabbed Tae Hyun's legs and lifted them. "I guess I like to look into your eyes. It makes me feel more connected to you."

Tae Hyun snorted. "More connected than having your dick

inside me?" Jason briefly frowned and quickly shook it off. But Tae Hyun still noticed. "I'm sorry. I didn't mean to–"

Jason leaned forward and kissed Tae Hyun, cutting him off mid-apology. "I love fucking you because I love you." His voice was low and throaty–almost a growl–as he pressed his cock against Tae Hyun again. "And I want to be sure you're enjoying it."

Tae Hyun gasped as Jason slipped back inside. He would've closed his eyes again but couldn't turn away from Jason's magnetic gaze. Instead, he wrapped his arms around Jason's shoulders, keeping their faces close enough that Jason's breath tickled his nose. Jason bit down on his lip as he fucked Tae Hyun even harder, which probably meant he was approaching his own climax. Tae Hyun hoped Jason would hold off long enough for him to–then, it suddenly hit him. He let go of Jason, fiercely crying out as a glorious wave of ecstasy washed over him, and his cum splattered across his chest and stomach.

Jason suddenly grunted. "Oh, shit. I'm gonna–" He pulled out, loudly crying out as he added his cum to Tae Hyun's. "Wow."

Tae Hyun breathed out a long, contented sigh as Jason fell beside him and rolled onto his back. "Yeah. Wow." He turned to his side and examined Jason's profile, watching his chest rise and fall as his breathing slowly calmed. The pale bedroom walls behind him had begun to take on the evening light's rosy hue. "Thank you, hyung. I needed that." He reached out and gently caressed Jason's arm. "Sorry if what I said was unkind."

Jason shook his head. "No, I was just being too sensitive."

"I mean it." Tae Hyun rested his hand on Jason's chest. "My favorite part about sex with you is that we still communicate. That we talk to each other. I don't want you to think you can't do that."

"Okay." Jason turned to face Tae Hyun and smiled. "And I think I get what you meant about your breakthrough. That felt different than this morning."

"It was." Tae Hyun pushed his face close enough to Jason's that their noses touched. "I love you, hyung." Then he leaned in a little further and kissed him. Jason responded, reaching behind Tae Hyun to run his fingers through his hair. The feeling was electric. Even having just been fucked out of his mind, Tae Hyun was still turned on enough that he thought he might get hard again. But he'd already cum twice that day. Passion or no, his body was spent.

Jason eventually pulled away. "I love you, too." Then he rolled over and sat up. "And I think I'm laying in your cum. We should probably change the sheets."

Tae Hyun chuckled as he got off the bed. "Could you take care of that? I'd like to clean up first."

"Yes, sir."

After Jason had changed the sheets and they'd both showered, they returned to the dining table and their half-eaten dinner. The sun had nearly set by then, and the distant ocean was ablaze with orange and scarlet light. But their dinner had gone cold, which meant the rice cakes were inedible. Tae Hyun scraped their plates back into his pots and returned them to the stove for reheating.

"Was Seong Woo still with you today?" Tae Hyun tested the sauce on a spoon, but it wasn't quite hot enough. "Or did he leave already?"

"No, he leaves the day after tomorrow." Jason frowned. "Actually, I have some not-so-good news from him. Is now a good time for that?"

Tae Hyun softly snorted. There was never a good time for bad news. But he'd had such a fantastic day he figured he could probably handle it. "Yes, I think so."

"Seong Woo's office heard back from the last venue in Seoul. They said no."

Tae Hyun quietly sighed. He'd expected that would be the case since all the other venues they'd asked said the same thing. "Because of KBR?" He huffed when Jason nodded. "I can't believe KBR is going to this much trouble to keep me from performing there.

Jason nodded. "Yeah, it definitely feels personal." He walked around the island to stand behind Tae Hyun, wrapping his arms around his waist. "But Naomi reminded us that we've got three dozen dates pretty much locked up, including BigCloud Arena. So it'll be a genuine world tour."

Tae Hyun set his spoon down and leaned back against Jason. "Still, I wish I could perform at home.

Jason gave Tae Hyun a gentle squeeze. "Isn't this home, too?"

Tae Hyun smiled as he wrapped Jason's arms in his. "Of course, it is. Home's wherever you are. But you know what I mean."

"Yeah, I know." Jason leaned in and gently kissed Tae Hyun's neck. "And what they're doing is shitty. But we'll figure something out."

Tae Hyun turned around and wrapped his arms around Jason's shoulders. "I know. And the fact that you've all done so much already makes me that much more anxious to release my album." He kissed Jason. "I really appreciate it." He kissed Jason again. "And I love you."

Jason smiled as he brushed Tae Hyun's bangs from his face.

"I love you, too. And everything's gonna be great. You'll see."

Tae Hyun smiled back, warmed by Jason's handsome face and firm grasp. He was like a rock that Tae Hyun could cling to, knowing it would never move no matter how bad the storm might get. And he couldn't imagine not having Jason by his side. "I know. Now, let's eat. I'm fucking starving."

04

Jason's phone rang as he turned from Laurel Canyon onto Sunset. He debated ignoring it since the top was down on his Ficaro Monaco convertible. He hardly ever drove the damn thing anymore. He hardly ever drove at all anymore, owing to his ever-present security team. Riding in an SUV was easier when you traveled with that many people. But the unseasonably warm temperatures spurred on by the bright, yellow sunshine had put Jason in a surprisingly pleasant mood. So he'd insisted on driving with the top down to his lunch date with Seong Woo. Seong Hyeon also seemed to enjoy the sunny ride. Jason even caught a hint of a grin on his face one of the few times he'd looked over.

But he had a sense that it would be Naomi calling, so he tapped the answer button on the steering wheel. "What's up, Naomi?"

"If you're in your car, I assume you're heading to lunch with Seong Woo."

Jason rolled his eyes. If there was one thing he could count on with Naomi, it was that she always knew what he was up to. Sometimes even before he did. "How did you know that?"

"He told me." Naomi paused for several moments. "Am I on speaker?"

"Of course. I'm driving, remember. So, yes, Seong Hyeon is listening."

"Oh. Hi, sweetie."

"Hello, Ms. Bell." The Song brothers had initially insisted on addressing Naomi as Chief Bell since she was Big Hammer's Chief Operating Officer, and that's what they would've done when speaking Korean. It had taken a few weeks to convince them that you didn't refer to someone by their job title in the US unless they were a Doctor or Professor or something.

"Hey. How come he's sweetie, and I'm just Jason?"

"I think you just answered that question yourself. Look, maybe you should call me after your meeting. I don't want to distract you when you're behind the wheel–"

Jason snorted. "Whatever. I'm an excellent driver."

"No, I think this can probably wait."

Jason huffed. "Seriously? You called me knowing that I'm driving just to tell me you don't want to talk to me while I'm behind the wheel?"

"I didn't expect you to actually answer one of my calls."

"That's not fair. It's been months since I avoided your calls." Jason snorted. "Besides, I didn't know it was you."

"Jason, I–"

"Just tell me!"

"Fine." Naomi sighed loudly enough to be heard over the wind noise. "You really want to know right now? Your father's office has been reaching out again."

Jason quietly growled as he tightened his grip on the wheel. He hadn't seen or spoken to his parents since the day he'd marched up to his father's oversized, marble-topped desk and told them he was done with them. He'd expected that would be the end of things. No, that wasn't true. He'd hoped that would be the end of things. But his parents were who they were, and their tolerance for Jason's increasing and increasingly obvious disrespect seemed to know no limits. They'd started reaching out after he'd made his first Big Hammer announcement. Of course, he'd already blocked their numbers, but they wouldn't stoop to reaching out directly anyway. Instead, occasionally, one of his mother's assistants or someone from his father's office would contact Naomi to discuss partnering with Big Hammer. And Naomi would politely but firmly tell them to fuck off. But the calls were only an excuse because his father only knew one way to talk to people. Business.

"You should just hang up on them. That's what I'd do."

Naomi remained silent for long enough that Jason thought the call had dropped. "Jason." Her ability to pack an entire scolding's worth of impact into a single word was always impressive, even if it never worked.

"Even if we were looking for a partner, which we're not, Brightstar is the last company I'd ever partner with."

"You know that's not what this is about."

"Of course, I fucking know." Jason swallowed the bile that had started creeping up his throat. Even the idea of talking to his parents gave him heartburn. "I'm not letting you guilt me into going back on my promise to them. And if Gerald Park really wants to ignore the fact that I cut him out of my life, there are a hundred other ways he could reach out to me."

"So, that's it then?"

"I'm telling you, just hang up on them."

"Alright, fine. They're your family. Far be it from me to tell you how to handle them."

As if Naomi hadn't just been doing that. Jason snorted. "Good. And we're just getting to the hotel, so I gotta let you go. Bye."

Jason tapped the steering wheel button again to end the call, still fuming. Naomi had warned him that the news could wait, but he'd insisted on hearing it right away. Still, if she hadn't wanted him to know, she could've waited to call him later. It felt like the universe conspired to ruin his mood on an otherwise lovely spring day. Well, it was welcome to try. He shook his head as he pulled up to the valet station at the Sunset Grand Hotel, revving the engine for added effect.

Jason waited for one of the valets to open his door before stepping out of the car.

"Good afternoon, Mr. Park. Welcome back to the Sunset Grand."

Jason was impressed. He was hardly an A-list celebrity, so it was nice to be greeted by name. Maybe it was due to his status as a *controversial public figure,* as Seong Hyeon had claimed. A second valet had opened Seong Hyeon's door but didn't offer him a personalized greeting. Jason nodded in thanks as he slipped his valet a hundred. He'd never before had a valet return his baby scratched and wasn't about to start.

"That was a large tip," Seong Hyeon shared as they walked under the entrance portico.

Jason snorted. "My car's worth more than a billion won." He'd guessed on the exchange rate, but at that level, it was close enough. "It merits a big tip."

Seong Woo had asked Jason to meet him for lunch on his last day in town. Since he was staying at the Sunset Grand, it was easiest just to meet him there. Plus, their security was enough to satisfy even Seong Hyeon. There wouldn't be anyone inside the hotel or restaurant that didn't have any business being there.

Jason was excited they were having lunch, just the two of them, since so much of their time together during Seong Woo's short stay had been business. It made sense that they were friends since Tae Hyun and Yoo Mi were so close. Plus, Jason really connected with Seong Woo. He figured it was because the man had spent so many years in California for college and grad school. He was still very much Korean, as opposed to Jason being Korean-American. But Seong Woo was Americanized enough that Jason related better to him than most other Koreans from Korea. It didn't hurt that Seong Woo had a model's good looks and athlete's body, even if he was depressingly straight.

After Jason checked in at the hotel restaurant's host station, he was led through the main dining room to a section of the pool deck set with outdoor seating. It wasn't warm enough for sunbathing, but a few pasty, die-hard tourists were attempting it anyway. Maybe they were from somewhere that sixty-five degrees was considered warm. Seong Hyeon peeled off soon after they were outside to take a seat at the bar while the host brought him to Seong Woo's table.

"Here you are, Mr. Park," the host said as she pulled out Jason's chair. "Enjoy your lunch."

Seong Woo chuckled as Jason sat. "Does the service staff here always greet you by name?"

"I'm a movie star. A lot of people know my name." Jason snorted. "Besides, you can't tell me you don't get the same thing everywhere you go in Seoul, Cho Seong Woo."

Seong Woo graciously nodded. "Fair enough. I–" He stopped when the phone sitting on the table dinged. He glanced at it and frowned. "What? Already?"

Trouble in paradise?"

Seong Woo half-rolled his eyes and shook his head as he picked up his phone. "No, just wedding stuff." He typed out a quick reply and set the phone down. "Sometimes I wish we'd just gone with a wedding castle."

Jason chuckled. "I'm sorry. A what?"

"It's a Korean thing. Weddings are different back there. All the stuff we're doing? The big ceremony with the attendants and fancy reception? That's all Western shit. Normally, we go to a place specializing in weddings, and we're in and out in a couple hours. It's a whole industry back home."

Jason smirked. "Sounds romantic."

Seong Woo shrugged. "I've been to American weddings. Don't tell me it needs to take a whole day to be romantic."

"I know, right?" Jason snorted. "I went to a Mexican wedding where they had a full mass in both English and Spanish. And they had an open tequila bar before dinner, which they didn't even serve until ten PM. It was a long fucking day."

Seong Woo laughed. "Well, you won't have to worry about that with us. Yoo Mi may want a fairy tale wedding, but she knows her guests will get cranky if she keeps them too long." He smiled. "Anyway, I appreciate you meeting with me today.

Jason frowned. "Meeting with you? I thought we were having lunch."

"Alright. Thank you for meeting with me for lunch."

Jason shook his head. "No way. Nobody says meeting *with* me for lunch. Meeting *with* me means business. And I know this can't be business. Otherwise, Naomi will kill us for leaving her out."

"Fine. Then call it personal business. I ordered you a Kingston, by the way."

Jason had an uncomfortable flashback to the Kingston bottle Ji Hoon had added to his office bar for the express purpose of smoothing over Jason during their meetings. "So this is a bad news meeting, then?"

"Not exactly." Seong Woo glanced over Jason's shoulder. "Ah, here come drinks. How about we order lunch now so you don't feel like I totally misled you."

Jason snorted. "Okay, but I'm ordering the most expensive thing on the menu now."

A server dropped off Jason's neat Kingston and a vodka martini for Seong Woo. Jason didn't order the most expensive thing on the menu because it was lunch, and he didn't need all that food. He settled for the pan-seared tuna on a bed of steamed greens instead.

Seong Woo held up his glass to make a toast. "To successful business ventures."

Jason lifted his Kingston in salute before taking a sip. "Okay, do we do small talk first, or do we get right to whatever's going on that you had to trick me into meeting with you?"

Seong Woo chuckled. "Let's save the small talk for after." He took another sip of his martini before setting the glass down. "I wanted to meet because my analysts have been hearing about strange things happening in the market lately."

"Strange things?"

Seong Woo nodded. "Nothing definite or official, mind you. But it seems like KBR might be liquidating some of its assets."

Jason nodded. "Okay. Pretend I don't have an MBA and explain why that's of interest to me."

Seong Woo chuckled. "I'm getting there. You see, on the surface, it means nothing. KBR has grown enough over the past decade to have multiple subsidiaries and partner companies. Mostly, it's typical vertical expansion stuff. Buying partial or controlling interests in venues, merchandise manufacturers, distribution networks, media outlets, that sort of thing. That gives them a greater degree of control throughout the entire production process." He paused to sip from his glass and give Jason a moment to digest what he'd said.

Ordinarily, Jason would tune out a lecture on corporate structures. But he knew Seong Woo would only bring up the subject if it was relevant. And he was paying for lunch. "Okay."

"The assets they're liquidating could be easily explained away as operational streamlining or divesting from unnecessary expenses."

"Could be?"

Seong Woo nodded. "Yes. Or, it could be belt-tightening. We don't know because it's a privately held company, so only the owners can see the books. But their deal with your father's company raised some flags with my analysts. And then that deal fell apart, raising more flags."

Jason frowned. "Why did the Brightstar deal raise some flags?"

"Because Pak Jun Ho's never done anything like that before. Ten years ago–hell, five years ago, Pak would've sooner sold one of his sons than get outside investors. So we're wondering if KBR isn't as financially stable as they'd have us believe."

Jason picked up his glass and gently shook it, watching the amber liquid inside slosh and swirl. It was his father's deal with KBR that had sent a blissfully unaware Jason to Korea, where he met Tae Hyun, fell in love with him, and nearly lost him. And it was the straw that finally broke the camel's back in Jason's already strained relationship with his father. "So, what? You think Pak needed my father's money?"

"Maybe. Or, maybe it was the prelude to a takeover." Seong Woo shrugged. "Like I said, we don't know. But my analyst team is pretty sharp. Even if they don't know exactly what's happening, they're sure something is happening."

Jason frowned again. "I still don't see why you're bringing this to me."

"Because my gut tells me that something's up. The deal with your father, liquidating assets, and the way they're fighting Tae Hyun?" Seong Woo shook his head. "I figured it's worth warning you to watch your back."

Jason snorted. "I mean, I've never stopped." He swallowed the last of his Kingston as he considered Seong Woo's warning. It still didn't make any sense. But if Seong Woo thought it was important enough to call a meeting, then–Wait. "But that's not all, right? You could've put all this in an email or a report I wouldn't read. There's something else."

Seong Woo gently sighed as he nodded. "Yeah, there's something else. Naomi's been running the numbers for Big Hammer and sent them to me for review. But my conclusion's the same as hers. At the rate we're going, unless the tour is successful, we'll run out of money before the end of next year."

Jason shook his head. "The tour and album will absolutely make money. If you didn't believe that, you wouldn't have invested."

"That's true. But the issue is that my investment is limited to my own money. You know my father would never allow me to spend Imperative Group funds on Big Hammer, right?"

Jason reluctantly nodded. While Seong Woo had no aversion to spending money to support a gay artist, the Cho family companies did. That was why Jason's return to Korean snack food commercials had been cut so short. "Of course. But what are you really saying here?"

Seong Woo frowned. "I'm sure Naomi will give you her version of this speech sometime soon. But I wanted you to hear this part from me directly. I'll gladly and happily sink all the money I have into this venture because I believe it'll succeed. And my point is that I've pretty much already done that."

"Ah." Jason sat back in his chair, willing the server to reappear with another drink for him. Of course, Seong Woo and Naomi believed in Big Hammer. They'd both personally invested in it. Even Tae Hyun had once he got his contract buyout payment. But the bulk of the money had come from Jason. And Seong Woo was telling him that, until they started making money from a tour and album sales, it would still have to come from him.

Hearing that didn't bother Jason as much as it could've. He'd known all along that starting a production company would be a risk. Hundreds of startups like his folded for every one that achieved any success. But those startups didn't have him. And more importantly, they didn't have a worldwide platinum-selling recording artist like Tae Hyun. If it came down to it, Jason would mortgage his house and sell his precious Monaco to keep Big Hammer afloat. "Okay. I get it. Thank you."

Seong Woo nodded. "Good. It's important that you know I'm coming from a good place here. I consider you to be a friend as much as a business partner."

Jason smiled. "As long as you're paying for lunch. But I gotta piss." He pushed his chair back and stood. "Order me another drink if the server ever comes back."

"You got it."

Jason glanced at Seong Hyeon as he walked toward the hotel's back entrance, shaking his head to indicate he didn't need assistance. He knew Seong Hyeon might still follow him, but he was more than capable of going to the bathroom alone.

Although Seong Woo's news didn't totally sit well with Jason, it also didn't surprise him. He knew he'd been impulsive to offer Tae Hyun his services as a producer, especially given his lack of experience. But he believed in Tae Hyun and his talents. More importantly, he loved Tae Hyun enough that he would absolutely sell everything he owned to fund his album and tour.

After a quick check on his hair in the bathroom lighting, Jason headed for a urinal and unzipped. He was in the middle of pissing when the bathroom door opened again.

"Well, if it isn't *the* Jason Park."

Jason immediately recognized that voice and audibly groaned. It belonged to Danny Crash, a notorious gossip columnist from the *Hollywood Hush*. For years, Jason couldn't trip on the sidewalk without ending up in Danny's gossip blog. It had been the primary reason Jason's father started buying off reporters and paparazzi. "Are you back to your old ways, Danny? Cornering celebrities while they've got their pants down?" He shook off the dribbles, stuffed his junk in his underwear, and zipped up. "Or is this your cruising zone? Cuz I didn't know."

Danny chuckled as Jason walked over to the sink to wash his hands. "Nobody cruises the Sunset Grand, Jason. Of course, you're just a baby gay, so you probably didn't know that."

Jason shook his wet hands before reaching for a towel. "I'd say it's a pleasure seeing you again, but we'd both know that's not true."

Danny briefly frowned. "I suppose I deserve that. Honestly, I probably would've gone easier on you if I'd known you were one of us."

Jason snorted. "I think we both know that's not true, either."

"Maybe, yeah. Look, I'm not here to corner you or anything. I honestly just came to pee. But, since you're here–"

"I'm not gonna fuck you, Danny."

Danny frowned again. "I suppose I deserve that, too. But, seriously. I normally don't share my gossip with the subjects of that gossip. But I've been hearing things about you recently."

Jason finished drying his hands, tossed the towel in the wicker bin next to the sink, and turned to face Danny. A few years older than him, the skinny, pale, freckled ginger had made his name on the backs of messy celebrities like Jason. The fact that he'd managed to hide his sexuality from Danny and all the other gossip queens was something of a minor miracle. "What things?"

"Well, nothing serious or credible. Otherwise, you'd be reading about it in my column. But someone's out there floating rumors about you. It's just stupid shit. Like you're cheating on Tae Hyun. Or that you brainwashed him into coming out, and he's your sex slave."

Jason snorted. "I brainwashed him? Come on."

Danny shrugged. "That's what I mean. Stupid shit. But it's

not just nasty netizens saying whatever evil shit they can think of because you wore the wrong color in your last interview. It's real people saying this stuff. Hell, two of my friends asked me if it was true that you're both sleeping with your hot security guards."

Jason scoffed. "Those guys are so very straight."

"I know, right? Any gay worth their weight in poppers can see that." Danny huffed. "Look, I know I owe you, right? For all those years when you were such a fucking mess. I gained so many readers from your dumb ass."

Jason chuckled. "I gotta say, I never thought the day would come when you'd say something like that to me."

"Yeah. Well, I saw Tae Hyun's declaration of love to you, along with the rest of the world. And it warmed even my cold, bitter little heart. You two are the closest thing our community has to a fairy tale these days." Danny huffed. "It's a shitty world out there. And we need more stories like yours. That's why I wanted to warn you."

Jason couldn't help but notice Danny said *warn him*. That made it his second warning of the day, and it was only lunchtime. "Do you think it's that serious?"

Danny shrugged. "Who knows? But I never hear this much shit talk about a celeb unless someone's running a smear campaign. And it seems like you've got a certain evil entertainment empire gunning for you."

Jason frowned. "You think it's KBR behind this?"

Danny shook his head. "I said nothing of the sort. But they haven't exactly been subtle about kicking Tae Hyun to the curb. Right?"

Jason had to agree. It was easy to point the finger at KBR, considering the lengths they'd already gone to fuck with Tae

Hyun. Who's to say their 24/7 global marketing machine wasn't pumping out a stream of shit rumors about him and his lover just to fuck with them some more. "Alright, Danny. Thanks for the heads up." He smiled. "Maybe it was good to see you, after all. But don't quote me on that."

Jason stopped halfway back to the pool deck. What were the odds that a fucker like Danny Crash would happen to run into Jason in the Sunset Grand bathroom while he was full of juicy rumors? Especially on the same day his father had reached out to Naomi. Something about the whole situation stank. It would hardly have been the first time his father had meddled in his life behind the scenes. He grabbed his phone and headed for the lobby, dialing Min Ji's number on the way. The Vital Agency lead answered on the third ring.

"Hello, Mr. Park, sir. What can I do for you?"

Jason's initial request for her would've been to stop calling him sir. It made sense to use the comparable honorifics in Korean. But it sounded pretentious in English. Still, he had other reasons for calling. "Hi, Min Ji. I just ran into Danny Crash at the Sunset Grand."

"Danny Crash," Min Ji repeated over the sounds of a keyboard clacking. "The *Hollywood Hush* gossip columnist? Is there a story you want me to kill?"

"No." Jason realized he'd begun pacing and forced himself to stop. "He actually warned me that there are suddenly a lot of rumors out there about Tae Hyun and me. Has your team noticed anything like that?"

"Ah. We haven't seen anything unusual on the sites we monitor. That's not to say that people aren't talking or saying nasty things about you."

"Naturally."

"What sort of rumors, sir?"

Jason huffed, reluctant to repeat them lest he unintentionally manifest them. "That I'm cheating. That I brainwashed Tae Hyun into being gay, and he's now my sex slave. That we're fucking the Song brothers. That sorta thing."

Min Ji paused long enough that Jason wondered if he'd offended her. Then her keyboard clacked away. "Okay. I'll have my team look into it. If people really are spreading those rumors, we should be able to find them."

"Any chance you could find out who's doing it?"

"We could try. Honestly, that would be something more appropriate to ask of Yu Min Kyu or your security team. Would you like me to reach out?"

"No." Jason shook his head even though she couldn't see him. "I'll talk to Seong Hyeon. And Min Ji?"

"Yes, sir."

"Could you keep this between us for now? I don't want to worry Tae Hyun with it if there's nothing to it."

"Of course, Mr. Park. Give us a little time to look into things. I'll call you if I learn anything in the meantime."

"Thanks, Min Ji. Talk to you later."

Jason hung up and stuffed his phone into his pocket. Then he turned to head back to the pool deck and nearly ran into Seong Hyeon. "Damn it."

"Sorry, sir." Seong Hyeon's expression didn't look the least bit sorry. "I followed you after you didn't return."

"Did you hear all that?" Seong Hyeon nodded. "Good. That saves me from telling you about it. Don't do anything about it for now. Let's see what Vital comes up with first."

Seong Hyeon nodded once. "Yes, sir. Also, you know Miss Kwon will certainly report on this to Mr. Cho."

"Yeah, yeah." Jason was Vital's client. But Seong Woo was Kwon Min Ji's boss. "I know. But there's nothing I can do about that." He gave Seong Hyeon a friendly clap on the arm. "But I gotta get back. I'm sure my lunch is getting cold." He moved to step around Seong Hyeon, who shifted to block his path.

"A moment, sir."

Jason's eyebrows peaked. It was out of character for his security chief to simply assert himself that way. Or, more precisely, it used to be out of character but had recently emerged as part of a new and improved Seong Hyeon. "What's up?"

"Don't forget where Cho Seong Woo comes from, sir."

Jason frowned. "What does that mean?"

"Mr. Cho's mannerisms and personality may seem very American to you. But he's not American. He's Korean. And, as such, his drive and motivations might not be what they seem."

Jason quietly scoffed. For a man who never usually shared his opinions about people, he sure seemed to have a lot of them lately. "So, you're saying I can't trust Seong Woo?"

Seong Hyeon shook his head. "No, that's not what I mean. I don't believe Mr. Cho is being dishonest with you. But he's beholden to his culture and, more importantly, his family in a way that I suspect you're probably familiar with."

Jason slowly leaned back as his body reacted to the broader perspective Seong Hyeon had just given him. His security chief was right. Jason hadn't really considered that, underneath all of Seong Woo's breezy swagger and flawless California accent, still beat the heart of the favored son of a not-quite chaebol family. Jason wasn't sure how that might change things between them. But he knew then that it definitely would somehow. He nodded. "Alright. Thanks for the insight."

"Of course, sir."

Jason's head spun as he ducked around Seong Hyeon, who discretely followed him toward the pool deck exit. He'd just experienced too many bad omens and insights for it to be a coincidence. If he were at all superstitious, he might be worried. But he wasn't. Because what Seong Hyeon probably didn't know was that Jason generally always expected the worst from people. His parents had taught him that by never once rising to meet his expectations. So, he considered Seong Woo to be a friend only as much as he was willing to allow the man to let him down. When push came to shove, he knew Seong Woo would always look out for himself and his own before anything else. It's what Jason would do, too. And he'd always known Danny Crash to be full of shit. So he gave it even odds that Danny's supposedly friendly gesture was meant only to stir the waters and see what came up. But he couldn't count on that. That day was the first time in Jason's life Danny Crash had brought news to him instead of the other way around. And it was all enough to set him on edge.

Hopefully, Jason had another Kingston waiting at the table.

05

Tae Hyun could hardly believe he was back. It had been almost four years to the day since he'd last set foot inside the Cooper Todd Memorial Concert Hall in downtown Los Angeles for the Music Video Awards broadcast. *XTC* had won four trophies that night, including Best Pop Song and Album. And they'd performed *Blossom* live on the award show stage. That year was easily the peak of his music career. Not that he had any idea at the time. But, back then, he was happy, in love, and riding the cresting wave of worldwide acclaim. A year later, he was serving army stew to bored, unhappy troops in a freezing mess hall within pissing distance of the northern border.

Tae Hyun had been full of nervous energy that night, too–but for a totally different reason. Where before he'd been buzzing with excitement after delivering the performance of his life–while not everyone agreed, most people thought *XTC*'s *Blossom* stage at the Music Video Awards had been one of their best–he was instead brimming with uneasy apprehension. Everything in his life was different than before. He was no longer the leader of *XTC* and hadn't been nominated for any awards. Instead, he and Jason had been asked to present the Best New Pop Album award during the broadcast. But he was still a bundle of anxiety, even if it was only the dress rehearsal. After all, it was his first major public appearance since he'd come out, and everything changed.

"Hey." Jason gave Tae Hyun's hand a gentle squeeze. "How are you holding up?"

Tae Hyun forced a smile and returned the squeeze. "I'll be okay. It's just that this place brings back memories."

"I'll bet it does." Jason smiled. "And we're about to make some new ones."

Tae Hyun wasn't just anxious. Truthfully, his feelings were all over the map. He was excited to be among so many of his peers again after his self-enforced Los Angeles exile. He'd almost had a chance to attend the Korean Music Awards the month before. He'd been invited, of course. But the show had ultimately rescinded his invitation. It didn't take much thought to figure out why. KBR was one of the Big Four and held a great deal of sway on its own turf. It was good that Los Angeles was well outside their domain, or he and Jason may have been forced to watch the Awards broadcast on TV. So Tae Hyun's emotions swung between the exhilarating anticipation of finally being part of the legitimate music scene again and the restless tension of not knowing exactly where he stood in that scene anymore.

And not-so-quietly hiding among those feelings was a shadow of worry about seeing Xiang again. Tae Hyun hadn't spoken with him since that fateful video release party beyond trading a few secret messages that he assumed Xiang had deleted afterward. But Xiang's video had been deservedly nominated for a Music Video Award after winning several at the Korean Music Awards. And Xiang would be there to perform the single live. Tae Hyun knew they probably wouldn't get to speak. But he hoped to at least get a few private words with him somehow.

Jason seemed to be having the time of his life. He was more animated on the ride to the theater than Tae Hyun had seen in a long time. And he wasn't shy when Tae Hyun had asked about it.

"I know," Jason replied with a grin. "Right? I haven't been in front of a camera since before I even met you." He briefly frowned. "Not counting that fucking CheezyFish commercial." Then his grin returned. "So, of course, I'm excited. Not that it's anything big. But it's a camera and a stage, so I'll take it."

After checking in with production–who told them they'd get called to line up with the other presenters after *Pluto's Orbit* finished their sound check and rehearsal–Tae Hyun fell into his old habits and started working the room like a pro. Of course, he knew quite a few of the artists he'd met over the years, most of whom were generally happy to see him and meet Jason. But not everyone wanted to talk. Some artists, including the boys from *DAZ3,* turned and walked away the moment they saw him.

Jason had just introduced Tae Hyun to Reggie Wakefield, a longtime veteran movie actor he'd briefly worked with on a film that never made it out of development, when someone called out his name.

"Well, goddamn, J!" Although he'd never met her, Tae Hyun recognized Raven Wild immediately. Raven's music spanned several genres, including indie rock, R&B, and hip-hop. And she was a rare example of a dark-skinned artist who'd become popular in Korea and other East Asian markets. Many K-pop labels had unsuccessfully tried to emulate her unique sound before giving up and simply hiring her to write for and perform with their groups. "Where the hell you been?"

Jason quickly ran over and threw his arms around Raven. The pair laughed as they hugged. They were obviously fond of each other. Then Jason excitedly took Tae Hyun's hand and pulled him closer. "Tae Hyun, you've gotta meet my friend Raven!"

Raven looked casual and breezy in distressed, bell-bottom jeans and a tight, black spaghetti-strap tank top that showed off her shoulders and curves. She shared a broad smile, her teeth brightly shining against dark aubergine lipstick that brought out the plum tones in her deep brown skin. "Shit, J. You ain't told me how fine he is."

Jason chuckled. "No, I'm pretty sure I told you."

"Maybe, yeah." Raven held out her hand, showing off glossy nails that matched her lipstick. "Hey, Tae Hyun. I'm glad to finally meet you."

"It's nice to meet you, too." Tae Hyun smiled as he shook Raven's hand. "I'm a little surprised we've never met before."

Raven nodded. "I know, right? I think KBR is the only label I never worked with."

"Which was lucky for us," Jason added. "Or you might not have given us the Gordo Hong hookup."

Raven chuckled. "Shit. As if I'd let a fucking record label tell me who I can or can't work with."

Tae Hyun couldn't keep himself from frowning in time. Then he decided he didn't care. His troubles with KBR had been an open secret lately, anyway. Why bother hiding his feelings about them to a fellow musician? "If only everyone felt that way."

Raven's smile turned a little sad as she touched Tae Hyun's

shoulder. "That's real. But hang in there, baby. I know you gotta feel like everybody been coming down on you. And, honestly, some folk really are. But lots of us love your music, including me. So, trust me. You'll come out on top of this."

Tae Hyun smiled to cover his embarrassment. Hearing that from someone with her standing in the industry meant a lot. "Thank you. That's very kind."

Raven nodded. "For sure." Then she frowned. "But it's pretty bad, right? I heard rumors about some of the shit KBR been pulling. I mean, I ain't worked with them. But they got no chill."

"It's not all that surprising," Tae Hyun confessed. "They are who they are."

Raven snorted. "Yeah. A bunch of sexist, homophobic–"

"Raven," Jason interrupted.

Raven nodded. "Okay, yeah. Sorry. Guess you know all that shit already. But lemme tell you something else." Tae Hyun nodded as she put her arm around Jason and pointed an aubergine nail at his chest. "Stick with this one. And don't let his bad boy rep fool you. I've known him since he was a scrawny teen idol."

Jason jokingly scoffed. "I was never fucking scrawny."

"Compared to now?" Raven laughed as she tried grabbing one of Jason's biceps. "You could do a lot worse than with this bomb-ass beefcake at your back, baby."

Tae Hyun grinned as he recalled how Jason had literally been at his back several times recently. "Actually, we take turns being in the back."

Raven's well-shaped brows briefly shot up before she barked out a laugh so loud she almost choked. "Oh shit," she called out, playfully smacking Tae Hyun's arm. "You're all right, Tae Hyun." Then she wrapped her free arm around his shoulder and pulled him close. "I see J finally met his match."

Jason snorted. "Oh, he outmatches me in every possible way."

"Maybe so. But I'm glad I ran into you cuz I want you both at my after-party tomorrow night. It'll be poppin'. And it's been too damn long since Jason fucking Park threw down at one of my parties." Raven gave Tae Hyun a little squeeze. "Plus, I'm sure I've got more folks for you to meet."

"We'll definitely be there," Jason assured her.

"Good." Raven gave the boys a final squeeze before she let go. "But I gotta go find my presenting partner. I know they're around–" She paused, frowning, as the group was approached by a frantic-looking woman carrying a clipboard. Tae Hyun's mental alarm bells immediately went off.

"Mr. Park? Mr. Woo? I'm Alicia from the production team."

Jason frowned. Maybe he'd had the same thought as Tae Hyun. "What's up, Alicia?"

Alicia's sad smile slipped a bit. "I'm afraid there's been some changes in our lineup, and we'll no longer need you as presenters tomorrow. I'm sorry to let you know so late."

Tae Hyun was surprised to hear that. He'd done enough presenting work to know that there were always a lot of last-minute schedule tweaks and assumed it would be something simple like a time change. To completely pull someone from the lineup during rehearsal wasn't unheard of. But it felt off.

Raven scoffed. "That's fucked up." She obviously agreed.

"What do you mean you no longer need us?" Jason's frown had become a scowl. "What kind of bullshit is that?"

Alicia visibly flinched. "I'm sorry, Mr. Park. I'm only telling you what they told me."

Jason's jaw muscles flared as he gritted his teeth. "What *who* told you?"

"The producers." Alicia's voice had gone so quiet Tae Hyun could hardly hear her.

Jason shook his head. "Well, if they want to fire us, they should have the fucking decency to tell us themselves."

"Yeah," Raven agreed. "Why don't you tell 'em to get they asses out here and do their own dirty work?"

Tae Hyun sensed everyone's attention turning their way, triggering years of public conflict avoidance instincts he couldn't ignore. The last thing he wanted was to end up on the front page of an entertainment blog under a snarky headline about poorly behaved idols. And, justified or not, Jason's anger wasn't helping anything. He put his hand on Jason's arm. "It's fine, Jason."

But Jason wasn't ready to let it go. Where Tae Hyun's instinct was to always smooth over public conflict, Jason automatically went to confrontation. "No, it's not fine. It's rude and disrespectful."

Tae Hyun was torn. The show's producers were disrespecting them and their time, and Jason was right to feel how he did about it. And Tae Hyun had already been anxious about his first public appearance before things started getting out of hand. And, as much as he hated to admit it, there was only one likely reason it was happening. His anger, carefully buried under his long-practiced mask of patient acceptance, threatened to burst out. He didn't want to be there anymore. Not if things were gonna be like that. "No, Jason. Let's just go."

"What?" Jason angrily huffed. "But you know why, right?

You know why they're doing this."

"Of course, I know why!" Tae Hyun's volume shot up as his control finally slipped, and his anger rushed to the surface and poured out. "It's the same reason why we can't get a venue in Seoul. It's the same reason why I haven't spoken with any of my friends at KBR in months. It's the same reason why I'm living here with you instead of back home!" Jason physically recoiled as if Tae Hyun had hit him. That was why he wanted to leave before he lost control. He'd said too much. "I'm sorry. I didn't mean that like it sounded."

Jason huffed. "It's okay. I know what you meant. And you're right, we should go." He turned to Alicia, still frowning, but the threat was gone from his stance. "I'm sorry I yelled. I know it's not your fault. But you can still tell your bosses I said to fuck off."

Tae Hyun took Jason by the hand as they walked away from Raven and Alicia. He mentally berated himself for daring to be excited about being a part of the industry again. He'd let his guard down and enjoyed meeting and talking with everyone at the rehearsal. And then his old label reached their clawed hands clear across the Pacific and snatched that from him, too. He imagined his former manager, Choo Ji Hoon, gleefully cackling behind the curtain as he sent out Alicia from production to dash Tae Hyun's hopes again. There was a point in the not-too-distant past when Tae Hyun had struggled to stand up to Ji Hoon. But that point had long since passed. If Director Choo ever showed his face to Tae Hyun again, he'd see a whole new side of his formerly favorite idol.

"Hyung, wait!" Tae Hyun automatically stopped at the sound of that voice. He hadn't heard it in months. But they'd spent years living and touring together, so he knew it as well as his own. He turned around as Xiang rushed toward him. "Please, don't leave yet."

"Xiang? What's going on?"

Tae Hyun's former group member ran up and put his hand on Tae Hyun's shoulder. "I just found out what happened." He huffed, sounding out of breath. "And I'm fucking sick of this shit. So I told Oh Min Su I wouldn't perform tomorrow if they didn't let you present the award."

Tae Hyun's mouth fell open. So much was happening he could hardly get his head around it. Xiang had confirmed Tae Hyun's suspicion that KBR was behind everything. But he'd also refused to perform? No. That wasn't okay. "You can't do that, Xiang. It's just an awards show. What if they fire you?"

Xiang huffed. "It's not just this awards show, and you know it. Besides, let them fire me. I've got competing offers from a half-dozen Chinese labels right now. I'll be fine."

Tae Hyun hesitated. So, it wasn't entirely altruistic. Xiang was manipulating Tae Hyun's situation just like KBR and–No. It was Xiang. He wasn't using Tae Hyun. He was just flexing his power as the biggest name in KBR's lineup. "It's so good to see you." Tae Hyun pulled Xiang into a firm embrace. "I missed you."

Xiang held Tae Hyun for several moments before letting go. "I missed you, too, hyung." Then he smiled at Jason. "It's nice to see you, too, Jason." He gave both of them a blatant once-over. "You're both looking good. I see Hollywood life suits you."

Tae Hyun chuckled, knowing that *Hollywood life* was definitely a euphemism. "It's all the sunshine. But you look good, too." Even dressed down for the rehearsal, Xiang was still incredibly well put together in a shiny black tracksuit with white piping and the hanja spelling of his name embroidered in white on his chest. He was still blond–or had gone back to blond–but his hair was so ash-toned it was nearly lavender. "I'd say solo life suits you."

Xiang chuckled. "It keeps me busy, that's for sure. As a matter of fact, I–"

"There you are, Xiang." A familiar Korean man walked up behind Xiang, wearing a KBR hoodie and light blue jeans. Despite it having been close to three years since Tae Hyun had last seen him, he still recognized Oh Min Su right away. He looked older than Tae Hyun remembered–and definitely older than his thirty years. His recently trimmed hair was thinner and his face a little softer, too. But he was still handsome, if a bit rough. "We need to–Ah." Min Su's face fell as soon as he noticed who else was standing there. "It's you."

Min Su was one of *XTC*'s former road managers, a highly-coveted position for many die-hard K-pop fans, given the amount of time they spent with the idols in their care. Of course, the position was hardly as glamorous as fans imagined it to be. Road managers often worked harder and for longer hours than even the idols. And Min Su had been no exception. A former KBR trainee, he'd moved into management after making several failed attempts to debut as an idol. Tae Hyun had hoped that his trainee experience would give him an understanding that other road managers didn't have. But the opposite turned out to be true. Tae Hyun didn't know if Min Su harbored a grudge about failing to debut or just didn't know how to deal with a road manager's stress. But he was often gruff and short-tempered with his idols, especially when they were on tour. Tae Hyun always tried to be understanding, knowing it wasn't an easy job. But Min Su was hard to like. At least Tae Hyun felt less guilty about sneaking around with Chang Min behind his back.

Since Min Su was in Los Angeles, he must've been given the job as Xiang's road manager after *XTC* went on hiatus. And the little empathy and understanding he'd shown Tae Hyun in the past was clearly gone. Tae Hyun could've hardly imagined a more awkward meeting, so he fell back on habitual politeness and bowed. "Hello, Oh Min Su. It's good to see you."

Min Su sighed and shook his head. "No. I could lose my job just for talking to you." He returned his attention to Xiang. "And you need to seriously think about what you're doing here."

Xiang loudly snorted. "You don't think I have, Min Su?" Tae Hyun was surprised at Xiang's defiant tone. Maybe Tae Hyun wasn't the only one dealing with Min Su's lack of understanding. "You know Tae Hyun and I have been friends since we were teenagers. We fucking grew up together." He shook his head. "Hell, just look at you acting like even standing next to him for too long will make you explode." He scoffed. "If you think I'm about to let CEO Pak tell me I can't even talk with my friend just because he–"

Min Su loudly grunted, cutting Xiang off. "That's enough. You've already caused me enough trouble here. We'll be lucky if CEO Pak doesn't have both our heads." He grunted again, roughly taking Xiang by the arm.

Jason, who'd been quietly hovering behind Tae Hyun, suddenly stepped up and yanked Min Su's hand away. "Hey, asshole," he said in Korean. For all of Jason's claims that English was his preferred language, he certainly had no trouble swearing in Korean. And Min Su's shocked expression was priceless. "Yeah, that's right. You've got an audience here. So maybe think about something besides your own ass for a minute." His tight-jawed grin made him look scary and a little unhinged. "And if you're looking to bully someone, why don't you try it with me and see how that goes?"

Min Su's shock quickly faded as he recognized Jason. His quiet chuckle was low and dark. "From what I've heard, you're not exactly one to talk, Mr. Park." He turned back to Xiang. "And if you're still performing, you need to come do your sound check." He gave Tae Hyun one last withering look before shaking his head and walking away.

A foul tension hung between everyone as they silently stood in Min Su's wake. Then Xiang shook his head.

"I'm sorry about all that, hyung." Xiang sighed. "Things are obviously different now." He took Tae Hyun's hand. "And I should probably go. But it was good seeing you. And I'm done with Pak's embargo now." He smiled and pulled Tae Hyun into a quick hug. "So I'll talk to you again soon." Xiang offered Jason a hug as well. "I thought I was good at standing up for myself, sunbaenim. But I see I could take lessons from you. Thank you."

Jason snorted. "I know how to be an asshole in three languages."

Tae Hyun frowned. "Three?"

"What?" Jason shrugged. "I grew up in LA. Of course, I know how to swear in Spanish, too."

After Xiang left, with another promise to stay in contact, Jason tracked down Alicia and sent her to confirm that they were indeed still on as presenters the next day. Tae Hyun anxiously fidgeted as he waited, knocked totally out of sorts by seeing Xiang and Min Su. Everything felt wrong. Min Su was even colder and harsher than he remembered. And, even with the little that Xiang had told him, it was clear that KBR's war against Tae Hyun came directly from CEO Pak. He'd suspected that was the case. But having his suspicions confirmed was much more upsetting than he would've predicted. How could he possibly go up against the CEO of a Big Four label, one of the most powerful people in the Korean entertainment industry? It felt increasingly likely that he'd never be allowed to perform in his home country again, which was something Tae Hyun didn't want to consider.

Tae Hyun tried his best to clamp down on his feelings, afraid he wouldn't stop them in time. But he felt the tears starting anyway. Then Jason wrapped his strong arms around Tae Hyun from behind.

"You've got this," Jason whispered in Tae Hyun's ear. "You're strong, capable, and talented."

Tae Hyun's heart warmed hearing Jason's gentle encouragement. "I still think I might cry."

"Then cry. You may be an idol, but you're a person, too. Let everyone see the real you. It's only gonna make them love you more."

Tae Hyun grabbed onto Jason's arms and squeezed. "Now you're gonna make me cry, hyung."

"Then cry," Jason lovingly purred. "But I've already seen the real you. And I love you the most."

06

After the roller coaster rehearsal day, the Music Video Awards taping was swift and slick without any major issues. When it was their turn to present, Jason and Tae Hyun went onstage to raucous applause compounded by a seemingly ad-libbed but, in reality, completely pre-planned on-camera kiss. Jason had expected Tae Hyun to veto the idea when he proposed it. But he was surprisingly in favor of it.

"It'll get people talking," Tae Hyun agreed with a grin. "Right?"

Of course, the kiss was nothing more than a peck–gotta keep it light for the broadcasters. But they made up for it in the back of the SUV on the way to Raven Wild's after-party. And the Song brothers worked extra hard not to notice anything happening in the back seat.

Raven's house sat perched atop one of the lower Hollywood Hills, meaning it offered a spectacular view but little in the way of parking, forcing Seong Hyeon to stay with the truck while he looked for a place to put it. Jason asked Seong Min to stay behind, too. He'd never known Raven to invite any trouble into her parties–at least, not the kind of trouble that required the beefy Seong Min's presence. Besides, they'd only be a phone call away.

The heartbeat thump of a deep house track poured from the doorway as Jason and Tae Hyun went inside. Jason wondered who Raven had hired to DJ, remembering with a bit of wicked guilt what he and another DJ had gotten up to in Raven's pool house once upon a time. At least, Jason hoped it was another DJ. He didn't want to imagine what might happen if he and Tae Hyun ran into one of his former lovers, especially considering how things had worked out with Tae Hyun's ex. Not that the DJ had been anything more than a makeout session. Or that Tae Hyun wouldn't be okay with it. But some things were probably best left in the past.

"Hot damn, you guys look fucking fierce!" Raven grinned as she approached the pair in the foyer.

Jason smiled. He knew he looked good in his Kimi Wakari-original award show look. She'd dressed him in a deep plum tuxedo jacket and pants and a sleeveless, cream-colored top constructed of two silk swatches layered and draped x-style across his shoulders and chest like a high-fashion gladiator harness. Kimi had dressed Tae Hyun in tailored, sapphire tuxedo trousers, a color-matched, high-collared, long-sleeve top made from a fine mesh that was nearly transparent, and a flouncy, regency style neck-tie. She'd actually come to Jason's house to dress the pair herself, then had her photographer do a quick fashion shoot on Jason's sundeck for posting on social media later. "Not looking half as sexy as you are, Ray Ray. Come gimme a spin, girl."

Raven obligingly offered a slow turn, showing off a silver mini-dress that looked to have been made from high-end chainmail with a plunging back that fell almost to the top of her curvaceous ass. "You likey?"

Jason nodded. "Me likey. How's the party going?"

Raven grinned. "Chill, sexy, and stylish, as always. The old Jason would approve. The new Jason'll have to judge for himself."

Jason caught a side-eye glance from Tae Hyun, so he rolled his eyes at Raven to deflect. It's not like Tae Hyun didn't know about how Jason used to be. But he didn't need any reminders. "Well, I think that's enough small talk. Is the bar in the same place?"

Raven snorted. "Ain't been that long since you been here. Everything's in the same place." Then she winked. "Including the pool house."

Jason playfully wagged a finger at her. "Don't start with me, girl. If everything's in the same place, that means I know where you keep the good hooch."

Raven rolled her eyes. "Don't fucking insult me. It's all good hooch!" Then she turned to Tae Hyun. "Hey, there's somebody here I want you to meet. When I see her again, I'll bring her your way."

Tae Hyun politely nodded. "Alright, thank you."

Despite Tae Hyun's neutral expression, Jason could see he was already in his professional mingling mode. That was fine for public events, but it was a party, so Jason would need to loosen him up. And he'd probably have to explain what hooch was. Hopefully, Tae Hyun wouldn't ask about the pool house. He grabbed Tae Hyun's hand. "Come on. Let's get drinks."

Jason led Tae Hyun away through the foyer into the main room. Raven's house, like Jason's, went top down, with the main living areas on the upper floor. The upstairs lounge also featured a wall of glass on the opposite side, offering a view of the LA basin that was almost as spectacular as his. Unlike Jason, Raven had spent a lot of time and money decorating her house. Her decor was an eclectic blend of mid-century modern and afro-futurist, with lots of dark woods and shiny chrome offset by animal prints and West African art and sculpture. Jason was always mildly jealous of Raven's style. Or, more so the fact that she had style. Yeah, everything in his house matched, but that was because his decorator had given up on him and did everything in shades of gray.

"This house is amazing," Tae Hyun gushed in Korean. "Raven has fantastic taste."

Jason swallowed his jealousy and nodded. "She does," he replied in Korean. "She's one of my favorite people."

"And it's nice that I finally get to spend time with some of your friends."

Jason almost frowned. He knew Tae Hyun hadn't meant that as a dig. And Raven was a friend, but only because she'd considered their relationship entertaining enough to put up with Jason's bullshit over the years. The sad fact was that almost all of Jason's so-called friends lately were people he employed or was in some kind of business relationship with. Hell, he'd even gone into business with Tae Hyun. Was he turning into his father?

"Hey. What's that look for? Did I say something wrong?"

Jason shook off the frown that had still snuck onto his face as he leaned in to kiss Tae Hyun's cheek. "Of course not. Nothing you say is wrong." He smiled. "What are you drinking?"

Tae Hyun shrugged. "Should I get something besides a gin and tonic? I wonder if they have soju."

Jason nodded. "I'm sure there's soju."

"Okay," Tae Hyun smiled. "I'll have that."

Jason walked up to the bar and flagged down the closest

bartender. He ordered a neat Kingston for himself and a soju martini with lemon for Tae Hyun, who put his arm around Jason as they waited. Jason glanced at Tae Hyun's hand draped over his shoulder. "That's new."

Tae Hyun half shrugged. "I know. Whenever you do this to me in public, I make you stop. So, I'm trying it out." He grinned. "It feels weird, but I like it."

Jason chuckled as he handed Tae Hyun his drink. "Good. Me, too."

Tae Hyun sipped his drink and nodded. "This is good."

Jason smiled. "I thought you'd like it." He swallowed some bourbon, grateful for its comforting warmth as it slid down his throat. "What do you think of the party?"

"It's nice. And not very crowded." Tae Hyun did a quick glance at his surroundings. "I assumed there'd be more people."

"There still may be more coming. But some folks will head to other parties, too." Jason grinned. "Between the big labels and other musicians, there's always a lot of award show after-parties."

"Ah." Tae Hyun nodded. "But we're just going to this one?"

Jason chuckled. "Do you want to see some of the others? I suppose we could–"

"No." Tae Hyun shook his head. "This is nice. At least the host knows me here."

Jason snorted. "Everyone knows you here, Tae Hyun. You're famous. Remember?"

"That's not what I meant." Tae Hyun frowned. "They may all know who I am, but I don't know any of them. And I'm not here to be on display."

Jason put his hand on Tae Hyun's arm. "I'm sorry. I wasn't

trying to–"

"I know. It's alright. I guess I feel a little out of my element."

Jason nodded. He'd assumed as much since they were still speaking Korean. "I could introduce you to some people."

"Sure. But let's just enjoy these drinks and the music first."

Jason took a generous swallow of his bourbon just as Raven emerged from the crowd with a familiar face in tow. He nodded over Tae Hyun's shoulder. "I think you might already know someone else here, too."

Tae Hyun turned to look just as Raven walked up beside them. "Riki?"

The familiar face in question was Riki, a Korean-American idol a few years older than Jason. She'd spent several years as leader of the K-pop girl group *Sugar Party* before going solo and splitting her time between Los Angeles and Seoul. She'd poured herself into a midnight-blue metallic body suit accented with a silver rope belt and chunky silver bracelets. And her chocolate brown hair was tightly pulled back into her trademark ponytail. She smiled at Tae Hyun. "I was wondering if you'd remember me."

Tae Hyun enthusiastically nodded. "Of course, I remember you. It's nice to see you again."

Raven nodded as if she was following along and turned to Jason. "I assume they already know each other?"

Jason hadn't even realized they were still speaking Korean. Had he gotten that used to hearing it all the time? He chuckled. "Of course, they know each other. They're both idols."

"Oh, I'm sorry, Raven." Tae Hyun switched to English. "That was rude. Thank you for bringing her to me."

"No problem." Raven smiled. "Sounds like my work here is done. Enjoy the party!" She grinned as she turned and bounced back into the crowd.

"I'm glad you're here," Riki continued in English. "I was excited to hear you'd be at the awards, but I didn't get a chance to say hello."

"Ah." Tae Hyun frowned. "I didn't know you were there."

"That's okay." Riki smiled as her gaze shifted from Tae Hyun to Jason and back. "You're way more on people's minds right now than I am."

Tae Hyun scrunched his face in embarrassment, which Jason rarely saw him do. "Oh. Where are my manners? Riki, this is Jason Park." He paused for a moment. "He's my, uh–"

"Boyfriend." Jason held out a hand in greeting. "I'm his boyfriend. And I wonder if we've already met."

Riki nodded. "I think so, maybe. I've been to most of your movie premieres." She smiled. "And it's actually Rebecca. Rebecca Han. Riki is only my stage name, although most people just call me that anyway." Then she turned back to Tae Hyun. "And I was excited to hear about your solo album. I've been a *Dreamer* ever since *Random Geography*. In fact, I listened to it all the time when I was working on my second album."

Tae Hyun's eyebrows shot up. "Wow! *Starlight Beatdown* was almost singularly responsible for getting me through my last breakup."

"For real?" Riki chuckled. "I think that's the first time I heard that one."

Tae Hyun bashfully grinned. "I was very angry at the time.

"Well, I'm glad I could help."

Jason had finished his Kingston while Tae Hyun and Riki talked, so he glanced toward the bar to see if it was busy and caught a glimpse of Tony Ruiz, the man whose messages he'd been ignoring. He quickly turned away, but not before they made eye contact, and Jason knew it was too late to escape. He pushed a casually friendly grin onto his face. "Hey, Tae Hyun. I'm gonna hit up the bar while you two catch up. Either of you need anything?"

Tae Hyun and Riki both shook their heads. "I'm okay," Tae Hyun said.

"Now I can ask him about you," Riki added with a wink.

Jason chuckled, outwardly casual, while he swallowed his irritation at having to deal with business at a party. He should've just let Tony know what was happening when he had the chance. But it was too late for that. He made sure to keep up his smile as he walked over to the bar.

"Hi, Jason." Tony had dressed low-key for the party–and presumably, the awards show–opting for his typical streetwear style of wide-legged, indigo denim pants and a slim, asphalt gray tufted vest over a white, long-sleeve tee printed with harajuku-style anime girls. He still had his trademark stubble but had cut his straight, formerly shoulder-length black hair short and went with a side part.

"I didn't expect to see you here, Tony."

Tony smiled. "I could say the same thing. You haven't been to one of Raven's parties in years." He nodded toward Jason's glass. "Still a Kingston man?"

Jason chuckled. "You know it."

Tony turned to the bartender and grabbed a bourbon for Jason and a clear cocktail for himself. "Here you go." He handed Jason his drink. "I take it you're done avoiding me now?"

"I haven't been avoiding you," Jason explained as he took the glass. "I've just been so damn busy. You know?"

Tony angrily frowned and rolled his eyes. "We're all busy, Jason. It's fucking Hollywood. But if you don't want the part, just tell me. You don't need to keep blowing me off like I'm some fucking back-office intern."

"It's not like that." Jason huffed. "Of course, I want the fucking part." He angrily shook his head. "But it's only been a few weeks, Tony. I'm busy. I've got a lot going on. So maybe back off a little. Okay?"

Tony's frown melted away. "Shit, Jason. I'm sorry. I might be a little drunk."

Jason reached up to rub the back of his head. He used the gesture to flirt most of the time, but it worked just as well for sheepish apologies. "No, I'm sorry. I should've just told you what I was thinking. Of course, I want the part. It's perfect for me. But I can't take it right now, not with everything going on."

Tony snorted. "See? That's all I need to hear." He shook his head. "I'll tell you something I *never* tell actors, cuz I know it always goes to your fucking head. But I've wanted to work with you again ever since we wrapped *Moon Shines Madly*. And I wrote this fucking part for you."

"Oh." Jason didn't know how to take that. He was obviously flattered. But he hadn't heard a peep from Tony since they finished all the movie press tours. "You did? How come you're just telling me now?"

Tony briefly looked at his chunky, pristine white high tops as he awkwardly shuffled his feet. "You know the score, Jason. It's a small town. You were persona non grata at Lodestar after the Marvin Lindsey thing. And I needed to keep working."

Jason reluctantly nodded. Tony hadn't told him anything new. A lot of doors had slammed in his face that day. Just because they were opening up again didn't change the past. "Yeah, I get it." He sighed. "So, what do we do? Will you wait for me?"

Tony laughed. "I've waited this long, haven't I? Of course, I'll fucking wait. I mean, you'll be producing it, too. Right? I hear that's your new thing."

"It's the only way I could think of to stop getting fired all the time." Jason chuckled. "I mean, it was that or stop beating up creepy old directors." He snorted. "No offense."

Tony playfully scoffed. "Does thirty-five count as old? I mean, I'm definitely creepy."

Jason laughed, remembering how his last director from the CheezyFish commercials had let a stranger onto a closed set to film him while he changed. "You're the least creepy director I worked with, man."

"You always say the sweetest things." Tony gently put his hand on Jason's shoulder. "Look, I'm sorry again for coming on so strong. I'm really excited about working with you again." He grinned. "And, like I said, I may be a little drunk."

Jason patted Tony's arm. "It's all good. I should get back to Tae Hyun. But I promise I'll be in touch."

"That was Tae Hyun?" Tony chuckled. "I thought he looked familiar. My wife's a big fan. She'd kill me if I didn't get a picture with him."

Jason snorted. Of course, even the director who'd admitted writing a script just for him couldn't help geeking out over the K-pop star. "I'll let him know you want one when I find him."

Jason had meant that as a joke, expecting to find Tae Hyun still chatting with Riki. But his idol was nowhere to be seen. He unsuccessfully checked all around Raven's main floor before finally stepping onto the balcony. The cool, nighttime air nearly overwhelmed him and made quick work of the sweat on his brow. He hadn't realized the party had gotten so hot. A few guests had also gone outside, quietly chatting and sipping their cocktails. But no Tae Hyun.

Jason let out a quiet sigh as he walked up to the railing overlooking the pool deck. Tae Hyun had to be in the bathroom, which Jason hadn't checked. Either that, or he'd gone home. Jason was about to check his phone when he spotted the wayward idol leaning on the railing down on the pool deck. Of course. He was at a party with some of the American music industry's hottest names, and Tae Hyun had done what he always did. He'd gone to enjoy the view.

Jason found the stairs down to the pool deck and wandered over to where Tae Hyun stood at the railing. "I should've known I'd find you here.

Tae Hyun turned to Jason and smiled. "It's almost as good as the view from your house.

Jason chuckled as he pointed toward the hills to Tae Hyun's left. "Look up there."

"What?" Tae Hyun turned to look where Jason pointed. "Wait. Is that your house?"

Jason laughed. "Yep."

"Oh, wow. I didn't realize we were so close."

"It would actually be walkable in a straight line from here," Jason explained, "if that was possible. But with all the canyons, it's easier to drive." Jason turned to look at Tae Hyun and was immediately captured by his profile–especially how the moonlight shone off his cheekbones and the curve of his nose. "But I prefer the view from here."

Tae Hyun turned to see Jason looking at him and sheepishly

grinned. Jason knew his ears were turning pink even if he couldn't see it. "You always do that."

"I have yet to find a better view than this one." Jason took Tae Hyun's hands and turned them to face each other. "No matter where we are, you're always what I want to see."

Tae Hyun beamed with a fairy blue glow in the reflected light from Raven's pool. "You always say the sweetest things, hyung." Then, he turned away to face the twinkling lights of the distant LA skyline. "Who was that you were talking to?"

Jason was caught off guard by Tae Hyun's awkward tone. Had he really gone outside because he'd seen Jason talking to someone else when he went to the bar? "A director, actually. Why? Are you jealous?"

Tae Hyun frowned. "No." Then he shook his head. "I mean, I know I'm not supposed to be. You always say you don't own me, so I guess it's the same for me with you."

"But you are?" Jason frowned at Tae Hyun's nod. "That was Antonio Ruiz. He wrote and directed *The Moon Shines Madly*."

Tae Hyun's mouth fell open. "For real? Shit." He shook his head. "I never imagined–" He sighed. "Now I feel stupid."

Jason took Tae Hyun by the hands and turned him back. "Please don't. You feel the way you feel." He gently caressed Tae Hyun's hands with his thumbs. "And you don't have to worry about me. I have no desire to cheat on you. Okay?"

Tae Hyun reluctantly nodded. "I know, hyung. It's not fair for me to put that on you. You're not Chang Min. You've always been honest with me."

Jason watched the undulating pool light paint the shadows of Tae Hyun's cheekbones and quietly sighed. "Well–"

Tae Hyun's breath caught in his throat. "Hyung?"

"No, no." Jason shook his head. "It's nothing like that." He sighed again. "Tony gave me a script a couple weeks ago. He wants to put me in his next movie." He risked a slight grin. "In fact, he just told me he wrote the part for me."

Tae Hyun's glowing eyes grew wide. "What?" He enthusiastically grinned, of course. He admitted once, on their first night together, that *Moon Shines Madly* was his favorite movie. "That's amazing, hyung!" Then his eyebrows fell. "When is it?"

Jason nodded. "That's the thing. I don't know when I'd even have time for a project that big." He shrugged. "That's why I haven't said anything. I don't want to turn it down, but I definitely can't do it now. Not with everything already going on."

Tae Hyun looked down, his frown dripping with guilt and shame. "Hyung, I can't be why you don't get this movie."

Jason let go of Tae Hyun's hand to lightly grasp his chin and lift his face. "In a way, you're why he even offered it to me. A year ago–hell, half a year ago, there was no way he'd consider handing me a new project. Then–"

Tae Hyun snorted. "Then I blew everything up."

"Then you made me the happiest man in the world." Jason leaned in to kiss Tae Hyun. He tasted soju and lemon as he gently prodded Tae Hyun's lips with his tongue. "And he knows I've got more important things going on right now. He said he'd wait."

Tae Hyun slowly ran his tongue along his lower lip. "Are you sure?"

Jason nodded. "Your album and tour are all I want to be doing right now." He grinned. "My turn can be next."

Tae Hyun's grin finally reappeared. "Maybe–" He paused as

he poked a finger at Jason's chest and slowly dragged it down to his waist. "Maybe it could be your turn right now."

"My turn?"

Tae Hyun nodded. "It's been a while since you were on the bottom, hyung."

Jason's eyebrows shot up. "Oh, you want to–" He paused as Tae Hyun nodded. "Oh."

Tae Hyun bit down on his lip as he cupped Jason's crotch and gently squeezed it. Jason's cock sprang to life, quickly getting hard under Tae Hyun's grip. "Can I fuck you, hyung?

Jason pushed forward and planted his lips on Tae Hyun's soft mouth. Tae Hyun responded, hungrily sucking in Jason's tongue as his hand moved to Jason's ass. Jason put his hands on Tae Hyun's hips and pulled him close enough to feel his erection press against his hip. And he wanted more. It had been months since Tae Hyun last topped him, and he'd never initiated it when he did. There was no chance Jason was letting the opportunity go to waste. He pulled off the kiss and leaned close to Tae Hyun's ear. "You really wanna fuck me?"

Tae Hyun quickly nodded. "Yes. We should go."

"No. I have a better idea."

Jason's grin was almost giddy as he took Tae Hyun's hand and pulled him away from the railing, circling the pool toward a small building on the pool deck's far side.

"Where are you taking me?" Tae Hyun's voice was little more than a stage whisper. But Jason could also hear his anxious curiosity.

"The pool house."

They stopped before a door on the side of the building. Jason flipped the keypad cover open and typed in the code he somehow still remembered. Not that he'd forgotten much from that night, the last time he was at one of Raven's parties. The red light above the keypad turned green as the door lock audibly clicked. Jason twisted the knob, shoved the door open, and pulled Tae Hyun inside.

"You want to do it in here?" Tae Hyun's tone had grown more anxious than curious.

Jason went to lock the door before turning back to face Tae Hyun. "Yeah."

Tae Hyun frowned. "I don't know, hyung. Are you sure–"

Jason silenced Tae Hyun with a kiss as his hand found Tae Hyun's still-hard cock. He grabbed hold of it, drawing a surprised hiss from Tae Hyun. "Yes, I'm sure."

"But what if someone finds us?"

Jason chuckled. "No one will find us in here." He knew what he wanted would push Tae Hyun out of his well-defined but increasingly expanding comfort zone. But he'd used Raven's pool house like that before. Hell, she'd even reminded him of that when he arrived. And Tae Hyun had surely done similar things when he was with Chang Min and always under the watchful eyes of his managers and minders? He grinned as he ran his thumb along the length of Tae Hyun's erection. "Tell me you don't want to."

Tae Hyun let out a surprised breath as Jason's thumb found the tip of his cock. "Hyung," he moaned. "You really want me to fuck you right here?"

Jason nodded. "Fuck yes. I want you inside me so fucking bad."

Tae Hyun's expression suddenly shifted from uncertainty to conviction as his lust overcame his doubt. He reached down and squeezed Jason's cock through his pants. "Then tell me you want me to fuck you, hyung."

Jason quietly moaned as Tae Hyun squeezed him. "I want you to fuck me."

"Tell me again," Tae Hyun commanded, squeezing him again.

"Fuck me, Tae Hyun. Right fucking now."

Tae Hyun let go of Jason's cock and undid the clasp on his pants. Jason's throbbing erection sprang free as Tae Hyun yanked his pants and underwear down. But Tae Hyun ignored it, turning Jason around and pushing him forward. Jason obligingly bent over, putting his hands on the wall beside the door for balance. Tae Hyun crouched behind Jason and spread his cheeks apart. Every part of Jason's body screamed yes. That's just what he wanted. Then Tae Hyun buried his face between Jason's cheeks and attacked him with his tongue. A rush of exhilarating warmth surged up Jason's spine as he fought to keep his balance. It had been too long since Tae Hyun last topped him. As much as he enjoyed fucking Tae Hyun, it was finally his turn.

Jason let out a low moan as Tae Hyun's tongue poked, prodded, and swirled around. He wanted to grab his cock, if only to shake off the precum he could feel leaking from it. But the rush of Tae Hyun's tongue pressing against him almost made him dizzy, and he was afraid to let go of the wall.

Then Tae Hyun backed away. "Are you ready, hyung?"

Was he ready? Jason took a moment to pull one of his hands from the wall and spit into his palm. Then he reached back, found Tae Hyun's cock, and wiped the spit on it. "Do it."

Tae Hyun took hold of Jason's hips to brace himself. Then Jason felt Tae Hyun's cock pressing against him. The anticipation nearly made him clench, so he let out a slow breath and tried to relax. The pressure grew, and Jason wondered if maybe he was too tight. Then Tae Hyun's cock slid inside, and Jason was suddenly in heaven.

Jason groaned. "Fuck."

Tae Hyun suddenly stopped. "Hyung, am I–"

"No, don't stop," Jason spat. "Keep fucking me."

Tae Hyun pushed again, sliding inside until Jason felt Tae Hyun's hips press against his ass. The whole world fell away as Jason's breath nearly caught in his throat, so he forced himself to breathe. He hadn't realized how much he'd missed the feeling of Tae Hyun inside him. It was warm, throbbing, and perfect.

Tae Hyun slowly pulled back before pushing himself in again, rewarding Jason with a burst of pleasure so intense he could almost see it. As Tae Hyun built up his rhythm, Jason finally risked pulling a hand away from the wall to grab himself. His cock twitched before he'd even touched it. Jason grabbed it anyway and started stroking in time to Tae Hyun's increasingly powerful thrusts.

Tae Hyun let out a stuttered moan. "Your ass feels incredible, hyung."

"So does your cock."

Tae Hyun's continued assault on Jason's prostate drove him closer to his impending climax, so he let go of himself. He didn't want to cum too soon, not if–

"Hyung, I'm gonna cum. Where should I–"

"Inside me. It's gotta be inside me."

Tae Hyun grunted as he fucked. His rhythm faltered as his thrusts shortened. Jason grabbed hold of himself again and began stroking. But he only reached the third stroke before his climax roared up from the depths and overcame him. He cried out, maintaining just enough presence of mind to point his cock down to keep from splattering the wall.

Jason felt his ass clench as he came, drawing a stifled cry from Tae Hyun as he emptied himself inside him. Still riding the chemical wave of his own orgasm, Tae Hyun's throbbing cock pressed against Jason's prostate and sent him into a quick second burst of welcome bliss.

Tae Hyun stayed in place when he'd finished, his breath low and heavy as he held onto Jason's hips for balance. "Damn, hyung. That was so fucking hot."

Jason chuckled. "I know, right? Not that I want to do this sort of thing all the time, but–yeah. Now, pull out slowly. I'd like to keep the mess to a minimum."

"Okay." Tae Hyun did as Jason instructed, leaving an unwelcome empty feeling in his wake. "But what do we do about–"

"It's a pool house," Jason interrupted, chuckling again as he pushed himself up and backed away from the wall. "There's plenty of towels." He turned around and planted a wet kiss on Tae Hyun's mouth. "Now, let me show you the shower."

07

Tae Hyun was barely awake and was already practicing. In his head, at least. Since he and the dancers had nearly perfected *Boy With No Shame*, they'd moved on to the next song, *Freefall Into You*. It was a love song, but it was specifically about the feeling of being caught in Jason's gravity whenever they were around each other. Even when they'd been separated by the world's largest ocean, Tae Hyun had still felt Jason's unceasing pull.

The song's choreo only used the twins, orbiting Tae Hyun as he danced and sang. He enjoyed dancing with them. They'd been a lucky find. Or, in reality, it had been lucky they'd found him. Big Hammer hadn't put out a general call for dancers, instead inviting specific performers that would mesh well with Tae Hyun onstage. But the twins had somehow found out about the opportunity anyway, presenting themselves as the perfect pair to express Tae Hyun's music. Truthfully, they were. Daniel Soo was gay and Korean, although he'd lived in the US for years. But he represented several aspects of Tae Hyun's identity. His twin sister Jenny Soo helped fill in the gaps, representing Tae Hyun's feminine side and his female fans.

The dance was choreographed to look like the three were

in conflict, with Jenny symbolizing his past self and Daniel his future. Each time one twin approached Tae Hyun, the other was driven away until Tae Hyun finally latched onto Daniel for the chorus. Then, the pair transitioned into a series of moves that could've been euphemistically described as intimate.

"Which song is that again? *Freefall?*"

Tae Hyun opened his eyes and looked to his side. Jason's eyes were still closed, but he was obviously awake. And Tae Hyun must've been unknowingly humming again. "Yes. I was mentally rehearsing the choreo. Sorry if I woke you."

Jason smiled, his eyes still closed, as he rolled to his side and cuddled up next to Tae Hyun. "It's okay." Jason snuck his hand onto Tae Hyun's stomach and slowly moved it south, his fingers lazily trailing across Tae Hyun's belly until he found his crotch. "Hmm. Looks like you're enjoying your rehearsal a little too much."

Tae Hyun chuckled. "That's just morning wood."

"I was gonna say–" Jason slid his bent leg over Tae Hyun's lower body, trapping him in place. "–I know you're going for sexy with this album, but this might be a little too realistic."

Tae Hyun snorted. "Finally."

"What?"

"You always claim to be jealous, but you never actually act that way. I think this is the first time."

Jason briefly frowned and opened his eyes. "What are you talking about?"

"You always say that you're insanely jealous. Then you let me do whatever I want. You've never once complained–not about what I do, or who I talk to, or–"

Jason furrowed his brows with confusion. Or maybe

concern. “Are you saying you want me to complain more?”

“No.” Tae Hyun sighed. “Never mind. I’ve gotta get up anyway.”

“Oh, no, you don’t.” Jason pushed himself up, straddled Tae Hyun’s pelvis, and pinned his arms to the mattress in a series of swift moves that caught Tae Hyun by surprise. “You don’t get to casually drop a bomb like that and leave me hanging.”

“Drop a bomb?”

“You know what I mean, so let’s clear this up. I don’t act jealous because I don’t have any reason to. And I don’t act possessive because you’re not my possession.”

Tae Hyun hadn’t meant to bring up jealousy–not after the other day when he’d gotten jealous of Jason talking to someone else at Raven’s after-party. It sort of slipped out in his early morning mental haze. He considered struggling free. Jason wasn’t even putting his full weight on him. But it was probably better to see it through. It was his issue, after all. Not Jason’s. “Are you honestly saying you don’t get jealous of Daniel?”

Jason smiled. “Are you kidding? Of course, I get jealous of the hot, sexy dancer who gets to spend all day wrapping his arms around my boyfriend.”

“But–”

“But I don’t act jealous cuz I understand why he does it. You remember what I do for a living, right?” Jason snorted. “Aside from being a producer.” Tae Hyun nodded. “And someday I’m gonna be in another movie. And I might have to kiss someone in that movie. Or, even more than that. Hell, in my last movie, I had a full-on nude scene.”

Tae Hyun’s eyebrows shot up. “You were naked?”

“It was just my butt.”

"Oh, but–"

"But that's not the point. The point is: Would that make you jealous? And would you tell me I can't do any kissing or nude scenes because of it?"

Tae Hyun swallowed his breezy retort as Jason's point sunk in. He'd first seen Jason in *The Moon Shines Madly,* in which he spent a not insignificant amount of time on screen wearing only his underwear. How would Tae Hyun feel about that now that they were boyfriends? It was at least as intimate–no, it was even more intimate than what Tae Hyun was doing with Daniel and the dancers. And the emotions Tae Hyun and Daniel expressed were just part of the dance. It wasn't real.

"No. I suppose not. But–" Tae Hyun paused, waiting for Jason to interrupt. But Jason said nothing. "But you've never been cheated on."

Jason raised a single eyebrow. "No. Are you cheating on me?"

Tae Hyun shook his head. "No. But what if I was?"

Jason shrugged. "I'd probably get really upset. And I'd wonder what was so wrong between us that would make someone like you think that's a good idea."

"Someone like me?"

Jason nodded. "You know what it's like to be cheated on. And you don't seem like the type who'd do that anyway. Hell, you've never been shy about telling me when I do something wrong."

Tae Hyun half smiled as he thought about all the times he'd had to calm Jason down. Or straighten him out. "I suppose."

"Then I don't have anything to worry about, do I?" Jason leaned down and kissed Tae Hyun's forehead. "I trust you.

That's why I don't act jealous. And I don't believe for a second that keeping you from doing what you love will prevent you from ever falling out of love with me and finding someone else."

Tae Hyun nodded. Jason may never have been cheated on, but he certainly knew the pain of losing the person he loved. Probably even more so than Tae Hyun. Then he smiled. "Okay. I love you. And I'm sorry for bringing it up."

"Don't be." Jason rolled off Tae Hyun and lay beside him. "I mean, it's a little early for existential relationship talk. But it's always okay." He grabbed Tae Hyun's hand and gave it a gentle squeeze. "Are we good? Cuz I seriously gotta piss."

Tae Hyun chuckled. "Go ahead. We're good."

Tae Hyun also had to go. But he let Jason use the main bathroom, trotting through the house to one of the guest bathrooms instead. He'd never imagined having more than one bathroom, but Jason's house had four, plus a half bath. And being able to use a different toilet every day felt decadent in the best way.

Jason made them smoothies for breakfast. Those were perfect since Tae Hyun needed the energy, but the last thing he wanted was a full stomach while he danced. Tae Hyun downed his as he double-checked that his gym bag had everything he needed for the day. Then he set his glass near the sink.

"What are you doing today?"

Jason pulled his smoothie glass from his lips to reveal a pale green foam mustache. "I'm coming to watch you practice."

"What?" Tae Hyun pushed his brows together. Had he forgotten about that? "Uh, okay."

Jason snorted and wiped his face with the back of his hand.

"I'm just kidding. I know you don't want me there. And I'm meeting with Naomi this morning to finalize the outstanding venue contracts, anyway."

Tae Hyun frowned. "I'm sorry. And I don't mind you watching me. I just don't want to distract the dancers. Having Seong Min there is bad enough."

Jason laughed. "Can you blame them? Seong Min's stacked like an Aztec pyramid." He stepped up to Tae Hyun and took him in his arms. "But I'll see you after."

Tae Hyun nodded before offering Jason a slow, gentle goodbye kiss. "I love you."

"I love you, too."

Seong Min was already waiting when Tae Hyun went outside. His ears warmed as he approached the SUV, thinking about the possibility that his bodyguard might've heard them talking about him. But, of course, he couldn't have. Tae Hyun climbed into the passenger seat and buckled up.

"Good morning, Seong Min."

"Good morning, Mr. Woo, sir." Unlike his brother, Seong Min wasn't afraid to smile. "To the dance studio, right?"

"Yes, please." Tae Hyun smiled as he set his gym bag between his feet. "How's your morning?"

"It's been pleasant, sir. Thank you." Seong Min pulled around to the end of the drive and out onto the street. "Are you rehearsing *Freefall Into You* again today?"

Tae Hyun tried to hide his surprise, realizing he had no reason to be. Of course, Seong Min knew the song's name. He'd been to every rehearsal. Hell, he probably knew the songs as well as Tae Hyun. "Yes, we are."

"Ah. I like that one." Seong Min briefly frowned. Was he fidgeting in his seat? "I mean, I like all the songs. All of your songs, sir. But I like that one the best." He clamped his mouth shut.

Tae Hyun imagined Seong Min was mentally berating himself for breaking some bodyguard rule about expressing opinions to his client. Too bad. Tae Hyun wanted to know more. "Why's that?"

"It makes me think that one day I may fall in love, too."

Tae Hyun frowned. "One day? Haven't you ever been in love?" Jason had asked that of Tae Hyun once before they'd started being honest with each other. And Tae Hyun had lied about it, saying no, only to later realize that he was really telling the truth. What he had with Chang Min hadn't been love at all.

Seong Min shook his head. "No, sir. As I'm sure you can imagine, this job doesn't allow much time for dating anyone."

"Oh. I'm sorry."

Seong Min smiled. "It's alright, sir. I'm not trying to guilt you. I enjoy working for you. Before I did, the farthest I'd been from home was Seoul. Now, I've been to Thailand and America. I've even been in Los Angeles long enough to know my way around parts of it. I love this job." He paused to check his mirrors before changing lanes. "Although I almost didn't take it."

Tae Hyun didn't bother hiding his surprise that time. He figured he already knew the answer but asked the question anyway. "Why not?"

"It was a very last-minute request, you'll recall. And I'd never done any celebrity work before." Tae Hyun nodded, realizing he'd guessed wrong. He'd assumed it was because he and Jason were gay. But Seong Min had never once said or done anything homophobic. And, as the celebrity in question, Tae Hyun knew that the demands on his security would be different from ordinary bodyguard work. "But then my brother found out it was you and told me he'd never speak to me again if I didn't take the job." Seong Min quietly chuckled. "He's a big fan, you see. He's been a *Dreamer* since the beginning."

Tae Hyun's jaw fell open. "Seong Hyeon's a *Dreamer*? He never said anything."

Seong Min quickly shook his head. "No, sir. I'm talking about our older brother, Seong Hun." He chuckled. "Although, I did catch Seong Hyeon humming one of your songs the other day."

"What?" That was almost as unexpected as thinking Seong Hyeon was a *Dreamer*. Or that there was a third, previously unknown Song brother. Tae Hyun's ears warmed as it dawned on him how little he knew about a man he spent so much time with. Only Jason saw Tae Hyun more. "I'm sorry. There's so much I don't know about you or your brother. Brothers, I mean."

Seong Min nodded. "It's alright, sir. I know you've got a lot going on. And you're the first person I've worked for who even calls me by name." He snorted. "Honestly, you're the first employer I've had who I think of as a person and not just a job."

Tae Hyun smiled, recalling how often KBR had made him feel more like a commodity than a human being. "I know the feeling. But, still. I promise to learn more about you. If you're willing to talk about it."

Seong Min chuckled. "I suppose you can't just look up my fan-wiki page, can you?"

Traffic was relatively light, so they made quick time driving to Alex's dance studio in Studio City. Tae Hyun had been unsure about it the first time he saw the unmarked building tucked between a small shipping company warehouse and a telemarketing office. But that uncertainty came from adjusting to how things were in Los Angeles. And he assumed there were plenty of similar places in Seoul. He'd been lucky enough to become a trainee with KBR at a young age and was used to their top-of-the-line facilities.

Tae Hyun waited for Seong Min to park and get out of the SUV before grabbing his bag. His bodyguard preferred a chance to survey their surroundings before letting him out. That was fine. The last thing he wanted to become was one of the clients that Seong Min had undoubtedly been referring to earlier.

Tae Hyun opened the door and stepped out when he got the all-clear. He hoisted his gym bag over his shoulder as Seong Min fell into place beside him. Then he spotted Alex and the twins lurking outside the building entrance. Their troubled, awkward stances immediately set him on edge. He waved to get their attention, but Daniel frowned when he looked over. Was something wrong? He was about to call out when Seong Min stopped him with an outstretched arm.

"Hold on a moment, sir."

Tae Hyun huffed. "What's going on?"

"I don't know."

Daniel tapped Alex's shoulder before pointing toward Tae Hyun. Looking at him, her expression was closer to anger than Daniel's concern. And her posture was stiff and controlled as she approached him. When she stopped in front of him, she practically loomed. It was the first time that she'd genuinely made him uncomfortable.

But Tae Hyun was also growing impatient. "Would someone please tell me what's happening?"

"We got tagged," Alex said.

Tae Hyun shook his head. "I don't know what that means."

"Someone spray painted graffiti on the building," Alex explained.

"Graffiti?" Tae Hyun peered around Alex's shoulders to glimpse what it could be. The graffiti was written in Hangul, which was both strange and telling. It couldn't have been random. It had to be meant for him. Then, as he read it, a cold spike of fear stabbed his heart. "Shit."

Alex huffed. "I don't know what it says, but it upset the twins a lot."

"It says *Remember Jong Soo*," Seong Min translated.

"Yeah," Alex agreed. "Okay, I already know what it says. I meant I don't know what it means. Who's Jong Soo?"

Tae Hyun took several deep breaths as he tried to calm his pounding heart while Seong Min snapped a photo.

Kwon Jong Soo used to be a member of *Cosine*, an earlier-generation KBR group that had debuted a few years before *XTC*. Tae Hyun remembered him as a sunbae who was never shy about offering praise or help–even just being a friendly face and listening ear when the going invariably got tough for the upcoming trainees. While they'd never been that close–Tae Hyun was too young to consider him a true friend–Jong Soo was a trusted and supportive hyung.

Jong Soo had also been famously rebellious, frequently acting out despite the regular apologies CEO Pak required of him afterward. And he was an outspoken critic of the tightly controlled, closed-off nature of conservative Korean society. But his rebel streak was cut short by his sudden, unexpected suicide. That had sent shockwaves through the industry–especially through KBR's hallowed halls. While rare, Jong Soo's death was hardly the only idol suicide. But it was KBR's first. Tae Hyun remembered well how tense things were in the KBR building for the first few weeks afterward. Ji Hoon, especially, had taken Jong Soo's death hard.

The official explanation for Jong Soo's suicide was untreated mental health problems, which conflicted with Tae Hyun's memories of a smiling, energetic hyung. But he knew well that appearances could be deceiving. Even ignoring the specifics of Tae Hyun's unique situation as a formerly closeted gay idol, being an idol at all could be mentally and physically grueling. For instance, KBR had given Tae Hyun a rigid diet when he first started as a trainee, leaving him hungry most of the time. While most people had already considered him skinny, it wasn't good enough for KBR. Idols were supposed to be perfect. But he ended up with the opposite problem after debuting, often struggling to take in enough calories to meet the demands of touring and performing. So he understood how something like that could damage someone's mental health.

After his death, a torrent of Jong Soo rumors swirled through the fan sites, message boards, and social media feeds. Netizens claimed he'd been caught using drugs. Or that he'd gotten someone pregnant. Or that he was gay. But a darker rumor had spread through the idol community, whispered backstage at performances or behind the curtains at media events. They said that Jong Soo had been driven to suicide by KBR, who'd given up on curtailing his outspoken ways in favor of permanently silencing him. As ruthless as CEO Pak could be, Tae Hyun had never honestly imagined something like that to be true. Of course, the outpouring of fan support for the remaining members of *Cosine* had directly translated into album sales and streaming numbers. KBR had even posthumously released Jong Soo's solo album–with the supposed support of his surviving family. And it had gotten a perfect all-kill on the charts that week.

Looking at the graffiti, Tae Hyun suddenly wondered if those dark rumors about KBR silencing Jong Soo were true after all. Of course, it was more likely the work of an angry fan who had somehow discovered where he'd been rehearsing. But just the fact that his rehearsal space was no longer secret was troubling enough.

"It's a warning," Tae Hyun finally admitted before briefly explaining Jong Soo's story.

"What the absolute fuck?" Alex growled. "Why would anyone do this? How would someone even know to find you here?"

Tae Hyun shook his head. "I don't know. But I'd love to know the answer to that, too."

08

"I don't fucking care." Jason's seething fury could've set Naomi's office ablaze. And he'd been thinking lately that maybe he'd moved on from losing his temper like that. But recent events seemed to indicate otherwise. Jason had vaguely remembered the story of the idol's suicide, but Tae Hyun had given him the insider's version, including the rumor that KBR had been the one to drive Jong Soo over the edge. And the idea that someone could get to Tae Hyun that easily with no one the wiser was too fucking much. He pointed an angry finger at Seong Hyeon. "Tell me how they even fucking found him in the first place."

Seong Hyeon's nearly ramrod-straight posture visibly stiffened. Jason imagined he didn't like being openly called out like that. But that was too fucking bad. His security team had seriously fucked up. At least he had Alex there. If anyone ever managed to get past Seong Min–an unlikely prospect at best–Alex could easily take his place. Jason had never told Tae Hyun, but he'd first met her as his taekwondo instructor. He'd only learned later on that she was also a dancer. And her dual pedigree kind of made her ideal in Jason's eyes.

"We're working on that, sir. We know that one of the dancers made a social media post with a photo of the location but no other information. That's our only lead."

"Which dancer?"

"Malik Collins."

Jason scoffed. "Well, he's obviously fired."

Tae Hyun shook his head. "Jason–"

"What? He signed an NDA, which he clearly violated." Jason had little sympathy for the dancer, considering the last time one of his employees violated their non-disclosure agreement.

Naomi sighed. "That's not helping, Jason."

Jason was tempted to tell Naomi where she could put her judgy attitude. But he was upset, not suicidal. "No? And what the hell do you suggest?"

"I suggest you calm down before you make things worse."

Jason huffed. It wasn't hard to imagine how things could be worse. And that was the primary reason for his rage. "You want me to do this now? Or during our meeting with Seong Woo?"

Naomi sighed again. "Fine. Just get it out of your system."

"Get it out of my system?" Jason nearly growled. He wanted to scream. "I don't understand why no one else is upset about this. KBR is obviously trying to fuck with us." He pointed to Tae Hyun. "To fuck with him."

"We don't know it was them yet, sir." Seong Hyeon's confidence was impressive. Jason wasn't sure anyone else would've spoken up to someone yelling like he was. "We're still looking into it."

"Looking into it?" Jason openly scowled. "Looking into it?" He scoffed. "You'd better give me more than that pathetic fucking line."

Seong Hyeon's only visible movement was slowly flexing

his hands open and closed. Jason knew what he was thinking. If he wasn't Seong Hyeon's employer, they'd probably come to blows. And, if it came to that, Seong Hyeon could probably take him in a fight. But it wouldn't come to that owing to the simple fact that Jason was right and Seong Hyeon was to blame.

"We're doing the best we can with our limited resources," Seong Hyeon finally explained. "Ideally, I should bring Yu Min Kyu into this."

Jason threw his hands up. "Then why the fuck don't you?"

"Because I told him no."

Jason whirled on Naomi. "You what?"

"We're hemorrhaging money, Jason. We can't afford any additional salaries and expenses."

"What?" Jason vigorously shook his head. "They fucking threatened Tae Hyun! What about that don't you understand?" He turned to Seong Hyeon. "Hell, you could be working on it full-time. Lord knows I don't fucking need you to watch me."

Seong Hyeon quietly cleared his throat. "With all due respect, Mr. Park–"

Jason shot Seong Hyeon a vicious glare. "And exactly how much fucking respect am I due here, Song Seong Hyeon? Is it enough that I don't have to worry about my boyfriend's safety anymore?"

"Stop it, Jason. You sound paranoid."

Jason whirled on Naomi and ominously leaned forward, planting his hands on her desk. "Paranoid?" He usually let her shut him down, but not this time. Instead, he stared daggers at her, displaying enough open hostility that she blinked and looked away. "We can't make a move in this fucking game without some jealous ex-lover or global media empire slapping us down." He pushed back from her desk with a low grunt. "All of you need to listen to me very carefully." Jason slowly panned from Naomi to Tae Hyun to Seong Min to Seong Hyeon. "Because I want to make this absolutely fucking clear." He pointed to Tae Hyun. "He's the only fucking thing that matters to me. So you all might enjoy the new and improved Jason, who's more thoughtful and considerate and less of an asshole. But I'll hold you all personally responsible if anything happens to him. And you don't want to see that Jason. Do you understand me?" Jason waited for an answer, but everyone was either too intimidated or annoyed to respond. "Well?"

"That's seriously enough, Jason." Naomi's tone was firm, but she still wouldn't make eye contact. "You need to calm down."

Jason scoffed. "If one more person tells me to calm down, I swear to god I'll–"

"Jason." Tae Hyun stood from his chair and walked to him. He grabbed Jason's hand and stood before him, his face calm and posture non-threatening. Jason wanted to scream at him. Or cry.

"I know why you're upset," Tae Hyun quietly shared. "But everyone's doing their best. And KBR is a monster. We're fighting a–" He stopped, briefly frowning. "What's the one with all the heads?"

Jason snorted. "A hydra."

Tae Hyun nodded. "Yes. KBR is a hydra. So they will come at us from many directions." He squeezed Jason's hand. "But we're better than them. So we'll still win."

Jason wanted to protest more, but the love in Tae Hyun's

soft brown eyes was too much for him to overcome. Tae Hyun had let him point and shout at everyone, knowing exactly why Jason was so upset. He was the only person in the room who knew what had happened to Jason during his first Seoul visit. Not even Naomi knew that story.

A quiet knock on Naomi's door interrupted Jason's train of thought before Lily opened it and poked her head inside. "Seong Woo's ready for you."

Naomi nodded and turned to Jason. "Are you done with your tantrum?" Jason glared at her and growled. "Fine. Have you fully expressed your justified outrage? Because we should talk to him."

Tae Hyun gently pulled Jason aside while Lily helped Naomi set up the video conference on the large flatscreen mounted on the wall opposite her desk. "Hey," he said in Korean. "Everything's okay. I'm okay. You're okay. So I'd like you to calm down."

Jason frowned. His fury still lingered. "I'm the only one taking this seriously. I'd feel better if I wasn't the only one upset about all this."

Tae Hyun shook his head. "You're not. I'm frightened and upset, too. But you're hoarding all the outrage right now."

Jason blew out a long, slow breath. "Alright, fine. You can have some of it back."

"Good."

"But if anything happens to you, I'm still going on a murder spree starting in this room and ending in CEO Pak's office."

Tae Hyun finally chuckled. "You'd fucking better."

Seong Woo popped up on the video display behind Tae Hyun's head. He looked tired. It was 8:30 AM in Seoul, according to the time display on the screen. "Let's see what

Yoo Mi's future husband has to say."

"Yes, my team's aware of it," Seong Woo admitted after straightening out their audio issues. "Someone posted a photo of the graffiti on an underground fan site. Fortunately, that site is hosted here in Seoul, so my legal team has subpoenaed the host company for their server records." He sighed. "It's a long shot, but it's something."

"So, how do we get these fuckers?" Jason almost chuckled as Seong Woo's eyebrows shot up. "I want to nail them to the wall, Seong Woo. To the fucking wall."

Seong Woo shook his head. "I don't know, Jason. But you should send what you have to Min Kyu's team. I'm sure he could help."

Jason glanced at Naomi, wondering if he'd have to overrule her in front of Seong Woo. But she nodded.

"We'd appreciate that," Naomi replied.

Tae Hyun leaned into the camera's view. "What if it's KBR?"

Seong Woo nodded. "We've considered that, too. If it was, it's unlikely that we'd find any evidence to support it. They're too careful and will certainly have covered their tracks. But, if we do, we'll definitely use it."

Jason nodded. "And if it's not?"

"We will find them," Seong Hyeon announced. "And we will make certain they do not do anything like this again."

Jason nodded again. "Good."

"In the meantime," Naomi interjected, "we should discuss the remaining tour arrangements and–"

Jason tuned her out. He was still too angry to think about the tour and all the potential safety issues that brought up. Until that morning, he'd been confident that the Song brothers and their security team were enough to protect Tae

Hyun. Then someone–probably someone sent by KBR–had shown him how wrong he was. After being effectively shut out of any Seoul venues and an attempt at shutting Tae Hyun out from even presenting at the Music Video Awards, they'd taken things to a whole new level. And Jason had no idea how to compete on that level. He was definitely out of his depth.

Jason glanced at Tae Hyun, who'd also tuned out and started scrolling on his phone. There was no telling what was going on in his head. Tae Hyun was hard to read at the best of times, and they'd hardly had time to speak since he'd gotten back from the dance studio. But he'd said he was frightened, which Jason could relate to. He was scared shitless–partly of what might happen to Tae Hyun in the future, but mostly of what he might've brought about by taking on the role of Tae Hyun's producer. There was a reason most of the popular music came from the big entertainment empires. Those companies were ruthless, and it took that same level of ruthlessness to compete against them.

Once the meeting with Seong Woo ended, Jason pulled Seong Hyeon out to the hallway to privately speak with him. "About what I said before–"

"There's no apology necessary, sir. I–"

"Apology?" Jason scoffed. "Oh, no. I meant every fucking word I said." He didn't raise his voice but ensured his tone was sharp and acidic. "You're the one who told me I need to take security more seriously. Remember?" He paused to give Seong Hyeon a chance to nod. "Well, you got your wish. So I want you to tell me right now, to my face, that you can handle this. Because, if you can't–" He shrugged, leaving his implied threat to hang between them.

Seong Hyeon frowned. Jason was sure he would've rather

cut out his own tongue than admit failure. "I'm sorry, sir. I'll–"

"No. I don't want your apology either." Jason huffed. "I want the man I love to be safe, Seong Hyeon. And I want you to tell me whether you can do that or not. Because every instinct I have tells me today was just a warning shot from KBR. And if you can't handle this, I need to find someone who can."

Seong Hyeon's jaw muscles flexed so tightly Jason thought they might snap. Then he nodded. "If I have the resources I need, then yes, I can handle it."

"You've got them," Jason said. "I'll talk to Naomi. And whatever she won't agree to, I will." He leaned in close enough to feel Seong Hyeon's breath on his face. "But the gloves come off. Do you get me?"

"I do, sir."

Jason examined Seong Hyeon's face for any signs that he was lying. And to ensure that the man really understood what he wanted. Satisfied, he nodded. "Good enough. Go get the car. I've seen enough of this goddamn building for the day."

Seong Hyeon offered Jason a quick bow before leaving him in the corridor. Jason returned to Naomi's office to collect Tae Hyun, who was speaking with Naomi next to Lily's desk. Tae Hyun smiled when he spotted Jason approaching. Naomi looked back and gave Jason a single nod before returning to her office.

"What was that about?"

Tae Hyun casually half-shrugged. "I may have been explaining how your anger before was entirely justified and that she shouldn't be so quick to dismiss it."

Jason's eyebrows floated up. "I'm very curious to know how

she took that suggestion."

Tae Hyun chuckled. "Reasonably well. I'm the diplomatic one. Remember?"

"I do." Jason smiled. "I'll never get tired of watching you charm your way through anything. I could learn a lot from you about that."

"It's only fair." Tae Hyun took Jason's hand. "I've already learned so much from you, hyung. You'll be my inspiration if I ever need to make anyone cry."

Jason almost frowned. "Are you teasing me?"

Tae Hyun smiled. "I am."

"Oh, how the tables have turned." Jason gently squeezed Tae Hyun's hand. "You know, next time, if you wanna shut me up, you can always just stick your dick in my mouth."

"Hyung!" Tae Hyun rolled his eyes. "You'll never let me win at teasing, will you?"

"No." Jason grinned. "But I'll let you keep trying." Then he let his smile fall away. "How are you? You know, seeing that message and all?"

Tae Hyun frowned. "I always liked Jong Soo, and I hate the idea that he'd suffered enough to take his own life. You know?" Jason nodded. He knew that feeling well. Losing Joo Won like that had been a blow that had taken him a decade to recover from. He didn't even want to consider what losing Tae Hyun would do to him. "And I never really believed that KBR had anything to do with it. Until today, at least." Tae Hyun visibly shivered. "It scares me to think that Pak might be capable of something like that."

Jason squeezed Tae Hyun's hand again. "It's a good thing you got out of there. At least, now, we can help protect you." He reached up to caress Tae Hyun's cheek. "And I meant what

I said before. If anything happens to you, I won't stop until everyone's paid for it."

Tae Hyun smiled, pressing his cheek into Jason's hand as his ears turned rosy. "Thank you, hyung. But let's hope it won't come to that."

"For sure." Jason gently brushed his thumb along the curve of Tae Hyun's jaw. "Are you ready to go?"

Tae Hyun emphatically nodded. "Yes, please."

Jason decided to skip saying goodbye to Naomi before leaving. He'd seen enough of her for the day, too. He was sure she probably felt the same way about him. So the pair went straight to the elevator, stepping into the empty car once it arrived.

Tae Hyun immediately pushed Jason against the nearby wall and attacked his mouth with a long, wet kiss. Jason was almost too surprised to respond. But he quickly grabbed Tae Hyun's waist, pulling their bodies together while their tongues clashed. He felt a warm, comforting flush spread from his belly to his chest, dampening the flames of his rage as it rekindled his love's fire. He'd spent so much effort ranting and raving about the vital importance of Tae Hyun's safety that he'd nearly forgotten why that was. Jason loved that man with a passion that made his fury seem mild.

But they only had eight floors to travel before they reached the lobby. So Tae Hyun, still ever conscious of avoiding public displays of affection, pulled away from their kiss. But he stayed in Jason's grasp for a moment longer, affectionately gazing at him with his soft, brown eyes.

Jason's heart melted a little. "I love you so much. I wish I could promise I'll never let anything bad happen to you."

"I love you, too, hyung." Tae Hyun stepped back and

grabbed Jason's hand at the ding signaling their arrival at the lobby. "And I know you can't promise that. Just promise me you'll always try. That's more than enough."

"I promise I'll always try."

Tae Hyun smiled. "Good. Let's go home."

09

Tae Hyun slowly drizzled the golden honey onto his granola and greek yogurt. Then he smiled as he dipped his spoon into the bowl and gave everything a good stir. He wasn't practicing that day, so he could actually eat something in the morning. And he'd never known that three simple ingredients could make such a delicious breakfast until Jason introduced it to him. Then he sighed, thinking about how much he missed dance practice. It had already been several days. And it would probably be at least a few more until they found a new studio. With Alex's studio becoming a security risk, it was no longer an option.

Tae Hyun brought his coffee and cereal to the table so he could eat while he scrolled through the news on his tablet. But he took in the view first. The sun had just come up, so the light shining down on the Los Angeles skyline still had a rosy golden hue. Jason was still asleep, or Tae Hyun would've made him come look at it. Not that Jason would've appreciated it. He probably would've insisted on saying something silly, like how he preferred the view of Tae Hyun more. But his ears warmed at the imagined compliment anyway.

Tae Hyun had eaten half his cereal and yogurt before finally tearing himself from the view and turning to his tablet. It was the end of the day back in Seoul, so the late news broadcasts would already be online to stream. As much as he'd gotten used to reading, hearing, and speaking English all day, he still liked to get his news in Korean. Especially if it was news about him.

Tae Hyun was still scanning the headlines when a news alert popped up on his screen. He'd programmed the alert for when a story was published mentioning both him and KBR. Most of them were the same rehashing of what he'd done to get fired, so he didn't expect much when he clicked on the alert. But his heart nearly stopped when he read the new headline on the web page.

KBR Cancels Release of XTC Tribute Compilation

Rumors have swirled around the possible release of an XTC tribute album featuring re-recordings of XTC hits by other KBR recording artists, including the DoubleDown Boys, Dyn4sty, and Cherry Squad. But KBR put those rumors to rest today, announcing that the project has officially been canceled. According to a recently televised interview with KBR Managing Director Choo Ji Hoon, the project had never grown beyond the concept stage, and moving forward with it was inappropriate "given recent circumstances." In the interview, Director Choo also–

"No." Tae Hyun shook his head. "Why would he do that?"

Tae Hyun had to see the interview. He shoved his chair back and stood, knocking over his coffee as he grabbed his tablet and rushed to the lounge. He barely noticed when the coffee cup smashed on the floor. Tae Hyun tossed his tablet on the couch, grabbed the remote from the coffee table, and turned on the giant TV. It took him a minute to find the web video streaming app and then a few more to find the news video. He hesitated before opening it. Did he really want to see it? There was no possible way it would make him anything besides angry. But that was just an excuse. He needed to know.

Tae Hyun clicked into the video, and a larger-than-life Choo Ji Hoon appeared on the screen, seated behind a desk on the set of an evening news program. Tae Hyun hadn't seen or spoken to Ji Hoon since his last day at the KBR building. Did he look older? Possibly. But the lower-thirds title above the news crawler immediately set Tae Hyun's nerves on edge. *KBR Managing Director Choo Ji Hoon sets the record straight about Woo Tae Hyun.* He quietly growled as he shook his head. Then he stopped putting it off and started the video.

"We're joined this evening by KBR Managing Director Choo Ji Hoon," said a bland news anchor Tae Hyun didn't know. *"Welcome, Director Choo."*

Ji Hoon offered the anchor the same smile he used when humoring the outlandish requests of his young idols. *"Thank you for having me."*

"We recently learned that KBR had been planning-"

The anchor continued, asking about the compilation album, which Ji Hoon then claimed had been shelved *given recent circumstances.*

"And those circumstances include the announcement made by former XTC leader Woo Tae Hyun earlier this year about his romantic relationship with the American actor Jason Park?"

Tae Hyun could see that Ji Hoon was annoyed but doubted the anchor would've noticed. *"I'm referring to our releasing Mr. Woo from his contract."*

The anchor frowned. *"You fired him."*

"That's not what I said."

"So the circumstances leading to KBR releasing one of their

top artists from his contract have nothing to do with Woo's announcement?"

Ji Hoon shook his head. *"It was a legitimate business decision made by CEO Pak Jun Ho."*

Tae Hyun angrily scoffed at Ji Hoon's obvious bullshit. He'd always been the benefactor of his former manager's ability to rewrite reality how it suited him. Being on the other side of that coin didn't feel as good.

"A business decision." The anchor's expression made it clear he didn't buy into Ji Hoon's line of reasoning either. *"Some segments of the fanbase have speculated that KBR is attacking Tae Hyun because he's gay."*

Ji Hoon shook his head. *"I don't appreciate the implication that protecting our legitimate business interests is attacking anyone. In any case, whether or not Tae Hyun is gay is irrelevant."*

"But he is gay. He said so himself. Are you saying that's not a factor?"

"It's not a factor." Ji Hoon's unyielding expression and firm tone were all too familiar. *"Woo Tae Hyun is welcome to pursue his solo career as he sees fit. But KBR has a duty to prevent any unfair competition with our current artists."*

"Competition?" The anchor's smile was unsettling. Tae Hyun was sure he was leading Ji Hoon into a trap. *"The music industry, in general, is booming. As is the K-pop industry specifically. Surely there's space for KBR artists and artists like Tae Hyun to coexist?"*

Tae Hyun groaned. *Artists like Tae Hyun?* What did that even mean?

"It's not a question of space. It's a question of why we would even offer it to someone who so willfully turned away from everything we gave him."

"Are you saying you'd have the same reaction if he'd declared his love for a woman instead of a man?"

Ji Hoon frowned. *"Well, no. Of course, not. But–"*

"Thank you, Director Choo." Satisfied that he'd gotten the answer he was looking for, the anchor turned to the camera. *"To explore this matter further, we contacted someone with intimate knowledge of the situation. We're joined now by Woo Jeong Ho and Byeon Sun Young from their home in Daejeon. Welcome to the both of you."*

Tae Hyun's heart stopped again as a pair of faces appeared in a split screen. They were faces he knew well. They were his parents. "No." The word was barely a whisper. What were they doing? In all the years he'd been an idol, his parents had never once talked with the media. That had been their longtime agreement in exchange for Tae Hyun's continuing financial support. An agreement they'd just broken.

"We're incredibly disappointed that our son has done these things," Tae Hyun's father spat, ignoring the anchor's greeting as words he'd undoubtedly practiced a hundred times in anticipation of his interview suddenly rushed out.

"No!" The word was a shrieking hurricane wind pummeling his already battered surroundings. "No!" Tae Hyun squeezed the remote until he heard it creak. Then he flung it at the TV screen. It struck near the bottom corner and bounced back, leaving behind a pale web of cracks. He must've also paused the playback somehow. His parent's faces had frozen, his father's angry finger still pointing at their webcam, his mother's an unknowable mask. Why would they do something like that? But he knew why. They'd been bought off. Ji Hoon, or, more likely, CEO Pak, had swooped in with an offer of support in exchange for turning against their son. Never mind that they'd kept taking the money he'd sent them. Never mind that–

"What the fuck, Tae Hyun?" Jason, finally awake, stomped from the hallway leading to their bedroom, bleary-eyed and rubbing his head. "What the hell are you doing? Why are you making so much noise?"

Words failed Tae Hyun, so he simply pointed at the screen.

Jason stopped rubbing his head to briefly rub his eyes as he focused on the faces floating on the lounge's far wall. Recognition struck after a moment. "Oh, shit." He shook his head. "Turn it off."

Tae Hyun's partially contained rage exploded. "What?" Words hadn't failed him after all. "No! I need to know. I need to hear what–"

"You don't need to hear shit." Jason glanced around the room in search of something. He briefly frowned as his eyes landed on the TV screen's damaged corner. "Where's the remote?"

Tae Hyun's eyes turned to where it lay on the floor between them, drawing Jason's attention. Tae Hyun sprang as Jason bent to pick it up, knocking them both on the couch and landing atop Jason with an exasperated groan. He desperately reached for the remote. "Give it to me!"

"What the fuck, Tae Hyun?"

Jason held the remote out of Tae Hyun's reach with his outstretched arm. But Tae Hyun knew he could still get it. He just needed to be quick. He crawled forward and–Whomp. Jason flipped over, knocking Tae Hyun off the couch. He fell to the floor, landing on his back with a dull thud. Then Jason crawled on top of him, sitting on his chest as he pinned Tae Hyun's arms to the floor with his hands.

"Stop this," Jason growled as Tae Hyun squirmed. "You're gonna hurt yourself. Or me."

Tae Hyun finally caught the pained confusion on Jason's face and immediately stopped struggling. Why was he fighting with Jason over the remote? Had he lost his mind? "I'm–" The word was a child's voice. He knew tears were coming and pushed out the second word before they arrived. "-sorry." Then his vision blurred as the tears flooded his eyes.

Jason breathed a long sigh through his nose as he reversed his hold on Tae Hyun's arms and lifted him to a seated position, wrapping his arms around Tae Hyun and cradling him to his chest as he cried. "It's gonna be alright. Everything will be alright."

"Nothing will be alright!" Tae Hyun's voice nearly cracked as he sobbed. "How could they do this to me?" He weakly pounded both fists on Jason's chest, which rang hollow. "Why would they do this?"

"I know it sucks right now, but you'll get through this."

Tae Hyun scoffed. "You don't know that." He didn't mind being comforted. No, he liked it. But he didn't need to be coddled. "You don't understand."

Jason gently pushed Tae Hyun back from his chest and looked down at him, his mouth twisted with a wry grin. "You're telling me I don't understand conservative Korean parents who'd rather publicly betray you than accept your being gay?"

Tae Hyun huffed. "Alright, yeah. I guess you do understand." He looked away from Jason and spotted the frozen tableau of his parent's disappointment. The last time he'd spoken with them, there'd been no talk of anything related to his relationship with Jason. His mother had called Jason his new friend. Jason was his colleague, according to his father. Tae Hyun knew they disapproved of him being gay. But he understood that they could at least carry on the semblance of a normal relationship as long as they didn't talk about it. Now, even that was gone. "I really wish they hadn't done this."

"I know." Jason pushed himself off his knees and stood before helping Tae Hyun to his feet. "The last time I spoke with my father, he told me he wished I was dead. So, I say fuck parents. If you don't want to deal with a kid being their own person, then don't have any."

Tae Hyun nodded, even if he disagreed. His nerves were still too jangled for anything else, and he'd already put Jason through enough. But Jason had such an American point of view about most things, including families. Obeying his elders, and especially his parents, was so ingrained in Tae Hyun's culture that even being gay had made him feel so guilty he kept up his charade with them after he'd publicly come out. He pointed to the TV. "I still need to watch this."

"Maybe." Jason frowned. "But let's do it together after you've had some time to calm down. After that little display–"

Tae Hyun bowed his head. "I'm sorry about the TV."

Jason scoffed. "I don't care about the damn TV. It's the cheapest fucking thing I own." He stepped close enough that Tae Hyun could feel his body heat radiating off him. "I care about you." He put his hands on Tae Hyun's hips and pulled their bodies together. "But you can't ever attack me like that again."

"I know." Tae Hyun sighed as he rested his head on Jason's shoulder. "I'm sorry, hyung. I was so upset I wasn't thinking clearly. Please forgive me."

Jason put his hand on Tae Hyun's head, gently pressing it to his shoulder. "I get that, too. Believe me. Just try not to do it again, please."

Tae Hyun nodded as he wrapped his arms around Jason and squeezed. "I won't. I promise."

"Okay. Let's clean up your mess."

Tae Hyun pulled his head off Jason's shoulder. "My mess?"

Jason nodded toward the kitchen, where Tae Hyun saw the pieces of his smashed cup sitting in a cooling puddle of coffee. He'd also managed to knock over his cereal bowl, spilling yogurt-covered granola on the table and chair. He sighed. "Shit. Sorry."

"It's okay." Jason smiled. "It's just stuff."

Tae Hyun cleaned up his mess while Jason visited the bathroom and brushed his teeth. He'd literally come right from bed after hearing Tae Hyun's shriek. Then Jason invited Tae Hyun to follow him downstairs to the gym. Tae Hyun couldn't think of why that would be a good idea, but he was in no position to refuse after his temper tantrum.

Like the rest of the house, the gym had mostly been done in shades of gray, from the dark gray padded flooring to the light gray walls. But it was bright and airy with a window wall that peeked out under the upstairs sundeck to offer a view of the grassy hillside.

Jason walked to the large, weighted bag hanging in the inside corner opposite the door. "Do you know what this is?"

Tae Hyun nodded. "It's a punching bag."

"Yep. Now I want you to punch it."

Tae Hyun frowned. "What?"

"I know you know how to make a fist and throw a punch. I've seen you do it."

Tae Hyun snorted, remembering when he'd attacked Chang Min after his ex-boyfriend and group member had tried outing Jason at Xiang's release party. "Okay, but–"

Jason huffed. "Stop arguing and punch this fucking thing. Pretend it's Ji Hoon. I know you want to hit that asshole."

"Well–" Tae Hyun took a deep breath as he considered Jason's suggestion. He really did want to hit Ji Hoon. "Okay." He walked up to the punching bag, gingerly putting his hand on it as if it would come apart if he was too rough.

Jason chuckled. "You can't damage it. Believe me, I've tried."

Tae Hyun nodded and pulled his hand away. Then he fell back into the basic self-defense stance he'd learned in the army, squeezing his hands into sharp fists. His lip curled into a sneer as a single thought of Ji Hoon's smug face rekindled his fiery rage. He threw a single forward jab and felt a sharp pain in his knuckles from the bag's rough surface. "Ow," he complained, shaking off the lingering ache.

Jason shook his head. "I thought you knew how to punch? If that's all you're gonna do, then never mind. You'll just hurt yourself."

"No. I can do this." Tae Hyun returned to his stance, holding his fists up in a defensive position. Then he shifted, sliding to the side as he launched a one-two combo with a right hook and left uppercut. The bag agreeably shook as each fist bounced off it. And it felt amazing. "Shit."

"I know, right?" Jason grinned. "Take it from someone with anger control issues. If you ever feel yourself spiraling out of control like that again, this is the first place you need to visit." He walked up to Tae Hyun and kissed his cheek. "I'm gonna head upstairs to make some more coffee and take a shower. Why don't you spend a little time beating this thing up and then maybe come join me?"

Tae Hyun smiled. "For the coffee or the shower?"

Jason shrugged as he walked away. "Your choice."

Tae Hyun was tempted to follow Jason right then. But he knew he needed to take Jason's advice first. He'd only ever gotten that angry twice before. The first time was when he'd walked in on his ex cheating on him. The second was when his ex had tried outing Jason. But both of those times were justified. His actions that morning weren't. He'd attacked the man he loved because he was so angry at his family's betrayal.

Tae Hyun knew he needed to find a way to come to terms with the situation. It was easy with Ji Hoon. He'd lost all his respect for the man the day he came out. The way Ji Hoon had barged into his table read with a pair of security guards in tow and snatched his phone from his hands was totally fucked up. And it dragged up memories of his early trainee days that he'd prefer to forget. Dealing with his parents would be another matter entirely.

But Tae Hyun didn't have to figure everything out right at that moment. He returned to his stance and punched the bag again, pleased with how satisfying it felt. Then he hit it again. Jason was right. It was exactly what he needed.

10

Even though he'd already flown into Incheon a handful of times, Jason was still impressed by how smoothly things ran there. It was like the polar opposite of LAX, which seemed to be designed primarily to confuse and disorient the multitude of travelers who passed through every day. The flight to Korea was mostly pleasant, owing almost entirely to having Tae Hyun seated beside him in first class. And it helped that the first-class attendants practically doted on them the entire flight. Being an out celebrity had some significant disadvantages. But flight attendants always loved you.

They were halfway to the luggage pickup area before the first person recognized them. Or, more specifically, before the first person recognized Seong Min. Jason and Tae Hyun had gone full ninja with baseball caps, sunglasses, and face masks. But the Songs hadn't, and one of the people at the airport happened to be a member of Seong Min's small but steadily growing fan club. Of course, once they recognized Seong Min, they knew who he was traveling with.

Tae Hyun, who'd never stopped loving his fans, agreed to pose for a photo. And it was game over once his mask came off. He'd posed for at least a dozen more photos as they slowly inched their way toward luggage pickup before Jason cued

Seong Hyeon to intervene. Jason might've felt differently if he hadn't just spent half a day in the air. But he knew Tae Hyun would've kept right on going if he wasn't stopped.

"I'm sorry," Tae Hyun whispered as they hurried away from his fans. "I know you hate that."

Jason shook his head. "Not at all. I'm just tired and hungry. And there'll always be more fans."

"I hope so."

Jason smiled as he reached up to put his arm over Tae Hyun's shoulder, then stopped, remembering they were in public. He patted Tae Hyun's shoulder instead. "Don't start with that. You're on your home turf now, so you'll be at your most powerful."

Tae Hyun chuckled. "I keep telling you I'm not a superhero."

"I know." Jason winked. "Your secret is safe with me."

Once they'd collected their bags, they proceeded to Arrivals, where Seong Woo waited with Yu Min Kyu, his head of security, and a small security team. Seong Woo looked surprisingly rested and happy despite his wedding being only three days away.

"Welcome back, my friends," Seong Woo said in Korean as he hugged them both. "I'm glad you made it."

Jason handed his bags to one of the dark-suited members of Seong Woo's security team. "I'm surprised you came yourself. Don't you have a wedding to prepare for?"

Seong Woo chuckled. "What? And miss a chance to see my two favorite people?"

"Yoo Mi kicked you out?" Tae Hyun asked with a smirk.

Seong Woo nodded. "Yeah. She said I was just getting in the way." He nodded to Min Kyu, who said something to his wrist before nodding back. "Let's head for the car. Airports make me anxious."

The car was, in fact, a massive, shiny black SUV, although of the Korean variety rather than American. Even then, it filled up fast with Jason and Tae Hyun, the Songs, Seong Woo, and Min Kyu. So a second SUV followed them with their luggage and the remaining members of the security team. Jason noticed the thicker-than-usual doors as he climbed inside and guessed the truck was probably armored. His suspicion was confirmed when he tried to open his window, which didn't budge. He glanced at Seong Woo, who nodded.

"I'm afraid the windows won't work," Seong Woo explained.

Tae Hyun tried his window, too, with the same result. "Are they broken?" He hadn't worked out the issue yet.

"No." Jason frowned. "Is there something you want to tell us, Seong Woo?"

"Alright." Seong Woo quietly sighed. "Yes, the truck's armored."

Tae Hyun's eyebrows shot up. "Armored?"

Seong Woo nodded. "We've been getting some threats. I think the tanks are probably overkill. But Min Kyu thought they were warranted."

"Always better to be safe than sorry," Min Kyu interjected.

"Threats," Tae Hyun repeated. "Because of me?"

Seong Woo shook his head. "No. Well, not directly, at least. You know how Yoo Mi has always had a, let's say, contentious relationship with her fanbase."

Jason snorted. "It's always the haters," he said in English.

Tae Hyun sighed. "I'm sorry if I did anything to make it worse, Seong Woo."

"Don't be." Seong Woo leaned back between the seats to get closer to Jason and Tae Hyun. "I'll tell you a secret. It was dating you that put her on my radar in the first place ."

Tae Hyun's eyebrows floated up again. "What? No way."

Seong Woo nodded. "It's true. So, if anything, we actually met because of you."

Jason reached over to put his hand on Tae Hyun's thigh. "See, there you go. No need to feel bad about Min Kyu's overzealous security response."

But Tae Hyun frowned anyway. "Please don't–"

"I know," Jason interrupted. Leave it to Tae Hyun to take his reassurance and turn it into something else. "I know. Don't humor you." He huffed and pulled his hand away. "Fine. Whatever."

Tae Hyun's eyebrows fell. "What's that supposed to mean?"

"Nothing." Jason sighed and looked away, suddenly wishing he'd actually humored Tae Hyun instead of sharing how he really felt. "I'm just tired and cranky from the flight."

Tae Hyun huffed. "Okay. Whatever."

Jason didn't even have to see Tae Hyun's face to know his expression. And if he wanted to blame himself for the threats and armored truck, Jason didn't have the energy to talk him out of it. He would've normally let that sort of thing slide. Most of Tae Hyun's annoying habits were minor. And many of them had changed or gone away once they committed to each other. But Tae Hyun's stubborn insistence that people not tell him what they thought he wanted to hear remained in full force. It didn't matter that he was wrong about it most of the time.

So the three passengers sat in awkward silence, surrounded by their equally silent security guards. Not that it was all that quiet. The road noise was thunderous at highway speeds, meaning the SUV probably had special tires, too. Only the best for the favored son of a not-quite chaebol family.

"I'm sorry," Tae Hyun finally announced. "I know you didn't mean anything by what you said."

Jason turned back to Tae Hyun and his composed, almost frosty expression. He obviously wasn't sorry that they'd argued, only that they'd done it in front of Seong Woo. But it was a fight about nothing. And appearances were important to Tae Hyun, so Jason decided to let it go. "Okay."

Seong Woo snorted. "Wow. I could learn a lot from you two. I think that's the shortest fight I've ever seen. One time, Yoo Mi didn't talk to me for twelve hours because I told her I didn't like her dress."

Tae Hyun rolled his eyes. "Try telling me you don't like what I'm wearing, and you'll get the same response."

Seong Woo chuckled. "No wonder you two get along so well."

Jason shook his head, pulled his phone from his pocket, and turned it on. He could imagine what it must be like to be on the receiving end of Yoo Mi's ire. She didn't strike him as someone to so quickly let things go.

After connecting to the local network, Jason sent Naomi a quick message to let her know they'd finally arrived. He knew Tae Hyun owed his sister a similar message but decided against reminding him of that, given their mutual crankiness. Hopefully, he'd remember before she got mad and messaged him to complain.

Passing through the gated community's security in a vehicle with Seong Woo inside was an entirely different affair than the first time they'd done it months ago. Then again, everything was different than it had been back then. But the group was ushered through security without delay and were soon whisked up to Seong Woo and Yoo Mi's condo via the penthouse elevator. When the doors opened, Jason was immediately overcome with the spicy, tangy aroma of what he hoped would be dinner. A pair of uniformed attendants waited for them in the marble-tiled entryway outside the elevator to take their bags.

Jason was impressed. "You have servants now?"

Seong Woo chuckled and shook his head as he led them into the condo's expansive main room. "No. They're temporary. Partly because you're both here and partly to support Yoo Mi before the wedding. Speaking of which, she should be around here somewhere."

"I'm right here," a smiling Yoo Mi announced as she emerged from an open doorway behind them. She wore giant, red oven mitts and had covered her smart, garnet sweater and loose, black pants with a frilly white apron. Then she frowned. "You boys look like you could use a drink."

Jason nodded. "Make that several, and you'd be right."

Tae Hyun sniffed the air. "Did you cook?"

Yoo Mi dramatically rolled her eyes. "Darling, you know I don't cook. I ordered dinner in. I'm just playing the part." She looked at Seong Woo. "Why don't you show them where they can wash up and change while I get dinner ready?"

"Of course."

Seong Woo walked up to Yoo Mi and gently kissed her cheek before beckoning for Jason and Tae Hyun to follow. Then he led them to the guest suite, where their bags had already been deposited. Like the rest of the condo, it was elegantly minimal, with light-colored, polished wood floors and expensive, Scandinavian-style furniture.

Seong Woo pointed to a door in the corner opposite the

room's entrance. "The ensuite is through there if you want to wash up. I'll go get your drinks ready in the meantime."

Jason snorted. "You're the second person to suggest we wash up. Do we really smell that bad?"

Seong Woo chuckled. "I'm having the car fumigated as we speak."

Tae Hyun wrapped his arm around Jason and pulled him close. "We won't be long. Thank you again for letting us stay here."

Seong Woo smiled. "It's no problem. See you in a bit."

Tae Hyun turned on Jason as soon as they were alone. "What was that about in the car?"

"Are you seriously still on that?" Jason shook his head. "I thought we'd moved on."

Tae Hyun frowned. "You know I don't like arguing in front of people."

"So, what? You've been saving this until we're finally alone so you can pounce on me?" Jason stripped off his shirt and sniffed one of his armpits. "Yikes. I guess I do need a shower." He turned toward the bathroom, but Tae Hyun stopped him with a hand on his chest.

"Stop avoiding the issue."

"What issue?" Jason huffed. "The fact that you're irrational about people being supportive? Or the fact that I called you out on it?"

Tae Hyun's frown was almost a scowl. Jason knew he'd probably been too blunt. But he was too tired and cranky to pull his punches.

"I'm not fucking irrational."

Jason decided to try and rescue things anyway. "Not about most things, no. But about this?" He shrugged. "The moment you think someone's humoring you, you totally shut them down."

"I don't–"

"You do. You were about to do it to me in the car, right?" Jason affected what he hoped was a playful scowl. "Please don't humor me," he said, wagging his finger for emphasis.

Tae Hyun huffed. "I don't sound like that."

Jason wagged his finger again. "I don't sound like that."

Tae Hyun scoffed. "If you won't take this seriously, then–"

"Then what?" Jason blew out his exasperation in a deep breath. "Is this seriously what you want to do right now? Argue? Because I'm tired, hungry, and stinky. And so are you."

"Wait." Tae Hyun's eyebrows popped up. "I don't stink, do I?"

Jason chuckled. "You smell like the finest gym locker room." He took hold of Tae Hyun's hands and pulled him closer. "Look. I don't think what I said was wrong, but I'm sorry I said it in front of Seong Woo. That wasn't very thoughtful. Okay?"

Tae Hyun pursed his lips as he considered Jason's apology. Hopefully, it was enough. It was all he was gonna get. He finally nodded. "Alright. I'm sorry, too. I'm probably making too big a deal out of this."

Jason smiled. "Good. Now can I please go wash off this stink?"

Tae Hyun shook his head as he tugged on Jason's hand and dragged him toward the washroom. "I think you smell so sexy right now, hyung."

Jason's eyebrows quickly rose, matching a similar motion in his crotch. "Here? Now?"

Tae Hyun shook his head as his ears reddened. "No way." He let go of Jason's hand and pulled his shirt off. "I'm too hungry." He unbuckled his pants and slid them down. "And we've already made Yoo Mi wait too long." Then he reached for Jason's pants and undid the top button. "But after?" He shrugged as he turned away and slid his underwear off, treating Jason to an outstanding view of his firm, round little ass.

Jason quickly stripped off his pants and underwear, following his bouncing erection into the granite-tiled shower behind Tae Hyun. "You little devil." He grasped Tae Hyun's waist and pulled them together, resting his cock between Tae Hyun's cheeks.

Tae Hyun quietly moaned as he pushed back, slowly grinding against Jason. "Stop being naughty, hyung."

"Me? I'm just standing here."

Tae Hyun reached forward to start the shower. Jason nearly yelped when he was briefly drenched in the icy spray. Then the warm water soon followed, and he felt his muscles begin to relax.

Tae Hyun grabbed the small bottle of body wash from an inset shelf beside the shower nozzle before turning around to reveal his matching erection. "We're here to wash up, remember?" He flipped the cap open and tilted the bottle to squeeze a small amount onto his hand. Then he returned the bottle to the shelf before lathering the sudsy wash between his palms. "I'll start."

Tae Hyun put his hands on Jason's chest, rubbing them around to spread the floral-scented suds across his body. His hands quickly drifted downward until they reached Jason's cock. Tae Hyun took hold of him and gently stroked, drawing an automatic groan from Jason. But two could play at that game. Jason quickly grabbed the bottle and helped himself to some before applying it to Tae Hyun's chest. He caressed Tae Hyun's smooth, slender form before his hands found his throbbing erection. Tae Hyun gasped as Jason slowly stroked it. And the two quickly fell into a harmonious rhythm, panting as they masturbated one another under the steamy shower flow. Tae Hyun came first, doing his best to muffle his cry. Jason soon followed, feeling some of the tension from his long flight melt away with each spurt.

The washing began in earnest after that, with Jason spending a little extra time working his hand between Tae Hyun's legs, earning him some renewed interest from Tae Hyun's cock. But Jason's stomach growled to remind him dinner was waiting, so they finished washing and dried off.

"I'm sorry again about before," Tae Hyun offered as he got dressed. "I overreacted."

"I'm sorry, too," Jason replied after pulling a clean shirt over his head. "I was just being cranky."

"I know." Tae Hyun sighed. "I could claim the same thing, but it wouldn't be true. I thought–" He paused, but there was no mistaking the surprising anguish in his voice. "I thought it would be different coming back here. But it feels the same."

"We just got here." Jason moved behind Tae Hyun and wrapped him in a reverse hug. "It'll get better. You'll see."

"And if it doesn't?"

"Then you'll still have me."

Once they'd finished dressing, Jason and Tae Hyun stopped by the bar to pick up a pair of drinks. Yoo Mi and Seong Woo were just sitting down when Jason and Tae Hyun arrived.

"Perfect timing," Yoo Mi announced before directing them

to their seats, putting Tae Hyun beside her and Jason on the opposite side next to Seong Woo. "I was about to send someone to fetch you."

Jason chuckled. "Were you worried we'd christen your guest shower?"

"That's sweet, darling." Yoo Mi flashed a smile Jason recognized from dozens of magazine covers. "But there's not a single corner of this condo that's gone unchristened."

Tae Hyun coughed in his drink and nearly did a spit take. "Yoo Mi!"

"What?" Yoo Mi casually shrugged. "It's just us. We don't have to pretend. Why? Did you christen the guest shower?"

Seong Woo loudly cleared his throat. "Yoo Mi."

Yoo Mi sighed. "Fine, fine. They're ready to serve us anyway."

Dinner started with kimchi pancakes and a soybean paste stew with pork and vegetables, followed by grilled pork belly with a spicy radish salad. It was delicious, of course, ordered from "a cute little place across the river" that Yoo Mi eventually admitted was actually Palate, a restaurant owned and run by expat celebrity chef Derek Goh.

"It's so subversive that an American makes the best Korean food in Seoul," Yoo Mi shared with a wink.

"It's excellent," Jason agreed as he stuffed a chunk of tender pork belly wrapped in a perilla leaf into his mouth. "Almost as good as Tae Hyun's cooking."

Yoo Mi playfully scoffed at Tae Hyun. "You never told me you cook. How come you never made anything for me?"

Tae Hyun shrugged. "I learned to cook in the army."

Yoo Mi elaborately pouted. "Well, tomorrow you're making dinner."

"Actually–" Tae Hyun put his food down and sipped from his gin and tonic. "I haven't talked about this with Jason yet, but I was thinking of going to Daejeon tomorrow."

Jason knew Tae Hyun would only be considering that for one reason. His parents were in Daejeon. "Are you sure that's what you want?"

Tae Hyun frowned. "No. It's the last thing I want. But I have to after what they did."

Jason nodded. He knew something of how Tae Hyun felt, having dealt with stern, unforgiving, homophobic parents for a lifetime. "Okay."

"You'll come?"

Jason chuckled. "Are you kidding? I'd march up to the gates of hell with you if that's what you wanted."

"Ooh, that's good." Seong Woo tapped Jason's shoulder. "I should put that in my vows."

Yoo Mi scoffed. "You haven't finished writing your vows? The wedding is only three days away!"

"Wedding?" Seong Woo winked. "What wedding?"

Yoo Mi grunted as she threw a rolled-up perilla leaf at him. "Don't you dare–"

"So, Daejeon?" Seong Woo announced, cutting Yoo Mi off as he plucked the leaf from his lap. "You're welcome to take one of the tanks. Although the train will be a lot faster."

"I saw that interview," Yoo Mi interjected. "Ji Hoon looked at least ten years older than the last time I saw him." She grinned. "I still have that video, by the way."

Tae Hyun smiled, but it looked forced. "Don't remind me. That's the last thing I want to remember from that day."

Yoo Mi snorted. "I still have that video, too." Then she frowned. "But what your parents did was awful. I never liked them. You know?"

Seong Woo breathed out an exasperated sigh. "Yoo Mi–"

"No," Tae Hyun interrupted. "She's right to say that. My parents were awful to her. I couldn't tell them what was really happening between us, so my father kept pressuring her to give up her career, and my mother kept asking when she would get pregnant."

Yoo Mi groaned. "I almost broke down once, near the end, and told her the truth."

"And now we know what they would've said." Tae Hyun sighed. "Sorry to bring everyone down like this."

"It's alright," Yoo Mi assured him. "I'd even offer to go with you if I wasn't so busy tomorrow. But you'll be back before the rehearsal the day after, right?"

Tae Hyun nodded. "We're not staying. We'll be back tomorrow evening."

"Oh!" Yoo Mi smiled. "Then you should join us for dinner out." She looked at Seong Woo and pouted. "Could you make us a reservation at the place I like?"

Seong Woo rolled his eyes. "Maybe we should see if our guests want to go first."

"Want to?" Yoo Mi huffed. "Of course, they want to go!" She turned to Tae Hyun. "You do, right?"

Tae Hyun didn't look so sure. "What if people find out I'm here?"

"You were already spotted at the airport," Jason countered. "Everyone who wants to know you're here already does."

"Oh, yeah." Tae Hyun still didn't look sure. "I suppose so."

Yoo Mi's elegantly blushed cheeks spread into a proper smile. "Fantastic! Then I guess it's settled."

After dinner, Yoo Mi surprised them with a dessert of

french crepes stuffed with a sinful chocolate hazelnut creme. Jason felt decadently full when they retired to the main room for after-dinner drinks. He noticed the view of Gangnam that he'd enjoyed the last time he'd come to Seong Woo's condo. But the city lights were obscured by low clouds and a foggy mist rising from the Han River. Then he felt a sudden urge to smoke. He hadn't smoked in months, but the cravings had yet to completely disappear. Thankfully, no one else there smoked, so he had no choice but to ignore it.

They'd been discussing their wedding plans–including a lavish reception and a two-week honeymoon to Tahiti–and the movie role Yoo Mi would take on when they returned. But Tae Hyun eventually started yawning and nodding off, which made Jason yawn, too. His 14-hour flight, the excellent food, and all the bourbon had finally caught up with him. So, Jason excused himself and headed for the balcony, thinking a little fresh air might do him some good. It was cool outside rather than cold, and the breeze blowing off the river helped perk him up a bit. But another cigarette craving made him second guess being out there. He turned to head back inside just as Yoo Mi walked up to the open sliding door.

"I'm sorry. Did you want to be alone?"

Jason shook his head. Something about his expression must've been off-putting, so he smiled. "No, no. Come on out."

Yoo Mi nodded as she stepped out. Then she handed Jason his unfinished Kingston. "I thought you might want this."

Jason chuckled as he took the glass from her. "Ordinarily, I would. But this day's really kicked my ass."

Yoo Mi shrugged and sipped her wine. Then she rested her arms on the balcony railing, leaned over, and deeply inhaled through her nose. "Ah, I love nights like tonight when it smells like the river and not fucking exhaust fumes." She glanced at Jason and smiled. "Remember the last time we were out here together?"

Jason nodded. "How could I forget? I was trying to be cool, and you saw right through it."

"It's a gift." Yoo Mi turned her gaze back to the distant city lights. "Not that you didn't do the exact same thing to me. I feel like we're alike that way."

Jason quietly sighed as he leaned on the railing beside Yoo Mi. "Yeah. We're like– wait. Do you know the English expression *two peas in a pod?*"

Yoo Mi chuckled. "I've never heard that one. But if you're talking about how alike you and I are, we'd say our hands and feet match."

"Maybe, but I could never pull off that nail color. I'm more of a fall palette."

Yoo Mi laughed. "You know, I always hoped things would work out for you two. You're good for each other. As anxious as Tae Hyun is right now, he's not even half as neurotic as he was when he first got home from the army."

"I used to be so self-centered," Jason admitted. "Until I fell for him. Now he's all I think about."

Yoo Mi stood up and turned to face Jason. "I know what you mean. I still feel guilty about making Tae Hyun pretend to date me so I could save my career."

Jason shook his head. "Nah. That's on you. I mean, it's your choice, I guess. But you're his closest friend." He smiled. "I doubt he'd change a thing about that."

"You're probably right." Yoo Mi chuckled again. "In a weird way, it's because of Tae Hyun that I'm with Seong Woo."

"We know. Seong Woo told us."

Yoo Mi frowned. "He told you what?"

"He said that dating Tae Hyun first put you on his radar."

Yoo Mi laughed. "Are you serious? That little shit. I had no idea." She shook her head. "I meant that spending that much time fake dating Tae Hyun was what convinced me I could do it for real." She smiled. "We may not have been in love, but I definitely love him. You know?"

Jason smiled. "I think I do. In fact, I should check in and see how he's doing."

"Oh, don't worry. He already went to bed. That's why I came out here."

"What? When?"

"He started nodding off after you got up," Yoo Mi explained. "So Seong Woo took him to bed."

"He what?"

Yoo Mi laughed. "Sorry, I meant put him to bed." She snorted. "He's the last one you'd need to worry about, Jason. It's you he's got the crush on, anyway."

"But Seong Woo is so very straight."

"Oh, no doubt. But you don't have to be gay to have a crush on another man." Yoo Mi chuckled. "I mean, he talked about you so damn much after that party. When you called him for help with security, it was like you'd finally asked him on a date. He was so giddy it was adorable."

"Giddy?" Jason snorted. "I'm glad you're not the jealous type."

"Why be jealous? I'm gorgeous, talented, and have great tits. He'd be crazy to fall for someone else." Yoo Mi smiled. "Plus, he trusts me."

"Trusts you? That man worships you."

Yoo Mi's smile grew a fraction wider. "I know. Why else do you think I'm marrying him? Speaking of which–"

Jason held up his free hand. "Please don't. We'll get there when we get there. Right now, our plates are totally full." Then he sighed, suddenly overcome with unexpected melancholy. "Plus, he's nowhere near ready for it."

Yoo Mi frowned. "He's not? I thought things–"

"Things are fine," Jason assured her. "We're both just as committed as ever. I meant that he's having a rougher time coming to terms with everything than I am. You know? First with KBR coming after him, and now his parents?" He shrugged. "I'm used to getting nailed to the wall by the public. But this is new for him."

"Okay." Yoo Mi's nod suggested that she wasn't agreeing with him so much as humoring him, which almost made Jason laugh. "But are you? Ready for marriage, I mean."

"Yeah. I'd do it tomorrow if I thought he wanted to."

Yoo Mi's eyes narrowed with obvious judgment. "If you say so."

"You don't believe me?"

Yoo Mi shrugged. "It doesn't matter if I believe you. It only matters if you do." Then she smiled. "But it'll happen when it happens, right? Now, get your ass inside and get to bed. You look like you fell asleep ten minutes ago."

Jason laughed, knowing she was probably right about that. Whether or not she was right about the other thing remained to be seen.

11

Tae Hyun had originally hoped to catch an early KTX train for Daejeon out of Seoul Station so they could be back before dinner time. But, between their jet lag and all the drinking at dinner, Jason and Tae Hyun overslept. Tae Hyun didn't even remember going to bed and woke in a mild state of panic until he found Jason's slumbering form lying next to him. After rushing through their showers and coffee, they ended up catching a train shortly after noon. And it was so cold and overcast in Seoul that Jason had to borrow a coat from Seong Woo. With the trouble they had just trying to leave, Tae Hyun wondered if going was a bad idea after all. Sure, he'd get to see Yun Seo again, but he didn't have to go all the way to Daejeon for that.

Seong Woo kindly sent Tae Hyun, Jason, and Seong Min to the train station in one of the tanks. Seong Hyeon had elected to stay behind. That was partly out of convenience since they didn't want to overwhelm Tae Hyun's parents with too many people and partly to allow Seong Hyeon time to meet with Min Kyu to consult about upgrading Tae Hyun's security. And they were traveling incognito. After the airport incident, even Seong Min agreed to go full ninja until they were on the train. But Yun Seo still spotted them as soon as they exited the massive, black SUV.

"So much for not getting recognized," Tae Hyun complained after a hug from Yun Seo.

Yun Seo rolled her eyes. "I knew what to look for, oppa. But no one'll recognize you otherwise." She chuckled. "You could be any K-pop group behind those masks and sunglasses."

They were just visiting for the day and had no luggage, so the group went straight for the train and boarded their first-class car. They'd purchased seats at the front of the train to minimize the number of people walking by them, which meant they could take their masks off. And Jason agreed to sit next to Seong Min so Tae Hyun and Yun Seo could have a chance to talk during the not-quite hour-long trip.

Yun Seo fidgeted in her seat while they waited to depart. Maybe she was trying to get comfortable. Maybe she was nervous. Tae Hyun certainly was.

"Are you trying to rock the train?" Tae Hyun hoped a little humor would help lessen their nerves.

Yun Seo took the hint and sat still. "Sorry, oppa. I'm just nervous about what's gonna happen there."

"What do you think will happen?"

Yun Seo snorted. "Are you asking because you don't know?"

Tae Hyun frowned. "I'm asking because I want to know what you think."

"I think there's no way this won't be weird and awkward." Yun Seo sighed. "The last time I spoke with our mother, she practically pretended you don't even exist."

Tae Hyun huffed. "I wished they'd done that when the reporters came calling. That was one more headache I didn't need."

Yun Seo put her hand on Tae Hyun's knee as the high-speed

train smoothly pulled away from the station. "Things will be fine, oppa. They'll eventually come around."

That was a fine sentiment, even if it was totally outside the realm of possibility. But Tae Hyun knew better. His parents had always been conservative to the point of being uptight. They kept to old-school Korean values and customs, with his father being the lifelong breadwinner and his mother in charge of the home. His father almost hadn't let Yun Seo go to college, but she'd convinced him that having a degree would make her a more attractive prospect as a modern wife.

Tae Hyun, of course, had essentially been allowed to do whatever he liked as long as it brought honor and prestige to the family. That was why his parents had let him train in the arts. His desire to sing and dance fell far beyond what his father had initially expected of him. But he worked hard, and his talents were undeniable. And being signed as a trainee when he was barely a teenager made his idol debut that much more certain and his parents that much happier.

Things changed for Tae Hyun when he finally understood that he was gay. That came with the realization that he'd never be able to tell his parents. Not that they'd been especially homophobic when he was growing up. But that was only because they didn't know any gay people. And any instances of gay representation in the media were almost nonexistent. But sometimes, the news of a local gay activist or media personality would reach them, and they made their feelings on the matter clear. Being gay was wrong. It was unnatural. And Tae Hyun doubted there was much he could do to change their minds about that.

As they rode along, Yun Seo reviewed Tae Hyun's schedule for the next few days since he'd be so busy with Yoo Mi and

Seong Woo's wedding. After that came his final review of the album master with Gordo and several meetings with potential stage and costume designers for the upcoming tour. But his most immediate appointment was the final fitting with the designer for his and Jason's tuxedos.

"I'm honestly surprised that Yoo Mi put you both in her wedding party," Yun Seo suddenly shared.

Tae Hyun frowned. "You don't approve?"

"Of course, I approve! How else would I score an invite to the year's hottest wedding? But I'm surprised she's even having a wedding party since it could distract from the attention on her."

Tae Hyun snorted. "If there's one thing to remember about Yoo Mi, it's that she's always managing her image. And she's never not three steps ahead of everyone else."

Yun Seo shrugged. "I suppose. I mean, her wedding is all the entertainment blogs are talking about." She leaned in close enough to whisper. "I even heard that one of the Big Four labels rescheduled an album release planned for the same day."

"You're kidding."

Yun Seo shrugged again. "It's what I heard."

Tae Hyun figured it was probably true. A lot of complex calculus was involved in determining release dates for the Big Four labels. As competitors, they didn't officially cooperate with one another. But Tae Hyun knew that, behind the scenes, things weren't so cut and dried. While he'd never heard an official reason for it, *XTC*'s debut had been pushed back twice to not coincide with releases from other labels. Of course, that unofficial courtesy didn't extend to any indie or even international labels.

It was sunny in Daejeon when they arrived, but still chilly. Back in his mask and sunglasses while walking through Daejeon Station, Tae Hyun was struck with the memory of when he and his parents had first boarded the train to Seoul for his KBR audition. He'd been so young then. And the station had seemed so much larger.

Since Daejeon only had a single subway line, and Tae Hyun didn't want to waste a precious hour of their short visit on the bus to Yuseong-gu, he'd had Yun Seo arrange a rental car for the afternoon. An attendant was waiting to hand over the keys outside the station. And they pretended not to notice as Yun Seo gave the keys to Seong Min.

Surprisingly, Seong Min already knew his way around Daejeon. "I have family here," he explained after asking for their destination's address.

Tae Hyun's parent's house in Yuseong-gu was on the northeast side of the city, a twenty-minute drive from the train station. Tae Hyun wondered as they drove if they should stop for a quick bite since he and Jason hadn't eaten much that day. He was about to suggest it when Jason spoke up instead.

"So, what should we expect?"

Tae Hyun frowned. "Honestly? I have no idea." Then he quietly sighed. "Normally, this would be a very standard visit. Our parents would welcome you as my friend, ask you a million questions, and feed us until we exploded. But today?" He shrugged.

Yun Seo leaned around from the front passenger seat. "I spoke with our mother this morning to let her know we were coming, and she seemed excited. But I could hear our father grumbling in the background."

Jason chuckled. "Sounds just like my parents."

Tae Hyun grabbed hold of Jason's hand. "It's important that you let me take the lead in there. At least until I have a sense of how things will go." He frowned. "I hope they'll be civil, but they may not be."

Jason nodded and squeezed Tae Hyun's hand. "Got it. I'll just smile and nod."

"I'm serious. My parents aren't going to like what I plan to say. My father might be very angry."

Jason frowned. "Define very angry."

"It's hard to say." Tae Hyun sighed again. "He'll rant and yell. He'll probably say some unkind things about me and you."

"I'm there for you. I don't care what he says about me." Jason shrugged. "Besides, I doubt he can be any worse than my dad. The last time we spoke, he told me he wished I was dead."

Yun Seo gasped. "He didn't."

Jason nodded. "Yeah. Gerald Park is a real piece of work."

Tae Hyun forced himself to smile at Jason. "Just be on your best behavior, please. And if things go badly, we can just leave."

Jason smiled back. "You got it."

Tae Hyun nodded. He knew Jason meant what he'd said. And he wanted to accept that Jason would follow through, but he knew him too well. Just like he knew his father. Still, he'd brought Jason along for a reason. If he really didn't want Jason to interfere, he could've gone to see his parents alone.

Tae Hyun's parents lived in a tidy, white, three-bedroom bungalow with a red-tiled roof set amongst dozens of similar houses built during district redevelopment in the late eighties.

Their home was older but well cared for. And it was a huge step up from the small, four-room house in Dong-gu where he'd been born. Of course, the Yuseong-gu house had been financed through his *XTC* earnings.

"It's cute," Jason said as he climbed from the car's backseat.

Tae Hyun was briefly surprised before remembering that Jason, for all his wealth and privilege, never complained about ordinary things. It was highly endearing. "Thanks. I actually helped them pick it out."

"And pay for it," Yun Seo quietly added.

Tae Hyun quietly huffed. "Please don't start." He bent down to see Seong Min still sitting at the wheel. "Are you coming in?"

Seong Min shook his head. "No, sir. With how you described the situation, it feels best if I stay out here. Unless you think you might need me for something."

Tae Hyun bit down on his lip as he considered the possibilities. He doubted the situation would get bad enough to require Seong Min's aid. "No. If you're okay waiting–"

"I am, sir. I'll probably go get something to eat while I wait." Seong Min retrieved his phone from the cubby behind the shifter. "But you can always call. I won't go far."

"Sounds like that's settled." Jason put his arm around Tae Hyun, causing his posture to go rigid. "Sorry." He sheepishly pulled his arm away. "Best behavior."

Tae Hyun sighed as he took Jason's hand. "I love you. And I appreciate you being here. Now, let's get this over with."

Tae Hyun let go of Jason's hand, walked up to the brightly painted, yellow front door, and hesitated. That was new. Then he shook off his nerves, turned the knob, and pushed. It didn't budge. Was it locked?

11

Yun Seo stepped up next to him and knocked. "They started locking it last year after the local news ran an exposé on local crime."

"What local crime?"

Yun Seo chuckled. "I know. But they bought into it."

The door swung open a moment later to reveal their mother's smiling face. "Oh, my lovely children are here." She gave Tae Hyun a thorough once-over before spreading her arms. "Come here."

Tae Hyun stepped into his mother's hug, feeling like perhaps he'd blown everything out of proportion. His parents must've already realized their mistake and wouldn't–

"You're so skinny," his mother announced. "Aren't you eating?"

Tae Hyun swallowed his sigh. She always said things like that. It was her way. "I'm eating fine, mother. Maybe we should go in?"

"Oh! Of course." She turned to walk inside. "Come in, come in."

Yun Seo grunted. "Where's my hug?" Then she walked into the house.

Tae Hyun quickly followed her. Jason came in and closed the door behind him while the others removed their shoes in the tiny entryway. Tae Hyun's parents were waiting in the sitting room. His mother was still smiling, but it was clearly a cover for something else. His father stood grim-faced with his arms folded across his chest. They both looked so much older than Tae Hyun remembered. Once black with silver streaks, his mother's hair had gone completely gray. And enough of his father's hair had fallen out that Tae Hyun could see his scalp.

Tae Hyun realized he was stalling and stopped putting off the inevitable. “Mother, Father? This is Jason Park.” He turned to Jason. “And these are my parents, Woo Jeong Ho and Byeon Sun Young.”

Jason offered them a bow. “It’s a pleasure to meet you both.”

Jeong Ho frowned. “Is he the American?”

“Yes, sir.” Jason briefly smiled and nodded. “I’m American.”

Jeong Ho seemed surprised at Jason’s reply, but his frown never wavered. “You have a Seoul accent.”

“My parents are from Seoul, sir.”

A thick tension settled between them as Tae Hyun watched his father’s mental wheels turn. That was the other reason Tae Hyun had brought Jason along. He was an unknown. His father knew how to push Tae Hyun’s buttons since he’d installed most of them. But that wasn’t true with Jason.

Sun Young gestured toward the dining table behind her. “You all must be hungry. Let’s eat before everything gets cold.”

The table was piled with enough food to feed a small army. Tae Hyun’s mouth watered as he enjoyed the familiar aromas of his mother’s dakgalbi. Of course, his parents had neglected to set a spot for Jason, even knowing he was coming. It could’ve been an oversight. Or, it could’ve been deliberate. After grabbing another chair from the sitting room, Sun Young and Yun Seo served everyone before taking their seats. The group sat in tense silence until Jason finally took a bite of his food.

“Oh wow. This is so good,” Jason announced.

Sun Young smiled. “Thank you, Jason. Have you had dakgalbi before?”

Jason nodded. “Yes. Tae Hyun recently made it for me.”

“Except we didn’t have any sweet potatoes,” Tae Hyun

added.

"Oh. Well, I usually use regular potatoes if that's the case," Sun Young explained. "Where did you learn how to make it? I don't recall ever teaching you."

"In my trainee dorm. It was–"

Jeong Ho loudly grunted. "You cook for the boy?"

Tae Hyun fought to keep from frowning. He assumed that *the boy* meant Jason, which was insulting on so many levels, not the least of which was that Jason was the older of the two. "Yes. Jason-hyung enjoys my cooking."

Jeong Ho's eyebrows twitched when Tae Hyun called Jason *hyung*. "And you're living together?"

"Yes, I've been living with Jason," Tae Hyun explained, "while I've been in Los Angeles."

"Living in sin."

Tae Hyun nearly groaned, but he knew it wouldn't help things. "We love each other, Father. And he makes me happy. Isn't that enough?"

Jeong Ho scowled. "Bah. Don't you dare call your sinful infatuation love. It was bad enough when you paraded around with that hussy–"

"Father!" Yun Seo called out. "Please don't–"

Jeong Ho silenced Yun Seo with a look. "Are both my children so willful and insolent?" He wasn't quite shouting, but Tae Hyun knew it was only a matter of time. "Do neither of you honor your parents any longer?"

Sun Young touched her husband's shoulder, drawing an irritated glare. "Perhaps we should discuss this after we eat? I made so much–"

"No." Jeong Ho shook his head. "There's nothing to discuss. And I'm not eating with the likes of him."

Yun Seo and her mother both frowned. Tae Hyun was struck by how much they were alike. In another life, without his father's influence, it may have been possible for his mother to be a friend and confidant, like his sister. Not that his mother was free from guilt. She'd never once failed to support her husband, even using her time alone with them while he was away or at work to coach the children into unquestioning obedience. After all, that was how she was raised, too. And that might've been fine for a family where the daughter wasn't intelligent, ambitious, and willful, and the son wasn't gay.

Tae Hyun sighed. "The likes of who, father? Me? Or Jason?"

Jeong Ho pressed his lips into a tight, thin line. "What's the difference? You're both immoral degenerates."

Tae Hyun angrily frowned. Then Jason barked out a sharp laugh. Tae Hyun's father scowled as he turned his attention directly to Jason.

"What's that? Is something funny to you?"

"Are you kidding?" Jason laughed again. "You're acting like such a stereotypical drama villain right now. I'd expect you to twirl your waxed mustache if you had one."

Tae Hyun's jaw dropped as he whirled on his boyfriend. "Jason–"

"I know, I know." Jason held up his hands in mock surrender. "You told me to be on my best behavior. I'm sorry, but I can't help it. This guy's just so fucking ridiculous."

His face bright red, Jeong Ho angrily shook his head. "I'd expect nothing less from a perverted deviant like you."

"Perverted deviant?" Jason loudly scoffed. "Please. I've been called worse by twelve-year-olds in the game chat. You'll have to try harder than that."

Tae Hyun knew he was losing control of the situation–if

he even ever had it. So he pushed his chair back and stood before grabbing Jason's hand and pulling him up. "Come with me."

Tae Hyun led a surprisingly compliant Jason back to the sitting room, stopping when he thought he'd be out of earshot. "Hyung, please," he whispered. "It doesn't matter what he says to me."

"To you, maybe. I can't just–"

"Let me handle this."

Jason sighed. "Alright, fine. Say what you came here to say so we can leave."

Tae Hyun nodded, knowing that was probably the best he could expect from Jason. "Thank you."

Tae Hyun returned to the tense mess waiting at the dining table. So far, Jason had been the only one who'd eaten anything. He thought about sitting down again but knew that would only make what he wanted to say harder. "Father, Mother, I didn't come here to argue with you. But we need to talk about–"

"We need to talk about how you've dishonored us," a red-faced Jeong Ho interrupted.

Jason grunted. "Let him speak."

Jeong Ho practically growled as he got up from the table. "I will not be spoken to like this." He stepped toward Jason, but Tae Hyun moved to intercept him.

"No, Father. Please leave him out of this. It's between you and–"

Tae Hyun was so surprised by the loud crack of his father's open palm striking his cheek that he didn't initially feel the pain. "How dare you defy me!"

Tae Hyun's father readied his hand for a second strike, but

Jason rushed forward to grab it. His father tried to wrench his arm away, but Jason's grip was too strong.

"So you like to hit people, do you?" Jason's face and voice were tight and controlled. His knuckles were almost white. How tightly was he holding his arm? "Why don't you try that with me and see how it goes?"

Tae Hyun's mother suddenly burst into tears. Yun Seo rushed to her, wrapping her in a tight hug that could've been meant to shield her as much as comfort her.

"I will not be disrespected in my own home," Tae Hyun's father spat. But Tae Hyun heard the change in his tone. He sounded unsure. His rigidly defiant stance had weakened.

"You want some fucking respect? Then try being respectful." Jason gestured toward Tae Hyun with his free hand. "This man is one of the world's top performing artists. He's literally changed people's lives for the better. Including yours." His voice was low and intense. "And you're treating him like this? You should be fucking ashamed of yourself."

Tae Hyun watched his father deflate under Jason's withering rant. And, possibly for the first time, he saw how old and fragile his parents really were. Their power over him had come from his inability to see them as people. But they weren't the larger-than-life demigods he'd always imagined them to be during his childhood. They were simply small, frail people from an older, ignorant generation that the world was rapidly leaving behind. And, just like he'd finally let go of Chang Min's hold over him, Tae Hyun let go of theirs, too.

"That's enough, hyung."

Jason loudly huffed, probably realizing he'd gone too far. "Fine. You want to listen to his crap? Then do it." He let go of Tae Hyun's father and stepped back. "I'll go wait in the car with Seong Min."

Tae Hyun didn't stop Jason as he stormed toward the front door, grabbed his coat and shoes, and went outside. His father grabbed his arm and massaged the angry red splotch where Jason had gripped it. Tae Hyun shook his head. Their meeting had gone sideways so fast that he hadn't even had a chance to say what he'd come there to say.

"I can live with your disapproval," Tae Hyun finally said. His voice was quiet but clear. "I know who I am now. And I'm okay with it whether you love me or not." He grunted. "But you went too far by trying to publicly shame me."

Tae Hyun's mother tore herself from Yun Seo's grasp and threw her arms around him. "I'm so sorry, my son," she sobbed. "We were wrong to–"

Tae Hyun's father loudly hissed, and his mother immediately fell silent. "You would choose this man over your family?"

Tae Hyun quietly snorted as he recalled Chang Min saying almost the exact same thing. His parents thought they owned him. Just as Chang Min had. Tae Hyun shook his head again. Nobody owned him. Not his parents. Not his ex. Not his former record label. Only Jason seemed to realize that. *You're not my possession,* he'd told Tae Hyun multiple times. Of course, he'd choose Jason over his family.

"It's you who's making the choice, Father." Tae Hyun looked at Yun Seo, who nodded. She knew it was time to go. "You can choose to accept me for who and what I am. Or you can choose to live in the past." He waited for his father to respond, still holding onto the small hope that he'd see how wrong he was and openly accept his son. But his father only stared past him, his stony expression never softening. Tae Hyun sighed.

"I hope KBR paid you well to betray me because you won't see any more money from me."

Tae Hyun returned to the entryway to retrieve his jacket and shoes. He wondered if Jason would be waiting like he said. Part of him knew for sure that Jason had run away after trying to bully Tae Hyun's father into accepting his son. It was exactly what Tae Hyun had told him not to do. And it was exactly what Tae Hyun needed. But he found Jason quietly sitting outside on the front step.

"Hyung."

Jason looked up at Tae Hyun. "Are you okay?"

Tae Hyun sighed as he sat beside Jason. "I don't know." He looked at Jason's profile. The cool afternoon sun brightly reflected off his cheeks, giving him an almost angelic glow. "I imagined a hundred different ways this could've gone. But I see now this was the only way it would be.

Jason nodded. "I'm sorry. I know I fucked everything up in there."

"No, you didn't." Tae Hyun ruefully chuckled. "It didn't help anything, but everything was already fucked up long before we even got here."

Jason shrugged. "Give them some time. They might still come around."

Tae Hyun chuckled. "You don't believe that."

"No, I don't." Jason shrugged again. "But what the hell do I know? Just because my parents are irredeemable doesn't mean yours are."

Tae Hyun felt a sharp sting from a sudden burst of cold wind against his cheek and wondered how red it was. He leaned against Jason's shoulder, so Jason lifted his arm, wrapped it around Tae Hyun's shoulder, and pulled him close. Tae Hyun enjoyed the comforting warmth of Jason's touch. "I'm sorry you had to see all that. But I'm glad you came with me."

Jason gave Tae Hyun a gentle squeeze. "I told you I'd march to the gates of hell with you, didn't I?"

Tae Hyun snorted. "Maybe. But my father's not the devil."

"No, he's not." Jason bent down and kissed Tae Hyun's forehead. "But I'd protect you from the devil himself, too, if I had to."

12

Jason regretted his behavior the moment he set foot outside. Despite his promise to behave, he'd done exactly the opposite. But seeing and hearing the way that old fucker treated the man he loved triggered the same reactions he had when he dealt with his own father. The two men were so much alike it was scary. Put Woo Jeong Ho in a mansion and dress him in a ten-thousand-dollar Italian suit, and they would've practically been the same person. But Jason had never laid a hand on his father. And he imagined that if he ever gripped Gerald Park's forearm like that, it wouldn't have felt as spindly and weak. Jason had no doubt about how easily he could've snapped it. But there was no way he could stand by and watch him slap Tae Hyun like that. The sound alone had awakened the rage he'd tried to dampen when he stepped into the home.

But Tae Hyun had let him off the hook with none of his usual lectures about image and appearance. And Jason briefly wondered if Tae Hyun had planned it that way all along. The thought disturbed him, but not enough to question Tae Hyun about it. At least, not right away. Jason was who he was. And he was nothing if not predictable. If Tae Hyun had truly not wanted Jason's interference, he would've left him behind.

The only good thing to come from their disastrous Daejeon

trip was the surprising, budding mutual crush between Yun Seo and Seong Min. Jason noticed Seong Min's half of the crush first, between his extra care and courtesy as he helped Yun Seo into the car and his constant glances toward her when he thought she wasn't looking. But the way they almost giddily chatted like school friends on the train back to Seoul was the clincher. Jason had no idea how they'd make anything work between them. But far be it from him to stand in their way.

Seong Woo and Yoo Mi were both out when Jason and Tae Hyun finally arrived at their condo, which meant they could avoid the initial *how did it go* questions and go straight to bed for a nap before dinner. That was fortunate since Jason was fucking exhausted. And he had no idea how to answer those questions yet, anyway.

Jason woke sometime later to someone gently shaking him. He cracked an eyelid open to see Tae Hyun smiling as he lay beside him. Jason smiled back. "Hi."

Tae Hyun chuckled. "Hi. We should get up soon so we have time to get ready for dinner."

"Okay." Jason snuck his arm underneath Tae Hyun and pulled him close enough to lay his head on Jason's chest. "So–"

Tae Hyun quietly sighed. "You want to talk about what happened."

"You don't? Cuz I kinda think we should."

Tae Hyun began to gently caress Jason's chest. "I don't know. It was awful. My parents are awful." He sighed again. "And I don't know what to do."

"Are you asking me? Because I don't think you want to do what I did."

Tae Hyun snorted. "Yeah, I don't know if I'm ready to

disown them yet."

Jason frowned. "Is that what you think you should do?"

"No. But it's what I think you think."

Jason quietly huffed. "Just because I did that with my parents doesn't mean it's what I think you should do. My parents have had a decade to come to terms with who I am. Yours have only had a few months."

"As if that would make a difference." Tae Hyun looked up at Jason, his soft brown eyes glistening with a hint of sadness. "They've always been like that. But they've never turned it against me before."

"I say fuck what they think." Jason softly kissed Tae Hyun's forehead. "You're worthy of their love. Being gay doesn't change that."

"But–"

"But nothing. I love you. Your sister loves you. Yoo Mi loves you." Jason grinned. "Not to mention your many, many fans."

Tae Hyun smiled, sniffling as he blinked away a few tears. "Thank you. And thank you for coming with me to the gates of hell."

Jason snorted. "You think that was bad? Just wait until you meet my parents."

After washing and getting dressed, Jason and Tae Hyun found Seong Woo waiting behind the granite-topped mahogany bar off the great room. He served them both a drink–which turned into two–while they waited for Yoo Mi to finish dressing. Seong Woo was about to pour them all a third when Yoo Mi finally appeared in a short, striped, sleeveless cocktail dress sparkling with black and white rhinestones. Tae Hyun excitedly asked her for a spin, then clapped to show his approval. Jason also clapped, even though he liked Tae Hyun's top with the black satin shoulders and a fine mesh that showed off his flat, toned midriff better.

Dinner was at Veil in Gangnam. Seong Woo couldn't get a private dining room but managed to secure a pair of tables on the mezzanine. Jason had been curious about Veil at first. But after having dined there a couple times, it felt too much like being an exhibit in a celebrity zoo. Still, it was Yoo Mi's weekend, and they were her guests.

After they were seated and made their orders, the conversation started out light and breezy. But the topic of Tae Hyun's Daejeon visit came up by the time they'd had at least a pair of drinks and were eating. Tae Hyun described what happened, glossing over some of the worst details and omitting Jason's actions entirely. Even then, it still sounded awful. His parents had made it clear that they no longer accepted him.

Yoo Mi and Seong Woo's faces fell as they listened to Tae Hyun's story. Jason could understand why. Their parents had probably never threatened to disown them.

"And so I told them I hoped KBR paid them off well since I wouldn't send them any more money," Tae Hyun explained as he wrapped things up. "And then we left."

"It was hard to witness," Jason added. "Even coming from a similar family dynamic."

Yoo Mi shook her head. "It sounds horrible. I don't understand why they'd feel that way. It's not like you're marching in gay pride parades or anything."

Tae Hyun frowned. "What's that supposed to mean?"

Jason wondered what she meant, too. But he had a sinking feeling he knew where she was coming from.

Yoo Mi's eyebrows briefly fell before she purposely relaxed

them. No wrinkles before the wedding day, right? "Exactly what I said. You're just Woo Tae Hyun, a K-pop idol who happens to be gay. It's not like you're shoving it down everyone's throat or anything."

And there it was. Jason hated what Yoo Mi was implying and was tempted to intervene. But he'd already done it once that day, to disastrous effect. Maybe it was better to let Tae Hyun handle it.

Tae Hyun's eyes narrowed as if Yoo Mi had suddenly gone out of focus. "I thought you didn't have any problem with my being gay."

"I don't!" Yoo Mi's defensive tone didn't bode well for the continuing exchange. "I kept your secret, didn't I? And then I stood up for you when you came out, which cost me my job. Hell, you're in my fucking wedding, Tae Hyun!"

Tae Hyun angrily snorted. "But only because I'm not one of those gays, right? You know, the ones shoving it down everyone's throat?"

Yoo Mi frowned. "I don't–"

"What would you do if I kissed Jason," Tae Hyun asked, cutting her off, "right here, right now?

"In public?" Yoo Mi's laugh was probably meant to sound casual, but it sounded forced. "I wouldn't even kiss Seong Woo right here in front of everyone. I mean, there's acceptance, and there's public decency."

Tae Hyun put his hands on the table and leaned forward. And Jason suddenly wondered if not intervening was the right call. "But you could do it, right? And there wouldn't even be half the scandal."

Yoo Mi's frown returned, only angrier. "That's not fair."

"No, it isn't fair." Tae Hyun snorted and waved his hand

toward Seong Woo. "You can kiss your boyfriend in public. You can legally marry him. And you'll even put me in the wedding as long as I'm not *too gay*. So tell me, who exactly is shoving what down whose throat here?

Yoo Mi's barely contained fury nearly erupted. If looks could kill, Tae Hyun's face would've melted off. "I don't think I want you in my wedding anymore."

"Good." Tae Hyun shoved his chair back and stood. "Come on, Jason. We're leaving."

Jason shared a brief, panicked look with Seong Woo, who offered the barest of shrugs. He obviously hadn't expected that to happen, either. So Jason pushed his chair back and stood, too, because Tae Hyun was his boyfriend. And because he was right.

Seong Hyeon and Seong Min, who'd undoubtedly heard the entire exchange, had already stood from the table they'd been sharing with Min Kyu and another bodyguard. Jason tried not to look at the other mezzanine tables to see who else had overheard them, knowing that everyone had, but no one would admit to it. The Songs followed Jason and Tae Hyun down to the main floor and outside through the front entrance. It wasn't until he stood on the sidewalk that he remembered they had no vehicle. He turned to Seong Hyeon, who nodded before Jason could speak. Then, he held out a set of keys.

"Min Kyu suggested I hang onto these for the time being."

"Is that for one of the tanks?" Jason let out a relieved sigh when Seong Hyeon nodded.

"Where should we take you, sir?"

Jason turned to Tae Hyun, who angrily huffed. "I don't care. Anywhere but that fucking condo."

Jason could empathize. He wasn't a big fan of Yoo Mi right then, either. But– "All of our stuff is there."

Tae Hyun shook his head. "I don't care. What about the apartment?"

Jason had taken a lease on a Nonhyeon-dong apartment for them to stay in during their Seoul visits. It wasn't even that far from the restaurant. But– "The keys are in my suitcase. Unless?" He turned to the Songs, who each shook their heads.

Tae Hyun shrugged. "Fine. Then let's go out."

"Out?"

"Yeah. Like, to a club, with drinks, music, and dancing." Tae Hyun's eyes suddenly grew wide. "Let's go to a gay club!"

Jason had never once set foot inside a gay club as an out gay man. Sure, he'd been to Cathedral and The Stallion in WeHo, but that was always in mixed company. And he'd always been careful to never seem too into it. But he was out now and had nothing to hide. And if they were gonna burn down their relationship with Mr. and the future Mrs. Cho, they might as well do it in style. Except they were in Seoul. "Are you sure that's a good idea? Maybe if we were in LA. Think about your–"

"My what? My image? My reputation?" Tae Hyun vigorously shook his head, and Jason wondered if he'd just become the new target of his boyfriend's ire. "No." He pointed back to the restaurant. "We just heard what my reputation is. Apparently, I'm one of the good ones."

Jason sighed. "Tae Hyun–"

"No. I know what you're going to say." Tae Hyun snorted. "But it doesn't matter what city we're in. Los Angeles, London, Tokyo–someone would recognize me. And then everyone would know, and I wouldn't just be the idol who happens to be gay anymore. I'd be the gay fucking idol."

"Tae Hyun–"

"I don't care, Jason." Tae Hyun shook his head again. "No. More than that. I want this. Shit, I'm already banned from performing here in Seoul. And now I'm banned from my fucking parents' house. All because I'm gay. So I don't want to be Tae Hyun, the idol who happens to be gay. I want to be the gay fucking idol who goes to gay clubs and kisses his boyfriend in public."

Jason chuckled. "For the record, I was gonna say okay."

Tae Hyun sheepishly grinned. "Oh."

"But that was a good fucking speech." Jason grabbed his phone and tapped the screen to wake it. "And I don't know shit about the gay nightlife in Seoul."

Seong Min politely cleared his throat. Everyone looked at him, including Seong Hyeon, who eventually nodded. "Actually, sir. We know of a club in Itaewon. Our brother manages it."

Jason chuckled. "Well, you boys are just full of surprises, aren't you."

The club Seong Min's brother managed was on Usadan-ro, a fairly major street by Itaewon standards, with two full traffic lanes. But the streets were too crowded to easily drive the tank through, so Seong Hyeon dropped them at the closest corner, leaving them in Seong Min's care while he found a place to park. Jason had repeatedly peeked at Tae Hyun on the drive across the river, checking for any signs that he'd changed his mind. But there were none. Even when they climbed out of the SUV onto a street filled with drunken revelers, Tae Hyun seemed calm. No. He seemed happy. That made Jason less anxious. He could deal with crowds just fine–even crowds of drunken gay Koreans. And seeing how much fun people were having made him feel better about the decision to go there.

Seong Min walked them past the line up in front of a nondescript building that could've just as easily been an insurance office. Only the sign that read Church in English, with the vertical stem on the "h" capped off with a steeple silhouette, gave the place away. That, and the horde of impeccably dressed, improbably muscled twenty-something men standing in line. The murmurs started before they even got to the bouncer at the door. But that was only because they had a security guard and were skipping the line. No one had recognized them so far.

The bouncer smiled when he saw Seong Min, offering him a half-handshake, half-hug bro shake before pulling aside the velvet rope to let the three of them pass.

Jason leaned in close to Seong Min. "He knows you?" He didn't have to whisper. The music was too loud.

Seong Min nodded. "I used to work the door here before I started working with Min Kyu."

Jason laughed. "You worked the door at a gay club?"

Seong Min shrugged. "A job's a job."

The club was smallish by WeHo standards, but the spectacular light show and booming sound system more than made up for it. And Jason understood why the line outside was so long. The place was already packed with hot, sweaty, shirtless men laughing, drinking, and dancing. He was a little bit awestruck.

Jason spotted the eldest Song brother as they approached the bar. He was just as tall and handsome as Seong Min but didn't have anywhere near his build. He smiled when he spotted his little brother. Then he saw Tae Hyun, and his jaw hit the floor. Jason understood his reaction. K-pop idols didn't show up in places like Church.

Seong Min's brother hustled to the far end of the bar, frantically gesturing for them to follow. He was waiting on the outside of the bar by the time the three managed to push through the crowd.

Seong Min leaned in close enough to Jason and Tae Hyun to be heard over the thunderous music. "This is my brother, Seong Hun."

Seong Hun offered a slight bow, then his hand, in welcome. Jason took it first. "Hello, I'm–"

"Jason Park, yeah." Seong Hun grinned. "I know you." He turned to Tae Hyun. "And Woo Tae Hyun. It's a privilege to meet you both, but what are you doing here?"

Jason snorted. "What? We can't go out?" He tapped Seong Min on the shoulder. "This place comes highly recommended."

Seong Hun frowned. "You know this is a gay club, right?"

Tae Hyun laughed. "You know we're gay, right?"

Seong Hun leaned back as a cloud of concern briefly dampened his enthusiasm. Then his smile returned with a vengeance. "Well, alright. Welcome!" He leaned in close, whispering something to Seong Min, who nodded. "He'll take you to a VIP booth. And I'll have drinks sent over." He grinned again. "I'm so happy you're here!"

Seong Hyeon showed up just as the group sat in their VIP booth. It was tiny, just big enough for the four of them. Seong Hun appeared soon after that with a bottle of Kingston and four glasses. Jason was immediately sold. Then Seong Hun asked to take a picture with Tae Hyun and Jason. Tae

Hyun looked at Jason, silently asking his permission. Jason shrugged and nodded before climbing out of the booth. He knew that was when people would probably recognize Tae Hyun. But that's what the gay fucking idol wanted. Jason hoped he didn't regret it.

Seong Hun posed between Jason and Tae Hyun, putting his arms around their shoulders, while Seong Min snapped a few photos with his brother's phone. Sure enough, the boys at the next table figured out who they were and immediately started fangirling. So Tae Hyun, ever the master of fan service, agreed to pose for photos with them, too. Jason chuckled as he grabbed the Kingston bottle, served himself a generous pour, and swallowed it in one go.

"So, you think you're one of us, now?"

Jason wasn't quite sure he'd heard the question correctly over the loud music. But he recognized the tone well enough. He turned around, automatically squaring his shoulders and straightening his posture. Jason doubted someone would be stupid enough to fight him there, but you never knew.

The speaker was a short, skinny, nondescript guy, probably Jason's age, whose casual sneer and sweat-stained shirt meant his beer muscles were doing the talking.

"What's that?"

"You think you're one of us now." Shorty defiantly lifted his chin in a way that nearly made Jason laugh. "You think you can just show up here and be accepted by us just because you came out."

They were accusations, not questions. But Jason saw right away that Shorty was no physical threat. He must've thought Jason and Tae Hyun were intruding on his turf and had something to say about it.

Jason leaned in close enough to be heard, staying far enough away to be non-threatening, a product of all the time he spent around Tae Hyun. "Let me ask you something, friend." He paused until Shorty nodded. "Are you out?"

"What?"

"You heard me. Are you out? At work, to your family, to your friends. Do they know you're gay?"

Shorty frowned as he processed Jason's questions. Then he shook his head. "No. Of course not."

Jason smiled. "Well, I am. There's not a single place I can go in this whole world where I'm not an out gay man. So, if anything, I'd say I belong here even more than you."

Shorty's frown deepened as he considered what Jason just said. Then his eyes went wide with a shameful realization. Shorty quickly bowed. "I'm sorry. That was so rude of me."

Jason reached out to touch Shorty's shoulder. "It's okay. You don't think I know that us being here is a big deal? So, no harm done."

Jason ended up posing for photos with Shorty, whose name was actually Ji Hu, and his friends. A year ago, he would've verbally shamed Ji Hu into a confrontation, then kicked the shit out of him in front of his friends. But that was the old Jason. The new Jason saved the violence for last–and only when he really needed it. Like when his future father-in-law thought he could hit his son.

After he returned to the booth, Jason barely had enough time for a second drink before Tae Hyun excitedly grabbed him to go dance. Jason almost said no. By that point, word of who they were had spread through the club, and he knew that a hundred people would be filming him as he danced with a fucking K-pop idol. But he smiled and said yes anyway. He'd already offered to march to the gates of hell with Tae Hyun. He could stomach some time on the dance floor.

Watching Tae Hyun move to the music, even on a crowded dance floor, was something of a religious experience. It was fitting that they were in a club called Church. Jason loved Tae Hyun's voice and listening to him sing. But Tae Hyun's effortless sensuality and phenomenal body awareness was a killer combo that struck Jason down every time. He didn't bother trying to keep up as he watched Tae Hyun get lost in the music. And he eventually backed away as a circle started to open around Tae Hyun, giving him the space he needed to show off.

Tae Hyun kept up the performance for the rest of the song before noticing Jason had moved away. He smiled as he approached Jason and put his arms over his shoulders. "Is it alright if I kiss my boyfriend right here, right now?"

Jason grinned. "You'd fucking better."

Tae Hyun stood on his toes and planted his soft, warm lips on Jason's mouth. Jason wrapped his arms around Tae Hyun and pulled him close as the raucous cheers rose up around them. And he suddenly knew why Tae Hyun insisted they come to the club. Jason had made out with a lot of people. But never in his life had he experienced the overwhelming joy of making out with someone on a dance floor full of screaming gays and their friends. He'd never felt so free. Or in love.

Things began to blur after the kiss. More drinking and dancing as the towering bass pumped through him. Tae Hyun onstage singing a surprisingly sensual karaoke cover of Raven Wild's *You Put Me Through It*. Rushing back to the tank, where Tae Hyun climbed onto Jason's lap for more kissing. And finally, stumbling through a darkened condo until they found the guest room.

Jason still had the presence of mind to close the door behind him before Tae Hyun attacked him, pressing their mouths and bodies together while Jason blindly navigated their intertwined forms across the room. Tae Hyun gasped when he ran into the bed. Then he chuckled when Jason pushed him onto it.

Jason couldn't get his clothes off fast enough, struggling to lift his shirt over his head as Tae Hyun fumbled with his belt buckle. His arms were still stuck over his head when Tae Hyun yanked his pants and underwear down. Then Tae Hyun's warm, wet mouth found his cock, and his knees nearly buckled. Jason pushed through the delirious haze and finally got his shirt off. He reached for Tae Hyun, gently grasping his hair to steady himself as Tae Hyun hungrily devoured him.

But Jason was hungry, too. He grabbed Tae Hyun's shoulders and pushed him back onto the bed. He half-grinned as he pointed at Tae Hyun's pants with his chin. "Get those off."

Tae Hyun grinned back as he undid his fly and shoved his pants and underwear to his knees. Jason grabbed them and tugged them off. Then Tae Hyun spread his bare legs as Jason fell to his knees before Tae Hyun's stiff, throbbing cock, and was immediately mesmerized.

"Are you gonna suck it, hyung, or just pray to it?"

Jason snorted as he leaned in close and opened his mouth. He was nearly overcome by Tae Hyun's sweaty, musky scent. It drove him wild as he greedily took Tae Hyun into his mouth. He was so intently focused on inhaling as much of that luscious cock as possible he barely heard Tae Hyun's animal groans. The salty sweetness of precum coated his tongue and the back of his throat as his head pistoned up and down, and he knew Tae Hyun must be close. Then Tae Hyun grabbed his hair and called out, holding Jason's mouth in place as he filled it with his thick, warm cum. Jason swallowed Tae Hyun's deposit as he came up for air, pausing to admire his cock, still glistening with his saliva. Then he set his sights a little lower and grinned.

Jason put his hands under Tae Hyun's thighs, pushed them skyward, and buried his face in Tae Hyun's ass. There was a point in the not-too-distant past when he never would've eaten an ass that hadn't been recently washed. But this was Tae Hyun, whose scent drove him wild. Jason attacked Tae Hyun's ass with abandon, pressing and curling his tongue against it to the distant sound of Tae Hyun's insistent moans. Then Tae Hyun grabbed Jason's hair and tugged. Jason pressed his nose into Tae Hyun's taint as he pushed his tongue inside him. Tae Hyun bucked and nearly pulled out a chunk of Jason's hair. Jason chuckled through the pain, knowing that Tae Hyun was ready.

Jason stood back, pointing his throbbing, dripping cock at Tae Hyun's ass. "You want it?" Tae Hyun, panting and nearly breathless with anticipation, enthusiastically nodded. Jason grinned. "I need to hear you say it."

"I want it," Tae Hyun replied with a leer. "Fuck me, hyung."

Jason dropped a knee onto the bed for balance, positioned his cock head against Tae Hyun, and pushed. Tae Hyun's ass resisted, and for a moment, Jason thought he might've tried to fuck him too soon. Then he plunged inside the velvety fire and, nearly overcome, fell to his hands. Jason remained still for a long, delicious moment, savoring the intensity of their physical connection until he felt Tae Hyun's hands on his back. He shifted, pulling halfway out before pushing in again. Tae Hyun groaned as Jason pulled back and gasped as he plunged inside, slowly raking his nails down Jason's back as he quickly built up his rhythm.

Jason knew he wouldn't last long when Tae Hyun pressed on his back, pushing their bodies together as they fucked. Tae Hyun's warm bourbon breath tickled Jason's ear in time to each stroke. And their bellies were soon slick with cum leaking from Tae Hyun's cock trapped between them. Jason urgently growled as the pressure rapidly built behind each hip flex until he knew it was nearly time. Then he sped up, pounding Tae Hyun harder and harder until he finally exploded.

Jason's heart thumped as he let his weight rest on Tae Hyun's chest. "I'm sorry, I forgot to ask–"

"It's perfect," Tae Hyun interrupted. "You don't have to ask, hyung. I always want it inside me. Just like I always want you inside me."

Jason pushed himself up and quietly chuckled at the wicked gleam in Tae Hyun's dark eyes. There was a point in the not-too-distant past when he'd worried that Tae Hyun would never let him inside his walls. Then Tae Hyun became the one to publicly declare his love for Jason to the world. And he was the one who'd initiated their very public makeout session on the dance floor of an Itaewon gay club. For as rough a time as they'd been having lately, Jason wouldn't have traded a moment of it. Everything between them felt so perfect right then. He never wanted it to end.

13

"I do."

Tae Hyun struggled to hold back his tears as he watched Yoo Mi doing the same thing while she made her vows. She looked like a fairy tale princess in her sleek, white lace and taffeta wedding gown with a three-meter-long train. Curls of her luscious dark hair spilled ever so artfully from beneath her jeweled silver tiara. She was the fitting centerpiece to her storybook wedding. You'd never know she'd been a sobbing mess the day before.

Tae Hyun hadn't believed that Yoo Mi would really kick him out of the wedding. After all, it was hardly their first fight and wasn't even close to the worst one. But it was the first time they'd fought in public, and the press had a field day speculating about the cause right up until the pictures and videos of his and Jason's Church outing hit the social media feeds.

I want to be the gay fucking idol who goes to gay clubs and kisses his boyfriend in public.

Tae Hyun got his wish and then some. Leaked videos of that kiss went viral overnight and were still trending on all the top social media platforms. And the international press celebrated Tae Hyun's impromptu night out as a victory for gay representation, rushing out dozens of hastily written think pieces alongside grainy photos of his dance floor makeout session with Jason. All because of a kiss.

The local press was much less celebratory. Most Korean news outlets decried Tae Hyun's lack of decency for kissing Jason in public. A few refused to disguise their homophobia behind calls for decorum, openly complaining that Tae Hyun was setting a bad example for families and children. The same news outlet that had run the interview with Ji Hoon and Tae Hyun's parents hosted a lively debate that very morning featuring a prominent gay rights activist and a local Protestant church leader that got so heated that the pastor had to be physically removed from the set after he tried to assault the activist. All because of a kiss.

Tae Hyun and Jason had gone back to the condo after the club. Seong Woo had messaged Jason at some point, telling him they were still welcome there. And that Yoo Mi was already sorry. She'd apologized to Tae Hyun herself the following morning after Tae Hyun had a long shower, two of Jason's painkillers, and half his coffee.

"I'm so sorry," Yoo Mi wailed after throwing her arms around Tae Hyun. "I don't know why I was such a bitch to you last night. You're my best friend."

"You'd better not forget it," Tae Hyun demanded. "I can't have any more of my loved ones turning against me."

Yoo Mi tearfully nodded. "I know. I don't care how gay you are. And if you want to march in the Pride parade, I'll march right along beside you."

That's when Tae Hyun's tears started. "I love you."

"I love you, too."

So Tae Hyun and Jason had spent the day doing what they'd

originally intended, getting their final tuxedo fitting from the designer before attending the rehearsal and rehearsal dinner. Thankfully, both were private, so there was no press. Tae Hyun's night out still dominated all the entertainment news. He was grateful to have at least one day out of the public eye.

The wedding was another story. A press armada had been camped outside the hotel all morning, hoping to catch a glimpse of the happy couple and their guests as they arrived. Which was exactly what Yoo Mi had planned. She'd also signed an exclusive deal with *Flash* magazine to film and photograph the wedding, which meant Tae Hyun would be dodging their reporters all day.

But the press weren't the only people camped outside the Park Grand Hotel that morning. A small group of vocal protestors had gathered behind a police barricade across the street from the hotel entrance with signs and a bullhorn, shouting at bewildered drivers and passersby who probably had no idea what was even happening.

Tae Hyun had been worried when he saw the press trucks, but his heart sank when he saw the protestors, knowing they'd come because of him. "I'm sorry if that's my fault," he told Yoo Mi as their vehicle pulled through the security gates outside the hotel entrance.

Yoo Mi waved off his apology. "Nonsense. They were always going to be here, darling." Then she smiled. "But now I'll be the day's top story because of you."

Tae Hyun nearly chuckled when he remembered that and fought to keep his face blandly happy as he watched over the ceremony. Yoo Mi was more than happy to reap the publicity benefits of Tae Hyun's free-spirited recklessness. But she would definitely murder him in front of everyone there if he upstaged her during the ceremony.

A tiny part of Tae Hyun wondered if Yoo Mi had planned the whole thing, staging the argument knowing that Tae Hyun might do something foolish and draw that much publicity to her wedding. But that was just paranoia. She may have been an admitted master at maintaining her public image, but not even Yoo Mi was that calculating.

A storm of flashbulbs erupted as soon as the officiant, one of Seong Woo's uncles, declared the happy couple husband and wife. And Tae Hyun let his tears flow as Yoo Mi and her new husband walked back up the aisle, ensuring he'd appear appropriately joyful should any of the dozens of cameras catch him.

Once the guests started to leave their seats, Jason wandered over from the groom's side of the stage. He offered Tae Hyun a subtle kiss on the cheek. "That was quite the ceremony. I can't believe Yoo Mi kept her head up the whole time. All that extra hair alone must've weighed ten pounds."

Tae Hyun chuckled. "I'm sure she'd tell you she did a runway show once where they had to hold fifty-kilo weights on their heads the whole time."

Jason laughed. "Yeah, on a tightrope while spinning plates in her hands. How are you holding up?"

Tae Hyun smiled. "I'm fine. I've been mentally preparing myself for this for weeks. And it's only one day."

Jason snorted. "It's not really that bad, is it?"

Tae Hyun was about to say something flippant but stopped himself as he realized Jason was testing the waters with him again about their unplanned wedding. The last time Jason brought it up directly, Tae Hyun had testily complained that they were way too busy to think about it. And he'd never apologized for that either. So he smiled and shook his head. "No, not at all." He took Jason's hand. "But ours will be so much better."

The flashes went off as he leaned in to kiss Jason.

"Are you sure you want to do this?" Jason whispered.

"They're already watching. We might as well give them a show."

Jason's pouty lips curled into an adorable smirk. "Actually, I've got a better idea." He took Tae Hyun's hand. "Come with me."

Jason tugged at Tae Hyun, pulling him along as he scampered off the stage toward the back corner of the room. They headed for a door clearly marked as an Emergency Exit with a sign warning anyone who opened it that an alarm would sound. Tae Hyun winced as Jason pushed on the bar to open the door, but no alarm squealed. The door led to the ubiquitous, painted cinder block hallways that always ran behind everything at hotels. The last time he was in one–no. There was no need to revisit that memory. They stopped before a door labeled Emergency Management. Tae Hyun assumed it would be locked, but it opened when Jason tried the handle. Tae Hyun was surprised to see that it was essentially a closet with only a pair of empty metal shelving units along one wall.

"What's this?"

Jason chuckled. "When we were here for the rehearsal yesterday, I had Seong Min look around for places we could escape to if the press attention got too heated." He spread his arms. "And he found this."

Tae Hyun snorted. "And what are we supposed to do in here?"

13

Jason grinned as he approached Tae Hyun and grabbed him by the waist. "Whatever we want."

Tae Hyun pressed himself against Jason as he leaned in to kiss him. Jason practically inhaled Tae Hyun's tongue and let his hands fall to Tae Hyun's ass, giving it a gentle squeeze.

Tae Hyun squirmed and backed off Jason's mouth. "We shouldn't do this here. And I don't want to miss the paebaek."

Jason frowned. "The what?"

"It's a traditional ceremony," Tae Hyun explained, "where the couple is welcomed into their new families by their in-laws. It used to be a private thing, but most people make it part of the reception now. And Yoo Mi wouldn't dare pass up the photo op."

Jason nodded. "Fair enough." He let go of Tae Hyun's ass, but Tae Hyun quickly grabbed his hands to keep them in place.

"But I want to pick this up later when we're really alone."

Jason's smirk returned. "Sounds like a date."

After sharing another kiss, Tae Hyun and Jason snuck out of the back hallway and found their way to the ballroom in time for cocktails and the paebaek ceremony. Korean weddings were usually breezy affairs, with a short ceremony before cocktails and dinner at one of the country's numerous dedicated wedding venues. But Yoo Mi wanted her wedding to be a spectacle that people talked about for weeks afterward, if not longer. So she'd borrowed from the more popular Western traditions, including having a dozen attendants in matching dresses and tuxedos and having a full reception afterward. That included flying in DJ Wicked Twister all the way from London and offering a top-shelf open bar for her guests. Thankfully, it didn't include speeches.

Guests slowly began to filter toward the dance floor or the bar once they'd finished eating. Tae Hyun noticed his sister on the dance floor and thought about joining her, but he knew it would draw attention to him, and he'd had enough of that for the weekend. Then Jason offered to go to the bar and grab drinks for them, so Tae Hyun sat back and enjoyed watching the dancers. He was tired, but only because it had been a long day. His jet lag had finally gone away.

Jason soon returned with their drinks, and the pair sat holding hands under the table. It felt so warm and comfortable holding Jason's hand in public, even if they hid it from public view. When the music eventually slowed down, Yoo Mi wandered over to their table and asked Tae Hyun if he wanted to dance.

"This has been quite the day, Yoo Mi." Tae Hyun took her hand and put his free arm around her to lead. "I hope you're enjoying it."

Yoo Mi smiled. "Are you kidding? I'm thrilled. It's the wedding I've dreamed of since I was a little girl."

Tae Hyun smiled back. "Now that you've checked this off your list, what's next?"

"Oh, I still have a long list. Now that I've shifted my career from modeling to acting, I want to star in at least two feature films in the next five years. Plus, an indie or art film that gets me an award. Then I'll move into semi-retirement and focus on starting a family."

Tae Hyun chuckled. "Sounds like you're right on track."

"I'd better be." Yoo Mi snorted. "I knew Seong Woo wanted kids right away, so I told him ten years, then let him bargain me down to five."

Tae Hyun laughed. "You didn't."

"What?" Yoo Mi casually shrugged. "I've been negotiating contracts longer than he has. I knew what I was doing. What about you?"

"What about me?"

Yoo Mi quietly huffed. "What's your plan?"

"I honestly don't know. I've got the album and the tour, I guess. If that's successful, I'll keep doing it until it's not."

Yoo Mi nodded. "What about a family?"

Tae Hyun shrugged. "I've never imagined having children. I'm not sure Jason wants any."

"Do you?"

"I like the idea of having kids, but not the reality." Tae Hyun sighed. "We couldn't raise them here. We can't even get married here. And I don't think I want to raise kids in America."

Yoo Mi smiled. "Still–"

"What's that smile for?"

"I love hearing you talk about your future with Jason. Not that it's him in particular, although I like him very much. But that you found someone who loves you enough to spend a future together. It's something I've always wanted for you." Yoo Mi's smile disappeared as her face fell. "I'm sorry again about the other night, too. I don't know why I said all those things. I don't even believe them."

"I know. It's because that's how we were raised. It's what our elders think. Thankfully, there are a lot more people like us than there are of them."

Yoo Mi stopped dancing to embrace Tae Hyun. As they hugged, Tae Hyun noticed Seong Hyeon saying something to Jason. Then, he saw Min Kyu speaking with Seong Woo. "Something's happening."

Yoo Mi pulled back to look him in the eyes. "What? What do you mean?"

"I don't know. But–"

Bang! Tae Hyun didn't know what the sound was, only that he saw a cloud of smoke or fumes rising from the far side of the room near the entrance. Panicked people rushed around him. They looked like they were shouting, but all he could hear was a piercing, high-pitched tone. Then, his eyes began to water.

Min Kyu rushed up behind Yoo Mi and took hold of her arm. "We need to go now, ma'am."

Yoo Mi's eyes darted back and forth in obvious confusion. "Why? What's happening?"

Min Kyu didn't bother answering as he dragged her away. And Tae Hyun stood in shock, gently shaking his head to dispel the annoying ringing in his ears until Seong Min stepped into his line of sight.

"We have to go, sir. Come with me."

"But, Jason–"

"He's fine." Seong Min grabbed Tae Hyun's arm. "Come with me now, sir."

Seong Min didn't wait for Tae Hyun to agree before dragging him away. They were running toward the gassy vapors, and Tae Hyun's eyes began to sting. But no, they were actually avoiding a group of wedding guests gathered around someone who'd fallen to the floor. Seong Min veered left and towed Tae Hyun toward an unmarked door on the side of the ballroom. He kicked the latch bar and dragged Tae Hyun into another concrete hallway before turning and slamming the door shut. Then he bent over, put his hands on his knees, and took a deep breath. Only then did Tae Hyun realize Seong

Min hadn't been breathing.

Tae Hyun's eyes were watery and stung. He tried to wipe them with his sleeve, but Seong Min grabbed it and stopped him. "Don't, sir. You have some on your jacket. It will only make the stinging worse."

Tae Hyun absently nodded and let his arm fall. "Some what?"

"Tear gas, sir. Someone released a canister in the ballroom." Seong Min straightened up. "We have to keep going, sir. Mr. Park will be waiting."

Tae Hyun nodded. "Go find my sister."

"What?" Seong Min shook his head. "No, sir, I need–"

"To find my sister." Tae Hyun put his free hand on Seong Min's arm. "Please. Just tell me where Jason is, and I'll find him."

The pair silently stood there for at least ten seconds before Seong Min nodded. "Alright." He let go of Tae Hyun's arm and pointed his thumb over his shoulder. "Take this corridor all the way to the double doors at the end. My brother and Mr. Park will be waiting."

Tae Hyun nodded. "Go. And please be careful."

Seong Min nodded back. Then he approached the door they'd just come through, pulled it open as he covered his nose and mouth with his arm, and rushed back into the chaos. Once the door closed, Tae Hyun ran in the direction Seong Min had pointed, his squeaky footsteps eerily echoing off the cinderblock walls. His mind still hadn't accepted what happened. Someone set off a tear gas canister at Yoo Mi's wedding? It didn't seem real. She was probably furious–or thrilled, considering the publicity she'd undoubtedly receive.

Tae Hyun sped up when he saw the double doors Seong

Min had mentioned. Then he hurriedly pushed them open to blessedly fresh air and rushed outside to a broad alleyway. He sensed movement behind him and turned around. Someone had just come into the corridor from the ballroom. Was it Seong Min and Yun Seo? But the doors slammed shut before he could decide. And there was no way to open them from the outside.

"Tae Hyun!"

The sound of that voice was music to Tae Hyun's ears. He spun around to see Jason rushing his way with Seong Hyeon close behind. Jason practically tackled Tae Hyun as he threw his arms around him.

"Are you alright?"

Tae Hyun pressed his chin against Jason's shoulder, ignoring the smell of tear gas. "I'm better now."

"My brother?"

Tae Hyun looked up to see what might've been genuine fear on Seong Hyeon's face. "He went back for my sister, but I think he's right behind me."

Seong Hyeon nodded as the exit doors burst open. Seong Min clambered out, carrying Yun Seo in his arms. Her bright red eyes were swollen shut. She must've been caught in the tear gas cloud. "Yun Seo!"

"She needs a medic," Seong Min wheezed. His eyes were red, too, but still open.

"There are medics out front," Seong Hyeon confirmed. He reached out to his brother. "Let me help you."

Seong Min shook his head. "No. Just lead me to where they are."

Seong Hyeon nodded as he turned and hurried back in the direction he'd come from. Seong Min quickly followed after him. Tae Hyun was about to join them when Jason grabbed his hand.

"Tell me you're okay. You're not hurt?"

Tae Hyun shook his head. "I got some in my eyes and nose, but I think I just need a shower. What about you?"

Jason blew out a relieved sigh. "I'm fine. Seong Hyeon got me out of there before I could even smell the gas. But I was so worried about you." He smiled and squeezed Tae Hyun's hand. "Come on. Let's go see about your sister."

14

Jason went into crisis mode the moment Seong Hyeon told him there was trouble. His first reaction had been to find Tae Hyun. He would've leaped over the banquet table if Seong Hyeon hadn't forcibly held him in place. Then Seong Hyeon told him it was already handled and–

Bang!

Things got hazy–no pun intended–after the tear gas canister went off. Jason remembered frantically running while holding his breath, manically fretting about Tae Hyun's safety after getting outside, and then the sweet relief of finally seeing him again.

No one claimed responsibility for the reception attack, which left a few guests with minor injuries from the tear gas–including Tae Hyun's sister, who'd been practically standing next to the canister when it went off–and sent one elderly member of Seong Woo's extended family to the hospital for observation. But the medics had checked out and cleaned up Yun Seo on the scene before releasing her to Tae Hyun's care. She was sleeping on the pullout bed in Yoo Mi's day room.

Police were investigating the incident but had no immediate leads. Seong Woo, understandably, was furious that it had been allowed to happen in the first place. And once all the people in his care had been accounted for and delivered to safety, Yu Min Kyu promptly resigned as his head of security. Seong Woo told him to stop being an idiot and just find out who did it. Yoo Mi's only consolation for having her reception ruined by the attack was the news coverage. Instead of being relegated to a fluff piece about the glamorous wedding's over-the-top extravagance during a lifestyle segment, Yoo Mi's wedding was one of the top stories on news programs worldwide. Then Seong Woo suggested that they postpone their honeymoon.

Yoo Mi went nuclear. "What? You can't be fucking serious! After all the work I did to pull off the wedding of the year, it got ruined. And now you think I want to give up my honeymoon? No. Absolutely fucking not."

"But, Yoo Mi–" Seong Woo's pleading suggested he may have already realized his mistake. "–It's not prudent for us to travel after–"

"Not prudent? Not fucking prudent!"

Jason shook his head as he tried to ignore the argument. Seong Woo had just taken the dragon by her tail. He'd hopefully let go before she bit his hand off. Jason glanced at Tae Hyun as he stepped from the shower. Even after disposing of their ruined tuxedos in tightly sealed trash bags and thoroughly washing themselves, the bathroom still smelled of tear gas. He wondered if he maybe still had some up his nose. The sensation felt uncomfortably close to the times he'd done coke with Amber Merritt while they filmed the *Monday Night Club* movies. Hopefully, it wouldn't last. But he didn't notice it as much in the bedroom.

Tae Hyun rubbed his hair with a towel as the rest of his

body dripped on the bathmat. "They're still going at it?"

Jason nodded as he examined his face in the bedroom vanity mirror. His eyes were still red-rimmed and bloodshot, but he looked well enough otherwise. "Yeah." He tried on a casual smile he didn't feel. It was obviously false. There'd be no pretending for the near future, at least. "How are you doing?"

"Me?" Tae Hyun wandered in from the bathroom and began to dry off the rest of his body. "Aside from the long fucking day, I guess I'm doing alright. How about you?"

Jason blew out a long sigh. "I never liked weddings anyway." A loud crash outside their door caught Jason's attention. "And it sounds like that's not getting any better. Maybe we should–"

Their door suddenly swung open before Yoo Mi stomped through and slammed it behind her. Tae Hyun practically squealed as he quickly wrapped his towel around his waist and jumped back into the bathroom.

"What the hell, Yoo Mi?"

Yoo Mi snorted as she plopped herself on the end of the bed. "Oh, relax. It's nothing I haven't seen before."

Jason turned from the mirror to face his host with a raised eyebrow. "You have?" He was dressed only in gray boxer briefs. It was hard to ignore Yoo Mi's thorough once-over, especially when she focused on his crotch.

"Yes, Jason, I have. It was all those times Tae Hyun and I fucked." Yoo Mi rolled her eyes. "So many times." Then she scoffed and gestured toward Tae Hyun. "I'm not talking about him. That's the most skin he's ever shown me."

Tae Hyun huffed as he emerged from the bathroom, still towel-clad, grabbed his underwear, shorts, and shirt from the bed, and went back to get dressed. "Why are you even in here, Yoo Mi?"

Jason turned back to the mirror–partly to finish fixing his hair and partly to give Yoo Mi the full show. "She's running away before she loses her argument."

"What?" Yoo Mi snorted. "I never lose." Then she frowned. "It just so happens that Seong Woo is right this time."

Jason nodded. "Leaving town right now isn't a good look. It'd be a shame to throw away all that precious, hard-earned public goodwill."

Yoo Mi frowned. "Are you looking to argue, too, because–"

"Tell me I'm wrong."

Yoo Mi sighed. "No, of course, you're not. But just because I know we can't go doesn't mean I can't be upset about it."

Tae Hyun returned to the bedroom fully dressed and sat beside Yoo Mi. "What'll happen now?"

"Vital is working on our public statement right now. And I imagine I'll do press and interviews all week instead of relaxing on a Tahitian beach."

Tae Hyun shared a conciliatory smile. "Tahiti will still be there when this blows over."

Yoo Mi nodded, but Jason caught the initial flash of a frown in her reflection. He doubted Tae Hyun even noticed. Then again, Tae Hyun was often far more perceptive than he let on. Still, Jason was sure he knew what her look meant. He may have only met her a few months ago, but he could still read her like a book. "So, how long until you throw us out?"

Tae Hyun's jaw fell open as he turned toward Jason. "What?" Then he turned back to Yoo Mi. "What does he mean? Are you seriously throwing us out?"

"I don't know what you're talking about." Yoo Mi's surprised frown suggested that she really didn't. But Jason assumed she'd probably expected more time to ease into the announcement. "You know you're always welcome here."

Jason turned around to face the bed. He knew he was right when Yoo Mi wouldn't even make eye contact. "Let's not do it like this, okay? I mean, it's bad enough that he won't even come in here and tell us himself. But I'd love it if you treated us like grown adults and told us the truth."

Tae Hyun frowned. "Why are you saying that? She just told us it wasn't true."

"He's saying it because he's right." Yoo Mi sighed. "Shit. I guess I thought–" She threw her hands out and frantically waved them around. "We thought maybe it would sound better coming from me. And I thought I could maybe even get you to agree to it."

Tae Hyun's mouth fell open again. "You're serious? So, you came to–what? Gaslight us into leaving?" He shook his head. "That's fucking low, even for you."

Yoo Mi didn't reply, but her expression told Jason everything he needed to know. "She thinks it was our fault."

Yoo Mi scoffed at Jason. "Are you just going to keep doing that instead of letting me talk?"

"Fine." Jason shrugged. "So talk. But please skip past all the bullshit."

Yoo Mi dramatically sighed. "We don't know why it happened. We don't even know who did it yet. For all we know right now, it could've been someone on the guest list."

"Of course it was," Jason agreed. "It had to be, considering that your security let them in in the first place."

Yoo Mi turned to Jason again, giving him another thorough once-over. "Would you please put some clothes on?"

"Oh, I'm sorry. Am I making you uncomfortable?" Jason chuckled. "You're the one who burst in here without knocking."

Tae Hyun frowned. "Jason, please."

"What?" Jason scoffed. He'd spent the entire day smiling and making nice around people he knew for a fact were judging him for being gay. Or being a foreigner. Hell, he was pretty sure he'd heard someone call him a washed-up actor when they thought he wasn't listening. He typically didn't give a shit about what other people thought. Especially a bunch of strangers he knew he'd never see again. But Tae Hyun cared, so Jason had to at least play the part. "Don't tell me you're buying all this, too?" He turned back to Yoo Mi. "Just tell us the damn truth."

"Alright. Yes, Seong Woo's father told him it would be better if you weren't here for the time being." Yoo Mi sympathetically smiled and put her hand on Tae Hyun's thigh. "It's for your safety as much as ours."

Tae Hyun's brows crowded together over his narrow-eyed look of disbelief. "Are you serious?" He loudly scoffed. "This place is probably safer than the fucking Blue House." He shook his head and looked away, pulling his leg out from under Yoo Mi's hand. "But, fine. You want us gone? We'll go."

"Please understand, Tae Hyun. This is just–"

"I understand just fine." Tae Hyun stood. "This is just like the other night. Obviously, your apologies were all bullshit."

"That's not fair."

Tae Hyun barked out an angry laugh. "Not fair? The only reason we're even here is for your wedding. So don't tell me about what's fair when you're throwing us out on the street."

Yoo Mi impatiently groaned. "On the street? You have an apartment here!"

While that was indeed true, it was still beside the point. Tae

Hyun was right that the only reason they were even there in the first place was for her wedding. Otherwise, they'd still be back in Los Angeles. Jason opened his mouth to back up his boyfriend but was interrupted by a knock on the door. He snorted. "See, that's what you're supposed to do."

But Seong Woo didn't wait for anyone to invite him in. It was his house, after all. He looked exactly like someone who'd had their wedding ruined by a tear gas attack and then spent the next several hours apologizing to some very wealthy, influential people. And he frowned when he saw the way everyone looked at him. Then he looked at Yoo Mi. "I thought we were going to tell them together?"

Yoo Mi pushed her lip out in a pout that Jason would've appreciated under different circumstances. "I didn't know how long you'd be, so I thought I'd let them know myself."

Jason snorted. "If it's any consolation, it wouldn't have come across any better if you'd double-teamed us."

Seong Woo frowned. "That's not fair, Jason."

"Fair?" Jason shook his head. "You two must have a different definition of fair than the rest of us."

Seong Woo shook his head. "I was speaking with my father. He insisted that this would be the best thing for now."

"Your father?" Jason angrily grunted. "Do I have to die before I stop getting fucked over by someone's asshole father?"

Seong Woo's expression briefly hardened. "Please don't talk about my father that way. And you know better than any of us how men like him can be."

Jason chuckled. "That's right. I do know. Which is why I don't accept this bullshit from you. You're my business partner. You're supposed to be my friend. And yet here you are, kicking us out of your house."

"Jason, I–"

"Just go. Let us get dressed and packed so we can get the hell out of here. Or do you want to watch us pack in case we might steal something?"

Seong Woo shook his head. "No, of course not."

Tae Hyun stepped up beside Jason. "What about my sister?"

"We'll make sure she's okay when she wakes up," Seong Woo replied. "And then I'll have someone take her home." He turned toward the door. "We'll give you time to dress and pack," he added before leaving the room.

Yoo Mi stood from the bed and reached for Tae Hyun's hand, but he pulled it from her reach. She frowned. "I'm sorry it's come to this."

Tae Hyun said nothing, so Yoo Mi left as well. Then Tae Hyun grabbed Jason's hand. "We'll be okay."

Jason wasn't sure if that was meant as reassurance or a question. But his response was the same. "Yeah. We will."

Tae Hyun gave Jason's hand a gentle squeeze. Then he let go and went to the closet to retrieve his suitcases. "We're not leaving Yun Seo here, are we?"

Jason shook his head as he grabbed his pants from the bed. "No way. Aside from the fact that I can't imagine what she'd say when she woke to find us gone, I don't want to give them any leverage."

Tae Hyun frowned. "You can't think they'd use her like that."

"I wouldn't have before. But, now?" Jason shrugged. "All bets are off."

Tae Hyun breathed out a long sigh and nodded. They had much to discuss, but it wasn't the time or place. Jason quickly stuffed his clothes into his open suitcase. He didn't bother folding anything since they were only headed across the river. And he was too angry to bother, anyway. Surprisingly, he had no desire to hit anyone. Maybe it wasn't anger, after all. Maybe it was disappointment. That was worse in a lot of ways. Anger was easy. Somebody fucked around, and then they found out. But disappointment meant he'd had expectations that someone failed to meet. It was the consequence of all the time he'd spent going soft. The old Jason had no expectations of anyone and was rarely disappointed.

Seong Hyeon showed up just as Jason closed his suitcase, knocking on the halfway-open door before entering the guest room. His detached expression was a little stiffer than usual. "Mr. Park, sir."

Jason snorted. "Lemme guess. You're quitting so you can go back to working for Min Kyu?"

Seong Hyeon's elaborate scowl probably meant Jason got that one wrong. "Absolutely not, sir. That's–"

"I'm sorry." Jason sighed. "It's just been–I'm sorry."

Seong Hyeon shared a single nod. "Mr. Yu informed us that you'd be leaving. I came to tell you that we've secured a vehicle for the duration of your Seoul stay."

"It's not one of Seong Woo's, is it?"

"No, sir. It's not."

"Good." Jason looked at Tae Hyun, who'd just finished getting dressed. "You're ready?" Tae Hyun nodded, so Jason turned back to Seong Hyeon. "Have your brother wake Yun Seo and get her ready to go."

Seong Hyeon nearly grinned. "I already have, sir. She's using the bathroom before we leave."

Jason cracked his first genuine smile since before the

reception incident. "You're a good man, Seong Hyeon. Could you help us with the bags?"

Neither Seong Woo or Yoo Mi bothered to see them out, which was probably for the best. They sent Min Kyu instead, who seemed vaguely embarrassed about the whole situation. But Jason wasn't fooled by the man's quietly affable nature. He was sure Min Kyu wouldn't hesitate to forcibly remove them from the condo if necessary.

The vehicle Seong Hyeon had secured was an unarmored version of the same model SUV as the tanks. That meant the windows would go down, so Jason opened his to feel the cool evening air as Tae Hyun explained the situation to his incredulous sister. He offered to have her stay in their guest room, but she was more than ready to go home. And she let Seong Min walk her to her building's front door before waving and heading inside.

The apartment was cold and dark, having sat empty since their last visit to Seoul. It was appropriate, considering Jason's mood. He typically would've had a housekeeper come by to dust and turn on the heat beforehand, but they didn't have any warning.

As Tae Hyun and Seong Min deposited the bags in the main bedroom, Seong Hyeon pulled Jason aside.

"There's something you should know, sir."

Jason frowned. "Okay. Tell me."

Seong Hyeon nodded as he retrieved his phone from his jacket pocket. He woke it, opened the camera roll, and tapped on a photo. No, it was a video. "This is part of the footage from an early news story about Mr. Cho's wedding," he explained as he handed the phone to Jason.

Jason tapped the play button and silently watched as a

reporter did a stand-up on the sidewalk outside the Park Grand Hotel with dozens of protestors chanting and waving their signs in the background. "What am I looking for?"

"Read the signs, sir."

Jason quietly huffed as he scrubbed back to the beginning of the video and played it again. The signs were mainly in English–with a few in Hangul–displaying hateful messages about sinners needing to be saved or they'd go to hell. It was such a weird, disappointing scene that Jason almost missed one of the Korean signs. He paused, went back, and played it again, pausing when the sign came back into view. He had to read it several times before its message finally sunk in.

Remember Jong Soo

"Oh." The sign cast a whole new light on the tear gas attack. It was already pretty much a given that the attacker's motivation had something to do with Tae Hyun. But the sign meant the attack was probably more than a protest. It was also a message–the same one that someone had spray painted on the side of a building in Studio City. "Shit."

Seong Hyeon nodded as he took his phone back. "Indeed, sir."

"Does Seong Woo know about this?"

"I don't know, sir. But, if we found it, I'm sure Yu Min Kyu will find it, too."

Jason nodded. "Is there any chance of finding out who that is?"

Seong Hyeon shook his head. "He's masked, sir."

"Alright. Keep this between us for now."

Seong Hyeon frowned. Then he nodded. "If you think that's best, sir."

Jason huffed. "Of course I do."

14

After the Songs left, Tae Hyun–none the wiser about what Jason and Seong Hyeon had discussed–said he was hungry and rummaged through the kitchen cabinets for anything to eat. There wasn't any fresh food, of course. But he found an unopened box of crackers that had only recently passed its sell-by date. Jason went to the bar cart. He really needed a drink, and it didn't matter that the liquor wasn't fresh.

Jason glanced over his shoulder at Tae Hyun. "You want something?"

"I'll have one of those."

Jason took the two bourbons to the living room and sat beside Tae Hyun on the chocolate brown leather sofa. It was pointed toward the floor-to-ceiling windows that offered an expansive view of Gangnam, including a partial view of Seonjeongneung, a historic park that contained the burial sites for some of Korea's Joseon dynasty rulers. The apartment was nice enough, with two bedrooms, two and a half bathrooms, and an open kitchen. It was luxurious by local standards but paled in comparison to the penthouse they'd just been thrown out of. Not that Jason cared. It was only meant for short-term stays. It wasn't his home.

Tae Hyun took his bourbon from Jason and swallowed a mouthful. "I'm glad we're out of that place."

Jason turned to look at Tae Hyun's handsome profile, dimly lit and ringed in golden light from the entryway–the only light they'd bothered turning on so far. He couldn't ignore the image of the protest sign reminding everyone of the idol who'd committed suicide under mysterious circumstances. It made him furious that someone wanted to hurt the man he loved. But, more than that, it terrified him. And the idea that someone could get past the security of one of the most well-protected men in Seoul–seriously, the wedding security would've made a royal family jealous–meant that there was next to nothing Jason could do to prevent that from happening. That was why he didn't want to tell Tae Hyun about the sign. He was worked up enough as it was. Jason would tell him, but it could wait.

"I'm sorry that happened."

Tae Hyun nodded before sipping from his drink again. "I was gonna be mad at you for attacking Yoo Mi." He sighed. "But then you turned out to be right. How do you do that?"

Jason shrugged. He didn't know how he was so good at reading people. "Childhood trauma?"

Tae Hyun chuckled. "How long do you think before she apologizes this time?"

"You'd know that better than me." Jason gave Tae Hyun's thigh a gentle squeeze. "Will you forgive her this time?"

Tae Hyun sighed again, setting his glass on the coffee table before laying his head on Jason's lap. "I probably will. I've pushed her so far outside her comfort zone that I'm surprised she took this long to push back." He found Jason's free hand and threaded their fingers together. "The hardest part is that she's really my only friend. Everyone else I know has either abandoned me or been banned from speaking to me."

While that technically wasn't true, Jason still understood what Tae Hyun meant. Everyone imagined that being famous would bring all their problems to an end. They only saw the fancy houses, star-studded events, and exotic vacations. And the glitz and glamor were nice. But most people never saw the dark sides of fame–the objectification, fetishization, and often bone-chilling, soul-crushing loneliness. Some stars, like Jason, coped by shutting themselves off from the world–only showing the world what they wanted to see after convincing himself that he didn't need the rest. But the lie to that notion was lying in his lap. Jason needed the love and companionship as much as anyone else. Fame's biggest drawback was being a job. And keeping that job sometimes meant giving up the connections that ordinary people often took for granted.

"Well, you've still got me."

Tae Hyun smiled as he gazed up at Jason, his golden face pale in the city lights dimly filtered through the windows. "And you've got me, too. Forever."

Jason nodded. "Forever."

15

Tae Hyun anxiously fidgeted in his seat while waiting for the broadcast to begin. He knew it bothered his sister since she'd repeatedly scolded him for it. But he couldn't help it. He hadn't been to SBN's Vision Center in Sangnam-dong since the last time *XTC* appeared on the weekly music show *Chart Masters* three years prior. But he wasn't there to perform as K-pop idol Woo Tae Hyun. He was in the audience courtesy of Min Ji from *Cherry Squad*, who'd reached out to him about it during a cryptic phone call the day before.

"Tae Hyun? It's Min Ji."

"What? Oh my gosh! How are you? How did you get this number?"

"Never mind all that. I haven't got much time to talk." Min Ji sounded harried and nearly out of breath. "We're appearing on *Chart Masters* tomorrow, and you need to be there."

"What?" As much as Tae Hyun enjoyed hearing from a friend and longtime peer, he was reluctant to agree. Especially given the unpredictable nature of his recent public outings. "I don't know, Min Ji. It might be better if–"

"No." Min Ji quietly huffed. "Just trust me.

"But why do I–"

"Trust me and be there. I'll leave a pair of tickets for you.

Now, I've got to–

"Wait." Despite there likely being a hundred Woo Tae Hyuns in Seoul, he didn't want to take any chances. "Put them under my sister's name."

So, Tae Hyun was a bundle of nerves. After everything that happened at Yoo Mi's wedding, he would've preferred to keep hiding out at the apartment over being in another crowded public space. But he hadn't spoken to Min Ji since the *DoubleDown Boys* release party. And the fact that she'd gone out of her way to speak with him directly said something. Except he wasn't sure what it was. The worst possibility was that KBR had set some kind of trap for him. Except Tae Hyun, Jason, and Yun Seo couldn't figure out what it might be. Even if KBR had sent the tickets instead of Min Ji, there really wasn't anything they could do to him during a live international broadcast. So he'd accepted the invite.

Attending the show with Yun Seo was a calculated risk. Tae Hyun would've preferred to be there with Jason, if only just for the comfort of having him there. But it was hard enough to go incognito by himself. And there was no way he wouldn't be recognized with Jason by his side. Even having Seong Hyeon or Seong Min with him ran the same risks. But Yun Seo was still mostly unknown. Sure, people knew Tae Hyun had a sister and who she was. And a sharp-eyed *U4* could probably piece things together given enough time. But, sitting with the studio audience gave him a good deal of anonymity. People just wouldn't expect the person they sat beside to be an idol.

Fortunately, audience members frequently wore masks to avoid being recognized if they appeared on camera. So Tae Hyun did the same. But he still fretted. There'd undoubtedly be a commotion if someone recognized him.

Yun Seo huffed and put her hand on Tae Hyun's bouncy knee. "If you don't stop doing that, oppa. I'm leaving."

"I'm sorry. I'm nervous."

"I know. So am I." Yun Seo patted his thigh. "But everything's fine, right?"

Tae Hyun nodded, reminding himself that his sister had been just as hesitant as he was about attending. At least, with all the obvious security present, they were pretty much assured there'd be no tear gas attacks at the show. "Yeah, everything's fine."

"Then please stop fidgeting. Maybe try having fun?"

Tae Hyun sighed. There was no chance of that. But he didn't need to drag his sister down any more than he already had. "Okay, yeah. You're right. Sorry."

"I know." Despite calling him out for fidgeting, Yun Seo seemed just as uncomfortable. "I talked to Mom this morning."

Tae Hyun frowned behind his mask. "You did? Why?"

Yun Seo shrugged. "She called me."

"Oh." Tae Hyun huffed. "What did she say?"

"What do you think? She's upset, oppa." Yun Seo sighed. Tae Hyun saw her frown in her downcast eyes. "She thinks you don't love her anymore."

"She's upset?" Tae Hyun scoffed. "Whatever. I'm not the one who went on TV to shit-talk her. How does she think I feel?"

"You know that was Dad, right? Mom never would've done it if he hadn't made her."

Tae Hyun's low sigh was almost a growl. "As if that matters."

"So you're really cutting them off?"

"Why shouldn't I?" Tae Hyun wished Yun Seo hadn't brought the subject up. Then again, it was the first time the two of them had been alone–relatively speaking–since before the wedding. "We had an agreement. I'd keep sending them money as long as they stayed out of my career. Doing an interview about how disappointed they are with me is exactly the opposite of that."

"I'm not talking about the money."

"Oh." Tae Hyun looked at his lap. "I don't know. All I know is that I don't want to talk to them right now." He turned his gaze toward his sister. "What would you do?"

Yun Seo chuckled. "It's not the same."

"I know, but–"

"I mean, I've been dealing with this sort of thing my whole life. I've never met their expectations. Especially our father's." She chuckled. "Remember when I wanted to go to school?"

Tae Hyun nodded. That had been a battle that lasted weeks. Or possibly longer. Maybe even a lot longer. "Oh. Shit."

"Yeah. This is just the first time it's happened to you." Yun Seo chuckled again. "Of course, none of my stories made the news, so–"

Tae Hyun lightheartedly scoffed. "If you're jealous, I could make a few calls."

"Jealous? No fucking thank you."

"Yun Seo!"

"What? I'm a grown-up, oppa. I can swear if I want to." Yun Seo rested her hand on Tae Hyun's thigh. "And I'm not saying anything about you and them. I'm only saying think about it before you shut them out completely."

"If I think about it any more than I already do, I'll have to stop thinking about anything else."

Yun Seo snorted. "Right. As if ninety percent of your brain isn't focused on *you know who*."

Tae Hyun shrugged since she was absolutely right. But, as they say, turnabout was fair play. "Speaking of which, what's going on with Seong Min?"

Yun Seo's jaw dropped. "What?" She quickly looked away, but not before Tae Hyun caught a peek at her pink earlobes behind her long hair.

Tae Hyun chuckled. "Oh, so that's how it is?"

Yun Seo huffed. "I don't know what you're talking about."

"I mean this." Tae Hyun snuck a hand up and pinched her closest earlobe. "Be honest. You like him, don't you?"

"Oppa." Yun Seo mumbled something Tae Hyun didn't catch. "Alright, fine. Yes. I like him. But if you think–"

"Good."

Yun Seo's eyebrows popped up. "What?"

"I like him, too. He's sweet, thoughtful, and considerate." Tae Hyun chuckled. "Not to mention a total hottie."

Yun Seo bashfully giggled, not bothering to hide her rosy ears. "I would climb that man like a tree."

"Yun Seo!"

"Still a grown-up, remember?" Yun Seo huffed. "Besides, it's not like it'll ever happen. You keep him too busy."

Tae Hyun shrugged. There was no reason to deny the truth. "Yeah, that's true. And it'll only get worse once I go on tour." Then he chuckled again. "Of course, you'll need to come along, too."

"What? Seriously?"

Tae Hyun snorted. "Did you really think I'd leave my assistant at home while I'm on tour?"

"I–" Yun Seo hesitated. "I guess I hadn't considered that."

"But it's work, so the tour comes first." Tae Hyun chuckled. "Of course, if you need any tips on how to sneak away for a little bit of quick fun on tour–"

"Oppa!"

"What? I'm a grown-up, too, Yun Seo."

Before Yun Seo could respond, a production assistant went onstage to coach the audience members who'd never attended a taping before. Tae Hyun knew it happened before each broadcast but had never seen it himself since he'd always been backstage before the show. Then, the audience lighting went dark, and the show's theme music played in the studio.

Tae Hyun had a moment of near vertigo, remembering the dozen or so times he, Xiang, and Chang Min had performed their comeback stages there. Although he'd watched a hundred different *Chart Masters* episodes, he'd never once attended a taping.

The audience roared with thunderous applause as the show's current MCs, Sunny from *Miss Kiss* and Min Si Woo from *G-Go*, bounded onstage. Tae Hyun knew both of them, of course, although not very well. But he was quickly caught up in the surrounding excitement and soon forgot all about his parents. And Sunny and Si Woo had surprisingly good chemistry as they bantered–much better than the MCs from Tae Hyun's last appearance on the show.

Yun Seo leaned in close. "Si Woo is so handsome."

Tae Hyun nodded. He was very good-looking. And very straight. "You know he's married, right?"

"A girl can dream."

After their opening banter and sharing the night's lineup, Si Woo stepped offstage while Sunny stayed behind to introduce the first act.

"I had the pleasure of performing with our first group," Sunny announced, "at last summer's Kfest Japan. Here to perform a soon-to-be-released track from their upcoming album, *Habitual*, it's *Cherry Squad*!

The crowd began to scream as the floating partition blocking off the rear of the stage rose to the ceiling to reveal Viki, Min Ji, and Su Bin bathed in soft, pink light. They wore coordinated mini-dresses with a floral theme. And, of course, they each had their individual cherry hair accents. Viki had strands of cherry red hair mixed in with her long, black braids. Min Ji wore an impeccable cherry-red wig. And Su Bin had a bright cherry-red streak in her shoulder-length, bleached hair. But something was off. Their posture was stiff behind obviously forced smiles.

Yun Seo glanced at Tae Hyun, who shrugged. She'd seen it, too.

Min Ji, the center and leader, held her mic to her mouth. "Two, three–"

"Soft as a whisper," the three *Cherry Squad* girls called out, "fragrant as the breeze and elegant in pink. We're *Cherry Squad*!"

Their introduction felt forced, too. Even Sunny seemed to notice as she walked offstage. But the audience erupted into raucous cheers anyway when the *Cherry Squad* members moved into their positions. The audience lighting dimmed to near darkness as the giant video wall at the back of the stage displayed an anime scene of cherry blossoms blowing in the wind. That had to explain their floral dresses. It was part of their new fashion era.

Then the music started. And Tae Hyun's heart stopped. It was the intro for *Blossom*. Yun Seo looked at Tae Hyun with wide-eyed panic as the crowd around them roared. It couldn't have been a different song. Tae Hyun had performed *Blossom* hundreds of times. He knew it the moment he heard the first note. But it had to be a mistake. Someone must've somehow cued the wrong track. That had to be it. But Viki, Min Ji, and Su Bin all danced to the beat, moving from their starting positions to the center of the stage, just as Tae Hyun remembered doing. They were about to perform his song. That's why Min Ji had insisted he be there.

When Ji Hoon had done the interview about canceling the *XTC* tribute album, Tae Hyun had assumed that meant the covers wouldn't be released. But why would KBR let that money go to waste when they could repackage the songs as part of the artists' new albums? And they'd given *Blossom,* one of *XTC*'s biggest hits, to *Cherry Squad*.

Just when it was time for Min Ji to sing, she stopped, standing silent and still in the center of the stage. No, all three of them stopped. Someone should've been singing. Had Min Ji missed her cue? Tae Hyun didn't think that was possible. But he hadn't expected to hear one of *XTC*'s songs on the show, either.

The crowd finally understood something was wrong as the song moved into the chorus. Their enthusiastic cheers had fallen to restless murmurs as they tried to figure out what was happening. Was it a prank? Were they on a hidden cam? Then Min Ji reached up and tore her monitor from her ear, letting it dangle from its cord over her shoulder. Tae Hyun could only assume that she'd been getting an earful from someone in the tech booth. And it began to dawn on him what was really happening. The girls were deliberately not singing. It was a protest.

"Why aren't you singing?" shouted someone from the audience.

"What's going on?" called out someone else.

The video wall froze just before the track playback cut out mid-chorus. Tae Hyun imagined that the live viewers were seeing a cutaway screen proclaiming technical difficulties. Then, someone Tae Hyun didn't recognize rushed onstage and confronted the girls, shouting and angrily gesturing toward the audience. But Min Ji shouted right back. Unfortunately, Tae Hyun was almost too far from the stage to make out what she said. Almost. But he clearly heard one thing when Min Ji pointed her finger at her opponent. "Because it's not our song!"

Was that why they weren't singing? Were they protesting being made to sing one of *XTC*'s songs? One of Tae Hyun's? Suddenly filled with grateful admiration, Tae Hyun wanted to shout some words of support but knew that would only make things worse, especially if anyone realized he was in the audience.

Tae Hyun leaned close to Yun Seo. "I guess now we know what Min Ji wanted us to see."

"Are they going to get in trouble?"

Tae Hyun shrugged. "I don't know. I mean, they disrupted a live broadcast of the most watched K-pop music show, so, probably. Yeah."

Then someone else marched onto the stage, and Tae Hyun's heart stopped again. It was Ji Hoon, his face hard and set in an expression Tae Hyun knew all too well. He'd seen it hundreds of times. Maybe more. And a different memory surfaced–not of his last time performing on *Chart Masters*, but his first. Just weeks after *XTC*'s debut, a bright, young

Tae Hyun caroused backstage with Xiang and Chang Min as they waited their turn to perform. But Tae Hyun hadn't seen Xiang sipping his customary orange soda–a habit that had continued well past their debut–and accidentally knocked the cup from his hand, spilling it on his and Xiang's costumes. There had been no time to clean it and barely enough time to change. And Ji Hoon was livid, shouting at Tae Hyun and Xiang about how careless they'd been. Then Tae Hyun had dared to speak up, reminding Ji Hoon that he needed to keep his voice down. Of course, that only set Ji Hoon off even more and earned Tae Hyun a sharp slap across the face. Tae Hyun's hand automatically went to his cheek at the thought. Ji Hoon hadn't struck him like that since he was a young trainee–when it happened more times than he cared to remember. And the makeup team barely had enough time to cover the red mark Ji Hoon had left behind. A few commenters had mentioned the lingering redness but attributed it to nerves.

Tae Hyun gripped Yun Seo's thigh as a surge of paranoid fear made him light-headed. What if Ji Hoon looked into the audience and recognized him? But, no. He was masked. And he was the last person Ji Hoon would expect to see at the taping.

Yun Seo looked at Tae Hyun with wide-eyed concern, but he shook his head, forcing himself to breathe and let the fear dissipate. And the onstage argument quickly wrapped up with Ji Hoon escorting *Cherry Squad* off stage. Sunny and Si Woo returned shortly afterward. They were obviously flustered.

"We're very sorry about that," Si Woo announced. "Apparently, there were some technical issues with the sound. Unfortunately, we'll have to move on with the show without a performance from *Cherry Squad*."

"But let's still show them our love," Sunny added, "for coming out here tonight."

Sunny and Si Woo started clapping. A few audience members booed, but they were quickly drowned out by cheering and applause. Tae Hyun loudly clapped along with them even as his dread lingered. And he wondered if Sunny and Si Woo knew what had really happened–that *Cherry Squad* had refused to sing. They had to if they were watching the playback backstage. But Tae Hyun doubted anyone except the girls had known beforehand what they planned to do.

Tae Hyun recalled what Riki had said to him at Raven's party–that people were talking about what KBR was doing to Tae Hyun. And they were taking sides even before KBR had given away *XTC*'s songs to other artists. But re-releasing *Blossom* as a *Cherry Squad* song meant that, eventually, when people searched for it, that version would come up. It was a singular act of erasure. Tae Hyun wondered if, once they'd done that, KBR would even start pulling *XTC*'s catalog from the streaming services, too. That was a chilling thought. And it was a clear warning to any performers who might publicly support Tae Hyun. Do that, and your label could take your songs away.

Even though they'd already come to see what they were meant to see, Tae Hyun stayed for the entire taping. He would've insisted that they leave if he could've. But it was a live broadcast, and no one could leave until they were done. So Tae Hyun sat with his discomfort as it slowly became annoyance and then, finally, anger. He hadn't thought about all the times Ji Hoon or the other managers had hit him in years. Just like his father had hit him, too. But Tae Hyun forced himself to calm down by reminding himself that things were different. As much as KBR and his father may have wanted him to act a certain way, he was free to be whoever he pleased. Still, once they were finally allowed to leave, Tae Hyun had to fight his urge to shove his way to the door. But they eventually made it to the waiting vehicle without incident.

"I don't know what to think about that," Yun Seo said when they were finally underway.

After all the time Tae Hyun had spent remembering how awful Ji Hoon had been to him, he'd hardly thought about what the *Cherry Squad* girls had done. "Me, neither." They'd certainly made a bold statement to KBR, even if the audience wasn't aware of it. But there would have to be fallout, and he worried about what that might be. "Part of me wishes they hadn't done that."

"What?" Yun Seo's mouth fell open. "Why? They did that for you."

Tae Hyun shook his head. "No. They did it for themselves."

Yun Seo frowned. "I don't understand."

Tae Hyun wasn't entirely sure he understood his point either. It had just occurred to him. But it felt right. "I mean, yes, they must've been thinking of me. But they were trying to send KBR a message. Because KBR could just as easily do to others what they've done to me."

"I know KBR is controlling, oppa, but–"

"You have no idea what they're capable of." Tae Hyun's sharp tone stopped his sister's statement in its tracks. His memories of his early trainee days threatened to re-emerge, so he shoved them back down. They were the past. He was free of KBR, and that stuff didn't matter anymore. "There's plenty I've never told you about."

Yun Seo frowned again as she touched Tay Hyun's leg. "You know you can tell me about it if you want to."

Tae Hyun nodded. "I know." But he couldn't. Not really. They were memories he'd repressed for the good of his career. And the careers of his fellow group members and idols. They knew because it happened to them, too. But he'd broken free of all that. He was no longer crushed under KBR's thumb. Sure, they still reached out to try swatting him like an annoying insect. But that was all they could do. He had Jason on his side. Hell, he had the world on his side. Ji Hoon, CEO Pak, and his parents could shake their angry fists at him all they wanted. It wouldn't stop him from making and performing his music. It wouldn't stop him from living as his authentic self.

16

Jason had only ever taken a subway once before. But it was the Seoul Metro–which gave him a definite advantage when he took it again. He was headed to an address on Tongil-ro in Eunpyeong-gu, so he eventually found his way onto a Line 3 train and arrived at Gupabal Station. He was impressed with himself when his phone said he was still on course. He didn't want to ask for help in case his accent gave him away as an American, Mr. Woo's assertion that he spoke with a Seoul accent notwithstanding. The directions pointed him toward exit 3, but he couldn't find it. So he went with exit 4 instead and emerged on the street level across from a giant mall.

Jason frowned. "Did they bury you in a mall?"

"You're looking for the ossuary?"

Startled, Jason turned to the sound of a stranger's question to see an old woman's face staring up at him. He thought she was glaring at him before realizing she was just squinting to bring him into focus. "Yes, Grandmother." He hesitated. "How did you–"

"I just came from there. And I heard what you said. Not many places around here house the dead." The old woman smiled at her little joke. At least she didn't call him out for being American. She pointed to Jason's right. "It's up that way. Tongil-ro is on the other side of the mall, so you can either go through it or around it." She huffed. "I'd suggest going around."

Jason offered a smile before wondering if she could even see it. Then he decided to bow. "Thank you, Grandmother."

The old woman waved off his thanks. "Bah. It's thanks enough that you're honoring your ancestors. Too many young people these days–" She shook her head as if she'd said enough before walking toward the subway entrance.

Jason snorted, pleased that he'd successfully interacted with a local without causing any trouble. But his good feelings were short-lived as he started the trek around the mall. He wasn't visiting his ancestors, although he probably could've found them if he tried hard enough. While he'd supposedly been raised to honor his parents in all things–an assertion he quickly grew out of–his father worshiped at the altar of capitalism before any other. So he'd never passed along any of the Neo-Confucian ideals he'd been raised with to his son.

Jason was alone partly because Seong Hyeon and Seong Min were with Tae Hyun and his sister for the *Chart Masters* broadcast. Seong Hyeon had vainly made him promise to stay in the apartment until they got back, which Jason agreed to. Of course, Seong Hyeon was needlessly worried that Jason would hit up the local tavern in search of a bartender with generous pours. But he would've just drank at home if he wanted to get drunk.

Jason was alone mostly because he was headed to visit Joo Won–or, rather, Joo Won's ashes.

It was Joo Won's birthday. Jason hated knowing that, just like he hated that it had been a decade since he'd last seen his first love's smile or heard his laughter. But he was in Seoul again. And he was alone. And it was Joo Won's birthday. So, the siren call was too loud to ignore. And Jason couldn't think of a good reason not to go and pay his respects to the boy who'd forever changed his life.

It hadn't been hard to discover where Joo Won's parents had interred his ashes. He'd done it years ago with a simple web search. Korea made that sort of thing easy. Just like they made cremation easy since open space was a precious commodity and there were a tremendous amount of dead people. So they'd tossed their Joseon-era fetish for finding the ideal burial grounds out the window and started storing their ancestors in little jars. And Joo Won's parents had stored his little jar next to a big, fancy mall wrapped in neon with an elaborate fountain at the main entrance.

No, that wasn't fair. The ossuary was probably there first. And it was on the other side of the street, so Jason had to hustle across eight lanes of traffic before walking the final block to the low building with a row of fake Greek columns lining the storefront. It was nominally attached to a Buddhist shrine, but Jason didn't know exactly how that worked. He didn't think Joo Won's family was Buddhist, but he didn't know that they weren't, either.

Beyond the glass double-door entrance, the lobby was done in tasteful, polished gray and brown granite, with an alcove opposite the doors holding a golden Buddha statue. A simple wooden table sat to the left of the entrance, holding a newish-looking tablet on a stand. Jason approached it and tapped through the search interface to learn which alcove Joo Won's ashes sat in. According to the search results, he was at the highest level. Since the building only had a single floor, Jason assumed that meant his parents had given him a first-class alcove. He still deserved better.

With the alcove number in mind, Jason followed the brass plaque signage through the building's maze-like layout until he found the correct room. Floor-to-ceiling polished wooden shelving units lined the walls of the small chamber, each holding dozens of memorial urns locked behind glass doors with whatever mementos or keepsakes their loved ones had chosen to leave behind. A tiny seating area with a pair of upholstered, high-backed chairs and a small table took up most of the central space. And an older woman wearing a simple black dress stood facing away from the door. Jason nearly panicked when he noticed her dyed-black hair was styled in the same swooped helmet shape his mother wore. But it wasn't his mother. She only wore her hair that way because all Korean women her age did the same.

Jason followed the numbered alcoves around the room, looking for Joo Won's. When he finally found it, he realized two things. The woman was looking at Joo Won's urn. And the woman was Joo Won's mother.

"I wondered if I'd ever see you here," Joo Won's mother said without even looking at Jason. "But I had a feeling it would be today."

Jason's surprised rage blossomed from his long-repressed feelings about what happened the last night he'd seen Joo Won. It had been a decade, but it may as well have been the day before. Joo Won's room had smelled like sporting gear, teenage boy, and whatever fancy new cologne he'd put on for Jason's benefit. While Jason and Joo Won usually went through several stages of casual conversation, light gaming, and a little roughhouse play before they got to the kissing itself, that night, the two boys took no detours. It was just as Jason had described it to Tae Hyun. A force like gravity dragged them together. Jason could hardly keep his hands off Joo Won, especially after their shirts came off. Maybe it was his raging hormones. Maybe it was that Jason had become increasingly convinced he was in love. Maybe it was the cologne. Jason had been working his way up to suggesting that they take their pants off, too, when the words came unexpectedly tumbling from his mouth. *I love you, Joo Won.* And he'd been staring at Joo Won's shy, surprised smile when their parents all burst into the room.

But Jason held back on his anger. He wouldn't let himself be the person who lost his shit in a funeral home. He inspected Joo Won's mother instead, really seeing her beyond his dark, painful memories. She'd styled her hair that day but hadn't worn any makeup beyond a thin layer of lipstick. Her dress was worn but well cared for. Her black kitten heel pumps were scuffed and unpolished. She was a mere shadow of the demon that haunted the dreams of his final night with Joo Won.

Jason sighed. "How did you know I'd be here?"

"I saw on the news that you were in Seoul. And I suspected that you might remember what today is." Joo Won's mother frowned. "Was."

Jason reluctantly nodded. He didn't want to see her at all, let alone speak with her. But they were both there. And the idea that she not only remembered him but had put together that he might appear based on a news story intrigued him. "So, did you come today because you thought I'd be here or despite that?"

Joo Won's mother cracked the barest hint of a smile. "I know you probably hate me."

It was Jason's turn to frown. He wished she'd at least look at him instead of staring ahead at the remains of her dead son. But he wasn't about to rise to whatever selfish, guilt-ridden vibe she offered. "Where's his father?"

"Dead." Her smile faded. "He had a heart attack three years ago. Now it's just me." So it was pity that she was after. The poor, lonesome woman who'd outlived her only son and only husband. If she thought she'd get anything more than cool detachment masking a decade of rage, she was– "I'm sorry. For what it's worth." Then she finally looked at him. She was so much older than Jason remembered her. And the years hadn't been kind. "I don't expect you to forgive me. I haven't even forgiven myself. But I wanted you to know that."

Jason snorted despite himself. "Is that why you wanted to see me? To offer an apology a decade too late for me?" He pointed to Joo Won's urn. "Too late for him?"

But Joo Won's mother shook her head. "No. I thought you'd probably run off the moment you figured out who I was. But I'm glad you didn't." Her smile returned despite the harsh words he'd just flung at her. "Seeing you reminds me of him."

Jason huffed. None of it was what he'd wanted. Not that he was even sure what he wanted. But he knew it wasn't a conversation with a woman who'd ruined his life and ended her son's. Then he shook his head. "I just wanted a chance to finally say goodbye to the boy I loved."

Joo Won's mother winced. Good. Jason was tired of the bland, maudlin martyr routine. It was cliché. Except it wasn't. Whatever grief Jason had carried all those years–grief that he'd finally let go of on that beach with Tae Hyun–she'd carried a hundredfold. Sure, Jason had loved Joo Won. But he'd only known him for weeks. She'd known him his entire life. And she was part of the reason he was dead.

Jason sighed again. “I’m sorry. This isn’t what–”

“Would you sit with me?”

“What?”

“It’s just–” Her voice cracked, and Jason saw the glimmer of fresh tears in her eyes. “I know I have no right to ask this of you. But you’re the last unfinished piece of my Joo Won.” A tear broke free to run down a pale, naked cheek. “I’ll understand if you want to say no. I probably would if I were in your shoes. But I’m asking for this kindness anyhow. Let me finally put my Joo Won to rest.”

Jason’s rage flickered and flared. How dare she ask anything at all of him? But the monster he’d imagined her to be was no more. She’d become a tired, broken old woman who’d resorted to begging the one person in the world who wanted to see her the least to sit with her. Jason was suddenly tired, too. He was tired of carrying those feelings when he’d already moved on. He had a life. He had someone he loved. He didn’t need that anger anymore. “Alright. But not here.”

By her surprised expression, Joo Won’s mother had clearly expected him to say no. “There’s a little self-serve cafe off the lobby. We can sit there.”

Jason nodded as Joo Won’s mother moved toward the room’s entrance. Then he stepped in front of the alcove that held Joo Won’s urn. It was made of burnished gold or brass and engraved with the Hanja spelling of his name. Next to it sat a baseball mitt, a toy dinosaur, and a framed photo of a smiling Joo Won posing in a baseball uniform. A deep ache of sadness smacked him like the baseball bat Joo Won held in his picture. Jason closed his eyes to fend off the tears and swallowed his pain. Then he opened them again and sighed.

"Goodbye, Joo Won."

Joo Won's mother waited for Jason in the corridor, nodding when he joined her before turning and leading him back to the lobby. The cafe wasn't much more than an alcove holding a small table with four chairs. An automated coffee and tea machine sat on a stand in the corner. Joo Won's mother hit the button for matcha. When she was done, Jason chose a black coffee because the bitter heat matched his mood. He took his small paper cup and sat opposite Joo Won's mother at the table.

"I don't remember your name," Jason said.

Joo Won's mother frowned. "I'm surprised. It's the same as your mother's."

"Mi Young?"

Joo Won's mother nodded. "Yes. We had a few jokes about that back when–" She suddenly stopped and sighed. Then she shook it off. "You were such a handsome boy. I can see why Joo Won liked you."

Jason frowned. "You can?"

Mi Young nodded again. "I've had so much time to think about that night. And what happened because of it." She blinked, and another tear rolled down her cheek. "What we did was unforgivable. We had no idea what you meant to him. If only–"

"Do you think that makes it okay?" Jason interrupted. "Your ignorance?"

Mi Young shook her head. "No, of course not. There's nothing that could make it okay." She sipped her tea and winced from the heat. "I knew something was going on between you. But I thought it was a harmless crush. Two boys playing at something they didn't understand. It wasn't until afterward that I discovered how wrong I was."

Jason's rage made him want to push back at her meaningless platitudes. But he knew there was nothing he could say to her that she hadn't already told herself many times. So he kept quiet.

"I've followed your career," Mi Young suddenly announced. "I remember when they stopped playing your commercial. Seong Su would always make me change the channel when it came on. Then your first movie came out." She smiled. "You're quite a talented young man. I've seen all your movies."

Jason shook his head. "Why would you do that? To punish yourself?"

Mi Young quietly chuckled. "No. Simply living is punishment enough. But seeing you reminds me of him. It makes me think of how happy he was when you were together."

Jason's sigh was almost a groan. It was a mistake to be sitting with her. It was a mistake to have spoken with her in the first place. He should've turned and run like she thought he would've. Joo Won's mother was looking for an absolution he could never give her. Even if he'd genuinely forgiven her–which he definitely had not–it wouldn't be enough to erase the stain of her guilt. She was too damaged. She was a broken husk of a person held together by her grief and a worn black dress.

"I forgive you."

Mi Young's surprise wasn't nearly as much as Jason's. He wasn't sure where the words had come from. Maybe he did pity her. Maybe he just wanted their conversation to be over. But he'd left her speechless long enough that he took that chance to go, leaving his untouched coffee steaming on the table as he walked out.

Jason barely noticed the trip home. His body moved on autopilot while his mind processed what had just happened. He hardly remembered why he thought seeing Joo Won's remains was a good idea. He certainly hadn't considered that the woman who shared the same name as his mother would be there, much less ask for his forgiveness. It made it hard not to think of his own mother and how she'd held him while he cried after first learning of Joo Won's death. That was the last time she'd truly embraced him, except for the red-carpet photo ops she'd wormed her way into at his movie premieres. Movies that Joo Won's mother had watched, hoping to glimpse some part of her son in Jason.

Jason arrived home before Tae Hyun. He had no idea what time it was or how long he'd been gone. His first stop was the bar and his half-full bottle of Kingston. They still hadn't stocked up at the apartment beyond a few basic groceries. But it was enough for the moment. He gave himself a generous pour, swallowed it in one go, and poured himself another. After swallowing that, he poured himself a third, brought his glass and the bottle to the couch, and sat, staring at the nighttime city lights out the window. He avoided looking at the visible corner of the park that held the historic burial mounds. The last thing he needed was to be reminded of visiting the dead. The second to last thing he needed was to be sober.

The buzz hit him after he'd finished his fourth or fifth round–he wasn't really keeping track–and with it came the rush of feelings he'd been drinking to suppress. Jason could hardly believe he'd told that woman he'd forgiven her when it was the farthest thing from the truth. It was almost as if part of him had decided she'd suffered enough for her evils.

He tried reasoning with himself. It wasn't like he'd actually forgiven her. He was just cutting the ties she'd placed on him. It was for his benefit more than anything else. Maybe that was the part of himself he was punishing with a liberal application of imported bourbon.

But all the memories of Joo Won and his mother kept leading Jason to thoughts of his parents and their involvement in Joo Won's death. As he'd once explained to Tae Hyun, Jason had no idea if Joo Won's suicide had also killed his relationship with them. Things were already so bad. But, even if it wasn't the sole cause, it was what had pushed things over the proverbial cliff. It was the night he'd sat crying in his mother's arms after she told him what Joo Won had done that he'd made his vows. He'd already broken his vow never to return to Seoul. He'd also broken his unspoken vow to never tell anyone else he loved them. But he still held fast to his one remaining vow. He hated his parents and would never forgive them.

Jason had his phone out and dialed the number before realizing it. What was he even doing? No, that wasn't true. He absolutely knew what he was doing. The universe had moved all the planets and stars to put Joo Won's mother in his path. It was time to go full circle.

"Jason?" His mother sounded half awake. What time was it in LA? Not that he could've even figured that out when he was sober.

"It's Joo Won's birthday, Mom."

"What? What are you talking about, Jason?"

Jason snorted. Leave it to her to forget about the most tragic time of his life. "He would've been twenty-five today."

His mother sighed. "Oh, Jason. It's been months since we've

heard from you. And this is why you finally call?"

"Why'd you do it?"

"Jason, you know very well that your father and–"

"No," Jason interrupted. "Not that. The night you told me Joo Won killed himself. You told me and then held me and let me cry. Why'd you do that?"

"I don't understand. Are you asking me why I hugged you? You're my son."

Jason snorted. "Let's not pretend you're overflowing with maternal instinct or anything. You never hugged me. Why then? Why that night?"

His mother sighed. "I don't know what to tell you, Jason. It seemed like the right thing to do."

Jason nearly burst out laughing as his mother easily confirmed her lack of maternal instinct. She could've said it was because she loved him. But she never did that either.

"I saw his mother tonight." Jason waited for his mother's reaction, but her breathing was the only thing that broke the silence. "She's got nothing. That night ruined her life. And now she's alone."

"I don't know what–"

"I just thought you'd want to know how many lives besides mine you ruined that night."

"Your life is hardly ruined, Jason."

"And one day, whenever Dad finally croaks, you'll be alone, too."

"Jason! I–"

"Goodbye."

Jason hung up without another word. Then he let his mind drift, the bourbon slowly warming in his grasp. If you asked him why he called his mother, he wouldn't be able to answer.

But it felt good to say what he'd said. After all that time, she was just as selfish and uncaring as ever. At least she hadn't told him she wished he was dead.

The sound of the front door dragged him back to reality.

"Jason?" Tae Hyun slipped his shoes off before stepping into the darkened apartment. "Jason, are you–oh. There you are. Why are you sitting in the dark?"

Jason didn't know what to say, so he said nothing.

"Are you okay, hyung?" The obvious concern in Tae Hyun's voice as he walked over broke through his Kingston-induced haze.

"Yeah." Jason sighed. "Maybe."

Tae Hyun frowned, his face glowing pale gray in the city lights filtering through the window. He reached down to take Jason's glass from his hand and set it on the side table. Then he climbed onto Jason's lap and gently pulled Jason's head against his chest. "I don't know what's going on, but you're gonna be okay."

"I went to see Joo Won."

"What?" Tae Hyun pushed Jason's head back and pointed it at his face. "I thought he was–"

"At the ossuary," Jason added. "His ashes." He sighed. "It's his birthday."

"Oh." Tae Hyun sighed and pulled Jason's head back against his chest. "I'm sorry, hyung. Why didn't you tell me? Why did you go alone?"

"I didn't exactly plan on going. It just worked out like that. I'm sorry I didn't tell you first." Jason leaned back. "This is uncomfortable. Can you–"

"Sorry. Of course." Tae Hyun climbed off Jason's lap, sat beside him, and took his hand. "Better?" Jason nodded. "Okay.

Do you want to tell me about it?"

Jason nodded again as he grabbed his bourbon and took a drink. "His mother was there."

"What? Oh, no."

"Yeah." Jason related the story of his unlikely encounter. It hardly seemed real at the time and even less so as he described it. But he couldn't have imagined it. His mind just didn't work like that. "So, I told her I forgive her."

Tae Hyun nodded. "Do you?"

"Fuck no. What she did is beyond forgiveness." Jason huffed. "And it's not my place to forgive her, anyway. That can only come from Joo Won, and it's too fucking late for him." He sighed before sipping his Kingston again. "But she was so broken. And I know she kept showing up there hoping that one day I'd come, too, so she can apologize and let me see how much she's suffered. So, I said it anyway. She's punished herself enough. She doesn't need any more shit from me."

Tae Hyun leaned in and kissed Jason's cheek. "Well, I'm proud of you, hyung. That was very noble of you."

"Noble?" Jason snorted. "I don't know about that. I just didn't want her shadow at my back, always hoping that one day she could tell me she's sorry. It was selfish."

"No." Tae Hyun squeezed Jason's hand. "You could've yelled at her or ignored her and walked away. She deserved as much. Or you could've told her the truth–that she's beyond forgiveness. But you didn't. I think that's pretty noble."

"Maybe." Jason sighed. "And I called my mom."

Tae Hyun's eyebrows carefully rose. "Oh. I–"

"I didn't forgive her or anything. I just wanted to know why she hugged me that night." Jason huffed. "She never fucking hugged me. She hardly ever touched me except to smack me when I talked back to her."

Jason wanted to still be angry at her. But, between the visit to Eunpyeong-gu, seeing Joo Won's mother, and all the Kingston, he'd hit his feelings limit. He yawned instead.

"Oh, hyung." Tae Hyun lifted the glass from Jason's hand and set it on the table on his side of the couch. Then he gently pulled Jason's head into his lap. "Our parents really suck, don't they?" Jason closed his eyes as Tae Hyun started running his fingers through his hair. "But at least we have each other. And I'll hug you as much as you want."

17

KBR released a statement the day after the *Chart Masters* broadcast reinforcing the narrative that *Cherry Squad* had suffered from technical difficulties. And the segment had been completely cut from the streaming versions online. But anyone who'd seen it live, especially those in the studio audience, knew better. There'd been no audio issues. *Cherry Squad* had refused to sing. The rebellion had begun.

Tae Hyun could easily imagine how tense the atmosphere in the KBR building must've been. Their social media teams had probably been working through the night getting any photos and video from the taping pulled every time they were posted. But there wasn't much they could do about the small but steadily growing group of *U4*s who'd started protesting outside their front doors. And that protest had drawn a smaller but just as vocal group of counter-protestors from a homophobic, right-wing religious group. The move to give *Cherry Squad* one of *XTC*'s top songs had seriously backfired on KBR. Instead of drawing attention away from Tae Hyun and his history with *XTC*, it had only shined a spotlight on it. That was a rare misstep by CEO Pak, and Tae Hyun had no doubt that several people probably lost their jobs over it. But none of that was his problem anymore.

Instead, it was an opportunity. So Tae Hyun and Jason had gone to the Vital offices that morning and started taking advantage of it. After they confirmed that they were still a Vital client, that is.

"Of course, you are, Mr. Park, sir." Min Ji had flown in from Los Angeles that morning, which lent some weight to her argument. "We're under contract. Whatever may happen in your personal relationship with Mr. Cho wouldn't affect that."

Jason's frown seemed to suggest he needed more convincing. "But you work for him. He owns this company."

"Sir." Min Ji's deadpan delivery made Tae Hyun embarrassed by association. "Big Hammer Entertainment is the only reason Vital established a Los Angeles office. And it's the only reason I'm in Seoul right now."

Jason chuckled. "Alright, alright. If that's how things really are, then let's get to work."

So Vital quickly wrote up and released a statement from Tae Hyun claiming he'd been in the audience during the taping to dispute KBR's version of events. They followed that up with a mostly scripted live stream where Tae Hyun directly addressed the *U4*s and answered some of their questions. And that led to a rushed series of interviews with the American media amid their evening news broadcasts. Of course, they didn't get any interview requests from the Korean media. But a producer for KTN's weekly K-pop show *Afternoon Music Party* said they'd consider including part of Tae Hyun's statement in their story on the incident. Considering KBR's pressure on all the networks and other media outlets, that was something. But that pressure could only do so much. At some point, something had to give.

After completing the interviews, Tae Hyun returned to his makeshift dressing room with Jason to remove his heavy camera makeup. Tae Hyun sat at the dressing table, grabbed a wipe from the box beside him, and began to clean his face.

Jason stood behind Tae Hyun's chair and put his hands on his shoulders. "I love watching you do that."

Tae Hyun's ears warmed as he grinned. "Thank you. I have to admit I was nervous at first. But I think it went well."

Jason gently squeezed Tae Hyun's shoulders. "Are you kidding? I've only ever seen you pull out that level of charm in videos. Seeing you do it in person was like a work of art. For real."

Tae Hyun's grin spread into a bright smile. "Wow. Thank you, hyung." He tossed the used facial wipe into the trash bin beside him and grabbed another from the dispenser. "What are we doing after? Because I thought–"

Jason spun Tae Hyun's chair around and plopped down on his lap. "I'm serious." He draped his arms on Tae Hyun's shoulders and leaned in close enough that their noses almost touched and the humid spray of Jason's breath warmed his face. "You totally charmed me."

"Hyung, we–"

Jason cut Tae Hyun off with a warm, sensual kiss. Tae Hyun was caught breathless as he surrendered to Jason's surprise seduction. Then Jason moved his kisses to Tae Hyun's cheek, jaw, and, finally, his neck, just below his ear. "Listening to you mesmerized me," he purred. "All I could think about was getting you alone again." He sat back, capturing Tae Hyun's attention with a smoldering gaze as he slowly unbuttoned Tae Hyun's shirt.

Tae Hyun softly moaned. His heart pounded under Jason's

gentle touch. He knew they should stop what they were doing. It was the wrong place and time for anything like that. But he was powerless to turn away from Jason's stare. And he didn't want to stop. "Hyung, the door."

Jason quietly chuckled. "I locked it behind me." He slid his hand down between his legs and grabbed Tae Hyun's insistent erection through his pants. "But I can get up and check it if you–"

Tae Hyun gripped Jason's shirt and pulled their bodies together, silencing him with another kiss. He prodded the space between Jason's lips with his tongue before probing inside his mouth. And he gasped when Jason gave his cock a gentle squeeze, pressing himself forward into Jason's grasp. He almost didn't hear the sound of a key in the door lock.

"Hyung–"

Too late, the door flung open to reveal a shocked Yoo Mi. "What the–oh." She sighed. "Are you two fucking serious with this in here?"

Jason let go of Tae Hyun and pulled his hand from between them. "The door was locked for a reason, Yoo Mi."

Yoo Mi dangled the key chain she held. "I know. That's why I have a key."

A few weeks ago, Tae Hyun would've assumed Yoo Mi was messing with them. But that was before she'd tossed him out of her condo after her disastrous wedding. "What are you even doing here?"

"I'm supposed to film an interview today." Yoo Mi shook her keys. "And I'm here to use my dressing room."

Tae Hyun snorted. "I think you mean my dressing room. We're obviously using it."

"Well, finish using it. I need it."

Tae Hyun chuckled. "Oh? So, you're gonna throw me out of here, too?"

Yoo Mi's jaw clenched hard enough to bite through steel. "Listen. I only–"

"Oh my god," Jason exclaimed in English. He got up from Tae Hyun's lap, grabbed Yoo Mi's upper arms, and put her in the chair beside Tae Hyun's. "You two need to sort this shit out," he added in Korean. "I'll go wait in the hall. Don't bother coming out until you've stopped doing whatever the hell this is." He huffed for added drama before leaving and shutting the door behind him.

Despite avoiding her gaze, Tae Hyun could still feel Yoo Mi's icy stare. He took a ragged breath to calm himself and returned to wiping his face. He had nothing to say to her until she apologized. And, even then, he didn't imagine he'd–

"You're so fucking frustrating."

Tae Hyun huffed, finally turning to meet Yoo Mi's glare. "Me? You're the one who threw me out. Remember? Twice."

Yoo Mi scoffed. "You make it sound like you didn't have anywhere to go, and I put you out on the street."

"That's irrelevant." Tae Hyun frowned, tossed the barely used facial wipe into the bin, and grabbed another. "The only reason I was even in your fucking condo in the first place was because of your wedding. Which you also threw me out of."

"I know!" Yoo Mi shook her head. "And I felt awful about that. I still feel awful about it." She huffed. "But that was me being spoiled, thoughtless, and maybe a little psychotic. The other thing is different."

"Different?" Tae Hyun snorted. "Different how, exactly?"

"You know how." Yoo Mi pursed her lips so tightly the corners turned white. "Seong Woo's parents were at the wedding. His mother got tear-gassed. His father was out for blood. Your blood."

Tae Hyun pushed his eyebrows together until his forehead wrinkled. "So you're saying what happened was my fault. That kicking me out was for my own good?"

"Tae Hyun." Yoo Mi let out an exasperated sigh. "Are you telling me that would've happened if you hadn't come out?" She shook her head. "Yes, my fans can be problematic. All fans can be. But tear-gassing my wedding? That was something on an entirely different level."

Tae Hyun knew she was right. He'd always known. Of course, it had been because of him. But he wasn't ready to give her the satisfaction of admitting it yet. "If you think it was my fault, why even have me in your fancy, over the top wedding in the first place? Why not just get married at a wedding castle like everyone else and be done with it."

Yoo Mi wistfully chuckled. "Because I'm a vain, attention-seeking fame whore who thrives on being in the public eye." Then her expression softened. "And because you're my best friend."

Tae Hyun finally turned toward her and sized her up. He knew she was being sincere. He just couldn't believe it. "Am I?"

"Of course you are!" Yoo Mi snorted. "I've always stood by you, even after you came out. And I kept your secret for all those years."

Tae Hyun groaned. "I know. You never fucking let me forget it." He narrowed his eyes into a not-quite glare. "But let's not forget that I kept your secret, too."

Yoo Mi frowned. "My secret?"

Tae Hyun chuckled. "What? You don't think people would

want to know that my company pimped me out to yours so you could date someone squeaky clean and save your reputation?" Yoo Mi's suddenly stricken expression meant he'd made his point. "Yeah. So maybe stop hanging that one over my head every time we fight."

Yoo Mi shook her head and blew out a long, slow breath. "Shit, Tae Hyun. I'm sorry."

Tae Hyun nodded. "I know." He sighed. "And I'm sorry, too. I know I'm not the easiest person to be friends with."

Yoo Mi snorted. "Are you kidding? You're a fucking dream friend compared to most of the cackling hens at my agency."

"Yoo Mi."

Yoo Mi waved off his critique. "I know, I know. That's not very feminist of me." Then she sighed. "And don't get me started on my damn husband."

Tae Hyun's brows swiftly hit his hairline. "What? It hasn't even been a week, and you're already complaining?"

"Tell me about it." Yoo Mi huffed. "I'm supposed to be happy, right? I mean, never mind that I'm missing my honeymoon. Or that half my friends and family aren't speaking to me right now, and the other half won't stop talking to the press. But Seong Woo and I have hardly spoken since the wedding. He's been so busy battling with his family about all the fallout from what happened. And his father's already threatened to cut him off."

"What?" Tae Hyun couldn't ignore the brief pang of feelings stabbing at his chest. "That's–" What was it? Terrible, for sure. He knew well the feeling of being betrayed by his parents and frowned. "I'm sorry."

"Darling." Yoo Mi wagged a finger at him. "This is supposed to be my pity party. You'll have to have yours some other time."

Tae Hyun shook his head. He didn't feel sorry for himself. It was something else. What was happening was terrible. But it was absurd, too. So many people–people who didn't know him or whose lives were hardly affected by him–had taken a stand against him for one simple reason. He'd come out as gay, and his job, friends, and family had all been taken from him. That made him feel a lot of things, but none of those were pity.

"This isn't a pity party." Tae Hyun huffed. "I'm fucking sick of it, Yoo Mi." He shook his head. "I know I've got no right to be. I know there are so many people out there who've been dealing with this a lot longer than I have. But I'm tired of all this." He huffed again. "I'm tired of everyone thinking they know what's best for me. Or thinking they fucking own me and that somehow my being gay wasn't part of their carefully laid plans." He leaned forward, not caring that he probably looked a little unhinged. "Well, nobody fucking owns me, Yoo Mi."

Yoo Mi stared at Tae Hyun with wide-eyed shock for long enough that he thought he might've broken her. Then a crimson-lipped smile slowly spread across her face. "I suppose that goes for your best friend, too?"

Tae Hyun nodded. "You're damn right it does. But you're more than my best friend." Then he smiled back. "You're my only friend."

"Only friend?" Yoo Mi scoffed. "That's not even remotely true." She pouted. "But I haven't been a very good friend lately, have I?"

"Maybe not." Tae Hyun shrugged. "Who can say at this point?" Then he grinned. "But I'll probably skip out on your next wedding."

Yoo Mi scoffed and playfully slapped his arm. "Don't even joke about that. Seong Woo is stuck with me forever."

"Even if he gets cut off by his father?"

Yoo Mi nodded. "Of course. I didn't marry him for his money, darling." She grinned. "I've already got plenty of that."

Tae Hyun chuckled. "Not to mention more self-confidence than you know what to do with. Still, he's lucky to have you. Which I'm sure he'll realize again soon enough and start paying attention to you again. Otherwise, we'll have to–"

"Holy shit!" Jason burst into the dressing room on the heels of his exclamation. "That's great news! I'll tell him right away." Jason grinned as he stuffed his phone in his pocket. "Guess what. We may have found a Korean venue for the tour."

Tae Hyun frowned. "It's not in the middle of nowhere, is it?"

Jason shook his head. "No. Incheon. There's a new concert venue opening soon near Songdo Park, I think."

"Oh, I heard about that place," Yoo Mi said. "I think they built it as part of their international tourism initiative."

While it wasn't Seoul, it was close enough. And a concert venue in the middle of Incheon was still accessible from anywhere in the Seoul Capital Area. That was better than flying his Korean fans to Japan. But it also seemed too good to be true. "And they're not worried about KBR?"

Jason shrugged. "Apparently not. They gave us first hold on the dates we requested. But we can ask them about it when we meet with them tomorrow."

"Tomorrow?" Tae Hyun nodded. "Okay." He smiled. "It'll be my first arena tour."

17

“Should I let Seong Woo know?” Yoo Mi asked.

Jason raised a single eyebrow. “Does that mean you two worked out whatever the hell’s happening between you?”

Tae Hyun nodded. “Everything’s fine.” He looked at Yoo Mi. “I think.”

“I tried throwing him out of here,” Yoo Mi admitted, “but he wouldn’t budge. So we have to be friends again.”

Jason chuckled. “That’s good. And, no. Seong Woo’s the one who told me about it.”

Tae Hyun was surprised to hear that. But it made sense, considering he and Yoo Mi had made up again. “Does that mean you two worked things out, too?”

Jason nodded. “For sure. I told him he was an asshole with no manners or loyalty, and he called me a rude American who assumes the whole world should bow at my feet.”

Yoo Mi laughed. “At least he talks to you.” Her smile vanished as she turned back toward Tae Hyun. “But I’ve seriously got to get ready for my interview, so you need to get out of here. Go do whatever you were doing at home.” Then her smile returned as sweet as ever. “Please.”

18

Jason always knew there was more than just an airport in Incheon. But there was knowing, and there was seeing. What he didn't expect was the traffic, which they hit as soon as they got on the Gyeongin Expressway, an eight-lane highway that would've been right at home in SoCal. He knew he shouldn't have been surprised by the number of other drivers since Seoul was something like the fourth-largest metro area in the world. But he was. At least the traffic was familiar. It almost made him feel at home.

They were on the road early since Seong Hyeon correctly assumed the traffic would slow their drive. But Jason used the early hour to do a much-needed check-in with Naomi. Between the madness of the past couple of weeks and the insane time difference, they'd mostly communicated via text.

"Jason." Naomi was all business, even at the early hour. Of course, it was only early for him. It was the end of the workday for her. "You're on your way to Incheon?"

"Yes, ma'am." Jason quickly stifled a sudden yawn.

"I read over the contract they sent, and it looks good. I'll have the lawyers give it a second look, of course, but–"

"But unless it's a smoking hole in the ground, we'll take it?"

Naomi chuckled. "I mean, if it's a nice hole–"

"That's what he said."

Naomi groaned. "Just keep your expectations realistic. Vital tells me to expect pushback from the city government."

"Of course." Jason sighed, earning him a concerned glance from Tae Hyun. He shook his head. "What do you suppose that means?"

"I don't know. There's only so much they can do since the venue is an independent entity. But it might mean they change their mind before we sign the contracts. Or the city could sue us. Who knows?"

Jason frowned, wishing he hadn't decided to check in with Naomi before the meeting. He already had so many problems weighing on him. He didn't need any more. "Alright. Anything else? I'm not entirely hopeless yet."

"Seriously?" Naomi sighed. "I keep forgetting how sensitive you get about this stuff. Just forget I said anything and go get this deal. As far as we know, they think they're trying to sell us. Right? So let them try."

"As far as we know?"

Naomi chuckled. "Yeah. And you can smell bullshit faster than me or anyone I know. So you smell any–"

"We burn the place down."

"I was gonna say walk away. Please, don't start any fires."

"No promises."

"Yeah, yeah, okay. Lemme know how it goes. And give Tae Hyun and Seong Woo my best."

"I'll message you after, Ms. Bell. See ya!" Jason hung up before Naomi could say anything else. He'd already heard enough. And Seong Woo wasn't even with them, anyway. But he wondered why Naomi didn't know that. Not that it mattered. Jason was capable of handling any negotiations himself. And he wasn't ready to let Seong Woo entirely off the hook for the wedding bullshit just yet. He'd mentioned that delivering the message from the venue was an olive branch, which would've meant more to Jason if it didn't benefit Seong Woo just as much. At least the man sounded genuinely sorry, which Jason appreciated. But he wouldn't forget how quickly and easily he'd cut off his support when the going got tough.

Jason smiled as he turned to Tae Hyun, who was already on edge. He was convinced Jason was hiding something from him. It didn't help matters that Jason actually was. "Naomi says hello."

Tae Hyun nodded. "Anything else?"

"Just the usual. The contract looks good, but nothing's final until it's final. You know? That sort of thing."

Tae Hyun offered a noncommittal nod. "So it's got nothing to do with your secret thing?"

Jason groaned. "There's no secret thing. I don't understand why you think there even is."

Tae Hyun's narrowed eyes and pursed lips said he wasn't convinced. "Okay, fine. But if I find out you're lying–"

"You can punish me," Jason interrupted with a grin. "Thoroughly."

Tae Hyun scoffed. "You're impossible sometimes, hyung."

Jason batted his eyelashes. "I know. It's part of my charm."

"Mr. Park," Seong Hyeon helpfully interrupted. He probably felt guilty about Jason forcing him to lie to Tae Hyun. "We're leaving the expressway now."

"Thanks, Seong Hyeon."

Jason had asked for the reminder just so he could see what Incheon looked like. But it was fortunate timing, too, saving him from continuing to lie to his boyfriend. Not that it was a bad lie. It was a good surprise. But the way Tae Hyun had immediately sniffed it out meant he probably wouldn't try surprising him very often. Especially if the payoff wasn't worth the hassle.

Of course, Incheon looked like every other part of Korea Jason had already been to, with wide, multi-lane streets and boulevards walled in by low and mid-rise office buildings, shopping malls, and apartments. It wasn't as dense as Seoul, but mostly just as tall. "Do you know your way around here, Tae Hyun?"

Tae Hyun reluctantly nodded and started playing tour guide, pointing out the buildings and landmarks he knew. The sun broke through the high, early morning clouds as they neared the Songdo district, splashing bright light on the Incheon Songdo Entertainment Center and Concert Hall as they approached from the southeast. The weather was supposed to be warm, maybe hitting the upper sixties, which would make any outside exploring pleasant enough. But Jason's attention was fixed on the Bubble, a semi-transparent geodesic dome that anchored the venue complex. Designed by a renowned Hong Kong architecture firm, according to the venue's website, the dome allowed for protected daylight shows in inclement weather and light shows visible from inside and outside the building via LEDs integrated into the dome's semi-transparent panels. It was an impressive facility compared to BigCloud Arena's covered concrete box and would undoubtedly make for a great show.

The Bubble sat across from the south edge of Songdo Central Park, a large, open garden space anchored by a seawater canal and lake. It was inspired, in name, at least, by New York's Central Park, even if it wasn't nearly as large. But it looked brand new, like everything else in the district, from the trees to the streets and buildings, including the recently opened Songdo Grand Hotel tower next to the Bubble.

After parking, Seong Hyeon and Seong Min led Jason and Tae Hyun to the marked staff entrance, where they found a uniformed escort waiting. The escort led the group past a security checkpoint to an elevator that brought them to a bright, open atrium with a park view. Jason was already impressed. Then the escort delivered them to an older gentleman with silver hair, a well-trimmed mustache, and thin, silver-rimmed glasses wearing a gray and taupe windowpane plaid suit. Jason immediately felt underdressed in his simple pullover and jeans. At least Tae Hyun, ever fashion-conscious, had dressed to impress in a long, oversized cream and charcoal button-up and wide, rust-colored chinos.

The older gentleman offered handshakes to Jason and Tae Hyun. "Mr. Park, sir. Mr. Woo, sir. I'm Director Kim Jeong Woo. It's a pleasure to meet you both."

Since Jeong Woo was older, Jason was momentarily confused about his formal language and honorifics. But Jason and Tae Hyun were the clients. And they were famous, so it sort of made sense in the complicated Korean rules of respect. Still, he wasn't Korean and didn't have to follow those rules. "Just Jason is fine, Director Kim."

"And I'd love if you called me Tae Hyun."

Director Kim smiled. "Very well, Jason. Tae Hyun. Please call me Jeong Woo. I'm excited to have you both here. Has your office had an opportunity to review the documents we sent, Jason?"

Jason nodded. "Yeah." He looked at Tae Hyun, who'd already adopted the smile he used for public appearances.

"And we're excited to tour your facility. It looks impressive even from the outside."

"Wonderful! I'm so glad to hear that." Jeong Woo gestured for them to follow. "Shall we get started?"

Jeong Woo took them to some behind-the-scenes areas, including dressing rooms that were sure to satisfy even the most demanding and temperamental artists, state-of-the-art production facilities, and an enormous below-ground staging area. Everything was brand new, well laid out, and clean enough to sparkle. And Director Kim was friendly and knowledgeable with a surprisingly easygoing manner. But it was all stuff Jason had seen on every other tour. Then Jeong Woo took them to a platform in the middle of the primary staging area.

"I have to admit," Jeong Woo said as he nodded to a staffer standing behind a console on the side of the room, "that this still gives me such a thrill." He grinned. "Mind your balance."

The platform lurched the tiniest bit–no more than an elevator would–before it slowly rose toward the ceiling. Jason looked up to an opening that appeared as the ceiling slid to one side. Daylight poured in, blinding him until he looked away and caught Tae Hyun doing the same. Then Tae Hyun grinned at Jason, apparently too excited to remember that he'd been nagging Jason about his supposed secret. Good. Jason grinned back.

The platform emerged in the middle of a giant stage. It wasn't as big as a football field, but you could probably still field a football game on it. The stage was surrounded by three seating levels, rising to meet the massive dome overhead. It was clear enough that, from the stage, they could've been standing outside. Jason stood, entranced by the fluffy white clouds floating overhead in the bright blue sky.

"Holy shit," Tae Hyun murmured in English.

The Director chuckled. "I thought you might be impressed. But this isn't even the best part." He pulled out a small radio, held it to his mouth, and hesitated. "I must apologize for this next part, but we don't have any of your unreleased music."

Jeong Woo spoke into the radio, and a moment later, inky blackness spread from the edges of the dome until night fell over the arena. Then the music started, bass notes thundering from unseen speakers so loud Jason could feel the vibrations in the air. He recognized the song immediately. It was *Blossom*.

But the Director wasn't just putting on a sound demo. A riot of color exploded overhead as a dozen massive flowers bloomed in time to the music. They were so clear Jason could've been watching them on his TV at home. The song's lyrics appeared near the bottom of the dome, scrolling around the arena with each word pulsing karaoke style in time to the song, which continued through the end of the first verse until the music and light show faded. Then, the blackness disappeared, too, replaced by the previous view of the sky overhead.

"That was all my tech team had time to work up on such short notice," Jeong Woo announced. "But I hope it's enough to demonstrate our capabilities."

Jason glanced at Tae Hyun, whose mouth hung open. Then he remembered himself, closed his mouth, and enthusiastically nodded. "I've never seen anything quite like it. It's absolutely amazing."

Jason nodded, too. "I'm with him."

Jeong Woo smiled. "Excellent. My team will be pleased to

hear that." He gestured away from the stage. "If you like, we can visit my office to discuss the terms of the agreement. And I'd be happy to answer any questions you–"

"I have a question," Jason interrupted.

Jeong Woo's smile briefly faltered before he nodded. "Of course."

"We've been stonewalled by every single venue in the Seoul Capital Area because of KBR. But you called us. Why? Aren't you worried about losing KBR's business?"

Jeong Woo reached up to smooth his mustache before nodding. "That's a fair question. My official answer would be that we don't yet have any of their business to lose. But I'm sure you'll agree we have the most unique offering in the current market. And I have no doubt that labels will clamor to book their shows here once they learn what we can do."

Tae Hyun narrowed his eyes in obvious suspicion. "But what's your unofficial answer?"

"Oh." Jeong Woo grinned and bashfully looked at his feet in an uncharacteristic moment of shyness. "Well, it would be that I'm also gay."

Jason's mouth fell open. "Are you serious?"

Jeong Woo nodded. "I don't think that's something most people would lie about."

Jason chuckled. "No, I guess not."

Jeong Woo looked at Tae Hyun. "I was shocked when you first came out. I couldn't understand why someone in your position would risk everything like that. And how KBR reacted confirmed my worst fears about coming out, too." Then he smiled. "But now, seeing how you've carried on–and even thrived–finally gave me the confidence to do the same. So, I came out as well. And that's why I reached out to you.

That's why I want you to perform here. I want people like you and me to see you performing on this stage despite everything and everyone working to prevent it."

"I'd be honored." Tae Hyun's tone was almost reverent. Jason could understand why. It was the first time someone in Jeong Woo's position had openly supported him.

After heading for Jeong Woo's office and discussing the relevant contract terms, Jason signed off on the proposal, signaling Big Hammer's intent to sign the contract. Naomi had basically told him to do it. And it was enough to secure their requested performance dates. Once they'd done another round of handshakes with a promise to follow through on the contract and payments, Jeong Woo followed up with one more announcement.

"Very good. Now, Jason. About that hotel suite–"

Jason quickly shook his head, but Tae Hyun had already noticed. "What hotel suite?"

Jason quietly huffed. "I was planning on surprising you with it."

Jeong Woo frowned. "I'm sorry. I had no idea–"

"It's fine." Jason waved off his apology and turned to Tae Hyun. "The Songdo Grand Hotel has a set of VIP suites for artists performing here, and I asked if we could stay in one tonight." He reached over to take Tae Hyun's hand. Tae Hyun briefly stiffened before remembering who they were with and relaxing. "I thought that, with everything that's happened, it would be a nice mini-vacation for us."

Tae Hyun snorted. "That's what you've been hiding from me?" Jason nodded. "Oh, hyung." He smiled. "Alright. Then let's go see it."

The hotel manager at the Songdo Grand personally escorted them to a giant, penthouse-level corner suite larger than their Seoul apartment. It included a main room with a full wet bar, dining and sitting areas, and two bedrooms with ensuite baths. A smaller pair of rooms were attached for staff or security–where the Songs would stay for the night. But the highlight was the rooftop veranda. It was almost as large as the main room and offered an expansive view of Songdo Central Park. After inviting them to contact the floor's dedicated attendant staff for anything they needed, the hotel manager took Seong Hyeon and Seong Min to their rooms. So Jason opened the bottle of champagne chilling on the dining table and poured each of them a glass, which they took out to the veranda. It was warm enough to be outside in their shirtsleeves, so the pair stood at the railing, enjoying their champagne and the view, until Jason spoke up.

"So, you're not mad about this?"

Tae Hyun chuckled. "Of course not. This is wonderful."

"Good. What do you want to do first?"

Tae Hyun thoughtfully frowned for a moment. "It's so nice out. Maybe we could walk around a bit. And I guess I want to go shopping. All the big labels have stores around here, and I don't have anything else to wear."

Jason smiled. "Actually, I packed a bag for you while you were in the shower. It's probably sitting in the main bedroom."

Tae Hyun frowned for real. "Oh." Then he nodded. "You probably don't think it's a good idea anyway."

"What?" Jason swallowed his frustration. He understood why Tae Hyun still expected that Jason wanted to control him somehow. Everyone else in Tae Hyun's life seemed to want that. But he wished that would go away at some point. "Why would that even matter? When have I ever told you no?"

Tae Hyun smiled. "Okay, good. Because I still want to go shopping."

After finishing their champagne, Jason summoned the Songs to accompany them for some outdoor enjoyment and shopping. Jason and Tae Hyun were masked, with Jason in a baseball cap and Tae Hyun in a bucket hat. Seong Min walked ahead and Seong Hyeon a few steps behind to make them less noticeable. Being recognized had grown into a riskier proposition lately, and neither one of them wanted to deal with fans, let alone protestors. But the shopping was hassle-free. Spend enough money, and shops would bend over backward to respect your privacy.

After Tae Hyun picked up several new outfits for himself–and one for Jason–at the Maximilien Cuvier, Haruhito, and Grammatico stores–all to be delivered to the hotel–they walked over to visit the park. The mid-afternoon sunshine was warm and pleasant, so the boys took a paddleboat out onto the lake while the Songs nervously stood by on the shore. But it was hard to pretend they were just hanging out, and Jason had to fight to keep from grabbing Tae Hyun's hand. So they decided to head back to the hotel. Jason and Tae Hyun were hungry anyway, and Jason wanted to give the Songs a break.

Jason ordered dinner to be sent up while they showered and changed. It was served by their bowtie-clad attendant, who Jason couldn't think of as anything except a butler. But the food came from the hotel restaurant Flore, the newest of Chef Derek Goh's growing Seoul-area dining empire. Named for Goh's French wife, the French-Korean fusion menu was daring and unexpected. It started with a pea and mint mousse with fish egg, pickled cucumber, and burrata. That was followed by scallops with asparagus, lemon and soy sauce, crumbled parmesan, and fennel. They finished with pear sorbet and almond milk ice cream with a kiwi and avocado sauce. Silence fell at the table each time a new course was served, and Jason and Tae Hyun anxiously tried the new dish.

The attendant had dimmed the room's lighting except for a pair of glass pendants hanging over the table, which set a deliciously romantic mood. And each course was paired with a new wine, which meant that Jason and Tae Hyun were comfortably buzzed by the time dessert came.

Jason raised his glass before trying the pear sorbet. "To our first Korean dinner date."

"Is it?" Tae Hyun tilted his head, his brow furrowed. "I guess it is." He lifted his glass. "And to a wonderful hyung who planned it and almost managed to surprise me."

Jason chuckled. "Almost." He sipped his wine. Then he dipped his spoon into the sorbet and had a taste. "Damn. So good."

Tae Hyun nodded. "Should we hire Chef Goh for our restaurant?"

Jason shook his head. "No way. This stuff was good, but I love your cooking so much more."

Tae Hyun bashfully grinned. "You're not just saying that?"

"I'm not." He leaned forward and winked. "There's nothing of yours I won't eat."

Tae Hyun chuckled as he patted his belly. "I don't think that's on the menu tonight, hyung. I'm too full."

Jason nodded. "Same here. Besides, I've got something better for us to do."

Something better was the hot tub on the veranda, which one of the hotel staff had set up for them while they ate so it would be ready by the time they were done. They changed into their swim briefs–with Tae Hyun wearing the pair he'd gotten from Jason in Thailand–while the attendant and his team cleared the table. And they found another champagne bottle chilling beside the hot tub, with two flutes already filled. Jason climbed in first, so Tae Hyun could hand him the champagne. The water's intense heat immediately went to work, loosening the stress-tightened muscles of his lower back. Then Tae Hyun gingerly climbed in beside him, slowly sliding down into his seat until only his head and shoulders poked above the water.

"Oh, hyung," Tae Hyun seductively moaned. "This is amazing."

"I know, right?" Jason sipped his champagne, set it on the edge of the hot tub, and quietly groaned as he slid further down into the hot, bubbling water. "I keep saying I should get one for the house, but I never do."

"Oh, we definitely should. I'd be out there soaking and enjoying the view every night."

Jason was surprised to hear that. While Tae Hyun had definitely made himself at home in Jason's house, he'd made it clear more than once that it was only because he had to stay somewhere in LA. "Really?"

Tae Hyun snorted. "Of course. This is so nice."

"That's not what I mean."

Tae Hyun frowned. "What did you–oh." He smiled and grabbed Jason's hand under the water. "I know I've complained about being homesick. But I've been home, and I'm not welcome there anymore. So, yes. Really. My home is wherever you are."

Maybe it was the wine. Maybe it was the heat. But Jason

unexpectedly felt himself tearing up from Tae Hyun's frank and simple admission. "I love you, Tae Hyun."

Jason squeezed Tae Hyun's hand as he leaned in for a kiss, finding Tae Hyun's warm, soft lips that tasted of champagne and pears. Tae Hyun draped his free arm around Jason's shoulders as he returned the kiss. It was slow, deep, and passionate, with the blurred mumble of the city streets and the twinkling lights of Songdo in the background.

Tae Hyun stopped, grinning as he pulled away from Jason. Then he shifted, moving into a semi-crouch before Jason, and began to sing.

You're my gravity,
Always pulling me closer.
No matter the distance,
Our love's the strongest force around.

Jason bit down on his lower lip as butterflies fluttered in his belly. Tae Hyun's voice was smooth and clear as he serenaded Jason in the hot tub.

Your love guides me
Over every ocean.
No matter the moment,
Two souls bound together, forever.

Between recording sessions, reviewing the masters, and Tae Hyun absentmindedly humming to himself, Jason had heard the song countless times. And Tae Hyun had already told him he wrote the song for him. But it was the first time he'd sung it just for him.

I freefall into you
Like the stars fall from the sky.
The song I sing for you
Feeling gravity defied.

Across galaxies, you always come to me
No force could ever tear us apart.
I freefall into you
Until our hearts collide.

Tae Hyun stopped singing as he pushed forward, still smiling, and resumed kissing Jason. Then he laid a hand on Jason's thigh and slowly inched it toward his crotch. Jason's cock, already semi-hard, sprang to life at Tae Hyun's gentle touch. And it surprised Jason enough that he broke away from the kiss.

Tae Hyun grinned. "Hyung, remember what I said earlier about being too full?" Jason slowly nodded. "I think I may have spoken too soon." He leaned in close enough to whisper in Jason's ear. "Are we alone?"

Jason craned his neck to catch a view of the darkened hotel suite and saw no signs of movement. And he doubted that the hotel staff would linger, considering what was likely about to happen in the hot tub. "Yeah, it's just us."

Tae Hyun's grin flashed wider as he reached under the waistband of Jason's swim briefs, grabbed his cock, and pulled it free. Jason shuddered as the combination of the warm water and Tae Hyun's firm grip sent a surprising surge of pleasure through his body. Then Tae Hyun tauntingly flicked his eyebrows up and down before lowering his head into the water.

Even knowing what was about to happen, Jason was still shocked enough to gasp when Tae Hyun took his cock into his mouth. Jason quickly grabbed the hot tub rim to steady himself as Tae Hyun demonstrated his remarkable breath control. Between the hot, bubbling water and Tae Hyun's slow, insistent blow job, the remaining tension melted from

Jason's body. He gently threaded his fingers through the drowned locks of Tae Hyun's hair, careful not to put any pressure on him but ready to drag him above the waterline if he stayed down too long.

Tae Hyun soon came up for air, breath heaving but smiling as he motioned for Jason to stand. Jason pushed himself from his seat and towered before Tae Hyun, his cock dripping with hot tub water and ample precum. The crisp night air felt ice cold on his pulsating erection after the water's steamy heat. But Tae Hyun quickly enveloped him with his warm mouth, tugging Jason's swim briefs off as he did so. Jason gasped as a cold breeze brushed across his wet nipples, forcing him to hang onto Tae Hyun's tight shoulders for balance.

The city and park spread out before him like a sparkling, jeweled carpet. And, just for a moment, Jason knew that if he let go of Tae Hyun, the breeze would pick him up and carry him away. But Tae Hyun's warm hands cupped Jason's ass and pulled him forward until he felt himself press against the back of Tae Hyun's throat. Jason nearly lost his balance again as the pressure building inside him threatened to erupt. Then, one of Tae Hyun's fingers found its way between his cheeks and brushed against his asshole, launching his explosive climax. He cried out, convulsing as he emptied himself inside Tae Hyun's mouth.

Tae Hyun held Jason in place until he'd swallowed every last drop of Jason's cum. Then he pushed Jason down into his seat and stood before him. After standing for so long, the water was almost too hot. But Jason hardly noticed. Tae Hyun had become a golden, glowing angel, his slick skin radiating the light reflected from the water below. His tantalizing erection strained against the thin fabric of his swim briefs until Jason finally released it. He took Tae Hyun into his mouth, gripping his hips for balance and control. Despite the chemical taste of hot tub water, Jason inhaled Tae Hyun's cock until his nose brushed against neatly trimmed pubic hair. Salty sweetness coated Jason's tongue as Tae Hyun left a trail of precum in his wake. Jason became ravenous, his insatiable hunger driven by Tae Hyun's panting moans as he sucked and slurped on Tae Hyun's steely stiffness. Then Tae Hyun grabbed the sides of Jason's head and thrust himself into his mouth. Jason, guessing that Tae Hyun would cum soon, repeated his lover's trick and snuck a finger between his legs to tease him. He may as well have pulled a trigger. Tae Hyun unleashed an animal cry, filling Jason's mouth with warm thickness.

Tae Hyun stood in place, holding Jason's head for balance, until he let out a long, contented sigh and sunk back into the bubbling water. Then he grinned. "Yeah. We're definitely getting a hot tub."

19

Things moved fast once they signed the Songdo Entertainment Complex contract. If Xiang and *Cherry Squad*'s protests had been cracks in KBR's dam, securing a Seoul-area venue had been the first genuine hole. After word spread that someone had openly defied KBR's unofficial ban against Tae Hyun, others soon followed suit. The Songdo Grand Hotel offered one of their ballrooms for an album release party. Several Korean tour logistics companies asked to submit bids to manage all or part of Tae Hyun's tour. And a KTN producer reached out to book Tae Hyun to appear on an upcoming episode of *Afternoon Music Party*. All the sudden attention made Tae Hyun's head spin.

Jason, Naomi, and Seong Woo were thankfully handling most of that. Tae Hyun was the talent and would've been lost if it were all up to him. But he still had many things to do–not the least of which was finalizing his tour's costumes and stage designs. He'd already considered proposals from several Los Angeles-based designers and designers from Vancouver, London, and Paris. Tae Hyun was leaning toward the Paris designer, who'd trained with Maximilien Cuvier and whose designs were closest to the dark, playful, sexy look Tae Hyun had in mind for *Boy With No Shame*. Then he got a message from Jeon I Jun.

A once-respected fashion and costume designer, Jeon I Jun had worked extensively with many KBR artists, including *XTC*, before a mysterious falling out with KBR derailed his promising career. The last time Tae Hyun worked with him was on the *Blossom* tour, where he'd designed all the costumes and stages. Tae Hyun had also long suspected that I Jun was gay and assumed that's what had soured things between him and KBR. And he was excited to hear from and potentially work with him. Plus, he seemed like a natural fit, given that they'd worked together before and had both been burned by KBR.

Jason and Seong Woo were meeting with a logistics company that day and couldn't join Tae Hyun for the meeting. So he went with Seong Min, who drove them across the Yeongdong Bridge from Cheongdam-dong to I Jun's studio in Seongsu-dong.

"May I ask you a question, sir?"

Tae Hyun looked up from the route map on his phone, surprised at Seong Min's solemn tone. His eyes were on the road, but his expression was serious to match. "Of course."

"It's about your sister, sir."

Tae Hyun stifled an inappropriate chuckle, recalling his chat with Yun Seo about Seong Min. "Alright."

Seong Min swallowed hard. He was obviously nervous, which was a first for Tae Hyun. He had to try hard not to prompt his bodyguard to spit it out. "I'd like to start courting Yun Seo, sir."

Tae Hyun shrugged. "Okay." Then he resumed watching the route map on his phone.

"I–" Tae Hyun tried very hard not to laugh when Seong

Min hesitated. "Are you sure?"

Tae Hyun finally let himself chuckle. "Of course, I'm sure. Why? Is there some reason I shouldn't be?"

"No, sir. Absolutely not."

Tae Hyun shrugged again. "Then, yeah, as long as it doesn't impact your job, I'm sure. Although, I've got to be honest. She might be more than you can handle."

It was Seong Min's turn to chuckle. "Oh, I'm well aware of that, sir. Believe me."

Tae Hyun laughed. "Good. And I think this is our turn."

Tae Hyun had never explored Seongsu-dong, an old industrial neighborhood revitalized over the years as its warehouses and factories were converted to shops, cafes, and artist lofts. Even Seong Min was unfamiliar with the area. So the pair got lost and turned around several times before they found the correct address and a nearby place to park. I Jun's studio was located above a coffee shop on Seongdeokjeong-gil, a few blocks from the river. A barista in the coffee shop pointed them to the building entrance off the alley, where Tae Hyun found the call box and pressed the studio's call button. The call box buzzed, and the door unlocked, so Seong Min held it open as the pair entered a long, narrow hallway with a small elevator on the far end. They rode the rickety elevator to the third floor, where the doors opened directly to I Jun's studio.

Tae Hyun was immediately concerned. Perhaps it was because he'd never worked with I Jun outside the KBR building or on location. But he'd expected the studio to be larger. Or, at least, nicer. The main room still showed the distressed signs of its industrial heritage, with bare concrete floors and exposed beams, plumbing, and ductwork. But, where the coffee shop downstairs had polished the concrete to a brilliant shine and stained their wood-clad walls and beams, I Jun had done none of that. Much of the space was filled with a group of long folding tables pushed together to make a large workspace with a half-dozen or more garments in various stages of construction laid across the top. The walls were covered by half-full clothing racks, at least ten fabric rolls vertically propped up against them, and a collection of dressmaker's dummies congregating in the far corner.

Tae Hyun and Seong Min shared a concerned glance before Tae Hyun sighed and accepted that an artist's surroundings weren't necessarily an indicator of their work. His choreographer's dance studio was an excellent example of that.

"I Jun? Are you here?"

Something clattered as it dropped to the floor, echoing from one of the pair of doorways leading off the main room. "Tae Hyun? Is that really you?" A smiling I Jun emerged from the doorway, arms spread wide in welcome. "I can hardly believe it!"

Tae Hyun quickly relaxed at the sight of his former designer, who, despite his shoddy surroundings, was impeccably dressed in a white, linen, tunic-style pullover with a thick black stripe across the chest, slender black pants or leggings, and shiny black leather loafers with pointed toes. His artfully jagged hair was bleached to a strawberry blond.

Tae Hyun smiled. "I Jun!" He walked over and accepted the designer's warm hug. "It's so good to see you." Then he gestured toward his bodyguard. "This is Song Seong Min."

I Jun offered Seong Min his hand. "Jeon I Jun. It's a pleasure to meet you." Seong Min nodded as he shook I Jun's hand but stayed silent, so I Jun turned back to Tae Hyun. "I can't believe you're actually here. Have you eaten? Would you like some tea? I was just setting the kettle to boil."

Tae Hyun shook his head. "No, thank you. But I'd love to hear about what you've been up to."

I Jun shrugged. "Nothing as newsworthy as you, I'm afraid." He shook his head. "The last time I saw you, you were finishing up the *Blossom* tour. But you've been busy since then, eh? The army? A solo career?" He grinned. "A boyfriend? Who I was hoping to meet today, by the way."

Tae Hyun chuckled. "Guilty on all counts. But Jason had other obligations today, so it's just me. I'm sorry about that."

"It's fine." I Jun waved off Tae Hyun's apology. "But I still can't believe my little Tae Hyun is really gay."

"Little? You're not that much older than me."

"I'm ten years older than you." I Jun smiled. "But I hope you're willing to work with a gay designer."

"So you are?" Tae Hyun awkwardly frowned. "Gay, I mean. I suspected you were, but–"

I Jun nodded. "But it wasn't something I could really talk about. So, I guess that makes two things we have in common. We've both been fired by KBR, too."

Tae Hyun laughed. "If we don't end up working together, we could always start a support group."

I Jun didn't quite cover his frown in time. "Of course. If I might ask, who are the others you're considering?"

"Absolutely." Tae Hyun listed off some of the designers he'd talked to. "But, right now, I'm leaning toward Renée Laurent."

I Jun's eyebrows fell as he nodded. "Maximilien's protege? Of course. I imagine he's shown you some brilliant designs."

Tae Hyun nodded. "Yes, but I haven't committed to anything yet. And I'm anxious to see what you can show me."

"Yes, yes. Certainly." I Jun gestured toward the back room. "Are you sure you won't have any tea?"

"I'm sure." Something felt off about I Jun. It could've been embarrassment or nerves. But it made Tae Hyun anxious to get the meeting over with. "Let's look at what you've got."

I Jun nodded and reached for a sketchpad sitting on the table. Tae Hyun glanced at Seong Min with his eyebrows raised while I Jun's back was turned. Seong Min shrugged and nodded toward the door, but Tae Hyun shook his head. He wasn't ready to give up on the meeting just yet. But he was glad he wasn't the only one who thought things were weird.

"Here we go," I Jun announced, spreading a set of sketches across the tabletop. "These are all rough since I haven't had much time to sketch."

"That's alright."

Tae Hyun approached the table and looked over I Jun's sketches. Rough was an understatement. The sketches Tae Hyun had made for himself were better than what I Jun showed him. He struggled to decipher what the designs were supposed to be. He picked up the leftmost sketch, which may have been a military-inspired look. But it was all wrong. He shook his head and set it down.

"Do you mind if I ask–" I Jun stopped and shook his head. "No, I probably shouldn't."

Tae Hyun had a sense of what his inappropriate question probably was, so his instinct was to agree. Still, it also might've given him some insight into what was going on with I Jun. "Ask me what?"

"It was Chang Min, right?"

Tae Hyun frowned. He immediately knew what I Jun was

asking but had no intention of confirming his suspicions. "What was Chang Min?"

I Jun shared a cautious smile. "You and Chang Min were lovers, right? He was who you mentioned in your video." His smile grew bolder. "I could see the way you two looked at each other and acted around each other. And, of course, KBR also fired him."

Tae Hyun clamped down on his surging annoyance. He and I Jun had worked together plenty of times but were hardly friends. And they hadn't spoken in years. "KBR fired Chang Min because his music wasn't selling very well."

I Jun didn't look convinced. "But, surely–"

"Could we just focus on why I'm here?" Tae Hyun picked up the next set of drawings. They looked familiar, but he couldn't place them. "Tell me more about these."

I Jun nodded. "Of course." He glanced over Tae Hyun's shoulder at the sketches in his hand. "These are a distressed look. Not quite post-apocalyptic, but more than urban streetwear." He started shuffling some of the items on the table around. "I think I have some swatches–"

"That's okay. I don't think that's the look I'm going for." Tae Hyun put the sketches down and grabbed the next set. They were definitely familiar. "What about these?"

"Oh, yes." I Jun gestured toward a clothing rack. "I actually have an example of something in a similar style." He walked over to the clothing rack and sorted through the pieces hanging there until he stopped and pulled one free. "Here it is."

I Jun held up an indigo, faux-suede jacket with intricate silver piping on the collar, sleeves, and lapels. It was lovely and well-made. And it probably fit Tae Hyun, too, considering he'd already worn it.

Tae Hyun frowned. "What's going on here, I Jun?"

"What do you mean?"

Tae Hyun huffed. "I know you said these are rushed, but they're not good. Or, at least, not original." He nodded toward the jacket in I Jun's hand. "I wore that during the European leg of the *Blossom* tour." He picked up the previous sketches, which he finally recognized. "These are *G-Go* costumes. And I can't remember where the others are from, but I know I've seen them before."

I Jun frowned as he replaced the jacket on the clothing rack. "I know," he finally admitted. "Like I said, I haven't had time to put anything together, and–"

"But you contacted us." Tae Hyun shook his head. "Why would you do that if you didn't have anything to show?"

I Jun stubbornly gestured to the drawings on the table. "I wanted to remind you of what I could do."

Tae Hyun frowned. He didn't get why I Jun was acting so cagey. "I know what you can do. I've worn your costumes before. That's why I'm here." Tae Hyun shook his head again. "But I think maybe it's time we left. If you like, you can–"

"Wait, please don't go." I Jun took hold of Tae Hyun's arm. "There's still more–"

But Seong Min quickly intervened, grabbing I Jun's forearm and pulling it away. "Mr. Woo said he's leaving."

I Jun yanked his arm free of Seong Min's grip, which meant he couldn't have been holding on very hard. "Alright, alright. You don't have to get rough." He shook his arm before massaging his wrist where Seong Min held him. "If you want to go, then just go."

Tae Hyun scowled. "I don't understand what you're up to,

I Jun. But I don't like it. And I don't think we'll be working together." He walked over to the elevator and pressed the down button.

I Jun moved toward Tae Hyun, but Seong Min stepped in between them and held his hand out. "Please stay back, sir."

I Jun scoffed. "Is this who you are now, Tae Hyun? Having your bodyguard rough me up in my own studio?"

Tae Hyun ignored I Jun as he and Seong Min stepped into the open elevator. He looked away, refusing to make eye contact, as the doors closed before him. Then he shook his head. "What the hell was that?"

"I don't know, sir. But I agree that something was off about him. It was a good idea to leave."

Tae Hyun nodded, running through the whole meeting in his head as the elevator slowly descended to the ground floor. He hadn't remembered I Jun ever being that sour and defensive. But a lot had happened since they'd last spoken. Tae Hyun had changed since then. It was certainly possible that I Jun had as well. Still, he'd had more than a day to prepare anything at all to show Tae Hyun. Yet, he hadn't. It almost felt like he'd simply wanted to see Tae Hyun again and used the costume meeting as an excuse. But, if that were the case, why hadn't he been more friendly or forthright? No, it didn't make any sense.

After taking a remarkably long time to travel the three floors, the elevator finally stopped. Tae Hyun's phone rang as the doors creaked and slid open, so he pulled it out to see Yun Seo calling. Seong Min reached out to hold the door for Tae Hyun as he answered and put the phone to his ear.

"Yun Seo?"

"Hi, oppa! I was calling because–"

Tae Hyun's attention quickly shifted to the pair of masked, black-clad figures walking into the narrow corridor from the alley outside. They looked like the sort of thugs you'd see in TV dramas, sent as henchmen by the show's villain to carry out his evil plans. But surely those things didn't happen in real life, did they? Concerned, Tae Hyun ignored his call and turned to Seong Min. But his bodyguard was already moving.

"Stay back, sir!"

Seong Min shoved Tae Hyun to the side and plowed headlong into the two strangers. A cold fear gripped Tae Hyun as he realized what was happening. Those men were there for him.

Tae Hyun had sometimes imagined what it would be like to see his mountain of a bodyguard in action. But things happened so quickly that he could barely keep up. Like Jason, Seong Min was fast. He ducked under one attacker's clumsy punch before knocking the second attacker to the floor. Then, the first attacker managed to get his arm around Seong Min's neck. But Seong Min slammed him into the wall behind him, forcing the man to let go.

Tae Hyun would've run, but the corridor was too narrow.

"Oppa! What's happening?"

Tae Hyun remembered his forgotten call. "Yun Seo! Some men have come for me. Get help!"

One of the attackers slipped past Seong Min and threw himself toward Tae Hyun, who yelped and jumped back. Then, his army training kicked in. That man definitely wanted to hurt him, so he needed to defend himself in any way he knew how. The stranger lunged for him, but Tae Hyun ducked to the side. He tried to kick the man, but he was off balance, and his foot barely made any impact. But it put him within arm's reach, so the stranger grabbed him and yanked him toward the door.

Fighting his panic, Tae Hyun switched tactics and surged forward, knocking his attacker to the floor before falling on him. His attacker struggled underneath him as Tae Hyun fought to pin his arms down. He wasn't sure what to do beyond that, but it was the only thing–

Bam!

A sharp noise temporarily deafened Tae Hyun as Seong Min slammed into the wall. The smell of gunpowder drew his gaze to the gun in the other attacker's hand. Seong Min had been shot!

Tae Hyun scrambled off the man he'd knocked down, desperately trying to get to his bodyguard before he got shot again. Then, the man with the gun swung it toward him. Tae Hyun barely had time to process the notion that he was about to get shot, too, before Seong Min lunged, knocking the gunman against the wall and opening a path to the door. He turned to face Tae Hyun as the gunman struggled under his weight.

"Run, sir. Run!"

Tae Hyun's feet moved before he'd even consciously decided to go. Some part of his animal brain knew it was his only chance to escape and wasn't waiting for his higher mind to agree. He ducked under the flailing arms of his bodyguard's shooter as he slipped around Seong Min, pushed the door open, and rushed outside. He turned toward the main road, hoping to possibly flag someone down, and nearly ran into a third masked man dressed in all black. The two silently stood before one another in a brief moment of surprised confusion before the stranger shouted and grabbed for him. Tae Hyun jumped back, out of his reach, and slammed into the side of a van parked behind him. He hadn't even noticed it until then. There was too much happening for his brain to process. But he used the momentum to propel himself away from the third attacker, dashing around the van and further into the alley. He had to get away. Seong Min had been shot. He was alive, but he'd been shot, and Tae Hyun needed to get away so he could–

Tae Hyun barely registered the presence of a fourth man in all black as he rushed around to the back of the van before exploding pain blossomed through his head, and everything went dark.

20

Jason never would've survived his meeting if it hadn't been for Seong Woo. Partly because having him there gave Jason a chance to test the waters on their reconciled friendship. But mostly because it forced Jason to pay attention as the people they met with droned on and on about travel and setup logistics. He knew the universe was punishing him for all the times he'd been shitty to producers and production assistants on his projects, so he needed all the help he could get to power through it. Even then, he still spent half the meeting daydreaming about suntanning on a secluded Thai beach with Tae Hyun lounging by his side.

It turned out he wasn't the only one who needed the help.

"We deserve a drink after that snoozefest," Seong Woo announced in English as they rode the elevator back to the lobby.

Jason chuckled, as much for hearing Seong Woo say *snoozefest* as anything else. "You didn't seem all that bored."

"It's a professional skill. Then again, neither did you."

Jason shrugged. "I didn't want you to get upset and throw me out of the meeting."

Seong Woo winced. "Ouch. Too soon."

"Is it? Shit." Jason grinned. "Now you're gonna throw me

out of the elevator, right?"

Seong Woo chuckled. "Damn. You're never gonna let me live that down, are you?"

"Nope." Jason stepped toward the elevator doors as they slid open. "You're too late, anyway. But you can still throw me out of the lobby."

Seong Woo snorted as he followed Jason from the elevator. "Will you shut up about that if I buy you a drink?" Jason held up two fingers, and Seong Woo laughed. "Okay, deal."

Seong Hyeon and Min Kyu waited in the lobby near the building exit, each seemingly trying to outdo the other's silent stoicism. Jason quietly snorted as he and Seong Woo headed their way.

"Great. Where should we go?"

Seong Woo glanced at a hundred-thousand-dollar Van Houte & Hospers timepiece on his wrist that must've weighed at least a quarter pound. "It's almost happy hour, and this is Yeouido. There's probably a hundred places to drink around here if you don't mind being around drunken office workers."

Jason shook his head. "I don't mind being around drunken anyone, as long as–" His pocket started vibrating, so he stopped to check his phone. He'd hoped it was Tae Hyun, but the call was from a Seoul number he didn't recognize. He picked it up anyway, remembering at the last minute to answer in Korean. "Hello?"

"Jason? It's Yun Seo!"

Tae Hyun's sister was the last person he expected to hear from. "Oh, hi. What–"

"Tae Hyun's in trouble!"

Jason's mind blanked, refusing to register Yun Seo's words or tone. There was no way Tae Hyun could be in trouble.

What did that even mean? "What?"

Yun Seo huffed. "I just called him, and I heard some commotion. Then he told me some men had come for him and to get help. I don't know what to do, so I called you and–"

Sudden panic tore through Jason as he finally grasped what she was saying. Tae Hyun was in trouble. People came for him. "That's all he told you?"

"No." Yun Seo huffed again. "Well, yeah. But I heard some fighting, and I think he dropped his phone, and the call disconnected. And, maybe–" She suddenly stopped speaking. All Jason could hear was the wheezing of her breath.

"Maybe what?"

"I might have heard a gunshot."

Holy shit. "What? Are you sure?" Seong Hyeon, hearing Jason's panicked tone, anxiously hovered nearby. "No, don't answer that. I've gotta go. Keep your phone handy in case he calls you."

"Okay. I'm sor–"

Jason ended the call before Yun Seo could complete her apology. There'd be time for all that once Tae Hyun was safe and accounted for. In the meantime, Jason's fearful panic battled his fearsome rage for dominance. But he ignored them both for the moment. There'd be time for that later, too.

Seong Hyeon opened his mouth to speak, but Seong Woo beat him out of the gate. "What's up?"

"Trouble." Jason turned to Seong Hyeon and relayed what Yun Seo had told him. "He was supposed to be at his designer meeting in–shit, I don't even remember where." He pulled up the tracking app on his phone to look for Tae Hyun. Sure enough, his phone was offline. Shit. Cold fear crept up from the darker corners of his mind, but Jason pushed it away. He needed to focus, so he checked the phone tracker's history. The last place Tae Hyun had his phone powered on was at his appointment with the designer in Seongsu-dong. "In Seongsu-dong." He pointed his screen at Seong Hyeon. "But his phone's offline."

Seong Hyeon nodded, pulled out his phone, and started tapping on his screen. "Seong Min's phone is offline, too."

Despite clamping down on his fear and rage, they weren't so easily dismissed. Jason roughly grabbed Seong Hyeon's arm, startling him. "You made me a promise."

"I know, sir." Seong Hyeon's voice was tight and controlled as he thumbed through another app on his phone. His brother had been with Tae Hyun, so he probably already felt his own worry and didn't need Jason adding to it. But that was too fucking bad.

"Then you need to keep it," Jason growled.

Seong Hyeon gave Jason a single nod before returning to his phone.

Seong Woo frowned and turned to Min Kyu. "What can we do to help?"

"Their vehicle is still parked in Seongsu-dong," Seong Hyeon announced.

Min Kyu nodded. "Okay. Send me the location, and I could have a team meet us there." He turned to Seong Woo. "With your permission, sir?"

Seong Woo nodded. "Absolutely. Whatever it takes."

Min Kyu nodded again, pulling out his phone as he turned away. "Everyone with me," he called out as he jogged off and put his phone to his ear.

Seong Hyeon didn't wait for Jason's okay to go with Min

Kyu.

"You heard the man," Seong Woo said to Jason before following after them.

Jason hurried to catch up to Seong Woo. "How big is your security team, exactly?"

"That depends on what we need."

Jason frowned. "How much security do you need?"

Seong Woo chuckled. "It's not all for me. There's Yoo Mi, of course. And we provide security for our clients, too. Like we did with you before you poached two of my best men."

Min Kyu waited for everyone at the elevator to the underground parking garage. He hung up his phone just before the elevator opened, stepped inside, and held the doors for the other three.

"My primary team is headed out now, sir. And I have the secondary team on standby."

Seong Woo nodded. "Perfect." He turned to Jason. "Everything's gonna be fine."

Jason gritted his teeth as he nodded. He usually would've blown off that sort of bland reassurance. But things were different with Tae Hyun involved. Jason could think of a hundred different ways his lover might be in trouble. And the more Jason considered the possibilities, the more his worry turned to fear. "And if it's not?"

Seong Hyeon angrily grunted. "Then I'll raise hell on anyone who gets in my way."

Jason snorted. If anything happened to Tae Hyun, it would be Jason who raised hell.

Because Seong Min had driven Tae Hyun in their truck, Jason and Seong Hyeon had ridden to the meeting with Seong Woo and Min Kyu in one of Seong Woo's tanks. Jason and

Seong Woo climbed into the back of the monstrous SUV while the two security men got in front, with Min Kyu at the wheel.

Once they were out of the garage and onto the streets of Yeouido Island, they were met with the sprawling mass of Seoul's evening rush hour traffic. But Min Kyu drove the truck like a sports car, somehow finding open lanes and maneuvering into them with clearances that made even Jason turn away. But watching the road was the only thing distracting Jason from his anxiety, anger, and fear. So his mind filled with scenario after scenario, each more troubling than the last, of all the ways Tae Hyun could be in danger. And most of those scenarios featured a certain evil entertainment empire.

"It has to be KBR," Jason suddenly announced.

Seong Woo shook his head. "We don't even know what's happened to them yet. Let's not go assuming anything until–"

"They got to him once." Jason's sharp, firm tone surprised even him. "They could do it again."

Seong Woo shook his head again. "We still don't know if that was them."

"Oh, come on." Jason scoffed. "They've been waging a PR campaign against us since Tae Hyun came out. Who else could it be?"

"I know." Seong Woo put a hand on Jason's arm. "I do your PR, remember? And we still don't know what's happened. Until then, let's not jump to any conclusions."

Jason huffed and pressed himself into his seat, silently willing the traffic to disappear. Then, he caught a glimpse of Seong Hyeon's reflection in the rearview mirror. Seong Hyeon made mirrored eye contact with Jason and offered him a single nod. He thought Jason was right. But Seong Woo was also right. They didn't actually know if anything had happened yet, let alone what that might be. So there was nothing to do but wait. He couldn't even call Naomi since it was probably the middle of the night in LA. Not that Naomi could do anything, either. Nobody could do anything other than what they were already doing. And Jason was stuck relying on a group of people who'd already let him down in the most spectacular ways to help him deal with the situation. He wanted to scream and pound his fists into the back of Min Kyu's seat. But he settled for not quite watching as Min Kyu weaved the tank through impossibly small gaps in the traffic and listened to the muffled scream of the truck's special tires on the pavement to drown out the voices in his head.

What would've probably been a twenty-minute drive with no traffic took a half-hour, even with Min Kyu's racetrack driving. But they eventually found Jason's rented SUV parked on the street. Another of Seong Woo's tanks was parked beside it, blocking traffic with its hazard lights flashing. Since they were approaching from the opposite direction, Min Kyu made a quick U-turn, cutting off both lanes of traffic, and pulled to a stop behind the other tank. Four men dressed in variations of Min Kyu's black suit, white shirt, and black tie stood guard around Jason's SUV as they waited for their boss to arrive.

Min Kyu left his truck running but turned on the flashers before jumping out and approaching his team. Seong Hyeon was hot on his heels. But Jason climbed across the rear seats to use Seong Woo's door so he didn't have to step out into traffic. Jason and Seong Woo anxiously hung back while the two security chiefs conferred with Min Kyu's team. Then

Seong Hyeon produced a set of keys, unlocked Jason's rented truck, and made a quick but thorough search for any clues to Tae Hyun's whereabouts. Jason began to fidget when he found nothing.

"Just let them work," Seong Woo said. "If there's anything here to be found, they'll find it."

Jason huffed. "I know. I just feel so fucking useless right now." Then he scanned the scene and noticed the coffee shop on the ground level of the designer's building. "Let's go ask in there." He grabbed Seong Woo's shoulder. "Maybe they saw something."

Seong Woo nodded while Jason pulled out his phone. He scrolled through his pics of Tae Hyun, including one he'd recently taken of the angelic, sleeping idol until he found one he could share with strangers. But it was unnecessary.

"Are you looking for Woo Tae Hyun?"

The barista must've recognized Jason. He nodded. "That's right."

"Oh, well, he was in here with his bodyguard a few hours ago asking about that designer that works in the building upstairs. But I haven't seen him since then." The barista frowned. "Is everything alright?"

Jason forced himself to keep a neutral expression. ""Everything's fine. He just lost his phone, and we're helping him track it down."

The barista nodded. "Oh, sure. Yeah, it's not here. Maybe it's upstairs?"

"We're headed there next." Jason grabbed Seong Woo and turned him toward the exit. "The upstairs entrance is where?"

The barista pointed to her left. "Around the corner in the alley."

"That was impressive," Seong Woo shared once they were back outside. "You didn't seem anxious at all."

Jason shrugged. "Best Actor winner."

Seong Hyeon, Min Kyu, and a pair of men from Min Kyu's team had already located the building's upstairs entrance and were waiting when Seong Woo and Jason arrived.

"The entrance is locked," Min Kyu shared, "and no one is answering at any of the buzzers."

Jason huffed. "Break it open."

Seong Hyeon shook his head. "That would probably set off an alarm, and I'm reluctant to involve the authorities at this point."

"We could call the landlord," Seong Woo suggested.

"Or, I could let you in." Jason turned to see the barista he'd just spoken with standing behind him, holding two large plastic garbage bags full of trash. "I mean, I assume it's important since there's so many of you here, you know, looking for a phone."

Jason ignored the almost unbearable tension in his jaw, knowing it would make him look furious, and forced himself to smile. "I'd appreciate it."

The barista shrugged and set the trash bags on the ground. "Sure." She dug through the pocket in her apron and pulled out a set of keys. "You're Jason Park. It's not like you're here to rob the place." She unlocked the door and pulled it open. "There you go."

Min Kyu grabbed the door from the barista. "Thank you. And I'd appreciate if you didn't–"

"Yeah, you were never here." The barista nodded. "I get it."

One of Min Kyu's men helped the barista with her garbage bags while Jason followed Min Kyu and Seong Hyeon inside.

Then Jason nearly ran into Seong Hyeon when he suddenly stopped.

"What's going–"

Min Kyu hissed and pulled a gun from inside his jacket. "Keep him back."

Seong Hyeon turned around and blocked Jason's path. "Give us a moment, sir. It may not be safe."

"What?" Jason craned his neck to peer around Seong Hyeon. "What do you mean not–" Min Kyu was inspecting some fresh blood on the wall next to what Jason was pretty sure was a bullet hole. Jason surged forward. "Damn it! Let me get–"

Seong Hyeon took hold of Jason by the shoulders and held him in place. "Wait here, Mr. Park, sir. For your own safety."

Min Kyu quietly swore before waving the two from his team behind Jason to follow. They squeezed past Jason and Seong Hyeon as Min Kyu went to call the elevator.

Jason struggled to get free. "Let me go! Tae Hyun could be hurt."

"If there's a shooter upstairs, then–"

Since Seong Hyeon wouldn't release his grip, Jason pushed himself close enough that their noses almost touched. "Do you really want to fight me, Seong Hyeon? Because that's the only way you're gonna keep me from following them."

Seong Hyeon grunted and let go. Jason ducked around him and ran for the elevator, but the door had just closed.

"Shit!" Jason angrily tapped on the call button.

Seong Hyeon put his hand on Jason's shoulder and nearly got smacked. Jason could feel himself losing control of his temper as he turned around. But the mixture of anger, frustration, and fear coursing through his veins was too hard to keep a lid on.

Seong Hyeon bowed. "I know I failed you, sir. But you need to let me do my job."

Jason recklessly poked a finger into Seong Hyeon's chest. "Don't start with that now. Just stop standing in my way."

"If something were to happen to you–"

Jason loudly huffed. "I don't give a shit what happens to me."

The elevator door opened, revealing Min Kyu's inscrutable face. "There's no one there. My team is scouring the place, looking for any clues about what happened."

Jason bitterly gestured toward the blood-stained wall. "That's not a clue?"

Min Kyu's eyes darted to Seong Hyeon, who carefully shook his head. "Mr. Park, sir. If you can't control yourself–"

"You'll what?" Jason scoffed. "I realize this is just a job to you. But there's nothing in this world more precious and important to me than that man. Nothing. So you can all give up that *Mr. Park, sir* shit right now."

Min Kyu, in an extravagant show of emotion, pursed his lips. Jason wondered if he'd finally crossed the line. Not that he cared. He was serious when he told Seong Hyeon that he didn't give a shit about what happened to himself.

The silent tension built between them until Seong Hyeon's pocket beeped. He quickly pulled out his phone and looked at the display. "I have Seong Min."

Jason whirled on his security chief. "What? Is his phone on again?"

Seong Hyeon shook his head. "No. But he has a secondary tracker for emergencies. He must've activated it."

For a moment, Jason was genuinely impressed with his security chief's spy craft. They might never have needed a secret emergency tracker. Until they did. "Okay, that's something. What now?"

"I could have a team meet us at that location inside thirty minutes," Min Kyu suggested.

But Jason kept his attention focused on Seong Hyeon. "I asked you."

"Sir?"

Jason huffed. "You're my security chief. You're responsible for Tae Hyun's safety. I want to know what you think."

Seong Hyeon nodded. "I agree with Yu Min Kyu."

Jason nodded. "Okay. Then what are we waiting for?"

Seong Woo's permission, it turned out. Thankfully, when Min Kyu updated him on the situation, he nodded. "Alright. I trust Min Kyu's judgment. Do whatever it takes."

Min Kyu pulled one of his men aside. "Find the designer and detain him." The man nodded and tapped a teammate's shoulder before they both rushed toward one of the tanks.

Seong Woo frowned. "Why are you doing that?"

"We need to know if the designer is involved somehow," Min Kyu explained. "He may have important information. And, if he's not involved, he may be in danger. Either way, it's necessary."

No, it's kidnapping, said the voice in Jason's head. But he didn't really care. His boyfriend was in trouble. And they were in another country, anyway. For all he knew, what they were doing was perfectly legal. As Min Kyu and Seong Woo returned to their truck, Seong Hyeon pulled Jason aside.

"I know you won't want to hear this, sir," Seong Hyeon carefully stated, "but–"

Jason snorted. "If you're about to tell me I have to stay behind, the answer is no."

Seong Hyeon shook his head. “No, sir. You’ve made your feelings on the matter clear.” Then he leaned in close enough that it took all of Jason’s willpower not to back away. “So, let me be equally clear. If you insist on being reckless and taking needless risks, I cannot ensure your safety.”

Jason grinned, knowing it would only make him look unhinged. But he didn’t care because Seong Hyeon had finally taken him seriously. “Good. Then let’s go.”

21

Tae Hyun woke to pain and darkness. The back of his head throbbed, and, for a brief, panicked moment, he thought whoever had hit him had damaged his eyesight. Sweat dripped from his forehead as he inhaled thick, musky air that smelled suspiciously like someone's breath. Then awareness returned and he realized it was his own breath. Someone had put a hood over his head.

Low, smooth vibrations rattled the floor beneath Tae Hyun. He was in a vehicle, probably a van or small truck, and was being taken somewhere. He tried to move his hands and discovered that they'd been tied behind his back. He had no idea how long he'd been knocked out. But his arms and hands hadn't fallen asleep, so it couldn't have been too long.

"The boss is gonna be pissed when he finds out you shot the big one."

Tae Hyun nearly jumped at the sound of the rough, raspy voice, but his mind was still too foggy for his body to react. The voice came from the direction his feet were pointing. That must've been the front of the van.

"I doubt it," answered a deep, gravelly voice from the same direction. "The big one's a bodyguard, not the target."

They were talking about Seong Min. Which meant Tae

Hyun's hazy memory of an almost deafening bang and seeing him slam against the corridor wall was real, and he'd definitely been shot. Muted panic swirled at the edges of his thoughts, interrupted only by a second realization. If Seong Min was the bodyguard, Tae Hyun was the target. And they were being kidnapped.

"Wait. He's not the guy's boyfriend?"

"Not unless he's got two." Deep Voice chuckled. "Did you even look at the photos the boss sent? For all you know, they're not even the right fucking guys."

Raspy Voice huffed. "Don't fucking start with me. I didn't shoot anyone."

Deep Voice scoffed. "Oh, come on. That guy was like hitting a brick fucking wall. It was the only way I could think of to knock him down." He scoffed again. "Besides, you're the one who hit the target over the head."

"Oh? So, should I have let him run away? Would that have made the boss happy?"

"He was pretty fast. Who knew idols could handle themselves like that?"

Raspy Voice snorted. "Probably all the dancing. And he already did his military service, too."

Deep Voice loudly scoffed. "That doesn't mean shit. My brother-in-law's in the army, and my grandmother could still knock him down."

Tae Hyun lay on his back, so he tried rolling onto his side and ran into something heavy beside him. He yelped before he could stop himself.

"Shit," Deep Voice exclaimed, "he's already awake!"

Tae Hyun mentally cursed himself for being so careless. He gingerly felt for whatever it was beside him as best he could with his tied hands and heard a gasp.

"Seong Min?"

"Sorry, sir. You startled me."

"Keep it down back there," called out Raspy Voice.

Tae Hyun ignored him. "Are you alright?"

"I don't know. I think so."

Raspy Voice scoffed. "Hey, I said-"

"We fucking heard you," Tae Hyun bitterly spat. "Tell me what the hell's going on. What do you want with us?"

"I want you to shut the fuck up."

Tae Hyun huffed. "You can't do this. You'd better let us go before–"

"I said shut the fuck up! Unless you want to get bashed on the head again."

"Didn't your boss say he wanted us unharmed?"

Deep Voice snorted. "Shit, how long has he been awake?"

"Yeah. The boss did say that." Tae Hyun heard the click of a seat belt buckle and someone shuffling in their seat. "But I already broke that rule once. Wanna see if I'll break it again?"

"Hey," Deep Voice said. "What are you doing? Sit back down, you idiot."

"You just focus on the driving and let me–"

"Are you even following the map? I don't know where the hell I'm going."

"Damn it, Do Hyeon." Raspy Voice huffed. "Do I have to do everything?"

"Did you just use my fucking name, dumbass?"

Raspy Voice huffed again. "They didn't know it was your real name until now, idiot. And you need to take the exit for Daedeoksan-ro."

"There. Was that so hard, Kun Woo?

"What? Now you're using my name? You fucking–"

The two kidnappers dissolved into petty bickering, so Tae Hyun figured they probably wouldn't notice him whispering to Seong Min. "How are you? Are you badly hurt?" It was killing Tae Hyun that he couldn't see anything or move his hands.

"I don't think so, sir. The bullet only grazed my upper arm, so it's mostly just a scratch." Seong Min quietly chuckled. "I won't be winning any arm wrestling competitions for a while." Tae Hyun frowned. Was his bodyguard delirious? "But it feels like someone bandaged up my arm a bit."

That was considerate. "Are you blindfolded, too?"

"Yes, sir." Seong Min quietly huffed as he moved around. "What about you? Are you alright, sir?"

"My head hurts. Otherwise, I think I'm okay." Tae Hyun huffed. "Have you been awake this whole time?"

"No, sir. I tried my best to keep them distracted while you ran. Then someone hit me over the head from behind when I ran after you."

"Me, too." Tae Hyun quietly huffed. "Do you have any idea where we are?"

"No, sir." Seong Min paused for a long moment. "Well, maybe. I think the street they mentioned is in Goyang."

Goyang? Tae Hyun couldn't think of anything there. "What should we do?"

"For now, just play along. If this is a kidnapping, they'll want you unharmed so they can make a ransom demand."

Ransom? Tae Hyun could hardly believe what was happening. Who would kidnap him? How much would they ask for? At least he knew why I Jun had been acting so strangely. The designer was obviously in on it somehow.

Seong Min said to play along, which was as good advice as any. Tae Hyun wished he had a way to contact Jason, but he couldn't feel his phone in his pocket. He must've dropped it at some point. Or his kidnappers had taken it. He almost shuddered, thinking about how Jason would react once he found out. Just the graffiti incident had sent his temper boiling. But that hardly compared to–Shit. *Remember Jong Soo.* What if it wasn't a kidnapping at all? What if it was something much worse? He'd been warned, after all. Was he suffering the consequences of ignoring the warning?

Tae Hyun wanted to mention that thought to Seong Min, but the van lurched to the side and rolled him onto his back. They must've reached the Daedeoksan-ro exit. Tae Hyun spread his legs to balance himself as they continued driving for a few more minutes. Then, they made a final turn and slowed to a stop. The van lightly rocked as the two people in front opened the doors and climbed out.

"You two sit tight," Kun Woo instructed. "We'll be right back."

"Quickly, sir," Seong Min whispered after Kun Woo slammed his door closed. "There's a device in my belt, but I can't reach it. I need you to find it and press it."

"A device?"

"A tracker. It's above my right pocket. If there are any wireless networks nearby, it will connect and send a signal to Seong Hyeon with our location." Seong Min shuffled closer to Tae Hyun. "Please hurry, sir. Before anyone comes back."

Tae Hyun reached out as he scooted backward until he found Seong Min's leg. He moved his hands up until he found Seong Min's pocket. Then he moved his hands up again and found Seong Min's leather belt. He ran his fingers along the belt until, sure enough, he found a spot where something button-shaped was embedded in it.

"I've got it."

"Okay, press on it until it beeps."

Tae Hyun pressed down with his finger until he heard a tiny beep. "Is that it?"

"Yes, sir. It'll keep trying to broadcast our location until I shut it off or the battery runs down. But Seong Hyeon will get an alert as long as there's a wireless network in range."

Tae Hyun quietly huffed as he pulled his hand away, ignoring the sweat that had started running down the back of his neck. The hood over his head was hot and stuffy. "I wish they'd take these hoods off us."

"The hoods are a good thing, sir. They only care about what you might see if they're going to let you go."

"Oh." Tae Hyun hadn't considered that. "So what do we do now? Just wait?"

"I can't think of anything else to do. I don't know for sure where we are or who's here. There could be four men or twenty. At least one of them is armed, so we have to assume they probably all are."

Tae Hyun huffed, wondering what Jason would do in that situation. He'd probably use whatever advantages he had to gain the upper hand. For Jason, that was his mouth, his temper, and, if need be, his fists. Tae Hyun had already tried fighting and running, which got him knocked out with the butt of someone's gun. He'd tried complaining, but not very hard. And that only got him told to shut the fuck up. His greatest strengths were his talents and charm. He didn't know how far those would get him with his kidnappers. Unless they happened to be *XTC* fans.

Someone opened a sliding door beside him with a loud thunk. They were definitely in a van, not a truck. "Alright, assholes," a new, shrill voice said as a pair of hands grabbed Tae Hyun. "Let's go."

Tae Hyun grunted as whoever had grabbed him yanked and pulled until he reached the door opening, then let him fall onto the hard, paved ground. He cried out more from shock than pain as he smacked the pavement. Still, it was enough to get someone's attention.

"Hey, dumbass," Do Hyeon called out. "The boss wants him unharmed."

Shrill Voice scoffed. "Yeah, with what the boss has planned, I don't think it'll matter if he gets a little bumped around."

Someone grabbed Tae Hyun and helped him to his feet. "Yeah?" It was Do Hyeon. "You're welcome to explain to the boss why you disobeyed his orders when he gets here." He gently pushed Tae Hyun forward. "Come on, it's this way."

Seong Min grunted and hissed as someone pulled him from the van. But, thankfully, there was no noise from him striking the pavement. Tae Hyun tried to pay more attention to his surroundings as he was led away. The droning rush of highway traffic wasn't far off. The pungent air had an earthy, oily, iron odor that he could smell even through the hood, reminding him of the motor pool at the army base where he'd been stationed. He knew he wasn't on an army base, but it could've been an auto repair or storage facility. Or, more likely, a scrapyard.

When the ground transitioned from rough to smooth, Tae Hyun assumed they'd gone inside. The echoes from his footsteps were wide and long, so it had to be a big space. A warehouse, maybe? Going inside also made Seong Min's labored breathing seem louder. Tae Hyun wondered if his bodyguard's self-diagnosis of *just a scratch* was even true.

"You shot my friend," Tae Hyun announced.

"I know," Do Hyeon confirmed. "I was there."

"Is he alright? He sounds terrible."

Do Hyeon scoffed. "Don't be so dramatic. He's well enough for now."

"For now? What's going to happen?"

"You'll find out soon enough." Do Hyeon stopped Tae Hyun. "Okay, sit here."

Tae Hyun heard Seong Min walk up beside him as Do Hyeon helped him sit on the cold, smooth concrete floor. Then Seong Min sat, too. And both their helpers left without saying anything more.

After a minute or so, once he could no longer hear anyone's footsteps, Tae Hyun cautiously whispered. "What do you think he meant by *what the boss has planned*?"

"I don't know, sir." Seong Min's breathing had calmed, but his voice was still strained. "And you don't need to whisper. If they want to know what we're saying, they just have to stand right next to us. It's not like we'd see them."

Tae Hyun shivered at the thought that they could literally be surrounded by people and not know it. Except, he didn't think they were. He wasn't sure how, but he sensed that the only thing near them was a pillar. Maybe it was having been trained as a dancer? He'd been naturally gifted with a strong, almost unconscious awareness of his surroundings that he'd honed through many years of dance training. Moving onstage without running into or tripping over the others near him was an essential skill for any idol who danced.

Or, that could all be bullshit Tae Hyun was using to comfort himself. Either way, he didn't think it mattered if anyone overheard them. He wasn't a spy. He hadn't been kidnapped by agents from the north to spill the state secrets he carried. Whoever had targeted him probably knew everything about him already.

"I don't think this is a kidnapping," Tae Hyun finally admitted.

"What's that, sir?"

Tae Hyun realized how silly that sounded. "I mean, I don't think the kidnapping part is the end goal." He swallowed, wishing he could have some water. "I keep thinking about the graffiti."

Seong Min let out a slow breath. "Remember Jong Soo?"

"Yeah."

"Oh." Seong Min paused for a pair of long breaths. "Okay, yeah. I hadn't been thinking about that, but I am now, and it's–" He sighed. "–troubling. Can you tell me how tight your restraints are?"

"What?"

"Are the restraints on your wrists very tight?"

"They're digging into my wrists a bit, but they're okay otherwise."

"So you can still feel your hands?"

Tae Hyun was briefly alarmed by that. "Yes. Can't you?"

"I'm fine." Seong Min shuffled a bit before spitting out a pained hiss. "Are yours loose enough to turn your hands or wriggle them without hurting?"

Tae Hyun bit down on his lip as he tried turning his hands. "No. These aren't coming off without a blade."

"Alright. Can you run with your hands tied?"

Was Seong Min proposing that they escape? "I'm a trained

dancer. Of course, I can. But what do you have planned?"

"Nothing yet, sir." Seong Min softly wheezed. "But we might not have much notice before we need to run."

Tae Hyun's concern for his ailing bodyguard grew. He twitched as he tried to move his arms before remembering his hands were tied. "Damn it." He swung his legs around to face Seong Min. "Are you sure you're okay? You don't sound good."

"My head hurts where they hit me, and my arm hurts where they shot me. And I-" Seong Min paused for a labored breath. "And I may have a concussion."

"Shit." Tae Hyun uselessly fussed against the bindings on his wrists again. "Well, hopefully, it won't take very long for your brother to find us."

"Hopefully, sir." Seong Min fell quiet again. Tae Hyun couldn't even hear him breathing. He was about to speak up when– "About what I said earlier, sir."

Earlier? What had he–Oh. Yun Seo. "Just for now, Seong Min, would you mind just calling me by my name?"

"Okay, si–" Seong Min chuckled. "Okay, Tae Hyun."

"What about what you said? Did you change your mind?"

"No, it's just–" Seong Min struggled for another breath. "If we don't make it out of here, I want you to know that I appreciate your faith in me. I–"

"Seong Min, don't. We'll–"

"Please, Tae Hyun. Let me finish." Seong Min paused long enough to ensure Tae Hyun wouldn't interrupt him. "I don't know your sister very well yet. But I like who she seems to be. Especially if she's anything like you."

Tae Hyun struggled to keep himself calm and was momentarily glad for the mask. "She likes you, too."

"She does?"

Tae Hyun scoffed. "Of course, she does. You're a sweet, thoughtful, handsome giant. Everyone likes you." He chuckled at the memory, then stopped. Maybe he had a concussion, too? "But she told me she likes you."

"Oh. Thanks for letting me know." Seong Min's smile was big enough that Tae Hyun could hear it in his voice. Then he snorted. "I can't believe she likes me back."

Was it the concussion that made Seong Min so loopy? Or was it the hood? They were thick enough to block out most of the light, which also made it hard to breathe. Tae Hyun noticed he was a little light-headed, too. "But you can't tell her I said that when we get out of here. Or she'll kill me."

"Sir. Tae Hyun, I–"

"Promise me, Seong Min. Promise you won't say anything."

Seong Min sighed, although it was more wistful than sad. "Alright. I promise."

"Good. Now–" Tae Hyun stopped at the echo of approaching footsteps and muffled voices. "Shh." He sat very still and listened very hard.

"–should know that there were some complications," Do Hyeon said.

"Complications?" A new voice. It sounded strangely familiar, but Tae Hyun couldn't immediately place it. "What complications?"

"The bodyguard was mildly injured from a gunshot."

"What do you mean by bodyguard?"

Do Hyeon's huff sounded like he was about done with everyone second-guessing him. "The primary target was only accompanied by his bodyguard. The secondary target–"

"That's just fucking great." The new voice was definitely

familiar, and not because he'd heard it that day. But he knew it from somewhere. "And you shot him? You were told to deliver them unharmed!"

"It was the bodyguard, sir," Do Hyeon explained, "not the target. And it's nothing serious." He and his angry companion stopped near the seated Tae Hyun and Seong Min. "We already bandaged him. See for yourself."

"Fine. Now, get that hood off him. I want to see his face."

"Sir, I–"

"Do it."

Do Hyeon sighed. "Alright, sir. But I–"

"No, not his, you idiot. The other one."

Do Hyeon sighed again just before something tugged at the hood over Tae Hyun's head. Fresh air flooded into his lungs as light even brighter than the hot follow-spots he used onstage made him close his eyes. Tae Hyun carefully opened them again and saw two figures looming over him at the edges of the light.

Tae Hyun blinked as he waited for his eyes to adjust. "What's going on? Why are you doing this?"

"I think you know why," answered the familiar voice.

Tae Hyun grunted. "Remember Jong Soo."

"Yes. Such a tragedy. He was such a talented boy. But he was also a boy who didn't know how to play the game."

Tae Hyun's eyes finally adjusted enough to make out the face of the person standing over him. He would've been more shocked, but several pieces of the puzzle he'd been wrestling with fell into place. And their previous interaction made a lot more sense. "Oh Min Su?"

Min Su's quiet chuckle was low and dark. "Hello, Woo Tae Hyun."

Tae Hyun shook his head. "Is that what this is to you?" He looked over at Seong Min sitting beside him. His upper arm had been crudely bandaged and showed the glistening red of fresh blood. He still had the hood over his head. "A fucking game?"

"This?" Min Su shook his head. "No. This is just the part of the game where you get to make a decision."

Tae Hyun huffed. "So this is KBR's desperate plan to silence me one way or another like they did with Jong Soo?"

"You're so fucking smug, Woo Tae Hyun." Min Su sneered. "All those years I followed you around, doing everything you asked of me, and you never once said thank you."

"Is that what you remember?" Tae Hyun scoffed. "Because I remember a manager who constantly complained about everything." He shook his head. "Maybe if you hadn't always been such an asshole to me, I would've been more thankful."

Min Su rushed toward Tae Hyun, grabbed his shirt, and yanked him to his feet. "You had everything I ever wanted just handed to you, you little shit." He angrily grunted. "And you threw it all away for what? Some second-rate American actor who doesn't know his own place?"

Tae Hyun snorted. He'd always assumed that jealousy was part of the reason Min Su had treated him so badly. Part of him couldn't blame the man. Tae Hyun would've been crushed to work so hard toward debuting only to get denied by KBR. But that didn't make the way he'd acted okay. And it definitely didn't excuse kidnapping him. "It's not my fault you never debuted, Oh Min Su. That's on you. And KBR. You don't have to take it out on me."

Crack! Tae Hyun knew the slap was coming and had braced himself for it, but it still stung.

"Sir," Do Hyeon interrupted, "the boss is here."

Tae Hyun turned to Do Hyeon with a questioning look. If Min Su wasn't the boss, then–

"No." Min Su pulled Tae Hyun close enough that his hot, angry breath washed over Tae Hyun's face. "Don't look at him. Look at me. I'm the one you need to worry about." He snorted. "And don't you dare think you know anything about–"

Tae Hyun took a page from Jason's book and decided it was time to fight back. He lifted his leg and stomped hard on Min Su's foot with his heavy, thick-soled boots. Min Su howled as he dropped Tae Hyun on his ass.

"You little shit! I'm gonna fucking–"

"That's enough." Tae Hyun and Min Su both froze. There was no mistaking that voice. Tae Hyun would know it anywhere. "It seems like I can't trust you to carry out even the simplest of tasks, Oh Min Su." Choo Ji Hoon sighed as he slowly emerged from the murky shadows. Ji Hoon was the boss. It had been Ji Hoon all along. "Perhaps I was wrong to trust you with this."

Min Su frantically shook his head. "No, sir. This can still work. There weren't any witnesses. We can still make this work."

"Bah." Ji Hoon scowled and angrily waved Min Su away as he walked closer. "As for you, Woo Tae Hyun, I can't tell you how disappointed I am in you." He shook his head. "Such talent. And it's all going to waste."

Tae Hyun wanted to protest but couldn't get his mouth to work. Choo Ji Hoon–a man who'd essentially raised him as a surrogate father only to throw him away the moment he dared to be himself–was behind everything. That couldn't be true. There was so much he wanted to say. But all those promises to show Ji Hoon the new and improved Tae Hyun flew out the window the moment he understood that this was exactly what they'd done to Kwon Jong Soo. He finally forced out a single word. "Why?"

Ji Hoon shook his head again. "You know why."

Min Su had said the same thing. But Tae Hyun was tired of people assuming he knew what was happening whenever they threw him a new complication. "Tell me yourself."

"I don't think you're in any position to make demands of me." Ji Hoon frowned. "Besides, it doesn't matter. This fuckwit–" He gestured toward a cowering Min Su. "–couldn't even carry out such a simple plan." He regarded a prone Tae Hyun with narrowed eyes. "Things didn't have to work out like this. You had a choice, and you chose this. Remember that."

"Don't do this." Tae Hyun's mind finally started letting him speak again.

Ji Hoon shook his head. "I think we both know it's too late for–"

Pop-pop-pop! The sound of small arms fire echoed through the large, mostly empty warehouse they were in. Startled, Tae Hyun pushed himself backward with his feet as Do Hyeon, a balding, middle-aged man who'd still kept himself in decent shape, grabbed Ji Hoon's arm.

"We need to get out of here, sir!"

Ji Hoon fruitlessly struggled against Do Hyeon's grip as the man dragged him into the shadow. Ji Hoon looked at Min Su before he disappeared into the darkness. "Finish the job," he called out. "Finish it if you want what I promised you."

Boom!

21

Tae Hyun's ears rang as an explosion echoed through the warehouse. Min Su used the distraction to rush toward him. He yelped as Min Su roughly grabbed his upper arms and dragged him to his feet. Tae Hyun tried to yank his arm free, earning him a firm backhand across his face. Then the room briefly flashed before Min Su followed up with a hard fist in his gut. Tired, in pain, and afraid, Tae Hyun slumped in Min Su's grip. So Min Su yanked on his arm and dragged him away.

22

"Can't this fucking thing go any faster?" Jason had given up all pretense of being in control of his feelings, which were rapidly boiling over in the back seat of the speeding armored SUV. But no one listened to him.

"I have an aerial view of the location, sir," Seong Hyeon finally replied.

Jason was about to ask what that meant when Min Kyu cut him off. "What are we looking at?"

Realizing that Seong Hyeon had temporarily shifted his allegiance to his old Special Forces commander, Jason quietly grumbled. But it was probably for the best. He may have played a super-ninja in his last movie, but Jason was no strategist when it came to daring rescues. He was better off leaving that for the experts.

"It appears to be a salvage yard, sir. Single entrance from the main road with a gauntlet approach. The defenders will have ample cover."

Min Kyu nodded. "And we have to assume they're armed."

"Yes, sir. But it's unlikely that they'll have anything more than small arms, which this vehicle is more than capable of withstanding."

Seong Woo patted the door next to him. "Remind me never

to question your recommendations again, Yu Min Kyu."

"Noted."

Jason sat forward at the mention of small arms. "Do I get a gun?"

"Absolutely not," Min Kyu and Seong Hyeon replied in near unison.

Jason frowned. "I know how to handle one."

"That's irrelevant." Min Kyu shook his head. "I can't trust you to do as I say. And I don't want any indiscriminate gunfire. We're not a police agency, so I only want defensive fire when necessary."

Jason angrily huffed. "So what am I supposed to do?"

"You're supposed to stay in the vehicle, sir," Seong Hyeon answered. "It's bulletproof."

"No way." Jason vigorously shook his head. "There's no chance of that."

Seong Hyeon aggressively grunted. "I'm not giving you a choice, sir."

"What?" Jason scoffed. "So you'll, what? Lock me in the car? Stand guard to make sure I stay put?"

"Yes. If I have to."

Jason scoffed again and slumped back into his seat. "Fuck. Alright, fine. Whatever." A voice in his head that sounded suspiciously like Tae Hyun reminded him that Seong Hyeon was only doing what he thought was best and maybe he should give the man a break. Then again, his best hadn't prevented Tae Hyun's kidnapping, had it?

Jason glanced at Seong Woo, who only offered a shrug. The fact that Seong Woo was there at all was something of a miracle. Jason couldn't imagine pulling off what they were planning with just Seong Hyeon and himself. If only he'd been at the designer meeting with Tae Hyun, the whole shitshow might've been avoided. Then again, he might've been the one who got shot instead of Tae Hyun or Seong Min. Hopefully, it was Seong Min. As much as he liked the youngest Song brother, it wasn't even a choice between him and Tae Hyun. Realistically, it had to have been Seong Min, anyway. He would've considered it a personal insult to not take a bullet for his charge.

"We don't know what we're up against, sir," Seong Hyeon continued. "Should we do any recon first?"

"We can send up a drone if we have time before the other teams arrive," Min Kyu replied. "Otherwise, we just go in together. Time is of the essence, and these people are clearly sloppy. I don't anticipate any difficulties."

The unflappable Yu Min Kyu's nearly unshakable confidence was probably the only thing keeping Jason from flat-out losing his shit. Even then, he tightly gripped the edges of his seat to keep himself from acting out. He'd spent the past few months managing his anger as best he could, but those efforts were rapidly failing. He thought back to his last movie where, as the wise-cracking sword-for-hire Kenji Shoda, he single-handedly stormed an enemy stronghold, dodging bullets and dispatching at least a dozen soldiers without suffering more than a few scratches and bruises. That's who Jason needed to become. Of course, that scene took a week to film using carefully choreographed movement and stage fighting. But Jason had done all his own fight choreo and stunts–partly due to the film's limited budget but mostly to take advantage of his martial arts training. He may not have been Kenji Shoda, but he was still Jason fucking Park. There was absolutely no way he was staying in the truck.

22

Once they exited the expressway, Min Kyu drove them a short way before spotting another pair of blacked-out SUVs idling in a buffet restaurant parking lot about a mile up the road. Jason had no idea where they were, and his surroundings gave him no helpful clues. Min Kyu parked beside the other SUVs so that he and Seong Hyeon could jump out and confer with the other teams while someone distributed radios, hard-plastic breather masks, and lightweight chest protectors from a heavy plastic storage box in the back of another truck.

Jason only caught pieces of their discussion through the open truck door and ached to get out and join them. He hated not knowing what was happening. But the essence of their rescue plan was to enter the salvage yard by force, sacrificing any finesse or stealth in exchange for the hope that Tae Hyun's kidnappers didn't have any weapons that could penetrate the trucks' armor. And they still had surprise on their side.

Once they'd finished their plan-making, the groups returned to their trucks. First, one tank, then the other tore from the restaurant parking lot and sped away. Min Kyu screeched his truck's tires as he hurriedly followed them. They passed along a full-height, corrugated metal fence that presumably marked the edges of the salvage yard and slowed as they approached a closed metal gate. Then the first truck sped up, ramming through the gate's rusty metal as if it had only suggested that they stop. The special tires on Min Kyu's tank shrieked as he stepped on the gas, pointing the truck's nose at the newly created opening, and powered into the scrapyard. It took the pair of men standing guard outside a dirty, partially rusted warehouse building almost the entire time it took the three tanks to drive across the open lot before they understood that they weren't supposed to be there. Then, they both pulled out handguns and started shooting. Thick armor dulled the sound of gunfire to muted pops, but their shots sparked where they hit the bodywork and left little spiderweb clouds where they struck the windows and windshield.

Jason thought that they might just drive right inside the warehouse. But Min Kyu and the other drivers pulled their trucks almost all the way to the giant, partly open sliding doors before skidding to a stop. Min Kyu quickly turned off his engine as he and Seong Hyeon jumped out, staying behind the doors for cover as they took shots at the guards. Between Min Kyu, Seong Hyeon, and the eight people on the other teams, it didn't take nearly as long for the pair of kidnappers to realize they were outmanned and outgunned. They both turned tail and ran into the warehouse. Then, one of the men from the other truck lobbed a small, gray metal cylinder through the open warehouse door and quickly looked away. Jason did the same just before the stun grenade exploded with a bright flash and muffled boom. When he turned back to watch the action, he caught the last of Min Kyu's men running into the warehouse.

"Fuckin' A." Jason was ready to jump out and run after them. But he anxiously counted to thirty instead, ensuring the coast was clear, before reaching for his door handle. He'd half expected Min Kyu to turn on the child locks, but it opened with no trouble.

Seong Woo gasped. "What are you doing?"

"What do you think? I'm going in."

"They said to stay behind."

Jason scoffed and turned the full weight of his repressed

anxiety, anger, and fear on Seong Woo. "Are you serious right now? Would you really fucking stay behind if it was Yoo Mi in there?"

Seong Woo briefly pursed his lips before reaching to open his door. "Okay, yeah. I–wait." He nodded toward the warehouse.

Jason turned just as a man dressed in all black frantically scampered out of the warehouse. He must've slipped past Min Kyu's squad somehow. Or they let him escape. Well, fuck that. Just as the man was about to pass by the truck, Jason kicked his heavy, armored door open. The runner had no time to stop, slamming headlong into the unbreakable window with a sickening thud and slumping to the ground.

"There." Jason triumphantly grinned. "I got one." He stepped out, looming over the fallen kidnapper for a moment before gently kicking him in the side. "Yep, he's out."

Seong Woo frowned as he walked to Jason's side of the truck. "We should tie him up so he doesn't run off."

"Do you think there's one of those assault team boxes in this thing? I bet they have zip ties."

Seong Woo shrugged. "Maybe. I don't know. Let me check." He walked to the back of the truck and opened the lift gate. "Yeah, there is. Hang on."

Jason fidgeted as he waited, his hands practically shaking as adrenaline coursed through his system. He thought about asking Seong Woo to grab a pair of chest protectors when some movement on the warehouse's far side caught his attention. Two more kidnappers had stumbled out of a small door farther up the side of the building and were awkwardly shuffling toward an old minivan parked nearby. No. One of the men had their hands tied behind their back. Then recognition hit. It wasn't a pair of kidnappers. It was a kidnapper and Tae Hyun!

"I see him!" Jason ran around the front of the truck and grabbed the driver's side door handle as the kidnapper shoved Tae Hyun into the minivan's passenger seat.

"What?" Seong Woo lifted his head from the open box in the back. "Who do you see?"

"Tae Hyun. They're fucking taking him again." Jason frantically scanned the dashboard and found the key Min Kyu had left in the ignition slot. He pressed the start button, and the engine roared to life.

Seong Woo yelped from the back of the truck. "What the hell are you doing?"

Jason gripped the wheel with one hand and shifted the truck into drive with the other. "I'm fucking stopping them. Go get Min Kyu!"

The minivan's tires kicked up a cloud of dust and gravel as it darted away. So Jason slammed his foot down on the accelerator, and the tank leaped forward. No wonder Min Kyu had been able to drive the thing so fast. It was a fucking monster. The minivan, already pointed away from the scrapyard's entrance, sped down a wide path bordered by tall piles of rusted metal junk. Jason didn't know where they were headed. Was there another entrance they hadn't seen? But he kept his foot planted on the gas pedal as he steered the unwieldy vehicle down the same path. He needed to catch up and stop them before they got away. There was no way he was losing Tae Hyun again.

But there was no other exit. Instead, the minivan barreled toward the corrugated metal fencing surrounding the scrapyard. Jason silently willed them to stop. That van couldn't possibly make it through to the road. Then, a distant screech of metal on metal wailed as the van veered into an impossible turn. Maybe the driver hadn't known there was no other exit. Maybe they were hoping to lead Jason away before doubling back. It didn't matter. They'd blown their one shot at escape.

Jason pointed the front of the tank at the van as it came out of its turn and slammed his foot on the brake pedal. He would've rammed them at full speed but couldn't risk hurting Tae Hyun. Even then, it was a heavy truck, and there wasn't much space to slow down. Jason braced himself with his hands on the wheel as the tank plowed into the front corner of the van. The airbag exploded in his face, drowning out the low crunch of crumpling metal as the truck finally stopped.

Dazed, Jason shook his head, threw his door open, and climbed out. The minivan's windshield was cracked but intact. And Tae Hyun sat in the van's passenger seat on the opposite side, slowly shaking his head behind a deflating airbag. A flash of movement to Jason's right caught his eye. He turned just as the van's driver took off, shambling back toward the warehouse.

"Fuck that." Jason spun around and ran, practically bouncing off the tank's rear corner as he rounded it and sprinted toward the running driver. They slowly ran with uncertain steps, possibly still dazed or even injured from the crash. So Jason quickly closed the distance between them like it was nothing. He ran for an hour practically every day. And he was angry. No, he was furious. They'd already taken Tae Hyun once, and that man had tried doing it again. Someone had to fucking pay, so it may as well be him.

As soon as Jason was close enough to hear the fleeing man's labored breathing, he leaped forward, wrapped his arms around the man, and dragged him to the ground. The man groaned as he struggled beneath Jason's weight. It was time to let him see the face of his captor. Jason pushed himself to a squat to flip the man over and–

Jason knew that face. He'd met and nearly fought with him at the Music Video Awards rehearsal. It was Oh Min Su.

Jason growled as he fell to his knees and straddled Min Su. Probably still stunned from the crash and again from being knocked to the ground, he finally looked up at Jason and gasped with recognition.

Jason sneered. "That's right, ass face. You know me." Min Su weakly flung an arm at Jason, who quickly knocked it away. "You've got one chance to walk away from this, Oh Min Su. Tell me why you took Tae Hyun."

"I don't–"

Jason cut him off with a tight-fisted strike to the side of his face. "Don't even try it. I said tell me why you took Tae Hyun." Min Su groaned and turned away, so Jason struck him again. "Fucking tell me why you took Tae Hyun!" But Jason didn't even wait for an answer before hitting him again. Then again. And again. He remembered his father telling him he was better off dead. He remembered Tae Hyun's father calling him a deviant. He remembered a stranger holding a protest sign telling him to remember what happened to a dead idol. But none of that came remotely close to what Min Su had done. He'd hurt Tae Hyun and needed to be punished.

Jason lifted his arm for another strike when someone grabbed it. He snarled and whirled on his newest foe, only to see Seong Woo holding his arm.

"That's enough. Go check on Tae Hyun. Min Kyu's on his way, so I'll watch this one until he gets here."

Seong Woo's grip was strong–probably stronger than Jason's–so there was no use fighting him. Plus, he was right. Jason had left Tae Hyun alone in the minivan as he chased after Min Su. He reluctantly grunted. "Okay."

Seong Woo helped Jason to his feet before letting go. "Is he–"

"He's Oh Min Su," Jason spat. "He works for KBR."

"Shit."

Jason nodded as he loomed over the man he'd just bloodied and bruised. It wasn't nearly enough, but it was a start. He left Seong Woo with the unconscious Min Su and rushed back to the minivan. Tae Hyun still sat in the passenger seat, but he'd slumped down, and his head was lowered.

"Tae Hyun!"

Tae Hyun's head popped up at the sound of Jason's voice. His frantic expression was obvious even behind the cracked windshield. "Hyung?"

Jason pulled the door open and gripped Tae Hyun by the arms, holding him steady while he inspected him for injuries. His cheek was red from being struck, but he seemed okay otherwise. "Are you hurt?"

Tae Hyun shook his head. "No, nothing serious. Did you get Min Su?"

"I did." Jason pulled Tae Hyun close, hugging him more tightly than he probably should've, considering he never planned to let go again. "I'm glad you're okay. I was so fucking scared."

Tae Hyun buried his head in Jason's shoulder. "You came for me, hyung."

"Of course, I came for you. I love you. I'll always come for you." Jason reached down to feel the thick, plastic zip ties binding Tae Hyun's wrists. "Let's get these off you." He glanced at the interior of the van. It was bare, painted metal scraped and scuffed from the countless crates and junk it had hauled. A cargo van. He turned to the glove box and popped it open. Sure enough, there was a box cutter inside. "Turn around, and I'll cut them off."

Tae Hyun twisted around in his seat, presenting Jason with his bound wrists. The skin was angry red fading to pink under the zip ties. "What happened to Min Su?"

"I dealt with him." Jason extended the blade on the box cutter and began to slice through the thick, black plastic. "Seong Woo's with him, now."

"Seong Woo's here?"

Jason nodded. "And Seong Hyeon, Min Kyu, and a bunch of Min Kyu's people." Tae Hyun suddenly gasped, and Jason quickly jerked the box cutter away. "Did I hurt you?"

"No." Tae Hyun shook his head. "No. Seong Min was shot."

Jason's heart plummeted to his stomach. In all the excitement, he hadn't thought about anyone but Tae Hyun. "Is he–"

"He's okay. The bullet only grazed him."

Jason breathed out some of his adrenaline-fueled stress. "That's a relief." He finished cutting off Tae Hyun's bindings. "There."

Tae Hyun pulled his arms free and shook them out before wrapping them around Jason. "Thank you, hyung. Thank you."

Jason and Tae Hyun tightly embraced each other as Jason's heart pounded in his ears. The fear, anger, and anguish he'd been bottling since getting Yun Seo's call threatened to break through his control and explode. But it wasn't the time. They were in some anonymous scrapyard somewhere in Seoul–if they were even still in Seoul–and needed to go home. But Jason held on for several moments before letting go. "Can you walk? We should get you out of here."

Tae Hyun nodded as he took Jason's outstretched hand. "What about Ji Hoon?"

"What? That asshole's here, too?" Jason snorted. He'd always secretly imagined his uncle was a villain, but his mind almost refused to process that he really was. "I only saw Oh Min Su."

"He was here." Tae Hyun deeply sighed and shook his head. "It was Ji Hoon the whole time, hyung. He's been the one behind it all."

"I fucking knew it." Jason helped Tae Hyun climb from the van, put his arm around him, and led him past the tank. "I've been saying it was KBR, and it was fucking KBR this whole time."

Tae Hyun briefly stiffened when he saw Min Su sitting with his hands bound behind his back between a pair of men from Min Kyu's security team. Then he surged forward, snarling, until Jason grabbed him and held him back.

"I think he's had enough."

Min Su was already sporting a bloodshot and bruised eye above a scratched, swollen, bloody cheek from Jason's beating. He glanced at the blood on his knuckles–Min Su's blood–then noticed Tae Hyun looking at it, too.

"Maybe," Tae Hyun replied, his voice low with restrained anger. "But he deserved everything you gave him."

Seong Woo, standing nearby, motioned for Jason and Tae Hyun to follow him before walking a few dozen feet from Min Su. He waited for them to catch up, frowning when he saw Tae Hyun.

"Are you alright?"

Tae Hyun nodded. "I am. I'm more worried about Seong Min. How's he doing?"

"His brother and one of my men are taking him to a company physician to get him checked out."

Jason snorted. "You have a company physician?"

"My father's company, of course. But we thought it would be best to keep him out of any public hospitals until we've decided what we want to do."

Tae Hyun frowned. "Decided what?"

"Whether or not we want to involve the police."

"Oh." Tae Hyun pursed his lips for a moment. "What are our other options?"

"Well, we can talk more about those. But, first, we should get our asses out of here. It's only a matter of time before someone official shows up and starts asking questions." Seong Woo grinned. "And there's something else you should probably know."

Jason huffed and shook his head. "Enough with the fucking theatrics, Seong Woo. Just tell us."

Seong Woo's grin fell away as he flinched at Jason's reprimand. Then it returned, just as bright as ever. "You'll never guess who Min Kyu has tied up in his truck right now."

23

Tae Hyun anxiously fidgeted on the folding chair he'd found leaning against the back wall of the makeshift office. He glanced at Choo Ji Hoon, who'd so far refused to answer anyone's questions. By his expression, you'd hardly have known that he'd been placed in his chair with his hands zip-tied behind his back. He could've been sitting in his office in KBR's Gangnam-gu headquarters, waiting for his next meeting. He was only missing his expensive office chair, a few plants, and a framed photo of his family on his desk.

Jason, Seong Woo, and Min Kyu had gathered in the corner of that same prefab office at some construction site conveniently owned by Cho Seong Woo's family, quietly conferring as they decided what exactly to do with the KBR Director. That left Tae Hyun to watch over Ji Hoon.

Tae Hyun's feelings toward the man sitting before him were complicated. They'd evolved over the years, just like any boy's would for a father figure. Because that's what Ji Hoon had always been to him. But Tae Hyun also had a complicated relationship with fathers, symbolic or otherwise. His desperation to please them and fulfill his duties as a son, trainee, and idol had come at the price of constantly lying. He'd always known that the love and support he enjoyed from his parental figures was conditional–they would surely withhold that love once they knew who he really was. And, for the most part, he'd been right about that.

Yet, Tae Hyun still struggled to reconcile who he'd believed Ji Hoon to be with who he actually was. This man had molded and guided him along his chosen path. It would be a lie to say Tae Hyun didn't owe much of his success to Ji Hoon and KBR. But Ji Hoon had sunk to staggering depths to silence him when his only crime had been publicly admitting his love for another man.

So the others could talk. Tae Hyun already knew what he wanted to do. He planned to break the man.

"It's not too late to stop all this," Ji Hoon suddenly announced. His tone was firm, but he'd kept his volume low. It was a statement meant solely for Tae Hyun.

"Not too late?" Tae Hyun tilted his head in confusion. "So, what? We just let you go, and everyone conveniently forgets about the whole thing?"

Ji Hoon shook his head. "Of course not. You'd still have to make your choice."

"My choice?" Tae Hyun frowned as he leaned closer. "No one's actually given me a choice yet."

"Yes, yes." Ji Hoon's face pointed at Tae Hyun, but his eyes darted to the men talking in the corner. Good. His easy demeanor was just an act. "We were interrupted by your men in black all playing at being soldiers. How long will they protect you from us, Woo Tae Hyun? How long do you think they can keep you safe?"

Tae Hyun deepened his frown. "You're still threatening me? Even now? Here?" He shook his head. "And you still haven't told me what this choice is."

"I think you know."

Tae Hyun sat back in his chair. It was always games with Ji Hoon. Just like it had been with Oh Min Su. Just like it always was with KBR. "Still, it might be better if you just spelled it out."

Ji Hoon sighed, showcasing a frown that Tae Hyun knew well. He was disappointed. Tae Hyun had let him down yet again. "You still play at ignorance. But we both know you're smarter than this."

Still a game. Tae Hyun was a little impressed. Ji Hoon had absolutely no power, and yet he still played things like he did. For all he knew, they planned to put a bag over his head and dump him in the Han, just like Tae Hyun had imagined would be done to him. But appearances mattered to Ji Hoon even more than they had to Tae Hyun. Ji Hoon taught him that lesson with a sharp hand to his face backstage before his first appearance on *Chart Masters*. So Ji Hoon kept up the appearance of power, if only for his own benefit.

Tae Hyun sighed. "You won't actually say it, will you?" He shook his head. "I used to respect you, you know?" He shook his head again. "Or, maybe not respect. Fear." He nodded, leaning forward. "I used to fear you. But that was before I knew you were a small, impotent, self-important shell of a man." He shook his head again. "Is that how you got Min Su to help you kidnap me? Fear?"

Ji Hoon wickedly chuckled. "Oh Min Su was more than happy to help us deal with you."

Tae Hyun nodded. Unlike Ji Hoon and his masterful composure, Min Su had folded like a paper lantern the moment he'd been stuffed into the back of one of the tanks, blabbing everything he knew to anyone who would listen.

Ji Hoon had apparently discovered that Min Su was in a relationship with Jeon I Jun. It made sense that KBR would look for that sort of thing after everything with Tae Hyun. But, instead of simply firing him, Ji Hoon had used Min Su's secret to blackmail him. He ensured Min Su's participation in Tae Hyun's kidnapping with the threat of firing him and publicly revealing why. I Jun still hadn't recovered from his falling out with KBR. It would undoubtedly have been the end of Min Su's career. Under different circumstances, Tae Hyun might've felt sorry for him. But things were how they were.

"Of course he was, considering what you threatened him with. But that's the only way you know how to operate, right?" Ji Hoon frowned at Tae Hyun's sudden grin. "You still think it's not too late to stop all this?"

The barest shadow of concern flickered across Ji Hoon's otherwise stoic face before he nodded. "It's not."

Tae Hyun quietly chuckled. "Wrong. It was too late the moment you had the graffiti painted outside my dance studio." He shook his head. "No. It was too late the moment you decided to do whatever you did to Kwon Jong Soo."

Ji Hoon briefly pursed his lips. "You have no idea what you're talking about."

"Then why don't you fucking enlighten me?"

Ji Hoon quietly chuckled. It wasn't clear if he was impressed with Tae Hyun's display of bravado or thought it was amusing. "Such a willful response. But that's to be expected from a boy ruled by his emotions."

Tae Hyun knew Ji Hoon was baiting him, but he wanted to keep the man talking. "You would know, wouldn't you? After all, you raised me."

Ji Hoon nodded. "You were my greatest success. And now you're my greatest failure."

"Even greater than Jong Soo?"

Ji Hoon's flinch would've been easy to miss if Tae Hyun hadn't been fixated on him. "Kwon Jong Soo is but a memory. You, however?" He frowned. "You remain a problem."

Tae Hyun snorted. "A problem you've made for yourself. You could've just let me go like you did with Chang Min."

"Chang Min?" Ji Hoon chuckled again. "He'll never amount to anything more than a moderately talented mess. I'd be surprised if we ever see another song from him. He's irrelevant to me." His face turned serious. "But you. You had potential. You had purpose."

"Purpose?" Tae Hyun could bait people, too.

Ji Hoon nodded. "Your charm? Your talent? Your impressive ability to stay relevant?" He huffed. "That was all meant for us. We gave that to you. And we would've made you the biggest name in KBR's history. Surely, even you can see that?"

It was Tae Hyun's turn to chuckle. "And I gave all that up, did I?"

Another flinch, but Ji Hoon covered it well as he nodded toward Jason. "For him."

"For love."

"Love?" Ji Hoon snorted. "Love? What do you know of love?" He shook his head. "You're an idol. You have a duty. You're supposed to love your fans. You're supposed to love your company." He snorted again. "Go ahead and fuck whoever you want. God knows you've certainly done enough of that when you thought our backs were turned. But love? No. You'll love who we tell you to love."

That was a lie. There was no way Ji Hoon would've

permitted his relationship with Chang Min had he known about it. He'd only found out afterward, most likely from Chang Min in a last-ditch effort to sabotage Tae Hyun. And Ji Hoon was using that knowledge to twist reality to suit him as he'd always done.

Tae Hyun forced himself to grin. "You don't own me."

"We made you."

"No, you trained me. But I've always been who I am." Tae Hyun's grin spread a bit wider. "And I'm already the biggest name in KBR's history."

Ji Hoon scoffed. "You're an aberration. A footnote."

"I would be if you had your way, and I ended up like Jong Soo." Tae Hyun leaned forward, his gaze dripping with sizzling charm. "Tell me the truth. What did you do to him?"

Ji Hoon frowned. "I don't know what–"

Crack! Tae Hyun's slap across Ji Hoon's face was loud enough to echo off the office's fake wood paneling. "Stop fucking lying." Tae Hyun shook his head. "It's childish and beneath you."

Ji Hoon's eyes frantically flickered between Tae Hyun and the three men behind him. "What? What's–"

"Don't look at them." Tae Hyun's words echoed Min Su's as he grabbed Ji Hoon's jacket and yanked him forward. "Look at me. I'm the one you have to answer to here." Ji Hoon's chest hurriedly rose and fell with his ragged, rapid breathing. Whatever he'd expected to happen, Tae Hyun getting physical with him obviously wasn't it. "And you know the answer I want."

Ji Hoon labored to calm his breathing, looking at Tae Hyun with narrowed, suddenly suspicious eyes. "Now, who's being childish?"

"And yet, I'm not the one who faked a man's suicide." Tae Hyun tightened his grip on Ji Hoon's jacket and pulled him close enough to feel the man's breath on his face. "Was he really that much of a problem? Was he so problematic that even the great Choo Ji Hoon couldn't keep him in line?"

Ji Hoon's control finally slipped. "You know nothing! You're a petulant, ignorant child who was handed everything on a platter and threw it back in our faces!" He scowled. "All you had to do was go away and quietly live your sick, deviant life."

"But I didn't." Tae Hyun forced his words through clenched teeth. "I haven't been quiet. Just like Jong Soo wasn't–"

"Enough!" Ji Hoon scoffed. "Stop saying that name." He shook his head, his eyes reddened with barely contained rage. Or was it something else? "You know nothing about Jong Soo. We did what we had to do to protect the company."

And there it was–the first crack in Ji Hoon's wall. The first admission that he was somehow involved in Jong Soo's death. But there was definitely something else there, too. Possibly fear. "Protect the company from what?" Ji Hoon pursed his lips again–this time in defiance of Tae Hyun–and looked away. Tae Hyun roughly grabbed Ji Hoon's chin and turned his face forward. "Answer me, damn it." There had to be more to the story, but Ji Hoon kept his lips pressed shut. Tae Hyun huffed and shoved him back into his chair.

"Did you get it?"

Tae Hyun glanced over his shoulder at Jason, who'd come to stand behind him, and nodded. "I got something, yeah."

"Good."

Ji Hoon's expression suddenly shifted from defiance back to fear as he realized that more had been happening than he knew. "What's going on?"

"Well, Uncle." Jason's tone was acid and sharp. "You see, we've been recording this whole session."

Ji Hoon huffed. "Nothing that I've said is admissible in any court." Tae Hyun had to hand it to him. Ji Hoon would always be Ji Hoon, even when his ass was already in the fire.

Jason barked out a sharp laugh. "Are you honestly that naive to think we're taking you to court?" He shook his head. "No, Uncle. We're using your own strategy against you and giving you a choice. You're going down. That much is certain. But you don't have to fall alone."

"Do what you will." Ji Hoon defiantly lifted his chin. "I have nothing further to say."

Tae Hyun scoffed. "Who do you think you're protecting here? You, of all people, should know exactly what CEO Pak will do if this all gets made public." He shook his head. "You tried to kidnap me, Director Choo. And now we know you were involved in Jong Soo's death, too."

Ji Hoon pursed his lips a third time, and Tae Hyun knew the conversation was over. Sure, they could probably still beat an answer out of him, but what would be the point? Even if slapping him had felt good. Really good.

Tae Hyun glanced at Jason again. "I think that's probably all we're getting."

Jason nodded. "Yeah, it seems like that." Ji Hoon's eyes went wide as Jason pulled a box cutter from his pocket and clicked the blade out several notches. "Oh, fucking relax. Unlike you, we're not murderers." He walked behind Ji Hoon's chair and started cutting through the zip ties.

Ji Hoon looked at Tae Hyun with heavy-browed confusion. "I don't understand."

Tae Hyun shrugged. "We're letting you go."

Ji Hoon's brows dipped further. "I'm to believe you'll let me simply walk out of here?"

Tae Hyun nodded. "Of course. Why wouldn't we?" Then he grinned. "We have more than enough to nail you to the wall." He glanced at Seong Woo just as he finished with the call he'd been on.

Seong Woo nodded. "Everything's set." While Tae Hyun had been talking with Ji Hoon, he explained, his security team had been recording video statements and getting signed confessions from Min Su and all the men they'd rounded up at the salvage yard. They'd send those, along with the recording they'd just made of Ji Hoon confessing to Tae Hyun's kidnapping and admitting his involvement in Jong Soo's death, to KBR CEO Pak. "So, the way we see things," he added, "there's no reason to involve the police. I'm sure Pak Jun Ho will take care of things for us."

Tae Hyun nodded. Most of the color had drained from Ji Hoon's face by then. "But it's not too late for you to stop all this."

Jason lifted the thick, plastic zip ties from Ji Hoon's wrists. "Otherwise, we'll happily drive you back into town." Ji Hoon, at a loss for words, simply nodded. So Jason shrugged and walked away.

Min Kyu showed up then with a pair of men from his security team. He briefly spoke with Jason and Seong Woo while his men, still wearing the black suits and ties they'd worn when they stormed the warehouse at the salvage yard, approached and stood on either side of Ji Hoon.

One of the men put his hand on Ji Hoon's shoulder. "Do you need any assistance to stand, sir?"

Ji Hoon had started his interrogation confident and in control. But he'd probably still believed then that there was a chance to talk his way out of trouble. A much different Ji Hoon inspected the hand on his shoulder and the man it belonged to, his confidence nowhere to be seen. "I, uh–what?"

Tae Hyun shook his head as he stood from his chair. "Don't give them any trouble," he warned Ji Hoon, "and you won't get any in return." Then he left Ji Hoon behind–hopefully, for the last time.

As much as he wanted to see the whole plan through, it had been a long day, and Tae Hyun had reached his limit. He found a seat on a cheap vinyl loveseat in the small meeting room outside the construction office. Then he leaned back, let his head gently rest on squeaky vinyl that smelled like cigarettes, and waited.

Seong Woo suggested that Jason and Tae Hyun go home and let him handle the rest. While he was involved with everything simply being a partner in Big Hammer, he was personally invested in punishing the forces that had ruined his wedding. The video confessions would probably be enough to scare the shit out of CEO Pak. But they'd still have the full weight of the Cho family's Imperative Group behind them. Tae Hyun doubted CEO Pak would go anywhere without looking over his shoulder for a long time.

Jason checked in with Tae Hyun after Min Kyu's men led a sullen, downcast Ji Hoon past him and out the door. "Are you ready to go?"

Tae Hyun nodded. It had been such a long, arduous day. Was it really, finally over? "I'm starving, tired, filthy, and sore. I'm ready to go." He lifted his head to see Jason's face. "Do you think someone here would drive us home?"

Jason nodded. "I do. Seong Hyeon and Seong Min are back. They're outside right now."

Tae Hyun quickly perked back up. "Seong Min's here? Is he alright?"

Jason nodded again. "He said he was. But maybe we should go see for ourselves?"

The sky had dimmed, and the air outside had cooled considerably in the early evening, but Tae Hyun was too excited to notice. Seong Min stood beside his brother, amiably chatting with two of Min Kyu's men. His right arm was in a sling, but he looked surprisingly okay otherwise. "Seong Min!"

The younger Song brother turned to Tae Hyun and smiled. "There you are, sir. You're looking well, considering."

Tae Hyun nearly sobbed as he rushed over and threw his arms around the mountain of a man. "Thank you for everything you did, Seong Min. I'm so glad you're okay."

"Careful there, sir." Seong Min winced and returned the hug with his good arm. "Of course, I'm okay. It'll take more than a few half-assed wanna-be gangsters like those fucking clowns to bring me down."

Tae Hyun laughed. "What did you say?"

Seong Min sheepishly shuffled back and bit his lip. "Sorry, sir. They may have given me some pain meds at the Cho family clinic."

"Don't be sorry," Jason sternly urged Seong Min. "You've earned it. In fact, I'm the one who should be sorry." He turned to face Seong Hyeon. "And I definitely owe you an apology for how much of an asshole I was today." To Tae Hyun's surprise, Jason actually bowed. "I'm sorry, Seong Hyeon. Please accept my apology."

Seong Hyeon, who most likely hadn't been given any pain meds, still showed his wide-eyed surprise. "Sir. I, uh–"

Jason chuckled. "Don't let it go to your head, Song Seong Hyeon." Then he offered his hand. "I also owe you my thanks for everything you did today."

Seong Hyeon, who still hadn't actually accepted Jason's apology, looked at his hand for a moment. Then he grabbed it and shook. "It was my job, sir. But it was also my honor."

"Good." Jason clapped Seong Hyeon on the arm. "Then please don't quit."

"Quit?" Seong Min laughed. "Are you kidding me? This job finally got fun. Why the hell would we quit?"

Jason chuckled again, but it sounded a bit forced. Tae Hyun could understand. It had been that kind of day. "I'm glad to hear that. I like having you around."

Seong Min brightly smiled. "I took my first bullet today. Now, I'm a genuine bodyguard. I feel fucking invincible!"

Jason patted Seong Min's good arm. "Maybe so. But you're not, so please don't do anything stupid."

Seong Hyeon drove them all back to the apartment while Seong Min cheerfully chattered for the whole ride. Tae Hyun tried to pay attention, but his day had caught up with him. After they got dropped off, Jason walked him to the apartment and helped him undress.

"You go take a shower. I'll order us some food, and then come join you."

Tae Hyun knew his smile was meager, but it was the best he could manage. "Thank you, hyung."

After Jason left, Tae Hyun started the water and stared at it for several minutes before stepping under the steamy spray. His headache had returned with a vengeance, but the soothing flow helped him calm down. The tears came out of nowhere. Tae Hyun hadn't realized how much he'd been holding them back until he couldn't stop them. It had all been too much. Too many people who'd supposedly cared about him had betrayed him. His ex. His parents. His company. All he'd done was get out of his own fucking way, and they'd punished him for it.

Then Jason appeared, quickly stripping off his clothes before stepping into the shower. Tae Hyun immediately stiffened at his touch, but Jason wrapped his arms around Tae Hyun's chest anyway, pulling him close and gently squeezing while he sobbed.

"Shh," Jason cooed. "I'm here. Everything's going to be okay."

Tae Hyun nodded as he cried. He had no words to express his overwhelming feelings. So he grabbed Jason's arms and held on until the tears finally slowed. Once he'd calmed down, Jason grabbed the body wash and a bath sponge and slowly, gently began to wash Tae Hyun. His touch was a comforting anchor, grounding Tae Hyun in that place and moment. He winced when Jason tried to wash his hair, so Jason stopped and rinsed him off. Then, he quickly washed himself before turning off the water. He wrapped a giant, fluffy bath towel around Tae Hyun and softly patted him dry before drying himself. Then he took Tae Hyun's hand, led him to the bedroom, and helped him dress in shorts and a loose t-shirt.

Jason smiled and carefully lowered the shirt over Tae Hyun's sore head. "There you are. Do you want to lie down while we wait for the food?"

Tae Hyun nodded, so Jason helped him into bed. "Could

you lay with me, hyung?"

"Of course." Jason climbed in beside Tae Hyun as he turned to his side. Then he wrapped his arms around Tae Hyun again and pulled him close. "Better?"

"Yes. Will you hold me for a while?"

"Are you kidding?" Jason leaned in close enough that his warm breath caressed the gentle curves of Tae Hyun's ear. "I'm never letting you go again."

24

Jason had always complained when watching movies or shows where one lover tenderly gazed upon another while they slept. It was creepy and, frankly, a little stalkerish. And yet, that's what he found himself unable to stop doing the morning after the kidnapping. He watched Tae Hyun sleep. And he finally understood why people did it. He'd been doing it most of the night, occasionally dozing off only to wake with a start and the absolute fear that Tae Hyun would no longer be lying there. He'd come so perilously close to losing the man he loved, and that was a pain he didn't think he could survive twice. And in the dead of night, Jason had vowed never to take his eyes off Tae Hyun again.

Staring at his serene, sleeping face, Jason could never have guessed everything Tae Hyun had endured the day before. His only visible reminders were the fading pink rings on his wrists from the hours he'd spent with his hands zip-tied together. Otherwise, he was perfect. Absolutely perfect.

Jason swallowed a sudden pang of immense longing–a deep-set ache so intense that it nearly made him sob. He reached up and ever so softly brushed Tae Hyun's bangs from his face as tears blurred his vision. Then he quietly rolled over and climbed from the bed, careful not to disturb his lover's slumber. Despite his recent vow, he knew he couldn't resist the urge to wake Tae Hyun and smother him with passionate kisses if he stayed there, and the man deserved his sleep. So he grabbed his phone as he softly padded from the bedroom to the bathroom. After using the toilet and quickly showering, he went to the kitchen. A quarter-full bottle of Kingston temptingly sat on the granite-topped counter, but Jason shook his head. He felt hungover, but it wasn't from drinking. It was from a day filled with the most urgent, primal emotions. And he'd been an actor long enough to know that the hair of the dog only made an emotional hangover even worse. He started making coffee instead.

As the kettle warmed, Jason grabbed his phone and went into the guest room on the opposite side of the apartment, hoping that would shield Tae Hyun from the call he was about to make. He didn't care if Tae Hyun heard it. He only wanted to keep from waking him.

Naomi picked up on the third ring. "Fucking hell, Jason."

Jason snorted. "Hell, for sure, yeah. But no fucking."

"It's only a figure of speech." Naomi sighed. "But how are you? How's Tae Hyun? Is he–"

"He's asleep. I don't know how he'll be today, but everything hit him pretty hard last night."

The deep ache surged as Jason remembered Tae Hyun's sobbing in the shower and his simple request to be held while he fell asleep. But he also remembered watching with something close to awe–or maybe pride–as Tae Hyun turned his charm and fury on an unsuspecting Choo Ji Hoon.

A tense conversation had led up to that plan. Had it been up to Jason, he would've just beat the answers from his maniacal uncle. Or, maybe, just beat him. In fact, Min Kyu and Seong

Woo had to physically restrain Jason from taking his rage out on Ji Hoon. But Tae Hyun presented an alternate plan, and Jason finally saw the truth of it. Tae Hyun had been Ji Hoon's target. But he also knew Ji Hoon better than anyone else in the room.

Naomi blew out a heavy sigh. "I can't–Fucking hell. I can't even think of something clever or hopeful to say. What about you? Are you okay?"

Jason forced himself to chuckle. "You know me. I tore through this fucking city, lighting every goddamn thing I could think of on fire until we finally found him."

"Of course you did." Naomi snorted. "I can't imagine you not raising absolute holy hell while he was missing."

Jason quietly sighed. He'd definitely done that and then some. His mind served him a few flashes of the climactic moments when he'd hammered Min Su's face, giving Jason an almost feral grin. That part of himself might've been inconvenient in more sedate social settings, but it sure came in handy when he needed it. "I think you would've been impressed with my self-control. Seong Hyeon only threatened to lock me in the car once all day."

"Wow." Naomi laughed. "How much of a pain in the ass would you have to be to get under that man's skin? He's so–I don't know. What's the word?"

"Stoic."

"Yeah, that. Like a statue." Naomi paused for a moment. "A gorgeously detailed, finely-carved marble statue."

"Damn, girl, settle down. I had no idea you were down with the Asian persuasion."

Naomi scoffed. "I'll only allow that because you were recently traumatized. And, because you were obviously right about KBR all along."

Jason swallowed his righteous snort, knowing Naomi would never lightly say something like that to him. "Maybe so. At least it's done with."

"And then some. Have you seen the news?"

"No. I just woke up."

"Shit. It's–" Naomi sighed again. Or maybe she was catching her breath. Jason recognized the sound. She was riding the emotional wave he'd already surfed. "Do you want the rundown? Or would you rather see it yourself?"

"Gimme the scoop, Ms. Bell."

According to Naomi, the fallout at KBR from Tae Hyun's attempted kidnapping was almost immediate. Ji Hoon announced his retirement as Managing Director to supposedly spend more time with his family. It wasn't as dramatic as a trial and possible prison sentence would've been, but Ji Hoon hadn't been wrong about his confession being inadmissible in court. Still, the confession existed, as did all the others Min Kyu's team had put together. And their threats to Ji Hoon, Min Su, and the other kidnappers were simple. Try anything, they were told, and we'll go public with all of it. For Min Su and Ji Hoon, that included giving up careers in anything related to the music industry. And the constant threat hanging over Ji Hoon's head was almost as good as prison.

KBR tried to keep the announcement quiet with a short and simple press release, but Vital quickly pushed it to any and every news outlet they could. Then they went on the offensive, planting rumors online about a feud between Ji Hoon and CEO Pak over how KBR dealt with Tae Hyun. Netizens immediately picked up the rumors and spread them far beyond the KBR social media team's ability to keep things under control.

"I guess that's something." Jason sighed. "They deserve every bit of that shitstorm and then some."

"For sure." Naomi snorted. "Pak Jun Ho is still a player, but we've taken him off the board. At least for now. And, now that we've got our hooks in them, he'll think twice about pulling any more shit against us."

"He'd fucking better. But I wish there was more I could do."

"You've already done plenty, Jason. Both of you have. Now it's my turn."

Jason snorted. "What does that mean?"

"It means it's time to let Mama Bear take a swing. They hurt one of my boys, and I'm gonna fuck 'em up for it."

"Hell yeah." Jason laughed. "Do your worst, Ms. Bell."

"Hyung? Hyung!"

Jason spun around at the sound of Tae Hyun calling out. "Hey, sounds like Tae Hyun's up. I should go."

"Say no more. Talk to you again soon."

Naomi disconnected without further comment, so Jason rushed from the guestroom across the apartment to their bedroom. Tae Hyun sat in bed, anxiously scratching his head through messy, slept-in hair. "Oh, there you are." He frowned. "Did I hear you talking to someone?"

Jason nodded and sat beside Tae Hyun on the bed. "It was Naomi. We were just catching up." He put his hand on Tae Hyun's thigh. "I'm sorry if I woke you."

"It's okay. I woke up, and you weren't here, so I panicked." Tae Hyun looked down at Jason's hand. "I'm sorry."

"Don't be." Jason leaned in and pulled Tae Hyun to his chest. "I'm sorry I wasn't here when you woke up."

Tae Hyun wrapped his arms around Jason and nestled his head against his shoulder. "Thank you. I know I'm being a baby right now."

"You just went through a lot." Jason gently tightened his embrace. "You don't need to apologize or explain anything."

Tae Hyun blew out a long, stuttering sigh. "Thank you, hyung."

"How are you feeling? Head still hurt?"

Tae Hyun nodded. "A little, but it's not too bad. How's Naomi?"

"Worried about you." Jason bent his neck and kissed Tae Hyun's forehead. "Are you hungry? I can make us something to eat."

Tae Hyun shook his head. "No. I'm not really that hungry."

Jason frowned. "Are you sure? You didn't eat anything last night before bed."

"I'm sure." Tae Hyun gently bit down on his lower lip. "Could you lay with me some more?"

Jason nodded. "Sure, of course." He climbed in next to Tae Hyun, who lay back and rolled to his side so they could spoon. "How's this?"

Tae Hyun pressed himself against Jason's body, more to ensure there weren't any gaps than anything sexual. "It's perfect."

"Do you want to talk about yesterday?"

Tae Hyun shook his head, brushing his hair across Jason's nose. "Not right now, hyung. Could we please just lay here for a while?"

"Yeah, sure. Sorry."

Jason tried his best to lay still, glad he'd at least used the bathroom before being called back to bed. Whispers of worry poked at the edges of his thoughts. It wasn't like Tae Hyun to stay in bed that late. He was almost always an early riser. It had to be everything that happened the day before weighing him down. At least he wasn't pushing Jason away. If he had to choose between neediness and the walls going back up, Jason would take needy every time.

Jason had no idea how long he lay there while Tae Hyun slept. It was hard to measure the time beyond counting his heartbeat. But Jason hadn't eaten anything the night before either and was starving. Since Tae Hyun's breathing had been calm and even for a while, Jason decided to risk carefully sliding his arm out from under him and quietly climbing from the bed. His heart hung a bit heavier with guilt as he softly closed the bedroom door, but he still needed to eat.

Jason had just stuffed a bite of cold bulgogi in his mouth when his phone buzzed. He glanced at where it lay on the counter, saw that Yun Seo was calling, tapped the answer button, and tucked his phone between his ear and shoulder. "Hi Yun Seo."

"Jason?" Yun Seo sighed. "What a relief. Tae Hyun said he'd call when he woke up. But he hasn't, so I just tried calling, and his phone's off."

"Mm-hmm." Jason swallowed his mouthful of meat. "That's because he's still in bed. It's nothing personal."

"Oh, damn." Yun Seo sighed again. "I guess that's to be expected. I'm sorry. I'm just–you know?"

Jason quietly chuckled. "Yeah, I get it. I think we're all gonna be a little *you know* for a while. And he seems pretty down, but he's okay otherwise, all things considered. What about you?"

"What about me?"

Jason chuckled again. "How are you doing?"

"Oh." Yun Seo chuckled, too. "I don't get asked that much. I guess I'm alright. Yesterday was–" Then she sighed. "It was a lot. I don't know that I'm cut out for this sort of thing."

"Hmm." Jason finished chewing and roughly swallowed. He hated eating on the phone but had to multitask. "I don't know if any of us are, Yun Seo. It's not like it happens all the time. You know?" He snorted. "Shit, I've been a celebrity since I was sixteen, and this is my first kidnapping."

"Still." Yun Seo's tone said she wasn't convinced. "It's about more than that. It's been so much this whole time. I thought I would manage his appointments and stuff, not go to war with his old label."

"Yeah." Jason huffed. If that's what Yun Seo had thought, then she obviously hadn't considered what being an idol's assistant would really be like. "Look, Yun Seo, promise me you won't quit right now. Tae Hyun doesn't need that stress. At least give it a few days."

"Who said anything about quitting?"

"So you're not thinking about quitting as his assistant?"

Yun Seo snorted. "Alright, fine. I guess I am. But you're right. It would be shitty of me to do it right now, considering everything." Then she chuckled. "I know I've said this before, but I see why he likes you."

Jason frowned. "Why's that?"

"You don't bullshit. Most people would, especially most people here. You know, saving face and all that. But you just come right out and say shit. It's–I don't know, maybe–"

"Irritating?"

Yun Seo laughed. "I was gonna say refreshing. But I know that pinpoint accuracy has pissed my brother off before, too."

Jason nodded. He knew how he could be. "We both have our quirks." He scooped up another spoonful of bulgogi. "So you're good? At least, for now?"

"Yeah. For now. But please have my brother call me when he wakes up anyway. I'd like to at least hear his voice."

"You got it."

"Thanks, oppa."

Jason smiled. "Anytime." He ended the call, set his phone on the counter, and stuffed the spoon in his mouth, thankful he'd managed to delay Yun Seo's knee-jerk quitting until things had at least settled down a bit. Hopefully, that would–

"My sister wants to quit?"

Startled, Jason nearly choked on his food. He turned to see Tae Hyun standing at the end of the kitchen island, his expression almost as cold as the bulgogi. Jason swallowed the partially chewed mound of food in his mouth despite the pain it caused in his throat. "She's just overreacting a little. I talked her out of it for now."

Tae Hyun's firm set mouth dipped at the corners. Not quite a frown. "You didn't need to do that. If she wants to quit, let her quit."

Whatever cuddly, warm neediness Tae Hyun had been feeling earlier was obviously gone. "That's the thing. She didn't really want to quit. She just wanted to say it out loud and have someone talk her out of it."

"You don't know that." Tae Hyun shook his head. "She's my sister. She wouldn't say it if she didn't want to do it."

No, that's you, Jason thought but didn't say. Yun Seo wasn't nearly as impulsive as her brother when it came to snap decisions. "I don't think that's true. At least not in this case. But she asked me to have you call her when you got up so you can certainly find out for yourself."

Tae Hyun huffed. "So you're putting it back on me?" He shook his head. "That's just typical."

Jason drew his brows together, unsure what Tae Hyun was getting at. "What does that even mean? Either you want me to get involved, or you don't. But I don't get what this is."

Tae Hyun huffed again, adding an eye roll for emphasis. Or more drama. "I didn't want you to get involved in the first place when she told you she wanted to quit. Then you told her she didn't want to. So now I'm the one that has to help her figure out what she really wants."

Jason's shoulders and lower back tensed as he shook his head. He saw what was going on. Tae Hyun wanted to fight, and Jason happened to be an easy target. "That's not what happened. If you were listening, then you heard me tell her just to wait a few days. I didn't tell her not to do it."

Tae Hyun threw up his hands. "Oh sure, as if that's so different." Then he slammed his hands on the countertop. "Stop trying to talk your way out of this. She's my sister and my assistant. Next time, let me handle things."

Jason snorted. "You could've handled things if you'd answered when she called. But you didn't. That's why she called me."

"You didn't have to answer! You could've ignored it like you do with half of Naomi's calls." Tae Hyun shook his head. "But, no. You just had to shove your nose into things like you always do. And then you leave me with the mess."

You are the mess right now, Jason didn't say. "I don't want to fight about this. Let's just–"

"Then don't fucking get involved!" Tae Hyun huffed, stormed from the kitchen to the main bathroom, and slammed the door.

Jason remained where he was, standing beside an open takeout container of bulgogi with a spoon in his hand. He blew out a long sigh as he rinsed off the spoon and put it in the dishwasher. Then, he closed up the container and returned it to the fridge. He longingly eyed the Kingston bottle but decided yet again to abstain for the time being. Instead, he turned to lean back against the counter, pressing it into the spot on his lower back that had begun to ache. Then he closed his eyes and focused on his breathing. That was part of an exercise he'd learned from his studio-mandated therapy as a teenager when he'd been unable to stop acting out on set. And it was one of the ways he'd been somewhat able to manage his anger over the past few months.

Tae Hyun was clearly hurting. And he'd never been given the benefit of mandated therapy, as far as Jason knew. Instead, he'd been brought up in a system of rigid control that forced him to swallow his discomfort in the face of abusive or oppressive authority until it manifested in often inconvenient ways. Jason had been surreptitiously helping him unlearn that behavior by giving him an environment where it was safe to speak up. But the trauma he'd just experienced was probably more than he knew how to process. Jason sure as fuck hadn't figured it out yet. If they were at home, he would've brought Tae Hyun down to the punching bag again. Or, at least, he would've gone down and taken a few swings at it himself. But their building's fitness center didn't even have a punching bag, so that was out. But Tae Hyun still needed to figure out how to process his base emotions in a way that didn't involve yelling at and picking fights with Jason. That was silly. If anyone else in the world yelled at him like that, Jason would've quickly reminded them of their mistake. But that was also why he allowed it. Jason had regularly been shitty–and even violent–to a lot of people who probably didn't deserve it. And he knew Tae Hyun didn't actually mean half of what he said. And the parts that he did mean really didn't matter, anyway.

Jason heard the sobbing as soon as he opened his eyes. Shit. It got louder as he rushed to the bathroom, so he didn't bother knocking and just opened the door. Tae Hyun sat in the shower crying, his head buried between his knees. Jason walked over, climbed in behind Tae Hyun, and wrapped his arms around him. At least he hadn't turned on the water yet.

"It's gonna be okay," Jason softly purred. "You're gonna be okay."

Tae Hyun began to wail. He'd probably been trying–and failing–to keep quiet. But he'd given up as soon as he'd been discovered. So Jason sat there, ignoring the ache in his back, and gently rocked Tae Hyun in his arms as he cried. Whatever lingering anger he might've felt had dissipated as he listened to his lover's sobs. The blossoming ache in his heart made his back pain pale in comparison. There was honestly nothing that Tae Hyun could've said to him that would've made him feel any differently. The man he loved was in much greater pain, and no amount of arguing would make Jason love him any less.

Tae Hyun's sobs began to quiet after a while. When he'd calmed enough to lift his head, Tae Hyun settled back against Jason's chest. "I'm sorry, hyung. I was being an asshole."

Jason gripped him even more tightly. "You were, but it's okay. I get it."

"I don't deserve you."

"No, you deserve a hundred times better. But I'm all you've

got."

Tae Hyun quietly snorted. "You're a hundred times better than you think you are."

"And you're a hundred times better than me."

Tae Hyun grabbed onto Jason's forearms and gave them a little squeeze. "I love you, hyung."

"I love you, too."

The pair sat in silence for a few moments and held one another as Jason mentally tried to soak up as much of Tae Hyun's pain as he could. Strangely, he thought of Joo Won's broken mother haunting the ossuary where she'd interred her son's ashes, waiting for someone to come along and release her from the pain. He'd tried to do that for her even if she didn't deserve it. But he'd secretly suspected that it's what Joo Won would've wanted him to do. He couldn't say why. One of the things he'd realized over the years was just how little he'd really known about the boy. Maybe it was just his own conscience telling him it was the right thing to do in a language he'd understand. But if he could do that for her, he could certainly do it for the man he loved.

"Hyung?"

"Yeah? What's up?"

"I think I want to go home."

They were already home, in a sense. "Home?"

"To Los Angeles. I think I'm done with Seoul for a little while."

Jason nodded and pressed his chin into Tae Hyun's shoulder. He would march to the gates of hell for Tae Hyun. He could certainly take him to LA. "Okay. Let's go home."

25

Tae Hyun's mood dramatically improved after Jason convinced him to eat something. Then, he explained the concept of an emotional hangover while they ate.

"You know how, say, you feel after a really great performance?"

Tae Hyun nodded instead of responding since his mouth was full of food. But he knew the sort of endorphin high he often experienced after a show that Jason referred to.

"Well, think of how you're feeling now as the opposite of that. You went through a lot, which takes an emotional toll. Plus, there's the effort to–I don't know. Keep it together? You basically borrowed against future emotional energy to do all that, and today, you're paying the price."

Tae Hyun nodded again. "Yeah. This is what it felt like after we fought in Thailand. Or when I caught Chang Min cheating." He quietly huffed. It was probably closer to the cheating thing. Tae Hyun had never experienced feeling that much raw emotion before. After his meltdown, he'd locked himself in his hotel suite's bathroom and refused to speak to anyone, even after Oh Min Su convinced the hotel staff to unlock the door. Min Su, who'd been hiding his own gay secret and certainly must've suspected, if not known, about

Tae Hyun and Chang Min. Min Su, who'd conspired with his lover Jeon I Jun to kidnap Tae Hyun. Min Su, who'd–No. He shook his head to clear it of those dark thoughts. "Except a million times worse."

"But you feel better now?" Tae Hyun nodded. "Good. Take it easy on yourself anyway. You'll bounce back, but it might take some time."

"I know." Tae Hyun looked down at the reheated leftovers and forced another bite. He wasn't exactly hungry, and the food tasted oddly bland. But he knew his body needed the energy, so he ate it anyway. "Are you sure you're okay going back to Los Angeles?"

Jason snorted. "Absolutely. I mean, don't get me wrong. This trip hasn't been all bad, right? We signed that new venue for your Seoul tour dates. And we finally muzzled KBR. At least, for now."

Tae Hyun couldn't help frowning. "Do you think they'll give up on their fight against me?"

Jason shrugged. "I think so, maybe. But, if not, we'll be ready for them. Plus–" He chuckled, and it sounded a little dark. "Plus, we're not done with them yet. Naomi's gonna take a swing at 'em, too."

Tae Hyun smiled as he thought of Naomi. She'd been a mystery to him until he'd first met her. Then, he understood why Jason had such a special relationship with her. She was more than a manager. She was a confidant, friend, and–not exactly a mother. More like an older sister, maybe. But she genuinely cared, and Tae Hyun had never once doubted her sincerity.

After they ate, Tae Hyun spoke with Yun Seo while Jason and Lily made flight arrangements to head home. Yun Seo didn't say anything about wanting to quit, focusing instead entirely on how Tae Hyun was doing. So he didn't bring it up, either. If she wanted to quit, he wouldn't stand in her way. Then he mentioned that he needed to pack and–

"Wait. What? Are you leaving already?"

Tae Hyun snorted. "Already? The last few weeks feel like a fucking year."

"Oh." Yun Seo sighed. "Yeah. I suppose I'm just being selfish and don't want you to go, oppa. Do you have to?"

"I do." Tae Hyun huffed. "It's just–I don't know. I don't feel safe right now."

"And being there will make you feel safe?"

"Not being here will."

Yun Seo didn't reply right away, so Tae Hyun let her have her silence. He didn't need to convince her of anything. He grabbed his suitcase from the closet and–

"Okay. I get it. You do what you have to, oppa. I'll be here for you no matter what."

Tae Hyun smiled. "Thanks, Yun Seo. I love you."

"I love you, too, oppa."

After showering, packing, cleaning up the apartment, and eating again, Jason, Tae Hyun, and the Songs headed to Incheon to catch their flight across the Pacific. Tae Hyun was a restless spirit as he wandered through the airport. Despite getting so much sleep, he was still worn out. It made most of the trip a blur. But the Songs sat in first class with them, which made Tae Hyun comfortable enough to sleep for most of the flight.

When they finally arrived at LAX, Jason abused their celebrity status to avoid a long walk through the International Arrivals terminal, instead talking their way into an escorted trip through a series of back hallways used by staff and VIPs. They still had a short distance across the sidewalk from the exit to the waiting SUV, but no one knew they were there, so no press brigade was waiting to pounce on them.

It was probably the jet lag, but being back in Los Angeles didn't feel any different than when Tae Hyun was in Seoul. Maybe it was because the city had become so familiar. Maybe he had chased the promise of comfort across the world's largest ocean for nothing. Wouldn't that be something? Was there nowhere in the world that he'd feel comfortable anymore? Was he destined to always be looking over his shoulder? No, that was just paranoia. But the thought that he might've wasted his and Jason's time pushing them to return to Los Angeles made him laugh to himself.

"Is that a smile?"

Tae Hyun snorted and looked out the window at the passing highway scenery. "We just got here, and you're teasing me already, hyung?"

"Never." Jason grabbed his hand and gave it a gentle squeeze. "I'm just happy to see you happy."

Tae Hyun wasn't sure if he was happy. But he wasn't the only one that had suffered recently. If it made Jason feel better to think he was happy, that was okay. "I think I am." Tae Hyun turned to face Jason. "I don't really have many bad memories of this place. And your home is here."

"Our home."

Tae Hyun frowned. "Hyung–"

"No. I'm serious. Even if we're not married, everything I have is yours, too."

Tae Hyun pushed a smile back to his lips. "That's good since I'm only with you for your money."

"Now who's doing the teasing?" Jason chuckled. "But you probably shouldn't have said that until after we're married."

Tae Hyun playfully pretended to frown. "Damn." He leaned in close enough to catch a whiff of Jason's cologne. "Will you forget I said that if I stick my dick in your mouth?"

Jason laughed and shook his head. "That only shuts me up. You have to get me drunk to make me forget stuff."

Their driver dropped them off at the house around dinner time–or breakfast, if Tae Hyun was going by his body clock. The Songs helped carry Jason and Tae Hyun's luggage inside before leaving to check in with the grounds security team. Lily had obviously been by earlier to ensure the place was clean and banish the chill of a house that had mostly sat empty for several weeks.

Despite Jason's assurance that it was his home, too, Tae Hyun still felt like a guest when he walked inside. It was a lovely house–far nicer than their Seoul apartment. But it was still Jason's. Then Tae Hyun spotted a pair of shoes he'd left behind sitting by the door. And, further inside, carefully placed on a shelf near a few other nicknacks, was the ceramic fox figurine Jason had bought him during their visit to the Ikseon-dong Hanok Village. That had been their first outing together, if not an actual date. And it was the first gift Jason had ever bought for him. It was a silly, cheap, thoughtful thing that Tae Hyun absolutely treasured, and Jason had displayed it in a place of honor. Overcome with a sudden warmth, his vision blurred with fresh tears as Tae Hyun realized what Jason said was true. It was Tae Hyun's home, too.

"What's this?" Jason appeared before Tae Hyun with a concerned frown. "Is something wrong?"

Tae Hyun quickly wiped his eyes with the back of his hand

and shook his head. "Nothing's wrong. These are happy tears." He gripped Jason by the waist and pulled them together. "I'm happy to be here with you, hyung."

Jason smiled and leaned in for a kiss. Tae Hyun inhaled his intoxicating scent as their lips met, then gasped when Jason snuck a warm hand under his shirt and ran it up the curve of his back. But Jason soon pulled away from the kiss and grinned. "Is now a good time for my surprise?"

Concerned, Tae Hyun's brows quickly bunched together. He definitely wasn't in the mood for surprises. "What did you do?"

Jason's grin pushed his cheeks a little wider. "You'll see." He took Tae Hyun by the hand. "Come on."

Tae Hyun let Jason pull him through the house and across the main floor lounge to the window wall that opened to the sun deck. He immediately spotted something new–a large boxy object covered with a tarp. He glanced at Jason, who still grinned as he slid the glass door open and yanked Tae Hyun outside. He had no idea what could've been under the tarp until they got closer. He stopped.

"Hyung? Is that what I think it is?"

Jason chuckled as he let go of Tae Hyun's hand, rushed over, and yanked the tarp off a large, brand-new hot tub. "Surprise!" He opened the framed cover, which folded onto itself and back over the edge. Steam rose from the placid, crystal-clear water until Jason tapped a control panel on the lip, and the jets kicked on. "What do you think?"

Tae Hyun started to laugh. After everything, he'd hardly thought about the night they'd spent in that Incheon hotel suite with a hot tub on the balcony when he said he wanted one. And Jason hadn't said a word about it since then. After failing to surprise Tae Hyun with their hotel stay, he finally pulled off the perfect surprise.

"I love it!" Tae Hyun rushed over and threw his arms around Jason. "You're the best, hyung."

Jason laughed. "I am the best hyung, aren't I?"

"You are. Can we use it now?"

Jason shook his head. "First, we shower." He grinned. "Then we can use it."

Tae Hyun smiled. "Okay"

Jason took Tae Hyun's hand again, leading him inside and down the hall to the main bedroom. Their suitcases neatly stood inside the bedroom door, but Jason bypassed them and brought Tae Hyun straight to the main bathroom. The pair wasted little time getting undressed and tossing their clothes on the gray slate-tiled floor, already warm from the radiant heating that had been turned on earlier in the day.

Tae Hyun's cock sprang to life as he watched a naked Jason step into the giant shower and turn on the water, marveling as the spray doused his fit, muscular body. He remembered the first night Jason had stayed with him in Seoul. Jason had come from the shower while Tae Hyun made dinner, dew drops of lingering wetness on his golden brown skin sparkling in the kitchen lighting. And he'd fretted about having such an attractive man in his apartment and what it might mean.

Tae Hyun followed his bouncing erection across the warm tile floor and stepped into the shower as Jason soaped up his body. "Hyung."

Jason turned around, wiping the suds from his face. "Hmm?" Then he glanced down and grinned. "Oh? Not even gonna wait for the hot tub?"

Tae Hyun shook his head. "No way." He put his hands on

Jason's burly chest and pushed him back to the shower wall. The spray from the rainfall showerhead drenched him as he passed under it and pressed their bodies together. "I want you now, hyung."

Jason, his eyes heavy with desire, gently bit down on his generous lower lip. Then he reached up to cup the sides of Tae Hyun's face as he leaned in for a kiss. Days–maybe weeks–of stress melted from Tae Hyun's body as they furiously made out under the water. Tae Hyun ran his tongue along the inside of Jason's mouth as he ran his hands down the sides of Jason's body. Then he found Jason's smooth, round ass, grabbed it, and pulled their hips together. Jason's lips vibrated from his moans as his iron cock pressed against Tae Hyun's hip and dueled with his erection.

Tae Hyun pulled back from the kiss and grinned. He reached up to grab Jason's arms and push them down to his sides. Then he licked his lips and bent down, softly tracing the outlines of Jason's chest with his tongue before taking one of Jason's nipples in his mouth.

Jason groaned as Tae Hyun flicked his tongue across the tip of his nipple. He flinched and tried to move his arms, but Tae Hyun firmly held them in place as he teased and sucked. Then he quickly moved to the other one, and Jason's groaning intensified.

"Oh, god. That's so good."

Tae Hyun lifted his head and straightened up. "I know." He let go of Jason's arm to grab his cock and gave it a firm squeeze. "But I'm just warming you up for what's to come."

Jason grinned. "What, not who?"

Tae Hyun laughed and squeezed Jason's erection again. "Why not both?" He bent his knees and crouched before quickly taking Jason's cock into his mouth. It had been long enough since Jason last trimmed that his thick, black pubic hair was noticeably bushier and brushed against Tae Hyun's face. He'd lost count of how many times he'd blown Jason, but it never got old. Just comforting and familiar. He loved how it felt and tasted. He loved how the thick foreskin pulled back far enough from the head to leave a ridge of exposed skin his tongue could play with. He loved using his tongue to trace a vein that ran from the base halfway up the shaft.

Jason gasped. "You should stop if you don't want me to cum right now."

Tae Hyun quickly pulled away, licking the remnants of Jason's salty precum from his lips. "I definitely don't." He slowly rose, leaving a path of soft kisses from Jason's belly to the nape of his neck. "I've got other plans for that." Then he turned around and presented Jason with his ass. "But you should wash me first."

Jason chuckled. "Yes, sir." He reached over to the inset shelf to grab the bottle of body wash, opened it, and squirted a generous amount on his hands. After rubbing them together, he put his hands on Tae Hyun. Starting from his shoulders, he reached around to run his hands down Tae Hyun's chest and stomach, rubbing them around to cover him in suds. Tae Hyun gasped when Jason's hands brushed his stiff, sensitive nipples. Then Jason's hands traveled south to his crotch, firmly grasping his cock and giving it long, gentle strokes. Tae Hyun breathed out a halting sigh as he dipped his head onto Jason's shoulder. Jason kissed his cheek and temple as he worked Tae Hyun's erection to a chorus of breathing and moaning, all the while pushing his cock into the fold of Tae Hyun's ass.

Jason soon replaced his cock with his other hand and ran his soapy fingers between Tae Hyun's legs. His touch was more caressing than washing, but that was the idea. And Tae Hyun felt himself pucker with each pass, growing increasingly eager until the anticipation left him nearly breathless. He shuddered when Jason slipped a finger inside, moving it in and out until Tae Hyun could no longer contain his hunger.

"Hyung," Tae Hyun moaned. "I want it now." He turned to face Jason, spying his tight-jawed, almost desperate expression, and grinned. "You should sit."

"Sit?" Tae Hyun nodded. "Okay." Jason slid down the tiles at his back, caught himself on his hands, and spread his legs on the shower floor. "Like this?"

"Yeah." Tae Hyun dropped into a crouch, grateful for his many hours spent getting back into shape on the dance floor. His legs felt strong and limber. "I want you to see my face while you fuck me."

Balancing himself with one hand on Jason's shoulder, Tae Hyun reached back and underneath himself with his other hand to grab Jason's insistent erection, positioned it against himself, and pushed himself down onto it. He let out a long, slow breath as he relaxed the muscles that would allow Jason entry until he felt the head of Jason's cock slide inside him.

"Oh, hyung."

Tae Hyun continued to lower himself as Jason's cock filled him, brushing against his prostate to send a delicious wave of electrifying joy up his spine. He couldn't possibly imagine anyone else fitting in him like Jason did. He closed his eyes as he crouched there, savoring the intensity of their carnal connection.

Once he was ready, Tae Hyun put his lithe, well-trained

leg muscles to work riding Jason's cock. He went slowly at first, finding his rhythm as he built up his speed. When he settled into a steady pace, Tae Hyun opened his eyes to see Jason staring up at him, his loving, deep brown eyes glistening with tearful joy. Tae Hyun bent his neck and found Jason's mouth, slipping his tongue between his lips as he rode him. The pair sang a crescendoing harmony of shared moans as they kissed and fucked on the shower floor. Each time Jason entered him, fireworks of ecstasy exploded in Tae Hyun's mind. Everything else fell away–the troubles, drama, pain, and hardships all disappeared until it was just Tae Hyun and Jason, connected and together, fucking in a formless, frenzied void. Then Jason came, loosing an ecstatic cry into Tae Hyun's mouth as he loaded Tae Hyun's ass with his cum. One of Jason's hands fell to Tae Hyun's thigh, holding it in place as he worked to catch his breath.

"God damn."

Tae Hyun laughed. "That good?"

Jason nodded, eyes closed in delirium. "And then some." Then he breathed a deep sigh and lifted his hand away. "Keep going."

"What? I thought you–"

"Keep going." Jason grinned. "You haven't cum yet, and I want to be inside you when you do."

Tae Hyun briefly bit down on his lower lip before nodding. He pushed up with his thighs, making Jason shiver as he rode his still rock-hard erection. Then Jason wrapped his hand around Tae Hyun's cock, holding it in place for Tae Hyun to fuck while Jason fucked him. The combined sensation was nearly overwhelming, but Tae Hyun held out for as long as he could. They hadn't fucked since before the hot tub in Incheon, and he didn't want it to end. But he could only keep holding off for so long, and soon, the thrill was too much to bear. Tae Hyun threw his head back and cried out with ecstatic joy as he came, riding wave after wave of rapture as he rode Jason's cock.

When he was spent, Tae Hyun let his head fall onto Jason's shoulder and breathed. The water cascaded down his back until he finally lifted himself off Jason and stood to give his stiff, overworked legs a bit of rest.

"Holy shit."

Tae Hyun chuckled as he glanced down at a seated Jason. "Yeah. That was amazing." He held out a hand. "Let me help you up."

Jason gripped Tae Hyun's hand and pulled himself to his feet. Then he flashed Tae Hyun a bright smile that made him weak in his already wobbly knees. "Feeling better?"

Tae Hyun nodded. "A million times better." Then he grinned. "Now, let's actually wash up and go sit in our new hot tub."

After washing themselves–and making out again–Tae Hyun and Jason dried off and wandered to the bedroom to retrieve their swim briefs. Tae Hyun had considered going naked until Jason reminded him they were one telephoto lens away from their blurry, grainy hot tub nudes hitting the internet. Then Tae Hyun picked up a pair of bath towels while Jason grabbed a bottle of Kingston and a pair of lowball glasses. Once outside, he poured a glass for each of them while Tae Hyun gingerly climbed inside the bubbling hot tub. The silky-smooth water was just on the unpleasant side of hot as he lowered himself into it. But he quickly adjusted and felt his remaining tension fall away.

Jason handed Tae Hyun his bourbon as he climbed in beside him. He swallowed a mouthful before putting his arm around Tae Hyun's shoulders and pulling him close. Tae Hyun rested his free hand on Jason's thigh as the pair sat together in the water, facing the dim twinkle of city lights in the hazy, late evening dusk. Tae Hyun had often enjoyed that view but never so much as he did at that moment. He couldn't imagine anything that would make it more perfect.

"God, I love this," Jason exclaimed. "I'm glad you talked me into getting a hot tub."

Tae Hyun chuckled. "Is that what I did?"

"As far as I'm concerned, yeah." Jason turned to kiss Tae Hyun's cheek. "I mean, I never would've gotten one if it weren't for you. I can't imagine even wanting to sit in one out here without you." He kissed Tae Hyun's cheek again. "I can't imagine doing anything without you."

It was hard for Tae Hyun to miss the change in Jason's tone. They still hadn't talked about what happened–at his request. They'd only talked around it. Maybe it was finally time.

"Do you want to know what happened?"

Jason took a long, deep breath before responding. "I do. But only if you're ready to tell me."

"I think I am. I haven't really thought about it since it was over." That was almost a lie. Tae Hyun had been constantly thinking about it, but not on a conscious level. Maybe talking about it would help get it out of his head a little. "I knew something was off as soon as we visited Jeon I Jun. But it wasn't until we left that things got bad." Tae Hyun described what happened, starting with the fight in the corridor and finishing with Min Su dragging him outside to the van when everything went crazy. "I wouldn't have made it without

Seong Min. Even with everything, including getting shot, he was like a rock that kept me anchored." To his surprise, Tae Hyun chuckled. "You know, he actually confessed that he wanted to date my sister when we were on our way to Seongsu-dong?"

Jason's laugh sounded a little forced, but Tae Hyun couldn't blame him. He'd just unloaded a whole day of violent trauma on him–a day that Tae Hyun had already had time to deal with. He'd happily give Jason some leeway as he processed everything that happened, too. "Finally. I wondered how long that would take."

"Yeah." Tae Hyun sighed. "And then we dragged him here with us."

"We could fire him."

Tae Hyun scoffed. "What? Why would we–"

"Relax, I'm only kidding."

"Oh." Tae Hyun snorted. "You're always teasing me, hyung."

"Do you want me to stop?"

"No."

Jason chuckled. "I guess I look at it like this. If you and I figured out a way to make things work, with everything and everyone working against us, they'll make it happen if they want to." He snorted. "At least as long as he thinks he's invincible."

"Yun Seo told me she would climb him like a tree."

Jason laughed. "She'd have to. He's at least a foot taller than her."

"Hyung!"

"What? I'm just saying."

Tae Hyun closed his eyes and settled back onto Jason's arm as he listened to Jason's slow, even breathing over the dull roar of the bubbling water. "And then you came for me." He opened his eyes to see the first stars dimly sparkling in the darkening sky. "I thought about what you would do in my place a lot. And I wondered if I was ever going to see you again."

Jason gently flexed his arm to pull Tae Hyun a little closer. "There was never a chance of that. I would've mobilized the army if I had to. I–" He stopped as his voice cracked, and Tae Hyun turned to see a tear running down his cheek. "I've marched to the gates of hell with you twice now. And I'll do it a hundred more times if I need to. There's nothing–absolutely nothing–I wouldn't do for you."

Tae Hyun's own tears began to fall as his heart filled with the pained anguish of a deep, profound love. Sure, there were probably many people in the world who'd say that to their lover. But Tae Hyun had repeatedly seen Jason acting on those words and absolutely knew they were true. This was a man that Tae Hyun had thrown his life away for. A man he'd written songs for. A man he'd also do anything for. "You're the love of my life, hyung. And I'll be by your side forever."

26

I'm the boy with no shame, a phoenix aflame, rising from the ashes–

Jason watched with unabashed joy as Tae Hyun sensually prowled around the stage surrounded by his six smoking-hot dancers. The Incheon Songdo Entertainment Center's luxury suite gave Jason a decent view of the central stage. But it also kept him comfortably away from the ten thousand singing, screaming, and dancing fans that had packed the venue for the opening night of Tae Hyun's *Boy With No Shame* concert tour. And the Bubble engineers had lived up to their promise of blowing everyone's minds by projecting a fancam view of Tae Hyun onto the overhead domed screens. Seeing that was absolutely mind-blowing.

Seong Woo, Yoo Mi, and Yun Seo surrounded Jason on the VIP suite's open balcony to watch Tae Hyun perform. The Song brothers were working, of course, coordinating with the venue's security and leading the recently expanded Big Hammer security team. But Jason definitely pretended not to notice earlier as Seong Min briefly stole Yun Seo away when he thought no one was looking. Kim Jeong Woo had visited them for a few minutes before the show but quickly stepped away to get back to work. Tae Hyun's show was the first large-scale event the venue had hosted and marked their official grand opening after they'd done a shakedown series of smaller soft opening events.

Jason couldn't have been happier. After a series of significant setbacks leading to a narrowly avoided disaster, things had absolutely turned around for Jason and Tae Hyun. Tae Hyun's tour had already sold out for most of the upcoming dates, and those venues scrambled to add more shows. His album had gone global platinum within a week of its release, peaking in the Top Ten on the American and European charts and even cracking the Top Forty on the Korean charts. And he and Tae Hyun had agreed that it would be okay for Jason to start official talks with Tony Ruiz about producing and starring in his movie, *The Devil's Detail.*

At the end of the song, Yun Seo, who stood beside Jason, suddenly slipped her arm around his waist and tugged Jason closer. Her open affection and affinity for casual touch was a fascinating insight into how her brother might've turned out had he not been run through the idol machine. Then again, that had made him the man he'd become–the man Jason loved.

Jason smiled at Yun Seo and reciprocated, putting his arm around her shoulders. "Enjoying yourself?"

Yun Seo enthusiastically nodded. "Are you kidding? I can't believe I almost quit!" She squeezed Jason. "Thanks again for making me think twice about that."

Jason half-shrugged. "I knew you really didn't mean it." Then he grinned. "Besides, how else would you get in your important tree climbing?"

Yun Seo snorted and playfully smacked Jason's arm. "I still can't believe he told you that."

Jason chuckled. "It's not like I didn't see it happening either."

Yun Seo excused herself to visit the suite's bar and craft table. So, Jason glanced at Seong Woo, who'd also embraced Yoo Mi from behind as they gazed out at the audience and stage. Then he found Naomi, who'd already been obsessively checking her phone, camped in the suite's far corner as she furiously typed a message to someone. He shook his head but didn't call out for her. If that's what she wanted to do at the concert, it was up to her. She'd more than earned her seat in the VIP suite with everything she'd done to support the tour–especially how she and Seong Woo had teamed up to put the screws to KBR and kick them while they were down.

It wasn't long after the kidnapping incident that things really began to fall apart for the evil music empire. Losing two of their key managers in Ji Hoon and Min Su meant KBR was forced to delay *Cherry Squad*'s upcoming album release and Xiang's North American tour, which caused a flood of complaints and forced KBR to start issuing refunds. But that was inevitable.

True to her word, Mama Bear Naomi had taken a big swing at KBR, coordinating with Seong Woo and Vital to tip off the Korean Fair Trade Commission about how they'd been using their market position to unfairly restrict competition among Seoul Capital Area performance venues. They routed the tip through one of Seong Woo's analysts, whom he'd poached from the Korean FTC the year before. Of course, the press had a field day with everything, forcing a rapid series of no-comment replies from KBR's press relations team amid speculation that Pak Jun Ho had fled the country. Even then, months later, most of KBR's promotional activities had ground to a halt as Pak defended his company against an increasingly hostile Korean government agency.

And, finally sensing his moment, Xiang announced a lawsuit against KBR seeking to terminate his contract with them, claiming they mishandled his business and illegally withheld his duly earned compensation.

Naomi eventually huffed, shaking her head, and stepped out into the corridor. Tae Hyun finished his costume change and returned to the stage, bantering with the excited crowd just before the intro for *Freefall Into You* began to play. Jason had been looking forward to seeing that song the most. He smiled as he remembered Tae Hyun serenading him in the hot tub at the Songdo Grand Hotel next door, then felt a tap on his shoulder. He turned around to see an almost stricken expression on Naomi's face.

"What's up?"

"Come with me. You need to hear this."

Jason shook his head. It was bad enough that Naomi had interrupted the song, but there was no way he was walking out on it. "Later. I want to–"

"Now, Jason." Naomi's stern expression left him no room for argument. "I'm serious."

That look meant it had to be important, but Jason couldn't think of any reason why Naomi would pull him away from Tae Hyun's performance to talk business. "Alright, fine."

Jason followed Naomi as she returned to the corridor, which was only marginally quieter than the luxury suite. But they could at least talk at a reasonable volume.

"I just talked to your lawyer."

Jason wasn't sure he'd correctly understood her at first. "What? What did–"

"Stop and listen to me." Naomi paused, waiting until Jason

nodded his compliance. He knew that tone well. She only used it when his bullshit was the absolute last thing she wanted. Then she took a deep breath. "Your parents died."

"What?" Jason heard and understood her words, but his mind refused to process them. His parents died? They were dead? He hadn't thought about them in more than a passing way since he'd last spoken with his mother the night he'd seen Joo Won. Truthfully, he sometimes wondered if he'd ever speak to them again. But it looked like he wouldn't. "Died? What happened?"

"They were killed in a car accident. Your father was driving, and they think he had another stroke." Naomi was clearly working hard to keep her tone even despite her obvious urgency. "But that's not important. What's–"

Jason scoffed. "What do you mean that's not important? My parents are–"

"Jason, listen to me." Naomi paused again until Jason nodded. "I just talked to your lawyer," she reminded him.

His lawyer? Why would his lawyer be the one to– "Wait. No." Jason shook his head. While he still hadn't quite wrapped his mind around the idea that his asshole parents were actually dead, he definitely knew why his lawyer would be the one to share the news. "No fucking way. Please don't say what I think you're about to say."

Naomi sighed. "I know you don't want to hear this. But you need to hear this, Jason." She paused again. Jason begrudgingly nodded. "Your father never changed his will. He left you everything."

Acknowledgments

I never imagined writing one K-pop-inspired contemporary gay romance, let alone two. But when my publisher asked for a follow-up book to *Idol Minds,* I could hardly say no. In fact, I'd already started working on it! I expected them to say no when I told them I wanted to make this book a little darker. But they said hell yeah. So, it's been a joy taking Jason and Tae Hyun on another journey–one where I could more deeply explore the highs and lows of queer celebrity life and how traditional cultures impact them.

Thanks again to Robert, Owen, Eric, and José for their help with the book–especially Owen, who coached me through writing my action scenes. And a special thank you to Jetspace Studio for allowing me to tell this story.

About the Author

KT Salvo (he/they) is a queer romance novelist and artist with a passion for gaming, anime, and K-pop. With a love for diverse and inclusive storytelling, KT's stories explore the complexities and joys of modern queer relationships. When not writing, KT can be found honing their artistic skills or enjoying a hearty, home-cooked, vegan meal. With a distinctive voice and a talent for crafting relatable and realistic characters, KT is quickly becoming a rising star in the world of queer romance fiction.

You can connect with KT at ktsalvo.com

Printed in Great Britain
by Amazon

43076511R00205